To Rob

Muchas Gracias-

FINDING ISHMAEL

Mi Amigo.

Michael Henry

MICHAEL HENRY

Michael Henry

Finding Ishmael
Copyright © 2014 Michael Henry
All rights reserved
Author Photography: T.G.McCary
Cover Design & Formatting: Laura Shinn
ISBN-13: 9781499122503
ISBN-10: 1499122500

Other books by this author:
Three Bad Years (2010)
At Random (2010)
The Ride Along (with William Henry – 2011)
D.O.G.s: *The Secret History* (with William Henry – 2011)
Atmosphere of Violence (with William Henry – 2012)
The Election (2013)

Finding Ishmael is a work of fiction. Names, characters, places and incidents are either used fictitiously or are products of the author's imagination. Any resemblance to actual events, locales, or persons, living or dead, is entirely coincidental.

For more on the author, visit http://henryandhenrybooks.com

Chapter One

Liam Connors fidgeted at the table closest to the door, wasting precious time. He had to calm himself. Clear his head. Come up with a plan to find Mimi. Liam glanced at the other patrons in the café. Menachem promised to meet him at five. Liam checked his watch—4:40 p.m.—and did some quick calculations.

28 and ½ hours—how long he and Mimi had been in Israel.

4 hours—how long Mimi had been missing.

Liam steadied his breathing and followed Menachem's suggestion. He opened the pocket-sized English language Pentateuch Menachem had given him earlier and tried to concentrate. Menachem had urged him to study the sixteenth and seventeenth chapters of Genesis to understand what Ike Palmer was talking about this morning. *This morning.* It seemed like a week ago.

Liam stood up to walk outside. *No.* He was to meet Menachem *in the café.* He sat back down. His brain was racing, his heart pumping, but he had to wait. *He didn't know whether to shit or go blind.* That's what his best toolpusher always said. Now Liam understood exactly what he meant.

He leafed quickly through the gossamer pages until he found the chapters in Genesis. No dice. He saw the words but nothing was sticking. All he could think about was Mimi. He closed the small book. The only phrase that resonated was the description of Ishmael as "a wild ass of a man...whose hand shall be against every man."

Liam leaned forward and crammed the book into his back pocket. He was raised Catholic and had learned his catechism, but the nuns taught him nothing about the Bible. What little he knew about Ishmael had come from the mouth of Crazy Ike this morning at breakfast in the tourist hotel, so the information was unreliable *per se.* Liam recognized the irony in Ike Palmer referring to Ishmael as a wild ass of a man. Ike had a lot of room to talk. As long as Liam had known him—since they were teens in Louisiana—Ike was *the* wildest possible ass of a man. When Liam described him to Mimi before they left the U.S., she said in her authoritative nursing voice that bi-polar disorder was not something Ike would grow out of. Mimi was not thrilled about the prospect of meeting with Crazy Ike, but she *was* excited about tacking on the three day stay in Israel at the end of their trip to Italy. If Liam had only listened to Mimi about Ike, she might never have been taken. It was his own fault.

Minutes dragged. *Ten 'til five.* Time was now an enemy. Before today, time had always been Liam's ally. In fact, time had made him a wealthy man. In his recent negotiations with Delaware Energy, Liam waited patiently at critical junctions. It seemed Delaware's lawyers and executives could not abide silence or the passage of time. They bid against their own offer again and again, sweetening the deal even before Liam could counter.

Liam had spent all of his working hours the last two decades finding and bringing to the surface viscous liquids or olefinic and aromatic gases trapped in rock strata miles deep inside the earth. The oil and gas deposits he searched for were the end products of a process that had begun a half a billion years ago, organic matter transforming under heat and pressure over vast periods of time.

Heat and pressure.

That's what he was feeling now. He tapped his foot and stared out the window. No Menachem in sight. He replayed the events of the previous 28 and ½ hours at warp speed, going over and over everything he and Mimi had done since their flight touched down at Ben Gurion International in Tel Aviv shortly after noon the previous day.

◆ ❖ ◆

"Just to see the sights," Liam said to the young Israeli customs agent. "We've been in Italy for ten days. We're spending three nights in Jerusalem then taking a direct flight home to the U.S."

The primary sight Liam planned to see was Ike Palmer, his wild-eyed buddy from Natchitoches, Louisiana who left the U.S. for Israel in 1988 to join a *kibbutz*. Until the Fed Ex envelope arrived at Grand Oaks a month earlier, Liam hadn't heard from him in twenty-five years. Ike had stuck a yellow Post-it note on his handwritten letter and scribbled, "Don't mention my name to anyone when you get here." He underlined "anyone" three times.

"Typical Ike," Liam thought when he read the note.

The young Israeli woman behind the customs desk held Liam's open passport. She looked at his photograph, then his face. She jotted something on a form, studied his photo and face again. All business. She didn't crack a smile while she verified his identity.

Even with her game face on Liam could tell she was a natural beauty, with dark hair and lively, intelligent eyes that needed no cosmetics. Feeling his oats, Liam gave her his biggest smile.

"No," she said and shook her finger at him.

Now he remembered. He erased his tourist grin and stood there trying to look as somber as he had a year earlier when he renewed his passport. The Shreveport photographer told him to do a "serious pose" because the State Department had sent out a bulletin indicating they reserved the right to reject a passport photograph unless the applicant was "unsmiling." Liam did as the photographer said, and in the name of public safety, his fifty-three years of training to "smile for the camera" went down the tubes.

Chalk up another victory for the terrorists.

Like all the female customs and security agents Liam observed that day at Tel Aviv's Ben-Gurion International Airport, the young woman behind the customs desk wore a drab uniform and no makeup or jewelry. She took her job very seriously. She seemed in good physical condition and was not unpleasant, a rarity for someone in her line of work.

She looked at Mimi's passport for two seconds and pushed it back to Mimi on the counter. She smiled at Liam—only at Liam. He noticed her teeth were bright white and straight.

"Welcome to Israel," she said to him. "You are very tall. Our men are not so tall, not so big."

"Let's go," Mimi said, poking and pushing Liam.

Moments later, Liam and Mimi were making their way through the airport. Liam was impressed. Ben Gurion International was state of the art, finer than most airports in the States. Every surface was clean as a whistle, shiny and welcoming. Each uniformed Israeli who worked in the facility seemed busy and focused. No one was standing around or wasting time. Customs was efficient, security tight and thorough, but not oppressive, focusing on the behavior of air passengers and how they responded to simple questions. It was a system based on human intelligence, not blind adherence to mindless protocols.

"I'm surprised she didn't frisk you," Mimi said.

Liam laughed.

"Oooh, you are so tall," Mimi said, trying to channel the agent's accent. "Our men are not so tall."

"She was just doing her job," Liam said with a smile. "They're taught to be friendly."

"And you just ate it up, didn't you, Mr. Big Stuff."

Mimi laughed and stuck her arm through Liam's. She pulled him close to her and snuggled against his arm as they walked.

"I don't blame that girl one bit," she said.

They entered the ground transportation area looking for Ike Palmer. Liam scanned the professional drivers holding signs in English, Hebrew, and Arabic. He had gone online before the trip to look at the two Semitic languages he knew he would encounter in Israel. The only thing he managed to learn was how to distinguish written Hebrew from Arabic. Hebrew characters were more upright and forceful than the elegant, cursive-styled Arabic alphabet. Walking through the airport he was pleased to see signs in English because he didn't know a single written or spoken word of Hebrew or Arabic.

"Look for a skinny guy with wild eyes walking like he's got a charlie horse," he suggested to Mimi, "talking really loud."

"I'll just keep a lookout for anyone strange," she said.

They passed a bronze bust of David Ben-Gurion, founding father and first prime minister of Israel. The bust confirmed what Liam noted about Ben-Gurion when he had first seen photographs of the prime minister in books and magazine articles: David Ben-Gurion, perhaps Israel's greatest statesman of all time, wore his hair in the same style as Larry Fine of the Three Stooges.

"There," Mimi said and pointed to a man holding a sign that read "Liam Connors."

They walked toward him. He was stocky, no more than 5'6", Liam estimated, and in his late fifties or early sixties. He wore jeans, Nike running shoes, a lightweight brown jacket, a tan fedora-shaped Tilley Hat on his slick brown head, and eyeglasses with lightly tinted transition lenses.

"Are you Mr. Connors?" the man asked in a heavy accent.

"I'm Liam Connors from Louisiana, U.S.A.," Liam said extending his hand.

"I am Menachem Wladyslaw," he said, exchanging a firm handshake and studying Liam with intelligent eyes.

"We were expecting to be met by Mr. Isaac Palmer."

"Yitzhak Palmer sent me to pick you up, Mr. Connors. I am to drive you and your guest to Jerusalem." Menachem caught himself. "Excuse, please. Yitzhak is Hebrew for Isaac."

"Well, let's go, Menachem," Liam said, trying to emit the guttural *ch* from deep in the back of his throat as Menachem had.

Liam had no hope of learning any Hebrew or Yiddish, but he did tell Mimi on the flight from Rome to Tel Aviv he wanted to learn how to produce the *ch* correctly while in Israel, so he could pronounce *chutzpah* and *l'chaim* correctly.

Menachem took Mimi's rolling suitcase and led them out of the airport. Within minutes Liam and Mimi sat in the backseat of Menachem's weathered gray Volvo heading southeast on Highway One, a well-engineered multi-laned highway.

"Look at the olive groves," Mimi said, "and all the trees."

While Mimi studied the landscape, Liam studied her. He loved to watch Mimi when her attention was elsewhere. Her hair was dark, almost black. She wore it very short in an asymmetric cut he thought was cool. Only a woman as beautiful as Mimi could wear her hair so short and still look stunning. Mimi said the length was ideal for her work as a nurse practitioner. Her skin was pale, smooth and flawless. Her nose was small and perfect. At thirty-eight, Mimi was fifteen years younger than Liam, and fourteen years younger than Liam's late wife, Annette.

Liam Connors was too big to be comfortable in the back seat of Manachem's Volvo. Broad-shouldered, 6'5" and 200 pounds, with high cheekbones and sandy blond hair beginning to show a little gray at the temples. Women thought him handsome. More than a few travelers in the Tel Aviv airport stopped to watch the striking American couple pass.

"Very good road," Liam said to Menachem, pulling Mimi toward him and kissing her lightly on the back of her lovely neck. She gave him a "what's that all about?" smile.

"Yes," Menachem said, making eye contact with Liam in the rear view mirror, "we have most excellent highways in Israel. Highway One is our main highway. It is the best, in my opinion."

"Where do you live?" Liam asked.

"Not far."

"In Jerusalem?"

Menachem nodded, more or less, and removed his Tilley hat. Liam studied the driver's head. The top of his head was smooth and tanned. Naturally bald, he shaved the sides to match.

"Let him concentrate on the road," Mimi whispered to Liam. "Some drivers don't like it when you talk to them."

Excited about being in Israel, Liam managed to keep quiet for about two miles. He asked Menachem if he were born in Israel.

"Yes. Near Jerusalem."

Liam pulled out his Lonely Planet travel book on Israel and the Palestinian Territories and turned to the section on Jerusalem. Mimi looked on with him. After a while, Liam's attention wandered to the thick pine and cedar groves on the hills they passed. The

Volvo was climbing steadily. He gave Mimi the book and leaned forward.

"We've been heading uphill since we left the airport."

"Yes. Jerusalem is a city on a hill, the kind your New Testament writer Matthew describes, whose light cannot be hidden. It is at elevation two thousand five hundred feet; the airport a little over one hundred," Menachem said. "Your first time in Israel?"

"Yes," Mimi said, looking up. "But we're only here for three days. Do you think it's safe?"

"Safer than Chicago," he said and made eye contact with Liam again in his mirror. "There's no danger for you inside Israel. Tourism is an important part of our economy and our government makes a great effort to keep our visitors safe. Tourism is not so good right now with the conflicts in Syria and Egypt and the continuing threats from Iran."

"Your English is very good," Liam said

His eyes on the highway, Menachem nodded and picked up something from his passenger seat. Over his shoulder he gave Liam his business card. Menachem Wladyslaw was printed in dark green bold print next to the image of an olive tree, together with his cell number and e-mail address. The card proclaimed Menachem a tour guide and interpreter of Hebrew, Yiddish, German, and English. Liam was impressed with Menachem's ability to navigate four difficult languages.

Liam felt ashamed of his own parochialism. Like most American travelers, Liam was fluent only in English. He retained some of the French he learned at LSU and a little Spanish from high school, but not enough to carry on an adult conversation in either language. His vocabulary was decent, but he spoke only in present tense and could understand little of what was said to him in French or Spanish unless the natives talked to him like a two-year-old.

Liam had worked his way through LSU on a ROTC scholarship and earned a degree in petroleum engineering. After fulfilling his military obligation and a stint with Chevron in New Orleans and Lafayette, he went out on his own and built from scratch an oil and gas exploration and production company, Clare Petroleum headquartered in Shreveport.

He stuck Menachem's business card in the pocket of his wrinkled white Oxford cloth shirt. Mimi studied the map of Jerusalem that unfolded from the Lonely Planet book. Liam patted her shoulder and gave her a wink. She smiled that playful smile of hers.

"It's three-thirty local time?" Liam asked Menachem.

"That's correct. Seven hours ahead of your East Coast. The date is February 27."

"How much longer to Jerusalem?"

"Only a few more minutes to the Old City."

"Is that where Yitzhak lives, the Old City?"

"That's where he asked me to bring you."

"Where does he live?"

"I don't know. I will let him know we're on schedule."

He picked up his cell and sent a text. Moments later, Menachem's phone buzzed. He read a message.

"Yitzhak will be late," Menachem said over his shoulder, "but not late too much. You must meet him in a different place."

Liam made eye contact in Menachem's mirror and nodded. Liam wasn't surprised Ike had changed the plans. He was an impulsive, smart guy with a quick wit and a mind that ran only at full speed. At LSU, when Ike was in a good mood, he talked nonstop and very loudly. He partied hard, drinking beer daily, smoking lots of weed, and carousing into the morning hours. Well-versed in things other than SEC sports, girls, and drinking, Ike kept up with current events and read a newspaper every day, a practice almost unheard of for an undergraduate in Baton Rouge. Ike's command of politics and international news had always impressed Liam.

"Do we have time to check into our hotel before we see Mr. Palmer?" Mimi asked Menachem.

"Yes, if you like," he said. "Your hotel?"

"The King David," Liam said.

"Very nice. Full of history."

"Is it far from the Old City?" Mimi asked.

"Not far. Walking distance."

"Are we meeting Ike Palmer in the Old City?" she asked.

"No. We will see him in Machne. Mahane Yehuda in your book. From the King David it is not far."

Menachem waited outside next to his gray Volvo as Liam and Mimi entered the elegant lobby of the King David Hotel. They checked in and looked around. The staff was crisply uniformed and attentive, anxious to serve. Before going upstairs, Liam took a quick peek in the Oriental Bar off the reception area, and the King's Garden Restaurant overlooking the hotel gardens and pool.

In their room on the top floor of the six-story hotel, a room described by the front desk clerk as a "deluxe Old City suite," Liam stood at the window overlooking the Old City. The hotel was built on a hill, and from the top floor Liam could see the domes and minarets of ancient Jerusalem. It had been a city for over three thousand years according to Liam's Lonely Planet, which he read while Mimi freshened up. According to the travel book, the southern wing of the hotel, used by the British as their administrative and military headquarters during the British Mandate, had been blown up by the Irgun in 1946. After the Brits took down their flag in 1948, the King David became prominent in the early history of the newly established Jewish State.

Liam walked barefoot into the large bathroom. Mimi sat in her bra and panties on a small, cushioned bench touching up her eye makeup. Liam knelt behind her and put his arms around her waist, looking at their reflection in the mirror. He kissed the back of her neck and buried his nose in her short, dark hair, inhaling deeply.

"You smell so good," Liam said.

She turned, draped her arms around his neck and kissed him lightly. Liam wanted more. He kissed her deeply.

"Are you interested, Mr. Connors?"

He kissed her again, this time exploring her delicious mouth with his tongue. He stood up, took off his shirt, and slipped out of his pants. Mimi watched him. She smiled and pulled off his boxers.

"Oh, Mr. Connors," she said aping the custom girl's accent, "you are interested." Eyes wide, she reached to examine him. "Our men are are not nearly so big, Mr. Connors."

Liam laughed and picked her up effortlessly, carrying her into the bedroom and gently placing her on the bed.

"What about Menachem?" she said removing her bra.

"I think he should stay with the car."

Before leaving the hotel, Mimi and Liam took time to read the names of the myriad world leaders and celebrities who had been guests in the King David, their signatures permanently displayed in floor tiles in the main corridor. Outside, Mimi commented on the towering palms lining the hotel drive and the rich landscaping. They walked toward Menachem leaning against his Volvo, talking on his cell. As they drew close, he ended his phone call and opened the car door. He drove them onto the narrow, busy King David Street in front of the hotel and headed north.

"Sorry you had to wait," Liam said. "I took a little nap."

"No. The timing is good. I have talked to Yitzhak. Just now. We will arrive at the market when he does. It is not far."

Mimi smiled and mouthed "not far" to Liam. She patted his knee as Menachem wove expertly through the traffic, veering west onto Hillel Street. After a few minutes he turned into a narrow alley and stopped. Menachem opened his phone and punched in a number. A battered aluminum garage door on the driver's side rolled up. He drove into the single parking space hidden between two buildings. It was a tight fit for the Volvo. Mimi squeezed easily through her partially open door, but Liam had a tough time getting his big frame out of the Volvo and into the alley. Menachem entered the number on his phone again and the door closed.

"Follow me," he said. "Stay very close."

No more than a hundred feet from where they parked, the narrow alley opened into a plaza adjacent to a crowded open-air market.

Menachem stopped to explain, speaking loudly over the market din. "This is Mahane Yehuda. Jerusalem's main market for locals. Tourists come here, too. You can buy anything, everything. All fresh. Very popular."

They walked through the plaza and slightly uphill on the market's main street. Around them locals pushed carts or carried bags of strange looking produce, calling out greetings to vendors they passed. The constant roar in exotic languages was punctuated by loud laughter and good natured shouting. Tourists gawked at the bustling spectacle as they followed their guides, trying not to trip on the uneven stone pavement.

"Sounds like the Tower of Babel." Mimi turned to Liam. "Fascinating. Some of the things for sale I don't even recognize."

Liam studied the merchants and buyers haggling. He understood nothing of what was being said, but saw one customer shake his head and his hand from side to side in the universal gesture meaning "that price is too high." Menachem paused to let a merchant pushing a wooden cart full of bananas pass. Mimi nudged Liam to look at the incredible variety of white and golden cheeses in the stall next to them.

Menachem raised his right hand over his head and turned ninety degrees to duck into a much smaller lane covered with a canopy of opaque fabric. There was little room. Liam and Mimi inched between vendors displaying fresh and dried fruits, vegetables, nuts, fresh fish and whole chickens on ice, pastries and breads, falafel, eggs, cheese, toys, candy, and clothing.

"Stay close," Liam said, putting his arm around Mimi.

"Gladly," she said smiling and looking up into his eyes.

Mimi poked Liam and pointed to gaudy sweatshirts and tee shirts some merchants hung overhead.

"You'd look fetching in that," she whispered.

They squeezed past other stalls where merchants folded their clothing inventory neatly on display shelves next to religious icons and prayer beads. The walkway was no more than eight feet wide, sometimes much narrower because of goods puddling out from the stalls. Liam and Mimi weaved around the merchandise and the steady flow of shoppers and workers, amazed at the ordered chaos.

Liam moved aside to allow a young boy to pass pulling a dolly stacked with crates of fruit, and found himself in a stall next to large, open burlap sacks of bright-colored spices, an amalgam of aromas Liam had never before encountered. Liam hustled to catch up with Mimi and Menachem, who had stopped past the spice merchant to turn into a stall offering dates, figs, plums, pistachios, almonds, cashews, and other fruits and nuts in open containers. A pigeon perched itself on the edge of a wooden crate, busily pecking at plump, cracked walnuts piled high in a display box.

Menachem exchanged a warm handshake and embrace with a small, grizzled man Liam assumed was the shop owner. The merchant gestured for Menachem to walk to the back of the store. Mimi and Liam smiled at the little fellow as they passed but he shook his head dismissively at the two Americans and gave a half-hearted wave for them to hurry inside. He growled and wiped his hands on a raggedy towel before flinging it at the walnut-eating pigeon.

They passed through a narrow doorway covered with a thin cloth into a café that was more spacious than Liam expected. Menachem gestured for Liam and Mimi to sit at a small table and barked something into the adjacent kitchen. A young, brown-skinned waiter came out to them wearing a wide smile. A jagged scar disfigured his left cheek.

"My name is Yusef. Coffee or tea?" he asked, very happy to see his new customers.

"The Turkish coffee here is very good," Menachem said. "I recommend you order their specialty—a remarkable date-filled pastry, the best in the entire market. Trust me."

Mimi said that was fine with her. Liam asked Menachem to tell the young waiter they'd have Turkish coffee and one of the café's famous pastries. It seemed to please Yusef greatly and he hustled into the kitchen.

"How do you think he got that awful scar?" Mimi asked Menachem.

"Who knows? He's Bedouin, in the desert or mountains somewhere. I can assure you it has been many weeks since he looked into a mirror. He does not give his scar much thought." Menachem glanced at his watch. "Yitzhak will be here soon. I must see a man the next street over. It will take only fifteen minutes. Enjoy your coffee and wait here for me please. No good to wander the market. It is possible to get lost."

"Don't worry," Liam said. "We'll stay right here. Do they take U.S. dollars?"

"Yes. Everyone in this market will welcome American dollars. I promise your U.S. currency is good almost everywhere in Israel. The Old City. In every sector, including the Muslim and Armenian Quarters. In Bethlehem or Nazareth or the other P.A. controlled areas on the West Bank, some merchants may not accept your money. Except maybe if they are not selling too much, then they will take your U.S. money."

"I could spend all day in this market," Mimi said after Menachem left, "just wandering around looking at things. The people, the stalls, the shops—it's all so exotic, so interesting."

"Like you," Liam winked.

Yusef brought the Turkish coffee, milk and sugar, and set the pastry between Liam and Mimi. He placed a smaller plate in front of each and handed them utensils wrapped in paper napkins. Liam thanked Yusef and served the pastry while Mimi doctored her coffee with milk and brown sugar. Liam looked for a moment into the dark, dense liquid in his small cup and took a sip, straight up.

"Whoa," he said. "That's strong. Kind of a smoky taste."

"Oh, my God," Mimi said after taking a bite of her pastry. "It melts in your mouth."

Liam was about to take a bite of his half when Crazy Ike Palmer lurched in from the kitchen. There was no mistaking Ike Palmer, still wiry and walking in his signature hyper herky-jerky manner. Liam stood and extended his big hand, but Ike pushed it aside and embraced him in a powerful hug. Liam felt Ike trembling.

Liam was surprised at how good it felt to see Ike again, crazy or not. Liam introduced Mimi and Ike gave her a big hug. "I'm so happy to see you guys," Ike yelled.

Ike started to say something else but choked up. Tears filled his eyes. Liam felt his own emotions welling up.

"Nice to meet you at last, Ike," Mimi said.

"Don't believe everything this peckerwood tells you," Ike said.

"I only told her the PG rated stories," Liam said, then hugged Ike again. "You are a sight for sore eyes. Sit down. Sit down. Let's get you a cup of coffee and one of these great pastries."

"Not for me, Liam. I need caffeine like an Eskimo needs ice. I'm high on the real thing."

Mimi looked alarmed but Liam started laughing. It was something they used to say when they were freshman at LSU.

"Gasoline!" Ike said and burst into an ear-splitting, open-mouthed laugh that sounded like a donkey braying. Liam hadn't experienced Ike's quirky laugh in two-and-a-half decades and was happy to hear it again, even if Ike's decibel output was out of control.

Ike was mostly gray, his remaining wavy black hair now relegated to streaks. He wore it long and combed straight back. A ten-day growth of salt and pepper stubble ranged across his cheeks. Liam guessed that Ike was still carrying about a hundred-and-fifty pounds on his six-foot frame. His face was tanned and deeply wrinkled, probably from the elements and most certainly from worry. Ike was a world-class worrier. His distinctive feature was still there—intense, very light, iceberg blue eyes that seemed to stare right through you. The color of Ike's eyes made Liam homesick for Shep, his eight-year-old Australian Shepherd, Liam's constant, faithful, ever cheerful companion as he explored the oil and gas fields of Louisiana.

"Tell me what you're doing," Liam said. "The last time we talked—1988—you were leaving Natchitoches to join a kibbutz on the edge of the Judean desert. Not a word from you since."

Ike smiled. A tremor at the edge of his mouth.

"How is Nathan?" Liam asked.

"Still making a fortune with his hedge fund. Living like a pagan. Denying his faith. I've given up trying to get him to return to temple."

"Do you talk?"

"Not really. The time differential between here and Wall Street makes communication tough, you know. Nathan's my only family but we live in different worlds. My older brother doesn't believe in anything."

"You ought to reach out to him," Liam said.

Ike checked the time on his phone.

"Do you think there's a bathroom in here?" Mimi asked.

"Sure is," Ike said. "Come with me."

Ike hopped up and led Mimi out of the dining area to a door just inside the kitchen. He told her to wait while he checked it out.

In for a few seconds, he came out nodding and hustled back to rejoin Liam at the table.

"That bathroom's not fancy but it's clean enough and works fine." He looked around to see if anyone else was in earshot. "I don't want to talk in front of Mimi."

"About your S.O.S.?"

"Yeah. Every word in my letter is true. I've found something in the desert that is going to change the political and religious landscape of the Middle East. The whole world. Huge ramifications."

"You never said what it was."

"I couldn't put it in the letter. Not safe."

"Mimi's going to have to know at some point."

"No problem with her knowing later. For now, it has to be just us."

"Why do you need me?"

"You're the *only* person in the world I trust one hundred per cent."

He leaned forward and took another look around the room just as Mimi returned to the table.

"Can you join us for dinner tonight at the hotel?" Mimi asked.

Ike held up one finger, reached for his pocket with his other hand, and pulled out his phone, looking at the screen.

"Excuse me," he said loudly, "Gotta take this."

Ike stood and disappeared into the kitchen.

Chapter Two

Mimi usually let Liam eat more than half of anything they shared. But not the date-filled pastry. Liam eyed what was left of her half.

"Keep your hands off," she said.

He pretended to pout and finished his strong Turkish coffee, occasionally glancing at the pastry just in case she changed her mind. She polished it off with exaggerated fanfare.

"This coffee is stout," Liam said. "Want another pastry?"

"Better not. I won't eat any supper."

"I could probably skip supper," Liam said patting his stomach, which was not as flat as usual, thanks to their previous ten days in Umbria and Tuscany.

Although he consumed too much pasta and red wine, the trip had been the most relaxing vacation Liam could recall. They had flown directly into Rome, where they picked up their full-sized Ford from Hertz and fled the city as quickly as possible. Liam had been to Rome, Venice, Florence, and Milan three years earlier with his wife Annette and a couple from Mississippi, close friends Willie Mitchell Banks and wife Susan. The Vatican and other historical sights were impressive and the urban energy exciting, but this trip he wanted to stay as far away from big cities as possible. Mimi, who had never been to Europe, had been eager to experience rural Italy, having read *Under the Tuscan Sun* over Christmas break during her first year of nursing school.

The ten days in Northern Italy had been everything Liam hoped for. He shed several layers of stress accumulated in finally closing on the transfer of the deep rights to mineral leases on fifteen thousand acres in Northwest Louisiana to Delaware Energy, overcoming aggressive attempts by the EPA and other federal agencies to prevent the sale. Liam's litigation with the feds was the most disheartening experience of his life, second only to Annette's death in an automobile crash. His own government advanced distortions, lies, and environmental junk science in an effort to derail the deal. Louisiana politicians he thought were friends treated him like a pariah, officially siding with the EPA and

Department of Energy. Liam had supported the junior senator from Louisiana in her last election. Her chief of staff offered a weak excuse for leaving Liam twisting in the wind. The staffer said the State could not afford to lose the money the EPA was doling out to Louisiana to assist in shoring up the coastal marshes disappearing because of salt water intrusion.

Liam informed both Louisiana senators he wasn't asking for a favor; he just wanted them to look at the facts. If they would take the time to study the issues, it would be clear that the government was overstepping its bounds. Liam was not in violation of any State or Federal regulations. The senators lied to Liam, saying they would take a look and get back right away. No word for a week, so Liam followed up. Each senator's chief of staff told Liam he was sorry, but their office was just too busy to get down in the weeds and study his situation. Then they repeated the real reason: there was too much funding at stake for them to question the EPA on Liam's behalf.

Liam decided to go it alone. He fought the agencies in Federal Court and won the right to conclude the deal with Delaware. The sale closed in December the previous year. Since the closing Liam had spent a lot of money finding out why he was targeted out of all the exploration companies in the Northwest Louisiana shale play. His friend Willie Mitchell Banks helped Liam get to the bottom of it. The lobbyists and investigators Liam hired with Willie Mitchell's help uncovered the source of his troubles—one angry career bureaucrat with a personal vendetta against Liam. Willie Mitchell broke the news the day they were leaving for Italy. Liam asked Willie Mitchell to tell his lawyers to keep their powder dry. He would handle it after his trip.

Liam had enjoyed the rolling hills of rural northern Italy, the local red wines with lunch and dinner, the long, lazy afternoons with Mimi. Late February was still low season for tourists. He and Mimi had expected cool temperatures, but they got lucky with what the locals pronounced an early spring. It was sweater weather, warm in the sunshine and cool in the late afternoons. They stayed at one centrally located B&B in Umbria, another in Tuscany. Every day was a laid-back, easy-going adventure of leisurely walks, wine tastings, delicious local cuisine, and love-making. Liam and Mimi took off on foot each morning, walking the gentle hills out from the inns, some days passing not a single tourist. Mimi was a good sport and lots of fun. Their time together in Italy was high romance.

Their first afternoon in Israel had been pleasant as well, with blue skies and mild temperatures. The King David was everything

Liam had expected and their walk through the open air market to the café was a treasure trove of people-watching. Liam patted Mimi's hand. He could tell she was anxious to leave the café and meander through more of the outdoor market. He didn't blame her. Liam was tired of waiting for Ike. He was ready to go, too.

"Looks like our luck with the weather is holding," Liam said.

"You should check on your friend," Mimi said. "He's been gone a long time."

Liam walked to the kitchen and poked his head in. The young Bedouin waiter Yusef smiled at him, making the raised scar even more prominent. Liam spoke slowly in English and used hand gestures to ask Yusef where his friend Ike had gone. The simple words that came out of Liam included *mi amigo*. Yusef understood somehow and pointed to an outside exit. Liam stepped through the door into a courtyard paved with limestone expecting to find Ike yelling excitedly to someone on his cell. No such luck. Ike had vanished.

Liam returned to the kitchen and tried to communicate with Yusef. The young man shrugged and smiled. He pointed to the courtyard. If Ike weren't in the courtyard, Yusef didn't know where he was. Liam rejoined Mimi at the table.

"Where is Ike?" Mimi asked.

"He went out the back door of the kitchen, according to Yusef. There's a courtyard back there but it's empty. He's gone."

"He's a bundle of nerves," Mimi said.

"I know that. He used to tell me he had been certified—he had papers to prove he was crazy."

"Does he always speak so loud?"

"No. Sometimes louder."

When Ike's FedEx letter arrived at Liam's Grand Oaks Plantation, five miles south of Natchitoches on the right-descending bank of the Cane River, Liam explained Ike's history to Mimi as they sat in the wooden swing on the wide porch of the raised plantation house.

Liam told her about meeting Ike for the first time in Natchitoches, when Liam's high school basketball team traveled seventy miles south from Shreveport to play Ike's high school. The two of them hit it off and began a friendship that continued through their college years in Baton Rouge. Liam explained that Ike was given to mood swings at LSU, dramatic highs and lows, which he self-medicated with Budweiser and weed. His many friends attributed Ike's swings to extreme moodiness, which became a part of Ike's profile everyone accepted. Just as some guys were known as ladies' men, mean drunks, goof-offs, or dopers, Ike was known for his moods. But there was an upside. In a good mood, Ike was more fun than anyone on the Baton Rouge campus.

Ike pledged a Jewish fraternity at LSU, Phi Epsilon Pi. None of the big frats rushed him. They were limited by their founding charters to recruiting "young Christian men of good character." Liam told Ike he was ineligible on two counts, he was Jewish *and* of bad character. The Phi Eps had dwindled to a dozen members when Ike pledged, and while they were in school the local chapter folded. No loss to Ike. Well-liked and a known hell-raiser, he partied at every fraternity house on campus.

As a Jew at LSU in the early eighties, Ike insisted to Liam that his paranoia was merely "heightened awareness." Ike explained that "even paranoid Jews can have real enemies."

The summer after graduation Ike returned to Natchitoches and married Irene Porter, the only child of a wealthy cotton and soybean farmer. Four years later, Ike was diagnosed with depression, bi-polar disorder, and paranoid personality by a psychiatrist in Shreveport. He struggled through two years of treatment, then divorced Irene and left the U.S. for Israel.

Ike's history made Mimi wary. But she was excited about the side trip to Jerusalem. She cautioned Liam against getting involved with Ike's scheme, whatever it might be. It became clear, however, that Liam was dead set on meeting Ike, so she told Liam in the swing on Grand Oak's porch that no matter how crazy Ike was, she could put up with anything for three days. Liam booked their flight from Rome to Tel Aviv. They would fly directly to Newark from Tel Aviv three days later.

Liam himself was having second thoughts about re-connecting with Ike when Menachem parted the cloth hanging in the café door. Liam gestured for him to join them at the table.

"Ike left us," Liam said.

"Yes. He called me."

"How could he be so rude!" Mimi said.

"It is Yitzhak's way. He wants another meeting tomorrow."

"Where will we meet him?"

"Just you," Menachem said to Liam as he removed his hat and scratched his smooth, shiny scalp. He looked at Mimi. "I am sorry but that is what Yitzhak decides."

"That's fine with me," Mimi said. "It certainly doesn't hurt my feelings. I can find something else to do."

Menachem handed Liam a cell phone.

"Yitzhak asked me to procure this rental phone for you. For calls inside Israel only. My number I have entered in the phone for you. Easier for you to contact me or for Yitzhak to call you. He has the number. You will not be able to call him. He changes phones and numbers many times."

"This is a little too much drama," Liam said to Menachem. "How well do you know Ike?"

"Hard to say. I drive him."

"I have known Ike since we played sports against each other in high school. We attended the same college. We partied and hung out together when he was married."

"You are old friends. He tells me he admires you."

"Ike's wife put up with a lot before the divorce. Thank God, they had no children. Ike had mental problems as a young man in Louisiana, mania and depression with a large helping of paranoia."

"I know of these things with Yitzhak. He was a troubled young man in America."

"So, what I want to ask you, Menachem, is whether Ike is...?"

Liam made small circles at his right temple with his index finger.

"No. He is not insane. Yitzhak has real enemies. Men follow us when I drive him. This happens more than once in the last two weeks. I have seen these men with my own eyes."

"Has he told you why he asked me to come to Israel?"

"No. He hires me to drive him. I hear him talk on his phone. I only know you are his friend from U.S."

"Has he told you about something he may have found?"

"I have heard him speak about that, but I know very little. He is careful on the phone. You know him. He speaks loud. But I must think Yitzhak a good person. If he says to you he found something I believe he tells the truth. You should give him another chance to explain."

"Who followed you? Is it someone from your government?"

"I do not think so. I do not know."

"Oh, come on. I'm tired," Mimi said. "Let's go back to the hotel."

"Absolutely," Menachem said.

Liam kept putting one dollar bills in the waiter Yusef's hand until Menachem told him "enough." The three filed outside into the maelstrom of the Mahane Yehuda market. It was later than Liam realized. They were losing the daylight. As they walked downhill on the ancient paving stones toward the Volvo in Menachem's parking place off the alley, Liam heard the call to prayer.

He looked for its source and found it atop a minaret next to a small blue-domed mosque outside the market. Instead of a devout *muezzin* singing a gentle Muslim prayer, Liam was disappointed to note a large set of speakers. The sound was tinny and intrusive— almost sinister. It did not make Liam feel like praying.

Chapter Three

"I should tell him to forget it," Liam said, "but when Ike walked through that kitchen door it was like he had never gone away. We picked up right where we left off. We really had some good times at LSU."

"That's nostalgia," Mimi said. "He reminds you of your youth."

"*Ute*. When we were *utes*."

Mimi thought a minute.

"*My Cousin Vinny.*"

"You make me very proud," Liam said.

Liam raised his Glenlivet over ice to her Ketel One and tonic with lime at their small table in the King David's stylish Oriental bar. Except for an older Indian couple in the corner and a fidgety forty-something Japanese banker-type seated at the bar, they had the place to themselves. They relaxed in low cushioned chairs, enveloped in soft, soothing music. The moment was serene. Liam touched his glass to hers.

"And you make me very happy," he said. "I love you."

Liam leaned close and kissed her lightly on the mouth, then took her hand and kissed the back of it.

"I love you, too. Such a wonderful trip. I don't want it to end."

Liam sat back in his chair. "I'm glad you suggested we go out when we first met," he said as a matter of fact. "I might never have worked up the nerve."

"You have a selective memory," she laughed. "I would have asked you if you hadn't asked me first."

Liam thought back to the first time he had seen Mimi in the doctor's office in Natchitoches. He was in for a physical. Mimi was Dr. Vercher's nurse practitioner. She handled his preliminary workup, asking questions in the exam room raised by Liam's answers on Dr.Vercher's new patient questionnaire. When she asked for his marital status because he had left it blank, he asked for hers. Liam termed himself a widower with two grown daughters. Mimi volunteered she was divorced, no children. It was the first time Liam had showed any interest in a woman since

Annette's death a year earlier. Flirting with Mimi felt right that day in Dr. Vercher's examination room.

"I'm going to give Ike the benefit of the doubt," Liam said, sipping his Glenlivet.

"I don't think you should. He acts like he's on speed."

"He's always been like that. Wound tight."

Liam took another sip. The melting ice softened the Glenlivet. No matter what the purists said, Liam liked ice.

"I'm going to call Menachem first thing tomorrow morning and see if he can take me to meet Ike again. I'll listen to what Ike has to say. If he's gone totally nuts, I'll forget about him and whatever he claims to have found. You and I can spend the next couple of days seeing Jerusalem and Israel. Perhaps we can hire Menachem to drive us around and show us the sights. We'll make the best of our three days."

"I know he's an old friend, but he gives me the willies. Be careful. Don't let him mix you up in something."

Liam thought back to the time Ike talked him and two other drunken Kappa Sigmas into climbing historic Memorial Tower in the center of campus. They hung out two bedsheets Ike had stitched together, on which he had painted IRAN SUCKS. It was the middle of the 1980 hostage crisis, and it created a firestorm among the Persian exchange students on the Baton Rouge campus. Ike was arrested for trespassing by the campus police but never ratted on Liam or the other two students. The incident could have cost Liam his ROTC scholarship had his involvement become known. Crazy Ike Palmer told LSU Campus Security he didn't care if they tortured him; he'd never give up his buddies. Liam imposed on a Kappa Sig acquaintance, a third-year law student, to write a First Amendment freedom of speech screed in Ike's defense for the "Daily Reveille." The Administration relented and dismissed the charges against Ike, resulting in more drunken revelry at the Kappa Sigma house.

"Don't worry," Liam said. "I know Ike's ways. It'll be fine."

"I'm going to wander around the Old City," Mimi said. "The concierge says it's an easy walk from the hotel. He gave me a map and said it's very safe. Jerusalem's history is fascinating."

"I find you fascinating," he said, kissing her hand again. "Let's do this. I'll plan on being back in our room by one o'clock. If I'm running late, I'll leave a message for you on the phone. We'll tour with Menachem tomorrow afternoon, get him to drop us off someplace nice in the new part of Jerusalem for dinner."

"The concierge said the first place we should go together is the top of the Mount of Olives. Get a panoramic view of the Old City and central Jerusalem."

"Deal," Liam said and raised his glass again, clinking hers. "To the most beautiful woman in Israel."

"Israel?"

"The Middle East."

She pretended to ignore him.

"The hemisphere."

"Which one?"

"All four. Northern and southern. Eastern and western."

She finally smiled his way. "How is your back?"

"Still a little sore."

"Just a muscle strain. Nothing to worry about. I'll rub it when we get back to the room. Use the physical therapy they taught us at nursing school."

He smiled. "Versatile. Ready for another?"

"Yes, but I have an idea. Let's do something daring."

"You have my undivided attention," he said.

"Let's ask the waiter to bring us a room service menu. We'll study our choices while we sip our drinks, then order dinner and a nice bottle of Israeli wine for the room and head upstairs."

"You, *Mademoiselle Mimi*, are a genius."

"In France, they continue to call divorcees *madame*."

"Even if they are young and beautiful and sexy?"

"*Oui, monsieur*. I looked it up. I thought you might want to take me to Provence while we're on this side of the Atlantic. El Al has a direct flight to Marseille."

"Why would I do something like that?"

"They think Provence is where human habitation in Europe began. And Avignon has the *Palais des Papes*. Didn't the nuns teach you about the dueling popes in the Fourteenth Century?"

"Not hardly. Come up with a better reason."

"The French were pioneers in modern medicine. Louis Pasteur was the first to create antibiotics. Other French scientists came up with the formulas for quinine, codeine, and aspirin. And they invented the stethoscope."

"Were any of these scientists from Provence?"

"Possibly. They didn't teach us that in nursing school."

"Unless you can tie one of these discoveries to Provence, I'm not convinced we should change our schedule. What else?"

"Okay," she paused and stroked his hand. "When you speak to me in French, it makes my knees weak and gives me very wicked ideas."

Liam pretended to think about it.

"Since you put it like that, let's see what tomorrow brings with Ike, then I'll talk to the concierge about Provence."

"I'm actually feeling very creative right now in Jerusalem."

Liam held her eyes and gently kissed the back of her hand.

"Should I try to guess what's in store for me upstairs?" he asked.

"You can guess, but I'm not at liberty to say. I do think you'll be pleased."

"*Garcon,*" Liam said as he signaled for the waiter.

An hour later, the white wine bottle on the bedside table was empty but the vintage domes covering dinner had not been touched. Liam lay on his back with his arm around Mimi, her head resting on his bare chest. She sighed.

"I guess I ought to put on my gown."

"I like this look," Liam said, lifting the fine cotton sheet.

"Should we have our dinner now?"

"I guess we should. Keep up our strength."

Liam walked across the room and lifted the silver dome. Mimi sat up against the headboard. Liam placed a pillow on her lap and the dinner plate on the pillow.

"Dinner is served, *madame.*"

"I've never been served by a naked waiter before."

"I hope everything meets with your approval."

"Yes. I am quite satisfied with your services—all of them."

Liam removed the plush white robe with "King David" stitched on its pocket from the bathroom door and admired their sixth floor view of Jerusalem's Old City.

"You know," Liam said, watching Mimi pick at the food on her plate, "if we keep up these two-a-days we might not have much time for sightseeing."

"Yes," Mimi said in the customs agent's Israeli accent, "that would be a tragedy, Mr. Tall Man. But some things can't be helped."

Chapter Four

The next morning Menachem answered Liam on the second ring.

"Menachem here."

"Can you pick me up at the King David?"

"Yes. Ten minutes. I have spoken to Yitzhak."

"Good. I'll wait for you on the street."

Liam asked the concierge to enter the King David's number on the rent-a-phone Menachem gave him. He tested it and walked outside.

Liam and Mimi had deliberately left their phones and iPads in Natchitoches. He gave his two daughters and everyone at Clare Petroleum the contact information for their B&Bs in Italy and the King David, but made it clear they were to contact him only in an emergency. It had been the longest time Liam had spent away from his computer and phone in many years—he felt liberated.

Out from under the *porte-cochere* he admired the impressive crowns atop a row of towering date palms lining the hotel driveway. Another gorgeous day. The palm fronds were silhouetted against an incredibly blue sky, more brilliant to Liam than the skies in northwest Louisiana. The elevation in Natchitoches was the same as Ben Gurion Airport, 2400 feet lower than Jerusalem.

Liam stood on the sidewalk and admired the arches and domes of the historic six-story YMCA central tower, directly across King David Street. His copy of Lonely Planet said the cornerstone was laid in 1928 and that the view from the top was one of the best in all of Jerusalem. He decided if the meeting with Ike was a bust he would ask Mimi to climb the steps to the top before they drove up the Mount of Olives.

Liam studied two young Israeli soldiers standing casually on the YMCA side of the street. They smiled at him and seemed relaxed, in spite of the machine guns hanging on straps from their shoulders. Liam estimated them to be in their early twenties. While he watched, they paid close attention to every pedestrian, every vehicle that passed, but never altered their informal, non-threatening demeanor.

Liam wondered if they were with the Jerusalem Police or the IDF, the Israel Defense Forces, but he was very familiar with their weapons—fully automatic Galil short assault rifles. The reliable Galil SAR was manufactured in Israel. During weapons training in the military, Liam had learned to use the Galil, as well as both the AK and H&K rifles.

When Menachem's gray Volvo came around the corner, Liam crossed the street and walked toward the car so Menachem did not have to turn in the hotel drive. Liam was ready to meet with Ike, figure out if Ike was blowing smoke about his big secret. Time to fish or cut bait.

"Good morning," Menachem said as Liam seated himself in the front passenger seat and closed his door.

"Okay if I sit up here?"

"Yes. It is better."

"Is Ike...Yitzhak expecting us?"

"We are heading there now. It is not far."

"This meeting with Yitzak. If it doesn't go well, could I hire you to show Mimi and me the city? You know, drive us to some sites like the Dead Sea and Masada? The next couple of days?"

"Surely. If you decide you cannot help Yitzhak I will be happy to drive you and your wife. He is very sorry about last night."

Liam opened the map of the city and tried to follow Menachem's route. When they turned east onto Shlomo Hamelech, Liam could see the ancient wall of the Old City ahead. They drove onto Jaffa Street, paralleling the track of the light rail that ran through the city.

"Damascus Gate," Menachem said, pointing to Liam's right.

The age of the limestone wall and its gates staggered Liam. In Louisiana, antebellum structures like his plantation house, Grand Oaks, were considered old because they pre-dated the Civil War. In Jerusalem, parts of the city walls, streets and remnants of buildings had been standing since the time of King Herod, two thousand years earlier.

Liam studied the city map and searched for signs on the street corners. As they passed Herod's Gate, Liam figured they were still on Sultan Suleiman, heading east. When they stopped at a red light, he held out the open map to Menachem and asked him to point to their destination.

"No need," he said, wagging his finger.

"Oh, I see. Let me guess. It's not far."

"Correct," Menachem said, looking very serious. "Finding the way on Jerusalem streets is a task for professionals."

Liam stared at his driver a moment and was relieved when Menachem cracked and began to chuckle. Liam laughed along with him and continued to try to follow their route on his map. The lack of signage forced him to give up. He only knew they headed north on a major multi-lane thoroughfare running through modern Jerusalem that was indistinguishable from freeways in any major city in the U.S. After fifteen minutes in heavy traffic, Menachem made a sharp exit off the main road without giving a signal. He executed several quick turns, eventually heading south. Four connected cars of Jerusalem's light train system passed them heading north in the median. Liam folded his map—he had no idea where they were. Menachem glanced in his rear view mirror and turned quickly onto a winding side street he followed for three blocks before parking behind an eight-story modern building. The sign read Palace Hotel. They entered through what Liam thought might be the employees' entrance. Liam followed Menachem through several connecting hallways. He was confused by all the turns, but it was obvious Menachem had come this way before. Finally, Menachem held open a door and they stepped into a huge dining room.

Waiters and tourists were moving in every direction. Menachem lead the way through the maze of crowded tables. White signs in the center of each proclaimed in English the names of the different tour groups enjoying their morning feed. Liam read the signs as they passed. Church groups, civic groups, school and university groups from all over the world.

Near the center of the dining hall, Liam got his bearings. He realized they had walked the length of one of the two wings of the big room. In front of them were six cafeteria-like serving stations offering breakfast foods and drinks—fresh breads and cereals, salads, spiced vegetables, and several types of hummus. There were egg, chicken, beef, and lamb dishes at another station, cheeses, yogurts, and Israeli-grown fruits available on another.

Waiters scurried here and there, replenishing deep serving trays to stay ahead of their ravenous guests. Tourists from both wings of the dining room circled the central food offerings like Hajj pilgrims circumnavigating the cube of the Kaaba at Mecca. Liam stayed behind Menachem as they walked carefully through a gaggle of Japanese pilgrims holding their empty plates tightly against their chests, their hungry eyes searching the stainless steel troughs before them.

When Menachem broke into the clear, Liam realized they had reached the far wing of the dining room. It was packed with at least two hundred more tourists. They passed a table of Koreans eating quietly, but earnestly. Then came a table of ill-dressed, overweight Americans talking loudly as they buttered their muffins and demanded more pastries and coffee. When they reached the far end, Menachem led Liam into a corner, where Menachem pulled back a wooden folding door and escorted him into an alcove tucked away from the diners. Menachem closed the folding door behind them and motioned Liam to sit at one of the tables in the small room.

Relieved their journey through the dining room was completed without incident, Liam was grateful the four hundred plus diners had not stampeded and crushed him beneath their Timberland and Rockport walking shoes. Why had Menachem brought him to this giant indoor feed lot? Surely, they were not meeting Ike in this place.

"Coffee?" Menachem asked.

"Yes, sir," Liam said and turned his cup right side up.

Menachem walked over, pulled the folding door back, and signaled. He returned to the table followed by a waiter holding an insulated pitcher of coffee. Liam glanced up as the waiter poured his cup full to the rim.

It was Crazy Ike Palmer.

"What the hell are you doing here, Ike?"

Ike had trimmed his stubble, had pulled his unruly hair back into a small, neat bun, and wore rimless glasses. He sported black pants and a white tunic like the other servers in the dining room.

"Best place for privacy is the middle of a crowd," Ike blurted loudly. "No locals here. Lots of noise. Nobody can record us."

Menachem touched his index finger to his lips.

"Too loud? Okay. Okay."

Ike placed the coffee pot on the table and gestured to Menachem, who walked to the folding door, cracked it a bit, and kept an eye on the horde of pilgrims and hotel personnel in the dining room. Liam could still hear silverware and glasses clinking, a steady buzz of breakfast conversation, and occasional loud American laughter.

"Sorry about last night," Ike said. "A lot of shit's hitting the fan."

"I guess it couldn't be helped."

"Seem strange to you? Me running off, dodging the bad guys?"

"Everything you've ever done seems strange to me, Ike."

"Ain't that the truth," Ike said. "I bet Mimi thinks I've got a screw loose or worse."

"She's sharp. A trained nurse. Looks at things analytically."

"Unlike me. I don't blame her. I got papers to prove I'm nuts."

"I told Mimi that, but this cloak and dagger stuff is...."

"Totally necessary," Ike said. "People want what I've found—and they want me dead."

Menachem turned to Ike and Liam for a moment, then back to monitor the crowd. The drama was getting to Liam, but he said nothing.

"I'll be up front with you, pal. When I first came here twenty-five years ago, I was a mess, crazy as a road lizard. You know how manic I could get. We did some outrageous shit at LSU, didn't we?"

"You did wild stuff sober. I only messed up when I was drunk."

Ike threw his head back and laughed his donkey laugh.

"Yeah. I was drinking way too much when I got here, taking any drug I could find. My first few years at my *kibbutz*—it's a miracle they didn't kick me out."

Ike stopped grinning. He seemed to calm down.

"But after a while...it's hard to explain. This place, this country became a source of strength and sanity for me. It's mystical, like this Israeli earth reached up and took me into its arms. For the first time felt at ease with myself. I should have lived here all my life. I don't expect you to understand." He paused. "You ever see Irene?"

"Now and then," Liam said. "Her husband Larry is a good guy. They have two sons. One in law school in Baton Rouge, the other farms her family's land in Natchitoches. He took over for Irene's dad."

"Good. She deserves a happy life. Leaving her like I did was the kindest thing I could have done. Had I stayed, I would have made her as miserable as I was. Thank God we didn't have children. I wouldn't wish my genes on anyone. Israel is where I belong. Should have been born here instead of Natchitoches. The only other Jews in the entire parish were beneath shattered tombstones in the Jewish Cemetery on Sixth Street. Next to the railroad tracks. Nobody cared for it. No telling what it looks like now. Go see it when you get back. Every one of those Jews is dead, but people want to keep inflicting pain."

Liam remained silent. Same old passionate Ike. Winding himself up, his heart on his sleeve.

"This land does have a powerful feel to it," Liam said. "I can sense it. Not sure what it is exactly, but I get what you're talking about."

"It's the spirit of millions of dead Jews," Ike said, his translucent blue eyes quivering with intensity. "All come to rest here—*Eretz Israel*. Six million killed in World War II, millions killed before them in *pogroms* and ghettos. Going back a century before the war in Europe and Russia."

Ike's eyes filled. His voice grew quiet.

"They're all here, Liam. You can see the faces and read the stories of three million of them at the Holocaust Museum, Yad Vashem. You gotta go while you're here."

"I'd like to."

"I don't own a thing in this country. No land, no stocks or bonds. The funny thing is, I don't feel the need to. Brother Nathan can't understand it and I don't expect you to. Back home it didn't matter how successful I was or how much money I was making, there was a big hole right here."

He poked his sternum with his index finger.

"I tried to fill it with alcohol and drugs. Now the hole is gone. It's been filled...with Israel. That's the only way I can explain it."

Menachem looked back at them again. Ike inched closer to Liam.

"My *kibbutz* is not far from here. It's called Tel Qidron. Northeast of Herodium in the hills above the Qidron valley. Near the Dead Sea. Don't stay there much now. I live in the hills closer to Jerusalem. I still work sometimes when they need me. Many good friends at Tel Qidron."

"You have a house?"

"No. Listen. You've heard of Herodium, right?"

"Not really. I meant to read up on everything before we got here but I never got around to it. I saw Herodium on a map and figured it has something to do with King Herod?"

"It's where he built his tomb. Let me ask you this: do you know who Ishmael was? From the Bible, you know?"

"We never studied the bible at Jesuit, Ike. But I remember the freshman English course we took at LSU. The first line of Moby Dick is 'Call me Ishmael'."

"Okay. Okay," Ike said, looking at his watch. "I don't have much time. Listen. The Bible, what Christians call the Old Testament, says Ishmael was the son of Abraham and his servant girl Hagar. Abraham's son by his wife Sarah was Isaac. Isaac is the one Yahweh instructed Abraham to sacrifice on that altar, to kill him."

"I remember that. God prevented it, too."

"Right. Muslims claim the Prophet Muhammad was descended from Ishmael, son of Abraham, and Jews claim descent from Abraham through Isaac. There's a bunch more to this, but...."

Ike glanced at Menachem then lowered his head and his voice. Liam leaned in.

"There's this dig at Herodium. Been going on for a long time. You know Qumran, where the Dead Sea Scrolls were found, right? The Book of Esther is the only Old Testament book not found at Qumran. Or so they say. What are the odds? One book out of all the books of the Bible missing? Sound suspicious? I believe there were many different versions of the Old Testament books among the Dead Sea Scrolls. The scholars had to decide which transcripts they were going to promote. I think they made a political decision: deep-six the version of Esther they found at Qumran. Same thing with the original Book of Genesis they found in the jars. That's why they kept the scrolls secret for so long. Infighting. You know. Put two Jews in a room you get three opinions."

"I've read about the Dead Sea Scrolls. Found in a cave. They're on display in a museum here."

"Right. The Israel Museum. Well, I've been in and out of every cave between Tel Qidron and Herodium, almost as far south as Masada, further north than Qumran, where the scrolls were found. It's all mountains, rocks, and desert. All arid and desolate, except for a few Bedouins and their goats."

"In the caves looking for what?"

"Just looking. I'm drawn to these places. I don't know. I've been doing it for a long time. Never found anything but goat shit and sheep bones. Until one day I found this old clay jar hidden in one of the caves not far from Herodium."

"When was this?"

"Five months ago. Anyway, this jar, like pottery, like terra cotta or something, like ancient jars, like those found at Qumran. It was sealed with some kind of wax. Anyway, I didn't open the jar. I've got a friend, an archeologist. He's pretty old. I took it to him. He's a genius when it comes to this kind of stuff. I knew him from the *kibbutz*. He was in one of the groups that studied the Dead Sea Scrolls while they were still secret. It took fifty years to release the contents to the public—I mean the scrolls they wanted the great unwashed to see. You knew about the delay in releasing them?"

"I know there was a controversy about who could look at them."

"Anyway, this jar I found had a well-preserved scroll in it when the archeologist opened it. I was there. He had to be careful, had to open the jar in a laboratory chamber thing so the contents wouldn't turn to dust."

Liam looked up at Menachem standing watch at the folding door, staring at the breakfast crowd, not moving a muscle.

"Well, anyway, this archeologist, he has a friend, a linguist who worked on the Dead Sea Scrolls with him. The Essenes wrote those scrolls in ancient Hebrew and Aramaic. The scroll in the jar I found is on parchment, and it's also in Aramaic according to the linguist. The two of them said the parchment is the same vintage as the Dead Sea Scrolls. The writing dates back to the first century after Christ died. Appears to be a portion of the Book of Genesis, specifically an unabridged version of chapters sixteen and seventeen. Passages contradict the story of the Egyptian slave girl Hagar and Sarah and Abraham in the Book of Genesis in the Dead Sea Scrolls."

Ike was talking faster and louder. He leaned in closer and tried to whisper.

"Hagar was already with child when she lay with Abraham. It says Sarah knew it because Hagar began showing pregnancy much too soon. It says Sarah knew Ishmael's birth came too early for him to have been Abraham's child.

"The Genesis version the secret government panel put out says Sarah expelled Hagar into the desert because Hagar began treating her with contempt. My linguist says the scroll I found lays out the real story. Sarah banished Hagar into the wild because Sarah knew Hagar had made a fool of Abraham. Makes perfect sense."

Liam sat quietly. Ike was staring a hole through him with those light blue laser eyes. Liam knew Ike expected him to be shocked, but Liam didn't know enough about the Bible to grasp the significance. Liam merely nodded while Ike told him the slave girl Hagar was pregnant with Ishmael before she slept with Abraham. Hagar's duplicity was explained in Ike's version of Genesis, not in the official version agreed upon by the Dead Sea scholars. But Liam was certain he could not repeat Ike's version to Mimi, confident of what he was saying.

Ike's eyes were on fire, his muscles tense. He grabbed Liam's forearm and squeezed hard.

"It means Hagar's child was not of the blood of Abraham. It means Muhammad was not a descendant of Abraham. It means the entire Islamic religion is based on something this scroll says isn't true. Do you see, Liam? If this scroll I found is correct, the Muslim world will be turned upside down. The provenance of the prophet set forth in the Quran would be wrong. Ditto their claim to be the one true religion.

"Here's what I believe. My scroll's version of Genesis was known to the scholars who studied the Dead Sea Scrolls. And that explains why the Scrolls were suppressed for so long. Fifty years.

Those scholars knew this accurate version of Genesis would bring on war immediately. A deadly insult to Islam. All hell would have broken loose. So, the scholars chose to destroy it or at least deny its existence. They didn't know there was another copy of the original in a tiny cave near Herodium. But there was. And I found it. I'm calling it the Ishmael Scroll because it establishes the true ancestry of Ishmael. It may explain why the author of Genesis said Ishmael was a 'wild ass of a man,' forever at odds with all other men.

Ike's fingers dug deeper into Liam's forearm.

"Damn, Ike," Liam said, pulling his arm away and shaking it to get the feeling back.

Ike leaned back against his chair and took a deep breath. "Sorry, Liam. It's just so incredible what all this means."

Ike lunged forward. Every vein in his neck was distended, his weathered face now red as a beet.

"It proves once and for all that Muslims have no legitimate claim on Jerusalem or Israel, the land God promised Abraham and his descendants. Irrefutable proof. God gave the Promised Land to the Jews and no one else."

Ike spoke with such convincing certainty that Liam was moved. Even if he couldn't quite comprehend it all, he did understand Ike's conclusion: the scroll Ike found would undermine the foundation of the Muslim religion and support Israel's historic claim to the exclusive possession of the Promised Land. It was also easy to see how possession or even knowledge of the scroll might put Ike in danger.

"Where is the scroll now?" Liam asked.

"Can't tell you. Best you don't know. But I'll take you to it."

"Will I meet the archeologist and the linguist?"

"Too dangerous. I've pledged to keep their identities secret. If their involvement became known their lives would be on the line, too."

Menachem closed the folding door.

"Quiet," Menachem said.

Eyes wide, Ike grabbed Liam's forearm. Menachem tapped his index finger against his lips. Liam felt the tension.

After a moment, Menachem cracked the door and stared into the big room.

"What is it?" Ike whispered.

"I saw a man looking this way," Menachem said. "But I think now it is nothing."

"Jeez," Ike said, letting go of Liam's arm.

Menachem resumed standing watch at the door. Liam whispered and pointed toward Menachem.

"Does he know everything?"

"He knows I found an ancient artifact, but doesn't know what its impact would be. I've told him it's worth millions. He knows people are after me to get it. Lots of people killed around here after making claims they found relics from Biblical times."

"Killed for religious reasons?"

"Yeah. And for the money. It's big money."

"And you want to give this scroll to me?"

"Only to you. You have to get it out of this country and into the hands of a man in Washington D.C. I'll give you his name later. An Israeli. Very high in our government."

"Who is after you?"

"They're not Jews, I can tell you that. They're Arabs, the ones I've seen. I don't know if they're with the Palestinian Authority or some Islamic group. Maybe a foreign government."

"How did they find out about all this?"

"I don't know. Wish I did. What's important now is getting it out of the country."

Liam had heard enough. What Ike was asking him to do brought Liam face to face with the real world, and he made his decision on the spot—no way was he going to take custody of Ike's scroll, regardless of the stakes involved. Mere possession of the scroll was probably a crime in Israel. Smuggling it out of Israel and into the United States would break a slew of laws in both countries.

"I can't do what you're asking, Ike. My advice is turn it over to your government, to the highest official you can get to. If you want I can call a friend of mine in Mississippi who has good connections in D.C., ask him to get our State Department and the U.S. Ambassador to Israel involved. I'm on the outs with my Louisiana delegation and every federal agency I sued. My friend in Mississippi has a son that works for Senator Skeeter Sumrall...."

"No," Ike bellowed, slamming his palm on the table, spilling Liam's coffee. "You don't understand. The Israeli government can't be trusted with something like this. There are factions that would destroy this scroll rather than authenticate it or make its existence known. They hold sway in the Knesset right now. They're the same people trying to give our land to the Palestinians. Make unenforceable deals with Arabs in the hopes of a lasting peace. Traitors! These people openly declare they want to drive us into the sea. It's what they live for. They believe we're descended from apes and pigs, the source of all evil in the world. They will never stop trying to wipe us out. How can we make a deal with them? No. I cannot give my scroll to my government. They would suppress this information in the name of peace with the Islamic world. It is out of the question."

Liam wasn't changing his mind. No matter what Ike said.

"Look, Ike. It's great seeing you again. You know me. I can't do something that breaks the law, no matter how good a cause. I play by the rules. Your FedEx letter—I appreciate the confidence you have in me. But I can't do this for you. It would put Mimi in harm's way. Require me to violate all kinds of laws and risk losing everything I've worked to build. It may be an historic and worthy cause, but there's a right way, a legal way to handle the scroll. Within the framework of the Israeli and international legal system, I'll do all I can for you. But no felonies. No matter how happy I am to see you again."

For a moment, Liam thought Ike was going to cry. He slumped in his chair and hung his head. It was as if Ike had never entertained the idea that his old friend might not go along with his modest proposal to smuggle an ancient scroll out of Israel.

"I'm sorry, Ike. I can't do it."

Ike straightened. He seemed spent.

Menachem closed the folding door. "We should go."

"Something happen out there?" Liam asked.

"The same man. A waiter. He cannot seem to take his eyes off this door." Menachem looked through the crack and signaled to Ike and Liam. "Stay where you are."

Menachem slipped outside and closed the door behind him. Liam strained to hear over the noise of the breakfast crowd. He walked to the door and opened it slightly. He saw Menachem speaking to a waiter. Menachem waved the man away. Liam opened the folding door for Menachem to enter.

"We should leave," Menachem said.

"What did he want?" Liam said.

"To bring us more coffee. That is what he said."

"Do this for me," Ike said to Liam. "For old times' sake. Just look at it. Let me prove to you I'm not crazy. Not the same Crazy Ike you knew years ago in Louisiana. Israel has offered me a cure. I know I'm still one weird Jew, but I have a firm grip on reality now. You're probably right. Your judgment was always better than mine. See the scroll. When I make it public, you can tell the folks in Louisiana that Crazy Ike wasn't so crazy after all. Tell them he did something momentous with his life."

Liam thought a minute. How could he say no?

"All right. I'll look. And it will be just me. No need for Mimi to come along."

Ike hopped up and squeezed Liam's hand, pumping it too long. "Deal, Liam. I'll let Menachem know the details." Ike grabbed the coffee pitcher and lurched out of the alcove.

Menachem stood at the folding wooden door watching Yitzhak disappear into the crowded dining room.

"Let's get back to the hotel," Liam said to Menachem.

"In a minute," he said.

Menachem continued to guard the opening. Liam was still reeling from the extraordinary tale he had just heard from Crazy Ike Palmer. Finally, Menachem turned.

"We can go now."

Chapter Five

Menachem brought the Volvo to a dead stop in bumper-to-bumper traffic. The third time in the same block. Liam spent most of the drive from the tourist hotel back to the King David in silence, assessing Ike's current mental state. Liam remembered the manic episodes he had witnessed at LSU and in Natchitoches. One night Ike broke into the LSU golf course storage shed and filled the trunk and back seat of his car with practice balls. When the campus police peeked in his car window and saw him sleeping half-buried in golf balls, they figured they had solved the great pro shop heist. Ike returned all the practice balls and paid for the damaged lock and chain he hacksawed in half. The campus shrink intervened and Ike dodged another prosecutorial bullet.

One October in Natchitoches, Ike decided to corner the local market in pecans, offering twice the going rate. Every pecan picker, recreational or commercial, stampeded to Ike's plantation store with as many pecans as they could gather. The Sheriff assigned two deputies to control traffic jams on the unpaved country road. Ike bought every sack or bucket tendered, filling empty cotton trailers and vacant row houses on the farm with Mayhans, Stuarts, Desirables, and even small, hard to crack Natives. When Ike's manic phase ran its course he took to his bed, where he remained for a week. Irene and her father managed to unload the pecans on wholesalers from Texas and Arkansas, who bought the nuts at the going rate, half of what Ike paid. From that day on, Irene made certain Ike took his lithium capsule every day.

Liam had seen Ike's car full of golf balls. He made a special trip down from Shreveport when Irene's family store was stuffed to the rafters with pecans. Ike's manic adventures were the stuff of legend, not so funny as Liam thought back on them. No, there was nothing funny about the flip side of Ike's personality. In college, Liam would binge on beer or liquor, then disappear for a week, so depressed he could not answer his phone. Irene called Liam several times during their marriage, pleading with him to drive down and talk to Ike. Irene was afraid of what Ike might do to himself. One time, Liam spent the entire day with Ike, finally coaxing him out of bed and taking him to the doctor.

Liam regretted having told Ike he would look at the scroll. Yet, he weighed the possibilities. If Ike's story about the scroll were the product of his diseased mind, Liam had no reason to worry. There would be no scroll to examine. On the other hand, if Ike had indeed found a scroll with profound historical significance, he should at least take a look at it and try to steer Ike in the right direction. Liam worried about the legal ramifications or physical danger involved in merely examining Ike's scroll. There was more than his own well-being to consider. He owed it to Mimi to do the responsible thing.

What would Mimi say? If he told her what Ike asked of him, Mimi would put her foot down. She would insist Liam forget about the scroll. She had a point. It's one thing to be courageous in an important cause, another to put yourself and others in jeopardy on behalf of a madman, former or otherwise.

"The guys following you and Ike," Liam asked Menachem, "you said you didn't know who they were. Did they look like criminals?"

"Hard to know. Sometimes the police and government agents look worse than the criminals. They were not Russians, I am certain of that. They were Semites."

"Russians in Israel?"

"After the wall in Berlin came down, one million Russians claiming to be Ashkenazi Jews moved to Israel. The government welcomed them with open arms, like prodigal children."

"They weren't Jews?"

"Who is to say? Some were. Many were just gangsters. The worst mobsters in this country today are Russians. They are much more dangerous than our home grown Israeli mafia."

"Ike believes the men following him are Arabs."

"I don't know. The men I saw—they could have been. I was driving. Yitzhak saw them better."

"When you were standing in that alcove watching the door, Menachem, you heard everything Ike said about the scroll, right?"

"Yes. Yitzhak cannot talk quiet. He talks so loud sometimes I think he must be unable to hear."

"He's always talked like that. Is he really on to something that would turn the world of Islam upside down?"

"It would be something important, I believe. Much depends on whether it can be proved to be authentic. Here in Israel, there have been many claims, discoveries that turn out later to be false. There is much...feelings about these things. People become very angry. I have a friend, a woman at Israel Museum, Dr. Sarah Mendheim, she must deal with false relics. It is her job. She and her scientists have confiscated many relics that criminals try to sell as real.

"And Yitzhak is correct. Many Israelis would rather suppress something that may cause more trouble for us with the Arab world. They don't care that it is truth. They are appeasers, according to Yitzhak. To me, sometimes I think they make good sense. Other times not so much. I don't know. Like everything in my part of the world, it is hard to know what is right."

"Who would want to suppress Ike's scroll?"

"The people in charge. The government. The politicians. The bureaucrats. Pacifists among the people. Yitzhak is correct when he says for fifty years, only certain scholars approved by the government were allowed to see the scrolls found at Qumran. These documents were the property of the Israeli people, but they were kept secret, away from public eyes. Only a chosen few could study them." He paused. "I do not know. Perhaps the appeasers are right and Yitzhak is wrong."

"If you were in my shoes, Menachem," Liam said, "would you meet with Ike again to see his scroll? I know what my Mimi will say."

"I cannot say. I think your wife would say this is not your fight and you should not step between Yitzhak and the people who wish him ill."

"Mimi's not my wife; my girl friend. And do *you* really believe Ike has found what he claims, that people would do him in for this scroll?"

"There are men who follow Yitzhak and me. On a recent drive and on one other day. This is all I know for certain. Who they are and why they follow him? I cannot be sure."

"Why do you drive him? Aren't you afraid you might be harmed as well?"

Menachem stopped the Volvo in traffic. He took his eyes off the street and looked directly at Liam.

"This is Israel. I have a friend, a woman. Her husband was having coffee one evening. It was ten o'clock, in a café in the Rehavia area of this city, a nice district not far from the home of our Prime Minister. I knew this man. He was merely drinking coffee that night, minding his business, reading his paper. A pacifist, a very devout Jew. He had spoken to me on many occasions before that night, always saying we should make peace with our enemies. He believed Israel had mistreated the people everyone now calls Palestinians. A suicide bomber, they think a Palestinian from Gaza, walked into the café, sat down next to this man I knew. The bomber blew himself up, along with the pacifist and ten other Israelis sitting in the café. More than fifty other Israeli citizens were hurt very badly that night but did not die. It was March 9, 2002. I remember it as though it happened last night."

The traffic began to move. Menachem inched the Volvo forward. Sitting in the passenger seat next to Menachem, Liam felt small. Menachem lived and worked in peril every day, driving through the most fought-over real estate on earth, on highways and streets laid over a simmering caldera of clashing belief systems fueled by hatred burning hotter than magma. For 1,400 years. His world could explode at any moment. Liam's life in Louisiana seemed ridiculously safe and prosperous. His battle with the U.S. Government over the Delaware sale was a legal and factual dispute, but no one was going to get blown up because of it. Just going about his business as a tour guide in Israel, Menachem was exposed to potentially lethal encounters every day. His buying a cup of coffee in a café or a newspaper in a kiosk might result in a sudden and violent death.

Liam had experienced some dicey moments in his military service, and a few in the oil field, but that was many years ago. In his current existence, the only gangsters Liam feared were in his own government. He could be fairly sure the feds had never considered killing him. Menachem's enemies plotted to kill Jews every day. For some of Israel's enemies, it was all they thought about.

"I had coffee in that café on March 8, the night before the explosion," Menachem said. "My friend the pacifist had three young children. In America, except for Oklahoma City, the World Trade Center, and the Boston Marathon bombings, your citizens have no real appreciation of this type of terror against innocents. We Israelis experience hundreds of these incidents. Militant Islamists kill our people. They hate us for being alive. We try to put it out of our minds as we go about our daily lives, but it is something we all live with here in the land God promised to Abraham."

Menachem pulled into the circular drive of the King David, opened the Volvo's glove compartment and grabbed a pocket-sized black book.

"Here," Menachem said, handing it to Liam. "It's the Pentateuch, the first five books of what you call the Old Testament. Read about Ishmael in Genesis, especially chapters sixteen and seventeen. The chapters are not long. It might help you understand what your friend Yitzhak is saying. I have been thinking about this story, about Hagar being pregnant before she slept with Abraham. It would explain something I have never understood."

"What is that?"

"At the end of Genesis chapter sixteen, it is reported that the angel told the slave girl to leave the desert and return to Sarah's house and submit to her. The angel then tells Hagar that her child Ishmael 'shall be a wild ass of a man, with his hand against everyone, and everyone's hand against him; and he shall live at odds with all his kin'. That is an accurate quote, I think."

"Why would Ishmael be such a problem for everyone?"

"Indeed," Menachem said, "if Yitzhak is telling the truth and his scroll is accurate, it could be because Ishmael was illegitimate and had no claim to the blood of Abraham. His mother Hagar knew the truth. Perhaps Ishmael found out and became bitter. I am no scholar of the Torah. I am just speculating."

"It's a mystery to me, Menachem."

"I will call you as soon as Yitzhak tells me the time and place for your next meeting."

"I'm not certain I'm going to meet with Ike again. I'm going to think about it. I'll let you know when you call me."

Liam walked into the hotel and took the elevator to his room. It had been made up; everything was neatly arranged: fresh towels in the bathroom; Mimi's makeup organized on her side of the double vanity. Liam knew the maid had done that, not Mimi. He opened the converted *armoire*, picked up the TV remote and plopped on the bed.

His first stop was the British edition of CNBC. The British commentators describing the day's U.S. financial market activity seemed more intelligent than the domestic CNBC hosts and contributors Liam listened to almost every day at home. He knew the commentators weren't actually smarter but their accent made them sound that way.

He surfed to his next stop, BBC World News, which really was news from all around the globe. He saw stories he never would have seen in the U.S. He stuck around for a few depressing reports of ethnic mayhem in several exotic locales, breezed through a replay of a soccer match between Manchester United and a team from Spain, several Israeli soap operas, and an Israeli reality show about home renovation. Of all the offerings, he spent the longest time watching a professional dart throwing match on a BBC station. The set resembled a pub and there was a play-by-play announcer and a color commentator—*for the dart match*—and lots of cheering.

Liam began to get antsy. Eleven-thirty. He hadn't heard from Mimi. He set their rendezvous for one p.m., so he had only himself to blame. He wished he had set it sooner, but he hadn't known how long the meeting with Crazy Ike was going to run. He turned off the dart match and took the stairs to work off some nervous energy. He nodded to the concierge as he left the lobby to march across the street to the YMCA. From its manicured courtyard he stared at the dome on top of the central tower and the stone arches above a balcony on each side. The top of the tower resembled a minaret. Cypress trees and columns surrounded him in the courtyard. Restless, he entered the lobby of the "Y" and climbed up the narrow stairway to the sixth floor. The panoramic view of Jerusalem from the top of the central tower was spectacular, but barely registered with Liam. He couldn't concentrate on anything but his watch.

Liam found the King David's number on his rent-a-phone speed dial. According to the receptionist, no message for him at the front desk and none waiting on his room phone. He left the YMCA and walked three blocks toward the Old City in hopes of intercepting Mimi, but after checking the map he decided there were multiple routes for her to take back to the hotel. His odds of running into her on the street were not good. He reminded himself their agreed upon time was one p.m. He headed back to the King David, trying to brush aside a premonition he could not shake.

He stopped at a small store down the hill from the hotel and bought a nine dollar cigar the proprietor assured him was a Cuban. It was 12:30. At the King David front desk he checked again for messages then hurried up the six flights to his room. He lay on the bed and surfed through a dozen channels, finally settling on the BBC dart match, which had turned into a nail-biter in his absence. One of the contestants was sweating bullets. The match was being telecast live. It was February 28. It could not have been unpleasantly warm in the facility hosting the match. The only physical exertion by the contestants was the delicate flick of the wrist needed to fling the slender darts onto the cork board. Liam figured the tension of the close match was getting to the contestants. He looked at his watch. Ten minutes of one. He tried to figure the dart contest's point system. No luck. Finally, it was one o'clock. He stared at the hotel phone, then at his rent-a-phone. Nothing.

Liam began to feel hollow inside. His head buzzed. His gut told him Mimi was in trouble. *Idiot.* He should have given her the cell phone. He didn't need the damn thing. And she should never have gone to the Old City by herself. Where was his brain? The concierge had assured her it was safe, but Liam should have been with her. Too damned focused on Ike's crap.

At one-fifteen Liam faced the concierge, displaying the Xerox copy of Mimi's passport he kept in his carry-on bag. The concierge's English was excellent, his pronunciation reflecting a hint of British upper-class.

"Yes, sir, Mr. Connors. I spoke to your wife before she left the hotel for the Old City."

Liam almost said "she's not my wife" but let it go. "Did she say exactly where she was going inside the Old City?"

"No, sir, Mr. Connors. I showed her the best walking route. I recommended the Jaffa Gate. Excellent shopping at the Mamilla Mall on the way there. I suggested she look for bargains inside the Christian Quarter. Perhaps she is enjoying lunch at one of the cafes."

"She would have called me if she was going to be late."

The concierge traced on Liam's Jerusalem city map the route he had recommended to Mimi. Liam thanked him and left the hotel to walk the same streets, hoping he would run into her returning to the hotel. What else to do? He couldn't just sit around.

By two-thirty he was back at the King David.

"I need to speak with hotel security," he told the concierge.

"By all means," he said.

The concierge disappeared through a door off the lobby. Five minutes later, he walked back through the same door with a strongly-built man in a navy blue sport coat and gray slacks. Liam guessed the man was in his early fifties.

"My name is Salzman. May I see the photograph of your wife?"

"My only copy," Liam said and handed him the Xerox copy of the passport. "She's not Mrs. Connors. Her name is Mimi Stanton. What can we do, Mr. Salzman?"

"Follow me," he said.

Liam walked behind Salzman down a narrow hallway. They stopped at a reinforced metal door. Salzman swiped an i.d. card through a slit near the door handle and waited. Liam looked into the camera mounted on the wall above them. The door buzzed.

Liam was impressed. One wall was covered with monitors showing hallways on guest room floors and in the common areas on the main floor—the front desk, the bar, and the main dining room. Four monitors on another wall were dedicated to the exterior of the King David. Two technicians in blue shirts and black ties sat at computers before the bank of monitors. Salzman said something in Hebrew to one of the technicians who responded with some questions. The technician tapped on his keyboard and pointed to one of the monitors.

Liam stared at the screen and saw Mimi walking past the front desk and out the main entrance. The screen changed and showed her walking beyond the hotel, eventually turning onto King David Street. The technician turned to the security man and said something.

"That is all we have," Mr. Salzman told Liam. "As you can see, the sequence is dated and timed. Her departure was uneventful."

For Liam, the hotel security cameras established two things: Mimi left the hotel at the time she told Liam she would be leaving, and she had not returned.

"Can we get the local police involved?" Liam said.

"I can call them for you and put you on the phone with them, but I must warn you, it is likely they will do nothing."

"Because it's only been two hours?"

"That is correct. These types of things happen every day."

"I understand. But I can assure you Ms Stanton would have called or left a message if she was going to be later than one o'clock."

Salzman nodded. There was nothing else to say.

"Can you tell me how to get to the local police station that would have jurisdiction over the Old City? Do you know any of the detectives or officers personally?"

"I would recommend an investigator. Akiva Peres. If you like I could call him. Request that he meet with you."

Liam nodden an okay and waited in the lobby, pacing a bit, checking his watch every few minutes.

Salzman came out.

"I spoke to Akiva Peres. He is expecting you."

On the map Salzman showed Liam the police station near the Jaffa Gate. Liam realized that he had been only a couple of blocks from the station an hour earlier. Salzman returned the Xerox of Mimi's passport. Liam thanked him and left.

Liam tried to walk fast but ended up running. In short order he arrived at the station. The sign on the building was in Hebrew. "Israeli Police, Jerusalem District" was stenciled in English on the glass door. Behind a thick security glass a woman in uniform sat talking with a man who had a camera hanging from his neck. Liam estimated the woman to be about sixty, with coarse gray hair, no makeup and an unpleasant voice. Liam forced himself to listen to her and waited his turn.

"I'm Liam Connors staying at the King David," he said to the woman at last. "Mr. Akiva Peres is expecting me."

She nodded, punched a button, and spoke gruffly in Hebrew into the phone on her desk.

"Give me her photo," she said with a heavy accent. "I will make copies."

Liam gave her the Xerox of Mimi's passport picture.

Behind her a short man with wavy black hair walked toward the glass. Liam noticed only one of the man's eyes seemed to focus on him.

"Mr. Connors?" he asked and pointed to a door. "Come this way."

Liam stepped through the door and followed him to a room with an open floor plan and six desks. Plainclothes cops sat behind four of the desks. Two of the men were on their phones. Liam sat down at an empty desk across from the man.

"You're Detective Akiva Peres, right?"

"Investigator. Yes. Salzman at the hotel called."

"I gave my only photograph to the lady out front."

"She is a sergeant in the Jerusalem Police," Akiva Peres said with a smile. "If you stood at that counter and listened to her for five minutes you would not call her a lady."

Liam nodded, unable to force himself to be jovial.

"May I see your passport?" he asked.

Liam gave it to him. Peres studied it a moment with his right eye and entered something on his computer. Liam watched him put on a pair of half-moon glasses to read the monitor.

"You arrived in Tel Aviv yesterday? Yes?"

"Yes, sir."

"Staying at the King David." He pursed his lips. "According to this, you are scheduled to fly from Tel Aviv to Newark after three nights."

"Yes."

"Our information tells us you are from Louisiana, U.S.A."

"That's in the South."

The desk sergeant plopped a stack of color copies of Mimi's passport photo on Peres's desk and walked out without a word.

"See what I mean?" he said, only his good eye looking at Liam.

"I know it's only been a couple of hours." Liam looked at his watch. "Two and a half now, but Ms Stanton has never been late for anything in her life. When we travel, she's always aware of the time, always punctual. She's a nurse. A good one. Something has happened."

Peres's phone buzzed. He picked up and listened a moment, making notes on a form. He looked up and caught Liam staring at his bad eye.

"A minor skirmish in the Golan," he said.

Liam started to say "sorry," but held his tongue and nodded, his anxiety increasing by the minute.

"We are a small country, Mr. Connors. We are surrounded by those who want to do us harm. Vastly outnumbered. So, we have cameras everywhere. They are an important part of our security. One of my assistants just scanned your friend's photograph and ran it through our recognition software, which was developed in our own country. Did you know we produce more patents per capita than any other country in the world?"

"No, I did not. What has your assistant found?"

"He said she entered the Christian Quarter through the Jaffa Gate a few minutes before ten this morning. That would be right, yes?"

"Yes, sir. According to the hotel security cameras she left the King David at nine-twenty. The concierge recommended she walk through the Mamilla Mall on the way. Do you have cameras inside the Old City?"

"Only on the major streets. Residential sections have such narrow, winding alleys and walkways. We are limited in what we can do. It's historical. Some residents object to our placing cameras. And because of political opposition we have few cameras in the Muslim Quarter." He paused. "Please give me your wife's height and current weight."

"She's my girl friend. My wife died over two years ago."

Peres studied Liam's face a moment. Liam added that Mimi was 5'6" and 120 pounds, and waited for him to enter the information into his computer.

"Did your system locate her inside the Old City, Mr. Peres?"

He looked at his monitor. "She passed by the Petra Hotel, then thirty minutes later left the Christian Quarter at the Pool of Hezekiah and entered the Armenian Quarter. Passing the Maronite Convent at ten-fifty, she walked toward the shops on the edge of the Armenian residential areas."

"And then?"

"That is the last time she is caught on our cameras. There is no evidence of her leaving the Old City. All gates have excellent camera coverage. She has not walked out."

"Can your men help me look for her?"

Peres rested his forearms on his desk and focused on Liam with his good eye. Liam knew what he was going to say. The universal police protocol regarding a person missing for three hours is to do nothing. "I will do this because I believe you. I will notify my men in the Old City to be on the lookout for your friend. Our technical people can send a text with her passport photograph attached to every policeman on duty inside the Old City, including those patrolling the gates. I will also have our information people send the text and photograph to all hospitals and clinics in the city, in case she became ill. Unfortunately, that is all I can do. I cannot place her on our website or begin a broader search at this point."

"I'm telling you something has happened to her," Liam said raising his voice, then catching himself. "Sorry. Sorry."

"It is all right, Mr. Connors. I can say it is my experience that most people eventually show up, unaware they have caused concern."

"Not Mimi Stanton."

"I know. You are certain. Millions of tourists pour through this city each year. This happens more often than you might think. Almost all of the persons re-appear. I believe that will happen for you."

"Thank you, Mr. Peres," Liam said, shaking hands. "When can I come back? How long must she be missing?"

"Our procedures require twenty-four hours before we can do more. I hope you understand."

"Can I have some of those copies?" Liam said pointing to the stack of photos.

"Certainly."

Liam grabbed about twenty of the copies. Peres took a final look at Liam's passport and gave it back to him.

"Be careful, Mr. Connors. It is easy to get lost in this city. Do you have someone you can call? A friend, perhaps?"

"My driver."

"His name?"

Liam gave him Menachem's card. Peres sat back down at his desk and typed on his keyboard a moment. While still reading the screen, he returned the card to Liam.

"How did you come to hire this man?"

"Through a friend."

"A friend in Israel?"

"Yes."

"What do you plan to do when you leave here, Mr. Connors?"

Liam was beginning to get irritated. What did Peres think he was going to do?

"I'm going to search for Mimi myself. Your cameras say she never left the Old City. That's where I'm going. I'll call my driver to help me if he will."

"Yes, yes, of course. I don't blame you." He paused a moment. "Your local friend, he is Yitzhak Palmer?"

A warning buzzer sounded in Liam's brain. How the hell did Peres know that? What exactly was Ike doing that put him on the Israeli Police radar? In their data bank?

"We went to college together in Louisiana. Old friends."

"Have you seen him since you have been in Jerusalem?"

"Yes. I had coffee with him this morning at some hotel."

Liam knew it was important to tell the truth. What he said was a factually correct answer to Peres's question. Liam wasn't going to volunteer additional information unless Peres asked the right questions. Liam would not lie to the Israeli Police, but he wasn't giving Peres any more information until he found out what was going on.

"Good luck, Mr. Connors. Please check in with me tomorrow. Let me know what has happened."

"Thank you, Mr. Peres. Could you give me a phone number where I can call you?"

He wrote a number on his card and gave it to Liam.

"This station number is on the card. I wrote down my cell phone as well, if you care to call me directly. Be careful, Mr. Connors."

Liam turned back to respond but Peres already had his back to him talking quietly to the investigator at the next desk.

Liam nodded at the female desk sergeant on his way out of the station. She ignored him. As soon as he was outside, he called Menachem.

Waiting for Menachem to pick up, Liam felt an adrenaline rush. He had to do something, get some process going to locate Mimi. But Liam recognized himself a stranger in a strange land. He was not sure which way to turn.

He felt like jumping out of his skin.

Chapter Six

Inside the Via Dolorosa Café in the Old City Liam glanced at his watch again. Still no Menachem. Liam double-checked his calculations: *28 ½ hours since they arrived in Israel. 4 hours since Mimi went missing.* He motioned for the waiter.

At exactly five p.m. Menachem entered the café and sat down at Liam's table. "I am happy you called me. To find her I will do all that is possible."

"Mimi. Her name is Mimi Stanton."

"You have children?"

"Not with Mimi. My first wife Annette and I had two daughters. They're grown women now. Annette was killed in an automobile accident. More than two years ago. Mimi is a nurse practitioner and works for a doctor in the small town in Louisiana where I moved after my wife's wreck. That's where we met."

"I am sorry your wife is deceased."

"Me, too. She was wonderful, the love of my life. But I've grown to love Mimi, too. I need your help."

Liam shared what he had learned from hotel security and Investigator Akiva Peres. He gave Menachem half of the Xerox copies and told him his plan. Show Mimi's picture to merchants whose stores lined every major street of the Old City.

"What do you think?"

"A good place to start."

"If no merchant tells us anything let's concentrate on the last place Mimi was caught on camera, the Armenian Quarter. Every street, walkway, and alley. Show every person we encounter Mimi's picture."

"We do this together?" Menachem asked.

"Together. Absolutely. It'll take longer, but I need an interpreter. Someone to help me get around. This place is a maze."

"Shall we begin then?"

Menachem stood up but Liam asked him to sit back down. "Wait. Wait. I'm chomping at the bit to get started, but you have to educate me on something," Liam said, leaning closer and speaking quietly. "I don't know how things work in your country and I don't want to make the situation worse. Investigator Peres asked me who my driver was. I gave him your card. He typed something into his computer. Then he asked me how I hired you. I told him through a friend from the U.S. who lives here now. Peres looked again at his screen. And you know what he asked me?"

"If your local friend would be Yitzhak Palmer?"

"How did you know that? What's going on here?"

"Again, I remind you. This is Israel, Mr. Connors, not your United States."

"Call me Liam. Please. Educate me."

"Liam. Very well. Population is small in Israel. No more than eight million. About three-fourths of us are Jews. Jerusalem city has only three-quarters of a million residents. You know yourself this is the most secure country in the world. So that we can survive. We Israelis have an unspoken agreement, an understanding with our government. We forget about privacy. For more security we do this. Things our police and the IDF do every day you Americans would say 'No, this you cannot do.' Your ACLU, your television people and newspapers would scream 'invasion of privacy.'

"You ask how government knows these things about me, about Yitzhak. My friend, let me tell you the Israeli Police know everything. There are thirty-five thousand employees in the Israeli Police force. As many police as you have in New York City."

"I see them...everywhere."

"Wait, Mr. Liam Connors, seventy-thousand unpaid volunteers the police. So for every policeman you see on the streets of this Old City, two civilians somewhere help him. They tell the police things they see, things they hear, things they know. Consider that. When I was last in New York City to visit my cousin Efraim, I see posters in the subways and in busses. These posters say, 'If you see something, say something'."

"Right. They remind people to do that."

"In Israel, we have lived that slogan since 1967. Is not necessary to tell Jews to say something. We tell officials everything we see that makes us suspicious. Seventy-thousand volunteers. Some people report too much. You know how your people are. Well, Jews are too suspicious. But we say better safe than sorry."

Menachem took off his Tilley hat and patted the top of his slick head, smoothing his nonexistent hair. "The Jerusalem Police, they know Menachem. They see me driving these streets almost every day. I speak to them. I introduce my clients to them. Sometimes, if a client or group forgets a camera or a credit card somewhere, it is Menachem who deals with the police for them."

"Do you know Akiva Peres?"

"A war hero. I knew him first when he wore a uniform and fought for our country. He knows my name and what I do. He sees me bring my groups through the Jaffa Gate. He always wave to me."

"Ike. Why is he in their system? He says he lives in caves in the hills east of here. Says he's no longer a regular at his *kibbutz*."

"Yitzhak spends much time at Tel Qidron. He sleeps there many nights, rather than in the caves above the Dead Sea."

"But still, why would his name come up when I gave them yours?"

"The police they know I drive him in Jerusalem. Sometimes I pick him up at Tel Qidron. Sometimes I meet him somewhere in the city. Drive him wherever he tells me. The police see me with him on the highways and on these city streets."

"You're not giving me straight answers, Menachem. Why do they care about Ike Palmer? Why keep tabs on him?"

Menachem leaned back against his chair. He picked up a packet of salt from the table, tore off the paper edge and sprinkled it into his hand. He licked the salt, grabbed a small paper napkin from the stainless steel dispenser on the table and wiped his palm. "Do you ever hear of Jerusalem Syndrome?"

A waiter dropped a coffee cup. Liam jumped when it exploded against the stone floor. Liam watched the agitated café manager rush over with a towel to wipe the floor and pick up the shards while muttering and staring daggers at the embarrassed waiter.

Liam turned back to Menachem. "No. What is it?"

"Jerusalem has strange power over some people. Especially people with some mental sickness. When we are not at war or under siege from Hamas in Gaza or Hezbollah in Lebanon, two-and-a-half million people visit our tiny country each year. Many are very religious. When they walk the Via Dolorosa or visit such sites as the Mount of Olives and the Church of the Holy Sepulchre, they follow the steps of Jesus and other prophets who walked this holy ground. Some of these visitors experience a change, believe they themselves are the Messiah, or the Virgin Mary. Sometimes a prophet. This Jerusalem Syndrome is real, not imaginary. It was first named by Israeli physicians in the 1930s. Every year it happens to many people."

"They have a mystical experience?"

"Yes, that is it. Over one hundred cases of this Jerusalem Syndrome every year. Some years, over two hundred."

"And Ike Palmer?"

"How do you say in the U.S, 'in spades?' He had been in the country no more than a few months when he began to say he was John the Baptist, making way for the Second Coming."

"My God," Liam said, shaking his head."

"I saw him once once in the Christian Quarter. But I heard many stories. He moved here from Tel Qidron and became well-known, walking barefoot, half-naked in the Old City, crying and praying very loud in English."

"He needed help."

"The police took him to a sanitarium, a mental hospital. After a few months he was allowed to return to the *kibbutz*, where he became productive, a valuable member of the collective. In the time I drive Yitzhak, he has not been crazy. Very intelligent and more religious than most Jews. And that is to include me. Yitzhak can sometimes be as devout as the *Hasidim* and other ultra-orthodox Jews. The *Haredim* as well. A responsible person. He tells me the truth, I think."

Liam glanced at his watch. "Good God, look at the time. Let's go. It's five-twenty." Liam spread his map of the Old City on the table.

"Where do we begin, Menachem?"

Chapter Seven

As Liam and Menachem left the café to start their search, a tall, slender man with a salt-and-pepper beard waited in his plaster-splattered Toyota truck thirty-three miles east of the Old City. The car park next to the mosaic factory on the western outskirts of Madaba was only half-filled.

Rohullah Samar, known to his associates as Hazara, positioned the Toyota truck so as not to miss Al Dub's west-bound white Fiat sedan coming up the dusty two-lane street. Hazara watched a few of the mosaic factory visitors, all men, drift outside and mill around the tourist busses remaining in the parking lot. Hazara suspected the men were bored with watching the Jordanian women inside the factory demonstrate how they made the intricate mosaic pieces for which Madaba had become famous. Hazara had seen the presentation one time too many.

Hazara spotted Al Dub driving the Fiat slowly uphill past the factory. He cranked his truck and pulled out onto the street, two cars behind Al Dub. They drove west toward Mount Nebo. Within a short time, Hazara was navigating the switchbacks and sharp turns, guiding his truck up the steep grade toward the Franciscan monastery at the top of the mountain. Hazara smirked. In his native Afghanistan, an 800 meter bump like Nebo on the landscape would never be referred to as a mountain.

He slowed as Al Dub drove the Fiat into the parking area below the monastery. After a few minutes, Hazara entered the car park and pulled into an empty space several hundred feet from the Fiat. He glanced at the giant construction crane jutting out of the center of the mountaintop facility. The Franciscans were constantly renovating their monastery, the museum, the cafeteria, and other facilities that catered to tourists. Each time in the past two years Hazara had come here to meet Al Dub, heavy construction was underway.

Hazara looked up. The sky was clear. Walking toward Mount Nebo's summit, Hazara paused to look westward over the northernmost edge of the Dead Sea into Israel. Jericho seemed close enough to touch. Further west and south, he could make out the eastern edge of Jerusalem. On many work days in Israel, he could see the construction crane atop Mount Nebo against the eastern sky.

Hazara thought Al Dub and the rich man he worked for were smart to station him in the Hashemite Kingdom of Jordan, east of the Jordan River and the Dead Sea. The airport in Amman was busy. Frequent flights left daily for cities around the Mediterranean. More important, Jordan was less security-minded than Israel. Passing through border controls in his truck at the King Hussein Bridge, and sometimes the Prince Abdullah Bridge, was much easier for Hazara than for other workers or tourists. Al Dub had delivered enough money to well-placed officials on both sides of the Jordan, arranging authentic Jordanian passports and West Bank and Israeli work visas for Hazara and The Black. All the tools, equipment, and supplies in the Toyota were real, exactly what itinerant masonry workers would carry to a job. Working and traveling the West Bank as Jordanian plasterers was a natural cover, especially since Hazara did a better job finishing plaster than the Palestinian laborers he worked beside every day.

Hazara had grown up west of Kabul working in his uncle's plaster business in the Hazarajat region of central Afghanistan. Twenty-six years earlier, when he was fourteen, he had joined the war against the Russian invaders. His real name was Rohullah Samar, but in the Taliban unit he allied with in Afghanistan, he became known only as Hazara, where he was born. At the time he was one of the few Shia Hazaras working with the radically devout Sunnis of the Taliban. Hazaras were looked down on by the Pashtuns and Tajiks in Afghanistan because they were Shias and because of their Asian features. At one time in his life the conflict and hatred between Shias and Sunnis meant something to Hazara, but not any more. He no longer cared about anyone's God.

He watched Al Dub walk up the hill ahead of him. He was in his mid-sixties, stocky and bald, but still strong as an ox. He admired the old man's approach to his work. Al Dub was no bureaucrat. He had proven he did not mind getting his hands dirty—or bloody. Hazara would not have welcomed a hand-to-hand fight with Al Dub. His barrel chest and strong arms were covered with thick, dense hair. Little wonder he was known in mercenary circles in the Middle East by his nickname, Al Dub, "the Bear." Hazara had been on many assignments for Al Dub and his rich sponsor in the past couple of years, had spent long nights on missions with "the Bear." Enough time to learn Al Dub's real name—Akmal Kassab. Enough time to grow weary of Al Dub's proselytizing about the Prophet and the evil infidels, claptrap that Hazara had dismissed as nonsense years before.

They were an odd couple. Hazara was 6'3" and slender, with skin the color of *café au lait*. Though only forty, his beard was beginning to show streaks of gray. In spite of the hint of Mongolian ancestry and coloring in his skin and facial features, many of his *jihadist* compatriots said he favored the holy martyr Usama bin Laden. He had lost the lower half of his left ear in 2006 in a losing battle to save the life of Al Zarqawi in Iraq. When Hazara walked he took long, graceful strides. His casual lope caused the ends of the chain belt he used to cinch his white cotton tunic to swing by his side. The stocky Al Dub did not walk with grace. He took short, aggressive steps. He dressed Western style, sometimes covering his bald head with a baseball cap.

Hazara reached Mount Nebo's highest overlook on the west side of the monastery. Al Dub was already sitting on one of the stone benches, gazing out onto the Jordan River Valley. Hazara sat on a different bench, more than ten feet from Al Dub. Alone on the overlook facing west, the two men alone watched the sun disappear behind the mountains running north and south bisecting northern Israel, the spine of the Jewish State on which Jerusalem was perched.

"Beautiful country," Hazara said.

"Infested with Hebrew vermin. What can you tell me?"

"She was taken without incident in the Old City late this morning."

"When will she be moved?"

"The Black tells me they will take her out of Jerusalem tonight."

"Do you need more men?"

"I have others to call."

"Can you trust them?"

"Yes," Hazara said calmly, but inside he did a slow burn. He was fed up with the stocky Syrian's monitoring his end of the operation. It was another insult to Hazara's professionalism. If the money weren't so good and the work so steady, Hazara would walk away, leaving Al Dub alone atop Mt. Nebo. Hazara decided to do some prying of his own.

"When do I get to meet our wealthy sponsor?"

"When I say so," Al Dub snapped. "Maybe never."

"I understand he is one of the richest men in the world."

"Who told you that?"

"No one in particular. I listen to people talk."

"Exactly the problem. Some people cannot keep their mouths shut. There's no reason for you to know him at this point. If *he* wishes to meet you, you may learn his identity."

Hazara couldn't afford to speak his mind just yet, but he knew the time was coming. And it would be soon. He had done the bidding of Al Dub and his rich financier for two years, and he had learned a few things on his own, in spite of Al Dub.

"Call me in Amman after you learn the woman is secured in the new location." Al Dub rose to begin the long walk down to his Fiat.

Hazara waited for ten minutes then picked up the binocular case Al Dub had left under his bench. He placed the strap over his head. In the dim light remaining, he unsnapped the lid and glanced inside. Tightly packed stacks of U.S. dollars and Israeli shekels filled the case to the brim.

The walk up Mount Nebo to the overlook had been no problem for Al Dub, the walk down even easier. Born into a middle-class family in Aleppo, Akmal Kassab was nineteen when he invaded Israel in 1967 with the Syrian Army through the Golan Heights. Al Dub and his army buddies weren't in the Golan long. Within a few days, they were almost wiped out by the Israeli Air Force. During their hasty retreat back to Syria, Al Dub survived, but not before suffering multiple broken bones, nerve damage, and a fifty per cent hearing loss in one ear due to the assault on his platoon by the better-trained, better-equipped Israelis.

He was back on the battlefield with the Syrian Army against the Jews in 1973 in the Yom Kippur War, invading Israel once again through the Golan. At the same time Anwar Sadat's Egyptian Army bridged the Suez Canal and invaded from the west. This time Al Dub was in Israel for several weeks before being driven back through the Golan almost to Damascus. Sadat's hastily arranged cease fire was the only thing that saved Al Dub and his fellow Syrian soldiers from further casualties and the occupation of their capital city.

Making it back alive after Syria's second confrontation with the Israeli Army, Al Dub decided he had enough of fighting Jews on the battlefield and resigned his commission. He decided to vent his hatred against the People of the Book and their "Illegitimate State" by engaging in activities less likely to break any more of his bones.

Al Dub worked for several years as a bodyguard and right-hand man for a PLO financier in Istanbul. He learned the mechanics of moving money from European and Middle Eastern bank accounts into the hands of terrorist cells bent on killing Jews and destroying the State of Israel. He was fortunate to be off duty the day the Turkish financier's steel-reinforced Mercedes was blown to bits on a side street in Istanbul by Israel's Mossad. Justifiably concerned for his own well-being, Al Dub quickly moved to Egypt and opened a currency exchange business. He did well for several years until his hatred for Israel caused him to grow restless in his prosperity. He began to search for a more open society in which to carry out his goal of destroying the Zionist state. He moved to the United States and settled in Brookline, Massachusetts, where he started a new currency exchange business. As his business grew, Al Dub found more time to spend with the pan-Arab *jihadists* who had settled in the power centers of the Great Satan: Boston, New York, and D.C. His work in their underground networks in the U.S. and Europe brought him to the attention of another financier, one who would change the direction of Al Dub's life, a Ukranian-born Jew named Anton Brodie. In 1989 Al Dub went to work full-time for Brodie. In the twenty-five years since, Brodie had gone from being described by financial media as "an extremely wealthy international currency trader" to being named by Fortune Magazine as the most secretive of "the ten wealthiest men in the world." Al Dub's terrorist activities had played a large role in Anton Brodie's accumulation of massive wealth.

Now as he drove slowly out of the parking area below the monastery, Al Dub looked forward to calling Brodie. The mission to steal the scroll the American Jew had found was not going exactly as he and Hazara had planned, but the scroll would soon be in their possession anyway. Brodie had insisted it be preserved intact when they finally took possession of the blasphemous document. Brodie stressed the scroll was vital to their plan. Every time they spoke, Brodie repeated his instructions: preserving the Ishmael scroll was of paramount importance.

No matter. Al Dub had already decided to destroy the scroll as soon as he possessed it. True, Brodie had been good to him in the past two-and-a-half decades, but the man was born a Jew and remained a Jew, the most villainous race of people in the history of the world. Brodie claimed that his being a Jew was an accident of birth; he did not practice the religion or subscribe to its beliefs. Al Dub had long suppressed his revulsion of Brodie's ancestry as a means to further Brodie's financial support of *jihad*. But Al Dub was growing tired of pretense. Brodie claimed he was only interested in possessing the scroll to make money. Brodie did not understand how offensive the claims of the scroll were to a true believer in the Quran like Al Dub. The very existence of such a false document was an abomination.

Al Dub knew destroying the scroll would not sit well with Anton Brodie, but he would accept the consequences. To be truthful, he was growing weary of Brodie and tired of his lifelong battle against the Jews and the Christian West. He had caused the death of enough infidels to guarantee him his reward with Allah. Maybe it was time, he thought, to let younger men take up the fight, time for him to sever his ties with the Jew currency trader.

"We shall see," Al Dub mumbled, as he turned his Fiat onto the main highway back to Amman.

Chapter Eight

It was two-thirty Friday morning when Menachem dropped Liam off at the King David. It had been a long, frustrating night. They stuck to the plan, finishing the canvass of the merchants on the major streets in the Old City shortly after midnight. They showed Mimi's picture to hundreds of men and women in the shops and in the markets. No one had seen her, but many of the cafes and stalls had already closed by the time they made the rounds.

Starting about one a.m. they walked the poorly lighted, twisting alleys and streets of the Armenian Quarter. After an hour, Liam realized they were wasting time. It was too late to be intercepting people on the street. The few residents they encountered were frightened. Liam couldn't blame them. Any rational person would be wary of two strangers on a dark street after midnight.

When Menachem stopped his Volvo in front of the King David, Liam reached into his wallet, pulled out all the U.S. dollars he had, and held them out.

"There's no need to pay me," he said, waving off the wad of money. "I want to help you."

"Please take the money, Menachem. You've got a business. Obligations. I need you full-time until we find Mimi."

"No, Liam."

Liam got out of the Volvo and reached through the open window to drop the money onto the passenger seat.

"You keep this money. I can't find Mimi without you. I'm hiring you. I want one hundred per cent of your time and attention. Cancel your other jobs. Work for me exclusively." Liam caught himself. He was giving orders to Menachem like he was one of his toolpushers or roustabouts. "I mean if that's all right with you."

Menachem pocketed the money.

"First place we need to stop is a phone store," Liam said. "I need to trade this local phone for one with international calling capability. Can you pick me up right here at eight?"

"The phone store will not be open at eight."

"Do you know the owner?"

"I know who he is."

"Call the owner first thing and get him to open early for us. Tell him I will make it worth his while. I want to be in Tel Aviv at the U.S. Embassy by ten."

"No problem."

"Before we go to the phone store we need to go to a bank or an ATM. I'm going to withdraw as much cash as I can on my credit cards and my bank debit card. Should I get dollars or shekels?"

"One-half dollars, one-half shekels. I will be here at eight."

"One more thing, Menachem. I want you to call Ike Palmer."

"I don't have his number."

"He calls you. It's in your phone."

"It is blocked when he calls. He constantly changes phones, changes numbers."

"Dammit, Menachem. Think. Use your wits. You know him well enough to tell me he's not crazy, so figure out how to contact him. I want to talk to him in the morning while we're driving to Tel Aviv. I want to see what he knows. Make it happen."

"I will try."

"I'm going to call the U.S. when I get to my room. I want them to be expecting us at the Embassy in the morning. We're not going to take a number and wait."

Menachem drove off. Liam walked inside and stopped at the front desk. No messages. He rode the elevator to the sixth floor, glancing at his reflection in the shiny brass doors of the car. In the room he checked the phone. The message light was dark. He took a five minute shower to wash off the grime of the Old City. Then he had the front desk place a call for him to Willie Mitchell Banks' cell phone. The lawyer answered.

"Hello? Who is this?"

"Listen, Willie Mitchell, it's Liam. Mimi's missing."

"What? Missing?"

"I'm in Jerusalem at the King David Hotel. She went shopping in the Old City. She didn't come back at one this afternoon like we had arranged. You know she's responsible, always on time."

"What time is it there now?"

"Almost three in the morning. She's been gone fourteen hours."

"Good God. What do you want me to do?"

"Use some of your connections in D.C. Help me. I can't call my Louisiana senators or my congressman. The EPA litigation. I'm a pariah in Washington."

"Just as well. They've shown you they can't be trusted."

"Could you talk to Scott and Senator Sumrall? Tell them Mimi's missing somewhere in Jerusalem. I've been to the local police. In six or seven hours I'm going to be at the U.S. Embassy in Tel Aviv. Could you ask the Senator pull to some strings with the State Department? Get some action out of them over here?"

"Skeeter will help us. I'll call Scott right now and set things in motion. Where were you when she was taken?"

Liam hated to tell him. He had talked to Willie Mitchell about Ike Palmer and the Fed Ex letter before he and Mimi left Louisiana.

"I had a meeting with Ike."

Willie Mitchell was silent on the other end for a moment. He had cautioned Liam to be careful fooling with Ike Palmer.

"You think Mimi going missing has something to do with Palmer?"

"It has to," Liam said. "There's no other explanation."

Liam felt his face grow hot. He had been recklessly naïve. Mimi demurred when they discussed the Fed Ex letter. He scheduled the three days in Israel anyway. Two meetings with Ike Palmer. A disturbed man up to his neck in God knows what. Now Mimi was gone.

"I can't believe I was so stupid," Liam said.

"Put that behind you. Focus on finding Mimi. What else do you want me to do?"

"I don't know right now. Just keep your cell handy. Make the calls to Scott and Senator Sumrall."

Liam gave Willie Mitchell the hotel contact information and his room number. He hung up and lay down on the bed for a moment. He considered himself lucky to have Willie Mitchell as a friend. Liam and Annette had met Willie Mitchell and Susan Banks in 2003 in Cozumel on an all-day snorkeling adventure off a huge catamaran. The two couples hit it off immediately and became close friends, traveling and vacationing together. Willie Mitchell and Liam spoke on the phone several times every week. Liam helped Susan in her negotiations to lease a hundred acres in DeSoto Parish in the northwest Louisiana shale play. Her acreage was near some of Liam's DeSoto Parish shallow production, so he knew what the companies were offering. More importantly, he knew what they were willing to pay. He coerced Delaware Energy to squeeze out a little extra bonus payment for Susan while they were salivating after him to sign his 15,000 acre deal.

But it was not only business that formed the basis of Liam and Willie Mitchell's friendship. It was character. They recognized traits in each other—honesty, integrity, perseverance, guts, a voracious work ethic. They shared these traits in common. The two men were in different regimens, but their intelligence and ability to reason and and strategize enabled each to be a valuable resource for the other. Liam used Willie Mitchell as a sounding board for legal issues; Willie Mitchell used Liam as a second opinion in general business, oil and gas matters. Liam recalled a conversation about a thorny title issue in a natural gas play he had been working. Willie Mitchell made an offhand remark about the title in question. The remark triggered a surge of creative energy in Liam and started him down the path to solving the problem and producing a sizable stream of income for Clare Petroleum.

Liam had been there for Willie Mitchell in what they both now referred to as the "three bad years:" when Susan and he were separated. Willie Mitchell and Susan helped Liam through the dark, miserable days following Annette's death. More recently, Willie Mitchell had given Liam good counsel in his fight and eventual settlement with the government in connection with the sale of his deep rights to Delaware Energy, a fight that Liam planned on picking up again when he returned to the United States with Mimi.

Liam reached up and turned off the lamp. He lay in the darkness trying to think. The faces he had seen in the Old City kept popping into his brain. There were hundreds of them, all shapes and sizes, different shades of brown, some smiling and gracious, some surly. In his mind's eye each of them had looked up from Mimi's photograph, stared at Liam and shook their heads. Instinctively they knew Liam was to blame.

You careless fool.

Chapter Nine

Mimi Stanton tried to open her eyes; she could not. She felt groggy, disoriented. Her head ached when she moved the slightest bit. Finally she forced her eyelids open. Too dark to see anything. She felt for her watch. Nothing there. It was hard to concentrate, but she forced herself to think. She was, after all, a problem-solving nurse practitioner.

Mimi felt her face and head. No bumps or sore spots. No bleeding or dried blood she could detect. She felt her torso. Everything seemed all right. Touching her blouse and skirt brought back a recollection. She was still dressed in the white linen blouse and narrow black slacks she had worn to the Old City, but the turquoise scarf Liam had bought her in Assisi and her large gold loop earrings were missing.

She rubbed her feet together; shoes were gone, too. Concentrating seemed to clear her head a bit. She felt the surface under her. She was on her back on hard wood covered by a thin blanket. Mimi extended her arms. Nothing above her. She pivoted on her behind and sat up. The effort made her light-headed. She steadied herself and carefully lowered her bare feet. The floor was cool, smooth, probably tile.

She took a deep breath and gagged. Something reeked—a vile smell of sewage or rot. Mimi pinched her nostrils, but she didn't want to inhale the rank fumes through her mouth either. She pulled her blouse over her nose to filter the odor. Mimi looked around. She was certain her eyes were working but saw nothing. She figured out the reason.

She was being held in pitch black darkness.

Being held.

The words were chilling. Mimi tamped down the fear that threatened to make her vomit. She reconstructed what she could. She recalled leaving the King David on the route suggested by the concierge, walking through the glitzy Mamilla Mall and entering the Old City through the Jaffa Gate. She remembered wandering through the Christian Quarter and browsing through five or six stalls before consulting her map and entering the Armenian Quarter. She remembered it being less commercial.

She recalled seeing Yusef, the waiter with the jagged scar from the café in Mahane Yehuda where she had met the infamous Ike Palmer. She remembered waving at Yusef in the crowd of people on the small, winding street. He did not wave back.

She remembered wandering into a store and asking the old shopkeeper if he had *mezuzahs*. Liam had wanted to get one while they were in Jerusalem; put on the door jamb at Grand Oaks. She remembered the merchant leading her to a counter in the back of the shop and placing several *mezuzahs* on a glass shelf for her to examine. She had picked one up when she felt someone behind her, a sweet smell, suffocation and darkness.

Ether.

That's why her head ached. She felt disoriented. Ether had a fruity, pungent odor. Not used in medical practice in the United States for decades. Her professor in nursing school had told them ether was still used in third world countries as an anesthetic. Israel was not a third world country, but it was surrounded by them.

Mimi eased herself to the floor, putting more weight on her feet as she grew confident she wouldn't fall. She let go of the table and stood with her arms in front of her, reaching to feel her way around the room. The darkness was unrelenting, yielding no clues.

She took a few baby steps and stopped when she struck her shin on something hard. Something cool and smooth at the level of her shin—something rounded. She jerked her hand back. She was caressing a toilet. No telling how nasty the thing was. Mimi shuffled around the toilet and touched a metal faucet. She turned the handle and felt a tiny trickle of cool water. At least she wouldn't die of thirst.

Mimi took her time feeling her way around the small bathroom in total darkness. No tub, no shower, no window. There was one door. She found the knob and tried to open it. She shook the knob but the door was sturdy and locked. She wasn't going anywhere.

She returned carefully to the wooden board. The thin blanket felt like wool. Why had she been taken? Why was she *being held?* Liam was wealthy, but no one in Jerusalem knew that. Only Ike Palmer knew they were coming to Israel, so unless she was the victim of a random kidnapping, Mimi figured Ike must have something to do with her situation.

Mimi sat in darkness for a long time, thinking. After a while, an encouraging hint of light came under the door. She wasn't hallucinating. The light grew brighter. Thinking it might be morning and someone might be on the other side of the door, she banged on it. No response. No sound or movement. She pounded the door again. Still nothing. Mimi leaned against the door, discouraged and afraid. She beat on the door and called out. "Is anyone there? Can you help me?" She waited a few minutes then screamed for help over and over. A voice beyond the door silenced her.

"Shut up, American whore."

Mimi's heart began to pound. She eased back to her wooden slab. Tears streamed down her cheeks. She might never see Liam again.

Chapter Ten

Hours later and a hundred kilometers west of where Mimi was *being held*, Menachem drove his Volvo slowly into the U.S. Embassy's security checkpoint in Tel Aviv. Stopped by the traffic control bar, he gave the Marine his driver's license, his business card, and Liam's passport.

"What is your business, sir?" the guard asked.

"The Ambassador is expecting us," Liam said leaning toward him from the passenger seat. "It's a missing person. I'm Liam Connors."

The Marine walked into the guard house and checked their documents. Liam studied the Embassy building. Five stories square, an eyesore among the other office buildings on HaYarkon Street. An unruly forest of satellite and communication dishes, insulated lines, and metal towers marked the roof.

"They could not have designed an uglier building if they tried," Liam said to Menachem.

Before leaving Jerusalem, Liam had loaded up with dollars and shekels from an ATM outside a local bank. Menachem had showed him how to request withdrawal instructions in English. Menachem had also succeeded in talking the phone store manager into opening early. Liam bought a new phone and gave the manager a healthy cash bonus for his trouble.

Menachem had not done as well with Ike. Menachem got him on the phone and extracted the promise of a phone call. Ike never called. Liam was angry.

"Do you think he intentionally lied to you?" Liam asked Menachem.

"I don't know. Maybe something happened."

Before leaving the King David earlier that morning, Liam had spoken to Mississippi Senator Skeeter Sumrall and Willie Mitchell's son, Scott Banks, on a conference call. The Senator assured Liam the Ambassador would be expecting him and do everything in her power to help. Scott Banks, Senator Sumrall's right hand man, told Liam he would other contacts who might help Liam.

The Marine working security at the Embassy returned their papers and raised the traffic control bar. They went through a more thorough security check at the building entrance, including a full body scan. A Marine in dress blues led Liam and Menachem to the Ambassador's office.

The United States Ambassador to Israel was in her sixties. She wore a navy blue business suit and pearls, red lipstick and too much rouge. The severity of her blue black hair dye suppressed its natural sheen. Senator Sumrall had told Liam she was the widow of a Silicon Valley pioneer, a big political donor, and savvy about Israel's internal politics. Skeeter said she and her late husband were active fund-raisers in the American Jewish philanthropy community and that the Ambassador had a reputation for being smart, but arrogant and prickly.

"Senator Sumrall called on your behalf," she said with a forced smile as Menachem and Liam sat down across a large, leather-topped desk. "But you are from Louisiana. Were your Senators unavailable?"

Menachem sensed a snag. He looked at Liam.

"I'm not sure. We've had our differences."

"Yes," she said, "the litigation." She knew the story.

Her condescension was subtle, but there it was. Liam suppressed his irritation. He had hoped to keep his lawsuit against the government on the Delaware deal out of the situation with Mimi. The thing to focus on was getting help from the United States government, no matter how much crow he had to eat. The Ambassador smiled at Liam over her reading glasses. The insincerity made his blood boil.

"We're going to put our resources to work for you. Help you find Miss Stanton. You must be very worried."

The Ambassador pushed a button on her phone and within seconds a young man opened the door and introduced himself to Menachem and Liam as James Exley, mid-thirties, very short hair, rimless glasses. The Ambassador stood and walked around to join the three men. Liam recognized the move. He and Menachem were being passed off to Mr. Exley. The Ambassador wanted to get back to something that actually interested her.

"Mr. Exley is *the* expert in the Embassy on this sort of thing. Lots of experience in security. He has liaised with Israeli Police on behalf of U.S. citizens on numerous occasions."

Liaised. Liam hated that phony government word. Exley gestured for them to follow him. Menachem looked at Liam long enough to signal that Menachem knew they were being patronized.

"We'll stay on top of this, Mr. Connors," the Ambassador said as they followed Exley out the door.

Exley's office was a few doors down from the Ambassador's. Menachem and Liam sat at his conference table. He took off his suit coat, tossed a legal pad on the table. "Now, what is your wife's full name?"

"She's not my wife."

Liam gave Exley the Xerox of Mimi's passport, disappointed that the embassy didn't already have her basic information. Liam related everything that happened the day before—a quick summary with exact times. He repeated the information he got from hotel security and described their meeting with Akiva Peres.

"Wait. Back up. This breakfast meeting at the hotel. With whom did you meet?"

"A friend from Louisiana. I hadn't seen him in a long time. He's an Israeli citizen, been living here twenty-five years."

"His name?"

"Isaac Palmer."

"And the purpose of the meeting?"

"Just to get together, see how he was doing. We used to be close."

Exley nodded as he made notes. He tapped his pen on the pad, a gesture Liam recognized from meetings with lawyers and businessmen in his negotiations involving oil and gas leases, litigation, and sales of production or assets. It meant Exley was reluctant to ask the next question.

"Do you and your..., uh, girl friend get along well, Mr. Connors?"

It was a question Liam would have asked were he in Exley's spot. They needed to rule out the possibility that Mimi had run away from Liam.

"No problems, very happy. This has been a wonderful trip. Ten relaxing days in Italy, this quick little side trip to Israel."

Exley wrote all this on his pad.

"She did not up and decide to leave me in Jerusalem, Mr. Exley. She went shopping. Something happened to her in the Old City."

Exley nodded and pursed his lips.

"Where might we reach this Mr. Palmer?" Exley asked.

"I don't know. I don't have his phone number or his address."

"How did you arrange to meet him for breakfast yesterday?"

"Menachem set that up."

Menachem nodded to Exley.

"Menachem drives Mr. Palmer around from time to time."

"That right?" Exley asked Menachem.

"Yes."

"Do you know where he lives, this Mr. Palmer?"

"No."

Exley arched his eyebrows. Liam could tell Exley thought something was fishy about his meeting with Ike Palmer, and he would put that something into his written report.

In addition, there was this odd element of Mr. Connors' meeting with one Isaac Palmer, an Israeli citizen and American ex-pat with whom Mr. Connors claimed a close relationship, in spite of the fact he did not know Palmer's address or how to contact him. To those of us in the Embassy accustomed to coming to the aid of U.S. citizens whose loved ones have become lost in this foreign country, the alleged relationship with Isaac Palmer seemed...off kilter somehow. Certainly a red flag. Additional facts we learned about this Isaac Palmer later in the investigation, something Mr. Connors withheld from us in our interview....

Liam knew what he was telling Exley didn't sound believable, but he could not mention the Ishmael Scroll.

"Let me check something," Exley said and walked across the room to his desk.

He tapped his keyboard and studied the monitor.

"I see you resolved your dispute with the EPA," Exley said.

"Yes," Liam said, irritated that Exley had brought it up.

"Right," Exley said, returning to the table. "I have enough to start working on this. I recommend you return to the King David and wait for me to call you. I will telephone Investigator Peres and coordinate with him. We no longer have a consulate in Jerusalem, but we do have offices. I'll scan in Miss Stanton's photo and send out an e-mail." He glanced at his watch. "By the time you return to Jerusalem, she will have been missing almost twenty-four hours, so Mr. Peres will be able to institute a search for her in accordance with their policy. I will urge him to use all the resources at his disposal to find Miss Stanton."

"Other than sending e-mail and phoning Akiva Peres," Liam asked, "do you have agents that can...."

"Not exactly," Exley said. "Primarily we coordinate with local law enforcement. Make sure they give the case proper attention. It's outside the purview of the State Department to actually search for U.S. citizens. We have no police powers. I am sure you are aware of that. Our role in this will be to aid the locals."

Exley stood up and put on his coat. He was ready for them to leave. He gave Liam his card and led them to the door.

"One more thing, Mr. Connors. If you should see Mr. Palmer again, get his phone number and address. And be so kind as to call me with that information? At this point I'm not sure how it might help us find Miss Stanton, but all the relevant information should be on file just in case."

"Certainly I will," Liam lied.

Menachem and Liam were escorted back to the entrance by the same Marine. They walked to the Volvo.

"Total waste of time," Liam said getting into the car and rolling down his window. "Such bull shit...."

"Wait," Menachem said holding up his index finger.

The Volvo passed the guard house and zigzagged around several huge concrete barriers positioned in the embassy driveway like slalom gates. Not until they were several blocks away did Menachem speak.

"They have parabolic receivers around the embassy," he said. "They capture the conversations of their visitors as they come and go. Many intelligence officers work in the Embassy. Sometimes the true intentions of visitors are found in the statements they make in their automobiles rather than what they say inside the Embassy."

That made perfect sense to Liam.

"How do you know about the receivers?" Liam asked.

"I drive many people. I listen to them talk when I am not describing the sights. Some do not know I speak English. Learn a lot by listening."

"Right," Liam said. "Let's go straight to the police station by the Jaffa Gate. See if Exley's call gets Investigator Peres moving."

"It will make no difference."

"You're probably right. Peres doesn't seem like the kind of guy who would be affected one way or the other by Mr. Exley."

Menachem pushed the Volvo, driving faster than normal. Liam tried to think. What could he do? Both Investigator Peres and the Ambassador's assistant Exley tried to be subtle about their interest in Ike Palmer, but it was clear they wanted to find him, too.

"After we check in with Peres," Liam said, "we have to locate Ike."

Chapter Eleven

Back in Jerusalem, Menachem answered his phone. He listened a moment, then offered it to Liam. "Yitzhak."

Liam mouthed "Speaker mode."

Menachem tapped a key and gave the phone to Liam.

"We need to talk, Ike" Liam said. "Where are you?"

"I can't say on this phone."

Liam slammed his palm on the console. Menachem jumped.

"Dammit to hell, Ike. I've had about all I can handle of this secret agent crap. Mimi's missing. It's got something to do with you."

Liam had no facts to back up his strong feeling, but knew from experience not to ignore his intuition. For a moment there was silence. That was all the confirmation Liam needed.

"I'm sorry, Liam. I really am."

"Sorry's not going to swing it. Tell me what you know. Who's got her? Where is she?"

"I don't know. And I don't know who is trying to kill me. If I did I would tell you."

"Who says someone's trying to kill you?"

"They sent word two days ago," Ike said. "Wednesday."

"Where'd they send it?"

"Tel Quidron. To a friend."

"Who's your friend?"

"She doesn't have anything to do with all this. No connection."

"Then how did they know she was your friend?"

"I don't know. Neither does she. She didn't see them in person. They called her. I'm to give them what I found. Or next time, they'll do more than tail me."

Menachem concentrated on the road. Liam tried a softer approach.

"You told me in the café I was the only man in the world you trust."

"Right. You *are* the only man I can trust."

"Then trust me now. Meet with Menachem and me."

"It's too dangerous."

Liam felt his ears begin to burn. "This is bull shit."

"If it's all bull shit why did they take Mimi?"

Menachem glanced over at Liam. Ike had a point.

"I regret I got you involved in this," Ike continued. "I'm really sorry they took your Mimi. These people will tell you they'll trade Mimi for the scroll. You cannot believe them. When they get the scroll they'll kill her anyway. Besides, no one has mentioned Mimi to me."

"Did they tell your girl friend they have Mimi?"

"No. They said nothing to her. It was Wednesday they called. Mimi went missing yesterday."

"Listen to me, Ike. If you don't work with me on finding Mimi, I will tell every official I run into about your Ishmael scroll. Everything you told me at breakfast yesterday about its significance. The Jerusalem Police might be interested to know they'll trade Mimi for it."

"Do what you have to do," Ike said after a pause. "If someone is holding Mimi as a trade for the scroll, I'm sorry. But the Ishmael Scroll is more important than the life of one person. It will settle an ancient dispute. People have fought wars over it for almost fourteen hundred years. Save hundreds of thousands of lives going forward. I'm not giving it to anyone who claims to be holding Mimi. They'll destroy the scroll, kill the girl, and continue their attacks on my people."

"Listen, Ike...."

Ike hung up.

Liam stared at the phone. Menachem braked the Volvo for traffic. A delivery truck pulled out from an adjoining alley and stopped inches from Liam's door. The driver sat on his horn, the blast piercing Liam's head like a knife. The driver's face was a mask of rage.

"Pay no attention to the fool," Menachem said.

The driver continued to lay on the horn and began to scream at them. Liam stared straight ahead through the windshield, mystified. After a moment, the noise of the horn seemed to fade, drowned out by Ike Palmer's chilling words that echoed inside Liam's brain.

They'll kill Mimi anyway.

◆❖◆

On the way to see Peres, Liam began to reconstruct for Menachem what Ike had told him at breakfast the day before.

"You don't have to go over this with me, my friend" Menachem said. "I was there."

"You were at the door. Ike was speaking low."

"Yitzhak cannot whisper. He talks loud, like an angry *yenta*. You know how he is. And I have very good ears."

"Do you believe him?"

"What does it matter? Whoever took Mimi believes him. I do not know what has happened. No one has talked to me about trading Mimi for the scroll."

"Do you know Ike's lady friend?"

"I have met her."

At one o'clock Menachem parked the Volvo and the two of them walked into the Jerusalem police station near the Jaffa Gate. Mimi's life was in danger. That was sinking in, working on Liam. They sat in the waiting room. The surly desk sergeant let them know that Investigator Peres might see them.

"I'll wait outside," Liam told the woman.

Menachem followed Liam out into the parking area. Liam suddenly had the urge to buy a pack of cigarettes and light one up. Menachem stood next to him staring at the Old City wall. Something was on his mind. He pointed to the Jaffa Gate.

"Herod the Great. He laid those stones. On the lower part of the wall there at the gate. After we secure Mimi, I will take you through the tunnels on the other side, below the Western Wall. Some stones are gigantic. A video reveals how they believe the builders did it."

"I pray to God we find Mimi."

"When we meet with Investigator Peres," Menachem said quietly, drawing closer, "it would not be wise for you to say anything about Yitzhak's scroll. Or about his friend, the girl at Tel Qidron. Let us keep those matters to ourselves for now."

"Why on earth, Menachem? Is there something you're not telling me?"

Liam felt the muscles in the back of his neck tighten. A familiar feeling, brought on by stress. Always confined to the back of his neck. Sudden. He rotated his head to work out the stiffness.

"Not at all. I have lived in Israel all my life. That information will not be helpful. Do not tell the police or any other official about Yitzhak's scroll. If it is as Yitzhak claims, people in authority here would sacrifice Mimi with ease. Such a document made public would support their hard-line policies toward Muslims." (He pronounced it *Moos-lims*.) "The hard-liners would say the scroll proves all the land Israel controls now is what God promised Abraham as recorded in Genesis. No part of the West Bank would be offered to the Arabs in any peace negotiations. Already now, they say the Promised Land runs from the Nile on the south to Lebanon on the north, from the Mediterranean on the west to the Euphrates on the east. Yitzhak's scroll would embolden them."

Liam pictured a map of the Middle East.

"That means Israel would have a claim to the Sinai in Egypt, most of Jordan, even parts of Iraq and Syria."

"*All* of Jordan. Part of Saudi Arabia. Right now, the *Moos-lims* claim this Promised Land through Ishmael, son of Abraham. Other members of the government and the Knesset, the appeasers, would want to suppress or destroy the scroll, avoid making the tension and the conflict we live with daily even worse. They would not care that the Ishmael Scroll proves Israel's claim to the Promised Land. Peace at any price."

"You and Ike both think involving your government is not a good idea. So you believe what Ike says about his scroll?"

"I only know what Yitzhak told you at the tourist hotel. I do not know if the scroll exists. If it is legitimate. If it is indeed authentic, it would explain Mimi's disappearance. The kidnappers would be using her as leverage to persuade you to force Yitzhak to turn over the scroll."

"Investigator Peres is ready," the sergeant growled.

"Twenty-four hours. It's been twenty-four hours," Liam said when Menachem and he sat down across from Akiva Peres.

"Yes. I initiated search procedures an hour ago." He turned to Menachem. "So you are Yitzhak Palmer's driver?"

"For quite some time."

"And you don't know how to reach him?"

"He calls me when he needs me. Maybe once a month."

"Do you pick him up from Tel Qidron at times?"

"Yes."

"Will you make me a list of the places you recall driving him over the last year?" Peres said and gave Menachem a note pad and pen.

"I began the search for Miss Stanton before your friend Mr. Exley called from the American Embassy," Peres said to Liam.

"Thank you," Liam said, "but Exley is no friend of mine, Investigator Peres. I went to the Embassy because I wanted to exhaust every avenue to find Mimi. I didn't expect much, and they met my expectations. They will not lift a finger to help me find my fiancé. If you find her they'll take part of the credit. My government has become bloated and worthless."

As Peres nodded in agreement, Liam noticed his good eye moved from Menachem but his bad eye didn't track. To be safe, Liam focused on the part of Peres' lower forehead where his eyebrows almost met. He would do nothing to offend Investigator Peres.

"In fairness to them, Mr. Connors, they are not in the business of finding people in Israel. Or any other country for that matter. Bureaucrats do not enjoy leaving their desks."

"Right. I understand. Can you tell me what actions you are taking?"

"We developed a web site that our volunteers and many other citizens check regularly. I posted Miss Stanton's picture on the site. Sometimes it is our best tool in these cases."

Peres described the other procedures he would implement. Liam was grateful, but the tactics Peres laid out might work to locate an elderly person with dementia who wandered away from a caretaker, not someone who had been forcibly taken and hidden.

"Mr. Connors, do you have any additional information that might shed light on where Miss Stanton might be? Or why someone would hold her against her will?"

"No," Liam said, following Menachem's instructions.

"Have you talked again to this Yitzhak Palmer?"

"Yes. He called Menachem's phone on our way back from Tel Aviv."

"May I see your phone?" Peres asked Menachem.

"I think he called using a pre-paid phone," Menachem said, handing his phone to Peres. "There is no phone number or information in my phone that will be of assistance."

Peres examined the phone and returned it. Menachem pushed the pen and pad toward Peres.

"Did Mr. Palmer say anything about Miss Stanton?" Peres asked.

"No," Liam said. "I asked him. He knows nothing."

"And you still do not know how to contact him?"

"No," Liam said.

"He is a member of Tel Qidron *kibbutz*," Menachem said, "but he says he seldom stays there."

"I know someone who does," Peres said. "If you think locating Yitzhak Palmer might help in the search for Miss Stanton."

"Great," Liam said. "I think we should search in the Old City again. Go to the vendors that were closed last night. Show them Mimi's photograph."

Investigator Peres made notes in his file and closed it.

"I have your contact information, Mr. Connors. Let us hope something will turn up."

"Thank you, Mr. Peres. I'll check with you later today."

"Best call here by six. But I always carry my cell."

Menachem and Liam walked past the desk sergeant. She ignored them. Her attitude poisoned the air in the waiting room.

"I did what you said, Menachem. Now, tell me what we do to find Mimi. Where to now?"

"Tel Qidron," he said and started the Volvo. "So now Miss Stanton is your fiancé?"

"If she'll have me after this fiasco. Why say she's my girl friend? It sounds so juvenile. She's more than that."

"Have you asked to marry her yet?"

"No. I pray I get the opportunity."

Chapter Twelve

Menachem had predicted Friday afternoon traffic would be a problem. A three-car accident held them up for twenty minutes. When they did start moving again, the Jerusalem police directed them to an alternate route out of the city. It continued to be slow going heading east on the multi-lane highway. Leaving Jerusalem, their drive was a steady incline. Liam studied his map. The Volvo began to run more quiet as they passed over the mountain ridge and began the downhill run toward the Dead Sea.

"That is Mar Saba over there," Menachem said. "A Greek Orthodox monastery in continuous use since the fifth century. Women may not enter the compound."

Liam nodded, but Menachem might as well have been speaking Hebrew. His travelogue was not registering with Liam. Mimi consumed him.

"I believe Akiva Peres will do his best to help," Menachem said.

"I hope so. He told me he lost his eye in a 'minor skirmish.'"

"Yom Kippur," Menachem said glancing over. "That 'skirmish' was a major campaign. His company held off the Syrian invasion in the Golan Heights and took part in the counter-offensive into Syria. Our troops were close to Damascus at the time of the first cease-fire because of soldiers like Akiva Peres. He lost his eye in the Golan, spent an hour in a medical tent to cover it with gauze and a patch, then fought in Syria, where he was wounded again. He carries those scars. Investigator Peres is a war hero. After the war the newspapers carried many stories of his bravery."

"A tough guy," Liam said.

Liam felt like a dilettante. He served out his commitment stateside. Military intelligence. Trained with all kinds of weapons but had never shot at a man. No one shot at him. He analyzed data for officers. Liam recalled Menachem's story about his pacifist friend's death in the coffee shop bombing. Merely living in Israel took courage.

At three o'clock they drove toward a thick grove of date palms on a small mesa overlooking what Menachem said was the Qidron Valley. Menachem guided the Volvo onto the asphalt drive that snaked through the palms and stopped at a long, low-slung cinder block building with a tile roof.

"Tel Qidron administration building," he said.

Liam stepped out of the car and looked around. A long tractor shed housed assorted agricultural equipment. Liam pointed to a group of small buildings.

"Residential buildings," Menachem said.

Liam followed him through the door of the building. The interior was Spartan. They stood behind a counter and waited. In a moment a thin older woman came out of an office. Her sun-ravaged face was pleasant but lined with deep wrinkles.

"May I help you?" she asked in heavily-accented English.

"Yes, ma'am," Liam said. "We're here...."

Menachem interrupted speaking Hebrew. Liam listened to the two of them go back and forth until the woman nodded and returned to her office. Through the open door Liam watched her pick up a telephone and begin making calls.

"This will take a while," Menachem said.

Liam slumped into one of the gray metal chairs lining the wall opposite the counter. He was bone-tired.

Menachem's light tap on Liam's shoulder waked him.

"How long was I out?" Liam asked, rubbing his eyes.

"Ten minutes," he said. "I want you to meet someone."

A young woman stood there, almost hidden behind Menachem. She wore khaki shorts and a light blue tee shirt with "Tel Qidron" printed in an arc over a white Star of David.

Liam extended his hand. "I'm Liam Connors."

"Shelly Feldman," she smiled.

She was pretty, with fair, tanned skin and ash blonde hair pulled back into a pony tail. Liam guessed she was about thirty.

"Shelly is Yitzhak's friend," Menachem said. "She's American."

"A small town in South Carolina. Not much of a place. But I can claim the University of South Carolina."

"Go, Cocks," Liam said.

"Haven't heard that in a while."

"LSU a few years back," Liam said. *A few years back* meaning thirty-one years.

"What do you want to know about Yitzhak?" she said.

"Do you know where he is?" Liam asked. "I'm an old friend."

"He's told me about you," she said, "but I never know where Yitzhak is. The last couple of months he's been coming and going at odd hours. Acting stranger than usual."

"How long have you been here at Tel Qidron?"

"Three years. I worked in Atlanta and D.C. as a paralegal after graduation, then moved here. What's this all about?"

"Let's go outside," Liam said and held the door for Shelly and Menachem.

"Ike phoned us this morning," Liam said. "He told us someone called you a few days ago and made a threat."

She looked at Menachem before she responded.

"Yes."

"What did the person sound like?"

"A man. An Arab, I'm fairly certain. He spoke pretty good English. He disguised his voice. I was helping in the kitchen. A lot of pots and pans noise on my end. I don't know. It's hard to say. But it wasn't a joke. The man sounded threatening."

"Tell me exactly what he said."

"He said to tell Yitzhak to give them what he found or they would do more than just follow him around, something like that."

"Did they say what it was they wanted?"

"Just what I told you. That's all."

"Did you know about Ike finding something in a cave, something ancient and very important?"

"I have to get back to work," she said and began to walk away.

"Wait. Just a few more questions."

She turned back to face Liam, her arms crossed against her chest.

"Ike told Menachem and me he found a scroll in a cave near Herodium," Liam said. "We know what it says. Hagar being already pregnant before she slept with Abraham."

"You know more than I do then, because he never told me that. He said he found something very valuable. That people were after him for it. Nothing about a scroll."

"It's what Yitzhak claims to have found," Menachem said. "I heard him tell Liam with my own ears. Liam's lady friend is missing, taken from the Old City just yesterday. The night before, Liam and she met with Ike at a café in Mahane Yehuda. They were seen."

"I'm sorry about your friend," she said to Liam, "but I don't know where Ike is. The man said nothing about any woman. If Ike comes here I'll call you. Leave me your number."

"How did people know you'd pass along a threat?"

"Everyone in Tel Qidron knows Yitzhak and I are...friends."

"How did you get in touch with him after the call?"

"I didn't. He called me and I told him. He said I wouldn't be seeing him for a while. That's the last thing he said."

Menachem wrote Liam's number on his card and gave it to Shelly.

"Call either one of us," Liam said.

"If he calls me I will let you know."

"Thanks," Liam said. "One more thing. Do you know of an archeologist who works here at Tel Qidron? An older man, older than I am, who studied the Dead Sea Scrolls?"

"No," she said. "Not here in the *kibbutz*. Most everyone here works on the crops. Agricultural work."

"What about a linguist?"

"Lots of smart people here do manual labor. I've never heard of a linguist," she said walking away. "I'll call if I hear from Yitzhak."

Menachem gestured for Liam to wait outside. He walked back into the administration building. Liam stared at another astonishingly clear blue sky above the date palm fronds. The temperature was mild for the first day of March. Liam thought what a great day it would have been to spend with Mimi visiting ancient sites.

"Let us return to Jerusalem," Menachem said when he walked outside to join Liam. "We have done all we can do here."

"What exactly did you do in there?"

"I know the woman who runs the office. I spoke to her about Yitzhak. She said she hasn't seen him in months but will ask around for us. She will call me with any information."

They drove through the date palms back onto the highway, heading west to Jerusalem.

"I don't know about the Feldman woman."

"She is all right," Menachem said. "I have picked her up with Yitzhak and driven them to Jerusalem several times. She only goes with him because he is an American. She is much younger."

"How does he pay you?"

"Shekels. He pays me well. It's why I put up with his unusual requests. Pick him up on some strange corner. Sometimes, it is very late. Past midnight."

"Where does he get his money?"

"He has an account at Hebrew National. I drive him there to make withdrawals from the outside ATM. It may be two or three o'clock in the morning."

"I mean where does he get the money to put into the account?"

"One time his withdrawal was denied. He got very upset. When he returned to the car he screamed on his phone to his brother in New York."

"Nathan?"

"Yes. Yitzhak was angry. He told his brother to transfer money into the account immediately. We went back to that same ATM two hours later and he made his withdrawal."

"You ever met Nathan?"

"No. I spoke to him on the phone one time when Yitzhak refused to take his calls."

"Is his number still in your phone?"

"It should be."

"I knew Nathan when we were kids. Maybe he can help us locate Ike."

"I do not think he can."

While Menachem drove, Liam thought about calling his office to get the number for Mimi's mother in Dallas but put it off, deciding it would do more harm than good. Mimi was an only child. She had no relationship with her father and wasn't close to her mother. Mimi despised her ex-husband. She had friends, but worked so hard she had little time for them, preferring to spend her free time with Liam. Liam knew he was her only support in the world. Consequently, rescuing her from her kidnappers was up to him. He made a silent vow.

I will find her. I will get her back.

"Let's drive to some of the places where you've picked up Ike, or dropped him off," Liam said, while Menachem drove west toward the mountain ridge. "He's bound to have a place in the city, Menachem. See if you can find his brother's number in your phone."

Chapter Thirteen

"Who the hell this?"

"It's Liam Connors, Nathan."

There was silence on the phone. Liam had Nathan on speaker so Menachem could hear.

Nathan cleared his voice. "What time is it?"

"I know it's early in New York."

"Liam Connors from Shreveport?"

"That's right. But I don't live there anymore. I moved to Natchitoches. Right now I'm in Israel."

"There can only be one reason you're calling. What's he done now?"

"My girl friend Mimi disappeared from the Old City yesterday. It's got something to do with your brother. Something he claims he's found."

"Run that by me again."

"Ike claims to have found a scroll. In a cave. Same age as the Dead Sea Scrolls. He says it invalidates any claim the Muslims have to the Promised Land."

"A scroll? Have you seen it?"

"No. Mimi and I just arrived Wednesday. We met with Ike at a café in a central market Wednesday night. I saw him again for coffee at a hotel yesterday morning. Mimi was kidnapped yesterday sometime before one in the afternoon Israel time."

"Why do you think he's involved with her disappearance?"

"No other explanation makes sense," Liam said. "I'm with Ike's driver, Menachem. He says men have been following Ike. I spoke to Ike on the phone today and he said he's been threatened. We just talked to a friend of his at Tel Qidron—Shelly Feldman from South Carolina—she says a man called her a few days ago threatening Ike. If Ike didn't give them what he had found he would regret it."

"And you think this same man took Mimi as leverage? To get this scroll Ike says he found?"

"That is exactly what we think."

"Have you received any kind of demand from the kidnappers?"

"No."

Menachem leaned toward the phone.

"It is Menachem Wladyslaw," he said loudly. "I spoke to you once when money for Yitzhak was not in the bank. I drive your brother many times. I believe these men took Mimi. To force Yitzhak to give them what he has found. It is the only thing I can believe, Mr. Nathan Palmer."

"Because you send Ike money," Liam added, "I thought maybe you might have some way to contact him."

"He doesn't talk to me unless something goes wrong with the wire transfer. He calls me. I don't have his phone number or his address. Only his *kibbutz*."

"We've just come from Tel Qidron. They don't know where he is."

"I can give you the bank account number when I get to my office later this morning. I have a breakfast meeting...."

"The bank is Hebrew National, Nathan, and I can't wait on your meeting. This is life and death."

"Hold on," Nathan said.

Liam listened to Nathan say "it's about Ike" to someone.

"Tell your wife I'm sorry to call so early."

"It's all right. I'll be at my office in thirty minutes. The bank information is there in a file. I'll call you."

"Text the account information to this phone number," Liam said. "And say, Nathan, why do you send him money? Is it part of his inheritance from your parents?"

"That's how it started," Nathan said. "That ran out years ago. I kept sending it out of my own funds after that."

"I wouldn't ask you this if it weren't important. How much do you send Ike?"

"Five grand a month."

"You're supporting him then."

"Ike tells me it's out of guilt. I don't go to temple any more. The money means nothing to me. I could send him five grand a day and not miss it. I don't know, Liam. He was so troubled over here in the States, and he seemed much better in Israel. He tells me he's found himself in the Promised Land. Shit, Liam, why do we do anything? He's the only family I got not counting my wife and kids."

"Thanks, Nathan. Sorry to put you out, but I must find Mimi. She's in danger, I know."

"I'm on board. I'll text you the account number. If I can do anything else, Liam, let me know." He paused. "You know how Ike is. How can you be sure if he really has found something? He used to be bad about making things up. If you find him, try to...well, just take care of him. I say he's doing better, but he's still Ike, you know."

"I know. I'll do what I can."

Liam ended the call and turned to Menachem.

"Thanks for doing that."

"What?"

"Talking to Nathan. Trying to help."

"I am on your side. I want Yitzhak to make it out of this, but if it comes to a choice between him and Mimi, I help you save her."

"Thank you," Liam said with a lump in his throat. "Thank you."

They entered Jerusalem before five. Traffic was still heavy and pedestrians seemed in a hurry. Menachem drove Liam to a dozen busy corners, cafes, and bus stops where he had picked up Ike or dropped him off over the last year. Liam marked each location on his city map with Menachem's help. He had yet to hear back from Nathan Palmer. As he was preparing to call him in New York again, Liam jumped when heavy metal music blared from his cell phone.

"Damn," Liam said grabbing the phone. "I've got to change that."

"Sorry to take so long, Liam," Nathan said on the other end. "Here's the bank account number."

Liam wrote the number on the back of his map.

"Thanks, Nathan."

"They might not cooperate with you," Nathan said. "Israeli banks are very security conscious, more so than ours."

"Okay, thanks, Nathan," Liam said and hung up.

"Let's get to the King David," Liam said to Menachem. "I've been meaning to ask you. Mimi went missing in the Armenian Quarter. Does that mean Armenians might be involved in this?"

"Not likely. Less than five hundred Armenians live there in the Old City. Most are students at the seminary or priests or people who work for the church. All property is owned by the Armenian Patriarchate. I would be surprised to find any illegal activity there for sure. Besides, Miss Feldman said the man that called to threaten Yitzhak was an Arab."

"Armenians aren't Arabs?"

"No."

"What are they?"

"Armenians."

Menachem pulled into the circular drive of the King David.

"Shall I wait for you?" Menachem asked.

"No. Let's valet the car. You come with me to the room. We'll make a couple of calls. I want to use a land line. While I'm on the phone you connect the Xs on my city map. Inside that ragged perimeter is bound to be Ike's Jerusalem apartment."

"Jerusalem is a crowded city."

"Maybe so, but we have to find that crazy son-of-a-bitch."

Chapter Fourteen

Menachem drove through the densely populated city center. Liam was frustrated. What sounded good in theory turned out to be a waste of time and gasoline. The area circumscribed by Menachem on the Jerusalem map was huge and included many neighborhoods that were packed with high and low-rise apartments, office buildings, and retail stores. Ike had done a good job varying the sites where Menachem picked him up or dropped him off. There was no discernible pattern. Ike's *pied a terre* might have been among the thousands of properties inside the perimeter of the search area, but it would be impossible to find.

"Crap," Liam said and flung his map into the Volvo's back seat. "Unless we see Ike walking on the street we won't find him like this. I've been watching too many cop show re-runs." He paused. "These men that were tailing Ike, the ones you saw, how did you lose them?"

"I did nothing," Menachem said. "I drop Yitzhak off where he tells me. What happens then, I don't know. He loses them on the street, walking I would guess. Yitzhak is very resourceful, very clever."

"No matter how sly Ike is," Liam said, "he would be no match for someone who knew what they were doing."

"Maybe they are not professional."

"Then that rules out your government and your police."

Liam grew quiet. He massaged the stiffness in the back of his neck. They were guessing. He watched the Israelis passing on the crowded sidewalk. The hopelessness of the situation was beginning to sink in. Finding Mimi was going to be impossible. They couldn't even find Ike. The Embassy was no help. Investigator Akiva Peres was willing to make the effort, but he had nothing to go on. Liam sunk lower. All the rushing around they had done in the last thirty hours was just busy work—groping in the dark by an American without a clue and his Israeli tour guide. Liam rubbed his sore neck as Menachem continued to drive.

Moments later, Liam jumped when his new cell phone blasted him with its heavy metal ring tone. He dropped the phone on the floor trying to answer. He snatched it up and answered, grumbling; he had meant to change the damned ring.

"We did," Liam said after a moment. "The Ambassador and her man Friday aren't going do anything but the bare minimum. Only what their protocol requires."

Liam listened and nodded.

"All right. Thanks. Please keep your cell handy."

Liam ended the call and looked at the settings on his phone, trying to figure out how to change the ring tone.

"Who was that?" Menachem asked.

"My Mississippi friend Willie Mitchell Banks. He says he's working with Senator Sumrall, but it doesn't look like we're going to get any kind of help from the government." He paused and turned to Menachem. "They managed to come at me with a half-dozen federal agencies to try to block my sale to Delaware, but the feds can't seem to generate *any* interest in helping me find Mimi. Bastards."

Staring out his window, Liam saw several merchants closing their shops as it began to get dark. Fewer pedestrians appeared on the sidewalks. Those remaining were moving faster. Then he remembered. It was Friday night, the beginning of the Jewish Sabbath. Stores and offices would be closed the next day.

"Nothing will be open tomorrow," Liam said.

"Not everything closes."

"What about the Jerusalem Police stations?"

"They will be open, but fewer officers will be on duty."

"I'm calling Investigator Peres."

Menachem turned the corner. Liam pulled Peres' card from his pocket and punched in his number. Peres picked up on the second ring.

"Liam Connors, Investigator Peres."

"Yes. Have you made any progress?"

"No, sir. Have you come up with anything?"

"I am sorry to report we have not."

"I'd like to come in tomorrow morning. As early as possible. Do you work on the Sabbath?"

"Every day I work, including *Shabbat*. I will be at the station at seven-thirty. Come in then."

"I'll be there," Liam said, "and I want to thank you for helping me."

There was silence on the other end for a moment.

"Mr. Connors," Peres said, "Everything in my power I will do to bring your friend back to you. Everything. I promise."

"Thank you. See you in the morning."

Liam closed his phone. "Dammit."

Liam rubbed the back of his aching neck. Menachem broke the silence, trying to get Liam focus on something else, even if briefly.

"May I ask you something?"

"Anything."

"Explain to me again why you cannot ask your state's representatives in Washington, D.C. to help you? Why do you go through your Mississippi friend's connections?"

"I don't trust my delegation. They don't like me, either."

"That is obvious. But why?"

"The short answer. The federal government tried to block the sale of my company's oil and gas leases to another company. My two senators and my congressman didn't lift a finger to help me. In fact, I found out they more or less sided with the government, told the agencies to do what they had to do. This was a once in a lifetime deal for me, and the government tried to stop it for no good reason."

"But you pushed it through, yes?"

"I did, but it wasn't easy. Saving the deal was more difficult and more intense than building my company."

"How did you get into the oil business?"

"I was around it as a kid."

"Are your parents alive?" Menachem asked.

"No."

They drove past a man in a sandwich board standing on the sidewalk, preaching to pedestrians hustling past him. The message on his board was in Hebrew.

"What's he saying?" Liam asked.

"Who?"

"That guy giving a sermon back there."

"Who knows," Menachem shrugged, glancing in his rear view mirror. "Every street minister in Jerusalem believes he has the answer." He paused. "Tell me what your father did for a living?"

"When I was young he was a promoter," Liam said, talking fast, "selling wildcat oil and gas prospects. That's how I got interested in the business. He got me summer jobs working on land rigs in north Louisiana. He was a big man with a ruddy Irish complexion, always fun to be around, the life of the party."

"Was he successful?"

"He was a great salesman, so good he began selling more than 100% of the working interest in his prospects, betting on dry holes. He had the misfortune of making two good wells in a row and couldn't pay his investors because he had oversubscribed the deal. The investors involved the Feds. He did two years federal time and when he got out he sold cars until he died."

"Like Zero Mostel in 'The Producers'," Menachem said. "Praying for a flop. 'Springtime For Hitler'."

Liam smiled.

"Same concept, but no joke. I loved my father, had fun being around him. I didn't realize his serious character flaws when I was young. He had a lot of energy on the front end of something, but wasn't big on doing the day-to-day hard work it took to make it successful. He never followed through on anything. I don't think he intentionally lied to investors. His pitch was so convincing he believed his own stories.

"My mother was the opposite. Whatever she said you could take to the bank. She worked every day of her life, teaching, running the household, taking care of me. She was quiet and understated, but she was the real hero in the family. My father was always talking about the next big deal, the one that would put him over the top. Mother listened and smiled and went on working. She must have loved him a lot because she accepted him the way he was, big talk and all. She wrote him everyday when he was in prison, and was there to pick him up when he was released. She never mentioned it again. Six months after he died, my mother passed away one night. She decided to stop eating. Didn't want to live without him."

"That kind of love is very powerful, my friend," Menachem said. "From the first time I met my wife, continuing to this day, I have never been interested in another woman. Now, tell me how you built such a successful business."

"Worked my way through LSU on a ROTC scholarship. Finished with a degree in Petroleum Engineering. Spent six years in U.S. Army intelligence to fulfill my obligation. Got out in 1989 and worked for Chevron in New Orleans and Lafayette, Louisiana. After a couple of years started my company, Clare Petroleum."

"After the county in Ireland?"

"Yes. There's been oil and gas drilling in Louisiana and East Texas going back seventy or eighty years. Lots of abandoned fields. While I was at Chevron I learned about new technology that made secondary and tertiary recovery in old fields possible. Went out on my own and got busy researching inactive fields. I looked at the old well logs and found the best shallow prospect I could, leased up the field with money I borrowed from a banker friend of mine in Shreveport, reworked the wells and started them producing again. Some fields had been shut in because they weren't economically feasible with oil at ten or fifteen dollars a barrel. In the late nineties and continuing today, with oil anywhere from seventy to a hundred dollars a barrel, those old fields and stripper wells I reworked gushed money. My first field was a home run; I was on my way. I used the profits to lease up more old fields until I had about 15,000 acres under lease."

"That one wants to convert us Jews to Christianity," Menachem said, pointing to a woman on the sidewalk passing out pamphlets. "I have listened to her. A fundamentalist Christian raising money to build the Third Temple at Temple Mount."

Menachem turned the corner before Liam got a look.

"Now. Go on with your story. Please."

"Then a gigantic shale play got underway in the parishes in northwest Louisiana where I had my shallow production. I signed a deal to sell the deep rights on all fifteen thousand acres to Delaware Energy."

"And that's when the U.S. government tried to stop you? Tell me why they did that."

"All because of one government bureaucrat. I hired investigators. They finished their report the week before Mimi and I left for Italy. A deal as big as mine takes a while to close. Leases and titles have to be re-checked."

"Who was this person?"

"That's another story. I'll tell you some other time."

"I'm glad you succeeded," Menachem said. "What would it have cost you if they had prevented the sale?"

"A tidy sum of money."

"I am happy for you that your government failed."

"Me too. But it's not over. Willie Mitchell is working right now, trying to get something done about the bureaucrat with the vendetta against me. After we find Mimi and I get back to the U.S. I will spend my time on another search."

"For what?"

"Justice," Liam said.

"Good for you," Menachem said as he pulled into the King David's circular drive and parked at the front entrance. "I will pick you up at seven in the morning. Be sure to have some dinner tonight."

"All right," Liam said, getting out of the Volvo. "See you at seven."

Chapter Fifteen

Liam ordered room service, showered, and tried to sleep. He may have slept an hour or two, but spent most of the night tossing and turning, thinking about Mimi, seeing her beautiful face. At some point in the early morning hours, he decided to tell Peres about the Ishmael Scroll. Liam no longer gave a damn about competing factions in the Israeli government wanting to suppress or promote a scroll they knew nothing about. All he cared about was Mimi.

At three a.m. Liam gave up. He turned on the light. His stomach was churning and adrenaline was rushing through his body. The back of his neck was still stiff. He had what his late wife Annette called the *heebie-jeebies*. He got out of bed and paced the room, trying to come up with a plan to find Mimi. But the synapses in his brain were misfiring. He jumped from one idea to another, none of them making any sense.

Liam pulled a chair to the window. He stared out over the Old City. Less than a kilometer square inside its ancient walls, Jerusalem was dark, much darker than the modern metropolis surrounding it. Liam felt the Old City draw him in. Jerusalem seemed a black hole with a powerful gravitational pull, the religious center of much of the world for three thousand years, the nexus of political conflict in the Middle East.

The mystical power of Jerusalem moved through and enveloped him. Liam closed his eyes and breathed deeply.

Annette appeared, walking slowly in the oak alley leading from the parish road to their raised plantation home. He was on the porch, watching her move toward him. It was a warm day in Natchitoches. A slight breeze out of the south stirred the Spanish moss hanging from the oaks and ruffled Annette's gown. She climbed up the wide staircase to the porch. She took his hand and smiled, kissed him on the cheek. She whispered in his ear, let go of his hand and went into the house. Liam turned to watch her go through the entrance hall and out the back door. He followed her and stopped on the high back gallery to watch Annette walk away between the rows of chest-high cotton plants in the field behind

Grand Oaks. She turned to wave at him and disappeared into the cotton.

Minutes later, Liam opened his eyes. Tears ran down his cheeks. The Old City before him remained dark and inert. But the disorder and turmoil in his brain seemed to have dissipated. He felt better physically. Liam got back in bed and pulled the sheet over him, picturing Annette walking through the cotton field, mouthing what she whispered to him on the porch: *Goodbye.*

At seven sharp Menachem picked up Liam at the King David. When they walked into the station ten minutes later, Investigator Peres was standing at the counter. Liam watched Peres and Menachem shake hands. Same height, same stocky build, same age, too. Probably early sixties. If Menachem had sported one bad eye and dark, unkempt hair, the tour guide and the war hero could have been twins.

"You are early," Peres said. "Good. Mr. Connors, I am sorry to inform you that all of our administrative personnel observe the Holy Day; you will not be seeing our gracious desk sergeant Leeba."

Liam tried to smile. No luck.

"Please. Call me Liam."

"Follow me," he said, leading them into his office.

"I regret to inform you. No reports of your fiancé came in during the night." Peres sat behind his desk. "The security camera image of her in the Armenian Quarter remains the last sighting. I have heard nothing from my police officers on the streets or from IDF forces or any other government agency. There has been no response to the posting on our web site. Nor has my counterpart at the Palestinian Authority received any information on her. I want you to understand, Mr. Connors, everyone in authority in my country considers the case of a missing tourist very seriously. A significant portion of our economy depends on foreign visitors, so it becomes a matter of national concern. Our searches and inquiries have turned up nothing."

"I have some things I want to whare with you," Liam said to Peres. "I should have told you before."

Peres leaned back in his chair, his hands folded over his slight paunch. Liam explained about getting the Fed Ex letter at Grand Oaks in Natchitoches, about the first encounter with Ike in the café at Mahane Yehuda and the subsequent meeting at the tourist hotel. He told Peres what Ike claimed was written about Hagar and Ishmael on the scroll. He also recounted what Ike had said on the phone the day before. Peres nodded at Liam, then turned to Menachem.

"Were you present when all this happened?" Peres asked Menachem. "Has Mr. Connors left out anything of importance?"

"I did not hear the conversation in the café Wednesday night, but I was present at the meeting in the hotel Thursday morning, and I heard the phone conversation yesterday. Liam has told you everything."

"Do you have anything to add?"

"Only that I do know for a fact that men followed Yitzhak in the last few weeks. I saw them on one occasion, maybe on one other, but I couldn't be certain."

Peres looked up at the ceiling for a moment, then at Liam.

"This changes everything, Mr. Connors. Why didn't you tell me all of this when we first met?"

"I asked him to keep secret the information about the scroll," Menachem said. "I am of the opinion there are those in our government who would either suppress such a scroll or misuse it."

"Anything else?"

"Yes," Menachem said to Peres, "I believe the men who took Miss Stanton are dangerous. If we do not find Yitzhak or the scroll, things will not go well for her. I am sorry to say that."

"I think Mr. Wladyslaw is correct," Peres said. "Certain politicians in our government would want to obtain such a scroll at any cost. They would not care so much what happens to Miss Stanton. May I ask, Mr. Wladyslaw, if you include me in that group?"

"I am cautious by nature. Please call me Menachem."

"Then let me ask you this. Do you think this Ishmael Scroll exists? Do you think it is authentic?"

"This is my opinion. Yes. I think the ancient scroll is real. Yitzhak is a strange one, but he has been truthful with me in the past."

"But neither of you has seen it, according to what you have told me. You take the word of a man whose mental state may be questionable."

"My first time in your office I could tell you knew who Ike Palmer was," Liam said. "And you knew Menachem was his driver."

"Yes," Peres said, "I know of Yitzhak Palmer since he played a half-naked John the Baptist on our streets, a voice crying in the wilderness."

Liam slid the page from the King David note pad containing Ike's Hebrew National bank account number and Nathan Palmer's cell number in New York. Peres picked up the page and read it.

"The number of Yitzhak Palmer's account at Hebrew National," Liam said, "into which his brother Nathan deposits five thousand U.S. dollars every month. We thought you might be able to get the address Ike used when he opened it."

"Yes," Peres said. "I can access this information. You understand, the address he used might not be his own."

"His brother told me Yitzhak has had this same account for many years."

"Excuse me while I check on this." Peres started to walk out, but stopped and turned back to Liam. "For the first time, Liam, Miss Stanton's disappearance is making sense to me. We do not have tourists disappear in the day time in the Old City, unless they leave of their own accord. From talking to you, I am sure she did not leave voluntarily. Someone has taken her—someone who knows of her connection to Yitzhak Palmer and his scroll. This is good news for you and Miss Stanton. They have a reason to make sure no harm comes to her. At least for now. For the purposes of our investigation, I will assume the scroll is real, or rather that the people who have your fiancé think it is authentic. Although they have not contacted you, I am certain they will do so. They know where you are staying."

"When they do call me, I want to have Ike or his scroll ready to give them and get Mimi back."

"The best result would be that we recover both Miss Stanton and the scroll," Peres said as he left them. "Let me get the address associated with this account."

"I had to tell him about the scroll," Liam said to Menachem.

"I understand. I would have done the same."

"Peres is sharp," Liam said. "With his war record I'm surprised he's not in a higher position."

"If you lived here and read our local papers you would know this. Two years ago Akiva Peres was suspended from our internal security service Shin Bet. Many call it by its Hebrew letters, Shabak. It is like your FBI. Akiva Peres was in charge of Yamas, Shin Bet's special operations division. There was a controversy about a Yamas raid on a terrorist cell in Nazareth. It is claimed that Peres was denied authorization to conduct the raid but he proceeded anyway."

"Were they terrorists?"

"Absolutely. It was a sleeper cell. Peres's men arrested five dangerous *jihadists,* confiscated many weapons and a large supply of explosives. He saved many lives that day."

"Why hadn't the operation been approved?"

"It was political. Something about notifying the Palestinian Authority, which governs Nazareth because of Oslo Accords. There has been no official pronouncement. In the newspaper, Peres admitted he had been denied the authority to conduct the raid. He said he knew the danger was real and conducted it anyway. He is a very—how you say in America—straight talker. Most everyone considers him a hero for his actions, but his bosses at Shin Bet suspended him the next day. He works as an investigator with the Jerusalem Police until his case is resolved with Shin Bet."

"Stupid."

"Yes. Every year our government gets more cautious. Afraid to make a mistake. It is a tragedy."

"Why didn't you tell me this before?"

Menachem shrugged as Peres returned to his desk.

"I have it," Peres said. "Yitzhak has this account for many years. The address he gave the bank is in Mekor Baruch. You understand he may not have this flat any longer. Let us go to this address. It is not far from here. Follow me in your car."

Menachem stayed so close to Peres's vehicle Liam was worried they might rear-end him if he stopped suddenly. Menachem seemed comfortable with the maneuvers, as if following within ten feet of Peres were routine. Liam guessed Menachem picked up his driving skills on the cramped and serpentine streets of Jerusalem.

"What is Mekor Baruch?" Liam asked.

"A nice area. Close to the light rail line. Convenient to the Old City and Mahane Yehuda."

"Is it inside the perimeter of the X's on the map?"

"Yes," Menachem said as he slowed the Volvo and stopped behind Peres. "This is Hahashmona'im Street."

They joined Peres on the sidewalk. He looked up at the four story apartment building.

"His flat is in this building. The Central Bus Station is just west of here. Tram stop only a block away. Good place to live for a man with no automobile and perhaps the need to travel quickly. Before we go in I want to ask you something. These men who have followed Mr. Palmer, how did they find out about the scroll he claims to have found."

"Ike Palmer has had a problem with mania ever since I've known him," Liam said. "In the U.S. it's part of a bi-polar disorder. He told me Israel has cured him."

"I am familiar with this bi-polar," Peres said

Peres spoke in Hebrew to Menachem for a moment.

"It is a mental disease with an organic source in the brain," Liam said. "I don't think it's something you can cure by moving to Israel. When I knew him in Louisiana, if Ike was in his manic phase he couldn't keep his mouth shut about anything. He talked non-stop. No way in hell could he keep a secret."

"So, you think he spoke about the scroll somewhere in Jerusalem?"

"Yes, and I think it's likely the wrong people overheard."

"What about you, Menachem?" Peres asked.

"That is probably correct. Very likely."

"Did you ever hear him discuss it when you drove him?"

"I knew he had found something. He was very excited during some phone conversations I overheard, but I never heard him say to anyone he had found a scroll."

"Let's go see the apartment," Peres said.

They followed Peres inside the building and climbed the concrete stairs to the third floor. Peres stopped at apartment number 32 and tapped on the door. He waited a moment and knocked harder.

"I don't hear anything," he said and tried the knob. "It's not locked. Stay behind me."

Peres cracked the door. After a moment, he opened it wide and the three men walked inside.

The apartment looked as if a tornado had struck inside the one room efficiency.

Every drawer was emptied and lay upside down on the floor. Cabinet doors were open, their contents strewn about. The mattress on the floor had been sliced open in several places, the stuffing ripped out and flung around the room.

Liam pieced together pieces of a print that had been torn from its frame and ripped in half. It was an ancient map of Israel. He looked around the main room and saw other maps that had been shredded. Liam took some time to put pieces and fragments together, enough to figure out that Ike's walls had been covered with maps of Israel from the time of Solomon to the present day. Ike's maps of modern Israel started with the declaration of statehood in 1948 and continued through the annexation of the West Bank and Sinai after the 1967 war. The most recent crumbled and torn map showed the current borders. Strewn about the room were pieces of black and white photographs of Theodore Herzl, David Ben Gurion, Golda Meir, and Moshe Dayan. Liam walked into the kitchen. Amid the pots and pans and broken dishes were the remains of several smashed liquor bottles. Liam picked up a sharp-edged piece of glass and sniffed it.

"Bourbon. So much for Ike's being on the wagon," Liam said.

"Maybe it was for someone else," Menachem said. "I have never known Yitzhak to drink alcohol since I drive him."

"That's because he drinks here," Liam said, flinging the jagged piece of glass across the room. "Lying son-of-a-bitch."

Investigator Peres opened the small bathroom door and walked inside. After a moment he walked out and punched a number on his cell.

"I'm calling our crime scene analysts to process what is left of Yitzhak's apartment. I doubt we will find anything."

"What do we do now?" Liam asked.

"Whoever came through here did not find what they were looking for," Peres said. "And I do not believe they have captured Yitzhak Palmer. My guess is these people will contact you very soon."

Chapter Sixteen

Peres had to wait at the apartment for his crime scene people. He suggested Liam and Menachem return to the Jaffa station. On the drive, Liam's heavy metal ring tone went off, making him jump again. He put the phone on speaker.

"Yes," he said. "This is Liam Connors."

"Salzman," the voice said, "with hotel security."

"Yes, sir, Mr. Salzman, tell me you have news."

"An envelope has been delivered here for you. I have not opened it."

"We're on our way."

Menachem picked up the pace. Traffic was still light compared to the previous two days, and they were soon back at the King David. Menachem slowed the Volvo near the *port cochere* and Liam jumped out before the car was fully stopped. Salzman was waiting at the front desk. He placed the five-by-eight envelope on the counter. *Liam Connors* was printed in pencil on the front.

"Do you have a pair of latex gloves?" Liam asked.

"Yes."

"Could you get me those and also a plastic bag, a large Zip Loc if you have one. Maybe from your kitchen?"

Salzman disappeared through a door as Menachem joined Liam at the front desk.

"What is in it?" he asked, pointing.

"Don't know yet, but I know we have to be careful handling it."

Salzman returned with the gloves and a Zip Loc bag. Liam borrowed a pair of scissors and a letter opener from the clerk at the front desk and snipped one corner of the envelope. He inserted the letter opener and sliced open the side of the envelope, careful not to disturb the glued portion of the flap. He put pressure on the edges and the side gapped open. A small piece of paper lay inside. He grasped the edge of the paper, pulled it out and dropped it and the envelope into the Zip Loc bag. A number was written in pencil on the paper. Nothing else.

"Does this mean anything to you?" he asked Salzman.

"It looks like a local phone number."

Menachem nodded agreement.

"How did the envelope get here?" Liam asked.

"It was left at the front desk by a young boy. I can show you the recording made by our camera."

"Did he say anything?" Liam asked.

"Not a word."

Liam made sure the Zip Loc bag was tightly sealed as Menachem and he followed Salzman into the security offices through the door behind the front desk. The image of the young boy was frozen on the black and white monitor. Salzman said something in Hebrew to the technician who put the image in motion—outside with the young boy walking across the grass toward the entrance. He was small, maybe seven or eight, and wore shorts, a tee shirt and sneakers. Liam watched as he entered the lobby and walked to the front desk. He placed the envelope on the counter, making sure the clerk saw it, and walked out.

"Do you have a better image of his face?" Liam asked.

"No," Salzman said. "As you see the boy kept his face down."

"Can I talk to the clerk?"

"Yes, but I have already questioned him. He said he paid no attention to the boy, except that his impression was of an Arab."

"Could I get a copy for...."

"We made this for you," Salzman said handing Liam a disc in a plain white envelope, "and Akiva Peres. Please tell him we will preserve the original in our system."

"Thank you," Liam told Salzman.

"If we can do anything else to assist you," Salzman said. "We at the King David want to find your friend."

"You've been a lot of help," Liam said.

Menachem and Liam hopped in the Volvo and drove toward the Jaffa station. He phoned Investigator Peres and told him about the note. Peres said the crime scene analysts had arrived at Yitzhak's apartment and he was on his way to the station.

Menachem parked the Volvo just as Peres pulled in. They followed him inside. In moments they were at this desk. Liam watched him examine the envelope and the small paper inside the Zip Loc.

"I only touched the edges and wore these latex gloves," Liam said pulling the gloves from his pocket. "Menachem and Salzman at the King David watched me the whole time."

Menachem nodded to confirm.

"How do you want me to make the call?" Liam asked Peres.

"The best would be to have our technicians place the call using their equipment. We could triangulate and possibly identify the location of the phone on the other end."

"You don't seem confident," Liam said.

"My best technical men are not working and will not answer my call if I try to reach them."

"*Shabbat?*" Menachem asked.

"Yes," Peres said. "This number is probably for a pre-paid phone we cannot trace to a person. Even if we locate the phone itself it does us no good unless we see someone holding it, which is very unlikely."

"Let's call," Liam said. "Right now."

Liam put his cell phone on the desk. Peres pulled a small tape recorder from one of the drawers, checked the tape and punched "Record." He gestured for Liam to dial. Liam tapped in the number, put the phone in speaker mode, and waited.

"Yes." A voice on the other end.

"This is Liam Connors. Who is this?"

"Do you have the scroll?"

"No."

"Where is Isaac Palmer?"

"I don't know. I'm trying to find him. Where is Mimi Stanton?"

"Call this number when you have what we want."

"How do I know she is all right?" Liam asked.

There was a click and the line went dead.

"Damn," Liam said. "Could you tell anything?"

"No," Peres said. "Tomorrow I will have my best people analyze the voice and try to discover something about that number. The call is probably routed through a public exchange, so I am not hopeful."

"Can't you call your people and say Mimi's life is at stake and...?"

"They will not answer today."

"They will not," Menachem said. "It is work."

"Dammit." He turned to Menachem. "Try to call Ike again."

"Yes," Peres said.

"He will not answer," Menachem said.

"Try anyway," Liam said.

Menachem pulled up the number from Ike's call the day before and hit re-dial. They listened as the phone rang and rang on the other end. After a while there was a click. He dialed it again and got the same result.

Liam stood up quickly, his chair clattered on the floor. Liam grabbed it and set it upright.

"Would you make me a copy of the note?" Liam said to Peres. "Keep the original for your people to examine."

Peres took the Zip Loc bag to the copy machine and returned with a duplicate of the note on one sheet of copy paper.

"What else can we do?" Liam asked.

"I plan to do some old-fashioned police work," Peres said. "I will make a few calls and visit some of my informants. It is not likely, but they might have heard something and may be in need of a few shekels. Of one thing I am sure. These fellows I will go see do not keep holy the Sabbath."

"Should we go with you?" Liam asked.

"No. These criminals would tell me nothing with you around. They must be careful who they talk to. After all, they are criminals."

"What should Menachem and I do?" Liam asked.

"If you are a religious man, you might pray."

"I doubt that will help."

"It cannot hurt," Menachem said and touched Liam's arm. "Let us go. Let Investigator Peres talk to his people."

Liam glanced at his watch. One o'clock. Mimi had now been missing for forty-eight hours.

Chapter Seventeen

Liam was feeling low when he closed the Volvo door. The bastards holding Mimi wanted the scroll. Liam didn't give a damn about the scroll—Mimi's life was infinitely more important. And Ike's behavior in the last two days had caused Liam to be less concerned about Ike's well-being. Had Ike not been so obsessed with secrecy and warned Liam about the potential danger of men following him, Liam would never have scheduled three days in Israel. And the s.o.b. had lied about being sober. Bourbon in his apartment. He'd had enough of Ike's bull shit. Liam tried to suppress his anger at his old friend. It was interfering with finding Mimi.

Liam was no detective, but he had done a good bit of investigative work in his business. On dozens of occasions, when Clare Petroleum had lost a pipe string or a drill bit thousands of feet down in the hole, Liam had brainstormed with drilling superintendents, troubleshooters, tool pushers, mud engineers and roughnecks to figure out what went wrong and come up with a way to try to save the well. They couldn't see what happened thousands of feet under them—they were drilling through solid rock and sand formations. They had to investigate, piece together clues from events that had happened before the breakdown in order to solve the problem. And they were successful, sixty per cent of the time. Liam kept a personal file in his desk on each drilling crisis. Every incident was different but each successful reclamation had this in common: Liam and his men gathered enough data from what had happened in the minutes and hours leading up to the breakdown to reconstruct the cause. Only after they figured out what mechanical failure shut the rig down could they come up with a solution to save the well. Surely, the same thought process could lead to finding Mimi.

"Let's go back to the café," Liam said when Menachem got in.

"Why would we do that?"

"Whoever took Mimi on Thursday had to have seen us on Wednesday. They needed at least that much time to plan the abduction. First possibility is the airport. They could have seen us there, too."

"Only if they had known about you before you arrived in Israel."

"Right," Liam said. "I'm certain Ike ran his mouth to someone he shouldn't have and that information got around to some folks who wanted what he says he found. If he talked about my coming to help him, I could see those people waiting for us to arrive at the airport or later at the King David."

Menachem and Liam were quiet for a moment.

"I don't think anyone was waiting for you at the airport or at the King David," Menachem said. "I think they follow Yitzhak. They see you and Miss Stanton there in the Yehuda Market café with him. They see you are good friends. I think Ike departs in a hurry to get away from them. Then they follow you and Mimi to the King David, and in the morning they follow her to the Old City. They take her there. They believe Yitzhak will give up the scroll to get her back for you."

"Makes sense," Liam said. "Once Ike gave them the slip Wednesday night, they could either follow us until we reconnected with Ike again. Or they could do what they did: kidnap Mimi and expect Ike to give up the scroll to save her."

Menachem turned off the engine and stepped out of the Volvo.

"What are you doing?" Liam asked.

"It's faster to walk to Mahane Yehuda from here, even on the Sabbath. Come with me. We go back to the café where this all began."

They walked along Jaffa Street in a westerly direction.

"Not many people out," Liam said.

"Neither orthodox or conservative Jews will come out today until after sunset," Menachem said, "when *Shabbat* has ended."

Liam thought back to the circuitous route Menachem drove from the King David to the breakfast meeting with Ike two days earlier.

"That's why so many turns and detours Thursday morning on the way to the tourist hotel," Liam said. "You were trying to lose anyone tailing us."

"I drive like that ever since I see the men following Yitzhak."

Menachem and Liam walked into the market. Unlike their first night in Jerusalem when Liam and Mimi had to weave through a sea of merchants, locals, and tourists, Saturday afternoon's market was quiet. Many vendors were open but few people were shopping.

"Jewish merchants will open after sunset," Menachem said. "The café will be open now. The owner is not a Jew."

"What is the old man?"

"An Arab. Once a Christian. He has no faith since his wife died. The waiter Yusef is a Bedouin, a Sunni."

Liam spotted the wizened old man standing next to his stalls of nuts and fruits. Menachem greeted him as he had Wednesday night—a buss on each cheek, then a big smile and an arm around the man's bony, sloping shoulders. Menachem drew the old man close and began talking quietly with him. Liam stood several feet away, pretending to be disinterested.

The man scratched his white stubble and answered Menachem. Liam saw the old man point toward the café in the back. Menachem thanked the man and walked through the stalls toward the café. Liam followed several steps behind, passing through the thin cloth hanging from the door frame. Not a single customer.

"Yusef," Menachem said in a loud voice. "Yusef."

The young Bedouin waiter with the jagged scar on his cheek came out of the kitchen quickly. His big smile faded when he saw Menachem and Liam, but he gestured for the two men to be seated.

"Coffee?" Yusef said, smiling nervously.

Menachem held up two fingers and spoke to Yusef in a language that Liam recognized as neither Hebrew nor Yiddish. Yusef bowed and backed his way into the kitchen.

"You spoke to both Yusef and the owner in Arabic but you don't list it on your card with the other languages."

"I speak enough Arabic to get by, not enough to take tourists around the city."

"Are there many...?"

"No," Menachem said, "very few Arab tourists. The Muslims who live in other countries come into Jerusalem only to see The Dome of the Rock and the Al Aqsa Mosque. No guide needed for that. They would not hire me even if I spoke their language fluently. They believe Jews walking on the Temple Mount is a sacrilege. When Prime Minister Sharon came to visit the Temple Mount during his first days in office it was an international incident." He paused. "I speak a little Farsi, too."

Yusef came in from the kitchen balancing two small cups and saucers. He sat them on the table and began bowing and backing away.

"Yusef," Menachem said, "do you have the date pastries?"

"Yes," Yusef said, avoiding eye contact.

"Bring us two, please."

Yusef hustled into the kitchen.

"Yusef seemed surprised to see us," Liam said.

"He is nervous, for sure. The old man, the owner, is not involved in Mimi's disappearance. I know him well enough to be confident of this."

"What about Yusef?"

"It is clear he is hiding something. He is not smart enough to conceal his anxiety."

Yusef returned and placed the pastry plates in front of them.

"Sit down a moment, Yusef," Menachem said.

Yusef shook his head no and pointed toward the front of the cafe.

"The old man...," Menachem said in an understanding voice, "well, stand here a moment with your tray. Let me ask a few questions. The old man cannot object to your being gracious to your customers."

In Arabic, Menachem questioned Yusef for five minutes. Liam didn't understand a word, but he watched Yusef react. He was disturbed. The young Bedouin kept his head down, afraid to look at Menachem. When Yusef's eyes were not darting about or blinking he stared blankly past Menachem. Liam noticed the death grip Yusef seemed to have on the flimsy aluminum tray he held. Finally, Menachem smiled and gestured to Yusef, who shuffled quickly into the kitchen.

"Whatever you asked him put him on the spot," Liam said.

Menachem pulled out his phone and held up one finger. He spoke quickly and quietly, listened a moment and ended the call.

"He said he has not seen Mimi since we were in here Wednesday night. No one has asked him about you and Mimi, or about Yitzhak Palmer. He said he knows nothing about Yitzhak, had never seen him before the other night."

"He seems scared to death," Liam said.

"He should be. He's lying..., how you say, through his tooth. Especially when he says he has never seen Yitzhak before. Yitzhak picked this café because it is his favorite in the market. Yusef is nervous because he is involved somehow."

"Who did you call just now?"

"A young man who will follow Yusef when he gets off work."

"Think we ought to call Investigator Peres?"

"No," Menachem said. "The young guy is on his way here. His name is Mahmoud. He is more cunning than the police. Or even Shin Bet."

Chapter Eighteen

"Stay here a minute," Menachem said after reading a text on his phone. "Keep an eye on the back door. Yusef may be leaving."

"Stop him?"

"No. Come to me out front."

"Where are you going?"

Menachem walked through the thin cloth dividing the café from the old man's market stall. Liam sipped the strong coffee. From the table he could not see Yusef, but he had a clear view of the back door leading to the courtyard, the same door Crazy Ike had used to desert Liam and Mimi Wednesday night. Discordant heavy metal from his pants pocket made him jump.

"Dammit," Liam said.

He looked at the number—a call from Mississippi.

"Anything on Mimi?" Willie Mitchell Banks said.

"No."

"I don't know if I should bother you with this right now. It's about David Bodenheimer."

Liam wanted to be bothered with news of the lying bureaucrat behind the onslaught of government agencies that almost derailed Liam's sale to Delaware Energy.

"Go ahead."

"The D.C. lawyers tell me the Energy Department is looking at what he did."

"They were no doubt proud of his work."

"They are finally looking into the conflict of interest."

"That's all. I just thought it might be significant."

"It is. I appreciate your staying on it." Liam paused. "In fact, Willie Mitchell, use your judgment if any decisions are needed. No need to call me. I got my hands full. Do what you think is best."

"All right. Sorry the State Department was no help."

"Not your fault. Our government can't do anything right."

"Call me when you can about Mimi."

Liam ended the call. He strummed his fingers on the table, keeping his eye on the door to the courtyard to make sure Yusef didn't sneak away.

"Liam," Menachem said, pushing aside the thin cloth covering the door opening and signaling for Liam to come with him. Liam pointed to the door in the kitchen leading to the courtyard outside. Menachem waved his hand dismissively, meaning "no problem." Liam walked out past Menachem, who stopped to pay the crusty old owner for their coffee and pastries. They left the stall and walked down the narrow passageway through the market. Business had picked up. Locals and tourists were shopping. Menachem stopped suddenly when they turned the corner. A young man stepped out from a closed market stall and waved them over. Menachem introduced Mahmoud. Liam figured him to be eighteen at most, probably younger. Liam shook his hand.

"Mahmoud and his younger brother will be watching Yusef for us," Menachem said to Liam. "His brother is behind the café right now, just in case Yusef decides to leave early. Mahmoud will watch the front. No matter what time Yusef leaves, they will follow him and report to us."

"Stay with him," Liam said to Mahmoud and shook his hand again.

Menachem led Liam through the bustling market onto the sidewalk along Jaffa Street. They had walked half a block before Liam said anything. "Who is Mahmoud?"

"A young man who has done work for me before. We will have to pay him, but he will not be expensive."

"Is he Jewish?"

"No. He's an Arab. A Bedouin, in fact. A very reliable young man who knows how to keep his mouth shut. He is much smarter than Yusef and will have no trouble following him. There is a saying in this part of the world. Loosely translated, it is this: It takes a Bedouin to catch a Bedouin."

"Good," Liam said. "We're finally doing something."

"So you are no longer willing to rely on your American government and the Jerusalem Police?"

Liam shook his head. "I got it figured, Menachem. If we want to find Mimi, we have to do it ourselves."

Menachem smiled and clapped Liam on the shoulder.

"How do you say it in America? Now, you are talking, my friend."

Chapter Nineteen

Mimi sat on the tile floor next to a toilet. The violent spasms in her stomach had subsided, but she was afraid to move back to the wooden table. It was increasingly difficult to get down from the table and make it to the toilet in time. She was getting weaker and dizzier with every attack of the intestinal virus she had picked up from the food they gave her or perhaps the water she was drinking from the faucet in the sink.

If she were taking care of a patient who suffered with what she had contracted, she would start them on Lomotil for the diarrhea and Phenergan for the debilitating nausea and dizziness. If the drugs were unavailable, she would advise them to drink plenty of fresh, clean water and eat only Saltines, Jello, and clear broth until their digestive system recovered.

Since neither the drugs, clean water, nor bland food were available, Mimi knew she would have to suffer with the effects of the bug until her gut became acclimated to the local water and food. She knew she was dehydrated from the vomiting and diarrhea, but looked on the bright side of her medical situation. She was in excellent health, so the digestive disorder was not going to kill her as long as she rested and kept hydrated. She wasn't eating any more of their food.

After a while, Mimi struggled to her feet and made it back to the table. She climbed onto the hard surface and glanced at the sliver of light coming through the crack under the door. The light had been there quite a while. It was the second time the light had appeared. She reasoned that today was her second day in captivity. Struggling to stay optimistic, she knew Liam was trying to find her. But lying in the darkness with her digestive system churning, Mimi frequently broke down in tears. She tried to control the crying, but could not. And while the tears were flowing, her mind piled on misery, dwelling on all the things that had gone wrong in her life.

Three surgeries to remove ovarian cysts when she was a young teen resulted in scarring that rendered Mimi barren. Her surgeons had told her that infertility might result from her surgeries, but she had no choice. The pain she suffered when the tangerine-sized cysts ruptured made her want to die. Her infertility was not confirmed until she was unable to conceive with her husband, Jimmy Mangum, after five years of trying. At first he said it didn't matter to him, he loved her no matter what. She discovered his love for her was so powerful Jimmy felt the need to share it with other women. When Mimi confronted him about his philandering, he blamed it on her inability to have children.

Mimi and Jimmy divorced. She reclaimed her maiden name. Mimi had plenty of suitors but no interest in them. She enrolled in nursing school in Shreveport, using her half of the meager proceeds from their community property settlement to pay tuition. She was determined to be independent, to support herself. Mimi borrowed money for her additional study to get the advanced degree required to be a licensed nurse practitioner. She was an only child, but her parents were no help. Her no-count father left home when she was ten. After Mimi finished high school in Shreveport, her mother married again, this time to a man from Dallas. Mimi chose not to live in the same house with her stepfather; he had a way of looking her over that made Mimi feel very uncomfortable. Her mother told her she was being ridiculous, bid Mimi goodbye and good luck, and moved to Dallas with her new husband. Mimi was on her own until she married Jimmy Mangum. A year into the marriage she realized it was a mistake. She should have left him then.

Years after her divorce, when she took the job as Dr. Vercher's nurse practitioner and moved to Natchitoches, she never expected to be swept off her feet by one of his patients, but that's what happened. Liam Connors was older and recently widowed, but when she met him for the first time she could hardly catch her breath. Liam had appeared in Dr. Vercher's office for his annual physical. Handsome and charming, a perfect gentleman, Mimi was in love with him immediately, well before she learned he was a successful oil man and the owner of Grand Oaks Plantation, five miles south of Natchitoches on the Cane River.

Mimi smiled in the darkness when she thought about Liam. They had been together over a year and it was by far the happiest time of her life. Mimi's smile turned into a grimace when her lower abdomen cramped and erupted again. She lurched off the table toward the toilet and barely made it in time. As she sat there in the darkness, doubled over in pain, she began to sob.

Moments later, she heard banging somewhere in the building. Her stomach quieted and she concentrated on the noise. Like a hammer on wood. The banging stopped and then resumed. She listened. Someone was outside her bathroom cell constructing something.

Mimi wondered what it was.

Chapter Twenty

Menachem's phone buzzed.

"We are already here at the King David," Menachem said. "We will wait for you in the bar."

"What was that about?" Liam asked.

"Akiva Peres. He is on his way here. He has information to share with us."

They walked inside the hotel. Liam checked with the front desk.

"No messages, Mr. Connors," the clerk said. "But Mr. Salzman asked to be notified when you returned. May I inform him?"

The clerk spoke quietly into his phone. After a few seconds the head of security came through the door.

"Any developments, Mr. Connors?" Salzman asked, the top button of his navy blazer straining from the pressure of his big chest.

"We're not sure," Liam said.

"What about the number left here by the young Arab boy?" Salzman asked.

"Investigator Peres helped us make contact," Menachem said before Liam could answer. "We are waiting to hear."

"Let us know if we can help in any way," Salzman said.

"Akiva Peres is meeting us in the Oriental," Menachem said.

Liam thanked Salzman. He and Menachem walked into the Oriental Bar and seated themselves in low, stuffed chairs around a small table. Liam ordered a Coke Zero and Menachem a club soda.

"Salzman is a good man, but we should keep what little we know to ourselves," Menachem said.

"Right," Liam said. "Do you think we need to hire somebody?"

"What do you mean?"

"We don't have guns. I guarantee you the people who took Mimi are armed to the hilt. We should even the odds."

"I do not think that would help."

"Where could we find some men? I mean if we decided we needed help?"

"They are all over the place in Jordan. Armed body guards. Tough guys. At any five star Western hotel. Like the Marriott or

Sheraton in Amman. Just have a drink and strike up a conversation with the Americans or British in the bar. They are looking for business. These men—when they drink they talk loud, like Yitzhak."

"Mercenaries?"

"Yes, but they do not call themselves mercenaries any more. These men now prefer to be known as contractors. Ex-military with special training. Some of them work as instructors at places like King Abdullah Special Operations Training Center. They teach the Jordanian military and their police force."

Liam studied Menachem.

"How do you know all this?"

"I have driven some of my customers into Amman from here. Only a distance of seventy kilometers, about forty-five miles."

"That's all?"

"How do you say, as your raven flies."

"Crow."

"Yes. But of course, the roads are not straight and there are only three border crossings. We meet delays going through customs and checkpoints, but usually you can arrive in Amman in three, maybe four hours, sometimes longer, depending on the passenger profiles and the current political situation. Driving any road in the Middle East, inside or outside of Israel, going through P.A. territories—one never knows what might happen."

"You've sat in those hotel bars? You've heard these contractors?"

"Many times. Usually my jobs are two-day, sometimes three-day round trips into Amman. One can hire men for anything in those bars."

"So we could get someone in Amman if we had to."

"I would not recommend it. The State of Israel makes it difficult for them to get in this country. You would be breaking Israeli law to hire such a person. These people are dangerous. There is the risk you might hire someone you cannot trust."

"You mean they might turn on you?"

"It has happened, yes," Menachem said.

Liam leaned toward Menachem. "You know a lot for a driver."

"In Israel, a good driver must be very resourceful."

"Obviously," Liam said.

The deep-cushioned chairs were comfortable and Liam felt a sinking spell. He sat up and glanced around the bar. Two men sat at a table in the near corner. One was an *Hasid* in a black suit and hat with long, curling sidelocks. The other man was a Scandinavian-looking blond in a trendy European-cut gray suit. The *Hasid*

Michael Henry

pointed to something in a black leather case open on the table
between them. The Scandiavian tapped his index finger to
something else in the case, leaned back and folded his arms across
his chest.

"What are those guys doing?" Liam whispered.

Menachem turned to look. "Diamonds."

"What about diamonds?"

"The *Hasid* is a dealer; the blond a buyer. From England or
Germany I would guess."

"They're doing a deal in this bar?"

"Diamond industry in Israel is very big. A world center for sale
of polished stones. The art of diamond cutting was developed by
Jews in Antwerp five hundred years ago. Very big export business."

"Why are they here?"

"Diamond merchants. It is what they do. They walk the streets
with millions in diamonds in their pockets to meet clients in coffee
shops, hookah bars, restaurants, all over. A tradition."

"Risky business practice," Liam said.

"Gentlemen," Akiva Peres said as he stood behind Liam.

Menachem and Liam rose to shake hands with Peres.

Liam towered over the two stocky Israelis, both a foot shorter
than Liam. He offered Peres a seat. Peres took off his jacket and
sunk deeply into the upholstered lounge chair, making him seem
even shorter. He looked around the bar with his good eye and
seemed startled when he discovered the waiter standing next to
him on his blind side.

"Water with gas," Peres told him.

"Thanks for coming," Liam said.

"It's better we talk about this here. Even late on a Sabbath
afternoon you can never be too careful in the station. People listen."

Peres leaned forward.

"One of my informants says he knows of the kidnapping of Miss
Stanton. He says it is a Hamas operation."

"The IDQ Brigade?" Menachem asked.

"Translate," Liam said.

"You know Hamas, the Palestinian Islamic organization?" Peres
said. "Very militant."

"I know who Hamas is. They're in charge in Gaza now, right?
They defeated Al Fatah in the election a few years back."

"Seven years ago. Their military wing is Izz ad-Din al-Qassam
Brigades, IDQ. They're the ones you see marching with black masks
and green bands across the front of their heads. They are dedicated
to the destruction of Israel."

"Hamas is Sunni," Menachem added.

"But I read that Iran is supporting Hamas in Gaza," Liam said. "That makes no sense. Iran is a Shia regime. Persians, not Arabs. Sunnis and Shias are fighting in Iraq. It's in the paper every week. They hate each other. I read an article in the Wall Street Journal. The Sunnis have tried to blow up the Karbala Mosque in Iraq many times, the holiest site in the world to the Shias. Can you explain to me how Sunnis and Shias can be working together in Gaza?"

Menachem looked over at Peres, then at Liam.

"It's complicated," Menachem said.

"Very," Peres said. "It would take many hours to explain. Let's just say they hate us more. Now. Back to what my informant said. He claims it is not the IDQ Brigades that took Miss Stanton. He says it is Hamas civilians under the direction of a single imam."

"Where they are holding her?" Liam asked.

"What I just told you is all he said."

"Is he reliable?" Menachem asked.

"He has been in the past. That is all I can go by. He is an insider and his information does not come cheap."

"I'll re-pay you," Liam said pulling out his wallet.

"Not necessary. We keep money at the station for this purpose."

"You think they might be holding her in Gaza?" Liam asked.

Peres and Menachem shook their heads at almost the same time.

"It's difficult to move between Gaza and Israel," Peres said, running his hand through his dark hair. "It is not likely they would risk holding her in Gaza."

"I agree," Menachem said. "Not in Gaza. There are sympathetic populations in many other areas controlled by the Palestine Authority."

"The PLO under a different title," Peres said.

"What are those areas?" Liam asked.

"Besides Gaza," Menachem said, "there is the area north of Jerusalem, including Nablus and Ramallah. Then south of Jerusalem, it includes Bethlehem and Hebron."

"And Jericho and East Jerusalem to the east of us," Peres said. "My guess is they would keep her in one of the occupied territories. Not so much scrutiny from strangers. As long as they are Arabs."

"Right," Menachem said, "in those cities their motto is 'If you see something, say nothing'."

"This is true," Peres said. "Not like here."

"So what do we do now?" Liam asked.

"I leaned on my informant," Peres said, "and promised him a big payment."

"I'll cover whatever," Liam said.

"I may need you to do that. In the meantime, I will make inquiries to my counterparts in the P.A. controlled areas. Some of them can be very cooperative at times."

"I doubt this is one of them," Menachem said. "News of a scroll that says Ishmael was not the son of Abraham is not going to be received well by any *Moos-lim*."

Liam watched as the *Hasid* and the blond shook hands across the small table. The blond slipped a small white envelope in his inside coat pocket.

"Ah," Peres said noticing the two men. "A deal has been struck. Let us hope our negotiations will end as peacefully."

Peres finished his sparkling water and stood to leave.

"Mr. Connors, again I say this is good news for you. If these Hamas Sunnis holding Miss Stanton are motivated by religious fervor, there is a good chance we can make an exchange. Assuming you can locate the scroll. My men continue to look for Yitzhak Palmer as well."

Liam stood up and shook Peres's hand.

"Menachem told me about your situation, the Nazareth deal."

Peres glared at Menachem with his good eye. Sunk deeply into his soft, low chair, Menachem met Peres's stare and shrugged.

"I hope it all works out for you," Liam said.

"Sometimes these tour guides in Israel talk too much, Mr. Connors. But it is true. My status as an investigator is not voluntary. If you like I can ask another officer, one trained better in police work to take over your case."

"No. No," Liam said. "Not no, but hell no. I am honored that you are working with us to find Mimi. I only mentioned it to let you know I admire what you did."

"I did what I had to do. No more. No less. The bureaucrats, they do not think like I do. I do not understand them, but theirs is the way of government. They have meetings and talk, then talk some more. Talking makes me tired. I will call you and your guide—who talks too much."

"I thank you for your help," Liam said.

Peres left the bar.

"You didn't say anything about Yusef," Liam said after Peres left the bar, "or Mahmoud and his little brother following Yusef."

"And you said nothing about hiring professionals with guns. Why did you not ask Investigator Peres for his opinion?"

"I figure we may have to do some things to save Mimi we don't want Peres or any other Israeli official to know about. Take the law into our own hands."

Menachem raised his glass to Liam.

"You are a quick study, Mr. Connors. If it becomes necessary I can obtain for you a gun. But let us not discuss guns any further. You know, I did not think you would be the kind of man willing to use a weapon here in Israel."

"I wasn't three days ago, but I am now."

Chapter Twenty-One

Mimi was almost certain the light under the door was dimming. But the more she studied it, the less certain she became. It was one of those phenomena best examined indirectly, like stars in the early evening sky.

The hammering had finally stopped, thank God. Mimi could not imagine what they were building on the other side of the door, but every hammer blow reverberated in her head and fragile stomach. She thought she heard low murmurs outside the door. Not sure. Her mind could be playing tricks on her in the fetid darkness of her bathroom cell.

Surprisingly, Mimi felt oddly optimistic about her situation for the first time. She was alive. They had not beaten her. Her intestinal attacks had diminished. She wasn't sure how long it had been. In the sensory deprivation chamber the bathroom had become, she could not be certain about the passage of time or the intensity of the light seeping under the door. If the light were dimming as she thought, it was the second time since her ordeal had begun. When she awoke the first time in the foul-smelling tiny room, the darkness was total. After hours in the dark cell, light had filtered under the door and continued for a long time, then disappeared. It had come again many hours ago. Then the banging had started and stopped, and now the light was leaving again. Since her head had cleared itself of the ether, she was developing some confidence in the general time line she had reconstructed. Mimi knew she had been taken on a Thursday, sometime around noon, while shopping in the Old City for a *mezuzah* to give to Liam. By her reckoning, it was now Saturday evening. She was approaching the end of her second full day in the tiny bathroom.

Mimi heard laughter on the other side of the door. Men laughing. More than two men. It was comforting in a strange way. Her captors had human emotions. Maybe they would consider mothers and sisters when deciding what to do with her.

But maybe that decision had already been made.

The door swung open. The glare hurt her eyes. After a moment, she squinted to see the dark outline of a man standing in the doorway. He seemed like a giant.

He grabbed Mimi's arm and jerked her off the wooden table. Her feet hit the tile floor hard. She lost her balance. Mimi's legs were shaky, wobbly from inactivity. The man's fingers dug into her. Mimi grabbed at his hand, trying to free herself.

"Out," the man said, squeezing her arm tighter and pulling her from the bathroom.

He flung her toward the center of the room. Mimi stumbled forward. She turned and yelled at the man to leave her alone. He wasn't a giant after all. He was less than six feet tall and slender. He was covered from shoulder to toe in a long, flowing white robe. The ends of the black and white *keffiyeh* on his head covered his face; only his eyes showed.

Mimi's knees grew weak when she saw other men sitting on the floor in a semi-circle, dressed the same way. She could see only their sandal-clad feet and the top half of their faces. The men were somber, no laughter like she had heard through the door. They stared at Mimi with hungry eyes.

The room seemed huge by comparison to Mimi's bathroom, but was no larger than a typical living room in the U.S. The windows were partially boarded up. There was enough light from outside for Mimi to see everything in the room, including a round wooden pole in the center. She glanced at the ceiling and floor where the pole had been crudely anchored with small boards and nails.

That's what the hammering was.

Mimi was right about the light under her door dimming. It was late afternoon, probably less than an hour before dark. She turned to the man who had dragged her from the room, still standing behind her. He pointed to the pole, stabbing at the air. Mimi glanced at the pole, then back at the leader. He pointed again toward the pole. She didn't move. He came closer and shoved her toward it.

Mimi stumbled again, ending next to the pole amid the half-circle of men. Her jailer sat himself on the floor to close the circle and growled. Mimi looked at the pole, then back at the leader, still pointing at the pole.

He wants me to dance. Pole dance.

Mimi's stomach cramped and she cringed. When the spasm passed, she stood still in the middle of the semi-circle of strangers, angry at her Arab captors. No way was she dancing for these animals. She would die first.

The leader stood up again and grabbed one of Mimi's hands, moving her toward the pole. Mimi jerked her hand away and the man slapped her hard. She had never been hit so hard. It knocked her to the floor.

He snarled at her. Mimi felt her aching jaw. Her hip hurt but she picked herself up and stood in front of the man. He gestured with his head at the pole, muttering something. Mimi stood her ground, defiant, staring into the leader's black eyes.

He slapped her again. Again she sprawled on the floor next to one of the men. He chuckled and touched her hair. Mimi moved away from the man's reach. She felt her jaw. It burned and hurt. She rose slowly to her feet. The leader moved closer to her, placing her hands on the pole. When he released her hand, Mimi let it drop to her side as if she had no control of it.

He hit her again, this time with his fist.

Again Mimi tumbled to the floor, striking her forehead as she fell. She was dazed but not unconscious. The cool tile felt good against her cheek. Her temple was throbbing where his fist had connected. The man pulled her to her feet, grabbed her forearm and twisted it, spinning her around. When she faced him again, he hit her in the stomach so hard Mimi thought his fist might have broken a rib. She lay on the floor gasping for breath, terrified. She fought to suck air into her lungs. He had knocked the breath out of her; she would not die from the blow. Mimi lay on the floor next to the pole in the middle of the men. The next blow might kill her.

Mimi grabbed the pole for support and pulled herself to her feet.

The leader sputtered angrily at her. He grabbed her by the shoulders, shaking her and barking orders. She shrugged her shoulders. What was he saying? He fingered the top button of her white linen blouse. Instinctively, Mimi slapped his hand away. He hit her in the face so hard it almost lifted her off the floor. She fell back onto the tile floor and lost consciousness.

Mimi felt water on her face. She opened her eyes. Someone was leaning over over her with a glass of water, ready to douse her with the remainder. She put up her hand and saw the person's face. It was not her captor; it was a young man in Western clothes—a young man she recognized from the café where she had eaten the delicious date pastries. Yusef—the waiter with the jagged scar on his cheek—the waiter she had seen in the Old City right before she was taken.

Was she seeing things?

No. Her tormentor pushed Yusef out of the way, jerked Mimi to her feet and pointed to her blouse. He wanted it unbuttoned. Tears ran down her cheeks. Mimi shook her head and closed her eyes so she wouldn't see the punch coming.

Her jaw exploded in pain, but only for a moment.

Chapter Twenty-Two

Menachem and Liam sat in the late afternoon shadows of the YMCA tower on a concrete bench across King David Street from the hotel. After the meeting with Peres, they left the Oriental Bar and bought *falafel* sandwiches from a street vendor, pita bread wrapped around a fried chickpea and fava bean patty. Liam managed to choke down a few bites before tossing his in the trash can. Menachem relished every bite, licking *hummus* from his fingers after throwing his wrapper away.

"Delicious," he said.

Liam heard the buzz of Menachem's cell phone. Menachem answered and spoke Arabic for several minutes.

"Mahmoud," he said.

"Any news?"

"Yusef left the café shortly after we talked to him. Mahmoud and his brother followed Yusef's bus to Jericho. They tailed him on foot through the city."

"Yusef didn't see them?"

"If Mahmoud and his brother don't want to be seen, believe me, they will not be seen. I have been working with them since Mahmoud was thirteen and his brother eleven. The best. It's in their Bedouin genes. Besides, as I said, Yusef is not very intelligent."

"They have a history with you then?"

"When tourism is down, a tour driver must be resourceful. They help me on different occasions."

Liam knew Menachem was being deliberately evasive. He let it pass.

"They're still in Jericho?"

"Mahmoud and his brother followed Yusef to a big house near the city center. Big wall around the house. Mahmoud and his brother watch Yusef climb over the wall and go inside through a back door. The windows of the house were boarded up. Like no one lives there."

"Did Mahmoud get a look inside?"

Menachem nodded. "Later, they hear an angry man talking very loud. Mahmoud climbs the fence and sneaks a look through the boards covering one window."

"Come on. Come on."

"He saw an American woman with short, dark hair."

"Was she all right?"

Menachem hesitated.

"Tell me."

"He saw a man knock her down with his fist."

Menachem drove them from King David Street to a run down service station and automotive repair shop. He huddled with a thin, gray-haired mechanic who continuously wiped his hands with a red rag pulled from his back pocket. The man proceeded to check and double-check all engine and electrical systems, hoses, tires, fans, and belts. He topped off every fuel and lubrication system and filled two twenty-liter plastic containers with his highest octane gas. Another with water. Liam helped load the containers into the trunk. The entire process took the mechanic less than thirty minutes, but it seemed forever to Liam.

"He is the only man in Israel I allow to touch my car," Menachem said as they drove off.

"You've turned this Volvo into a bomb."

"Don't worry. The gasoline in the trunk will not blow us up. We will be driving in darkness on lonely highways with no places to serve us. If we are forced to leave Jericho in a hurry, if people pursue us, we may go south from Jericho along the western shore of the Dead Sea. It is the Judean Desert. Then, perhaps the Negev Desert, where there is nothing but rocks and sand. Running out of gas or water in the desert is much more dangerous than carrying gasoline in an automobile. Trust me."

"Whatever," Liam said, unable to shake the image of a man hitting Mimi, knocking her down. "We need to get to Jericho now."

"Yes," Menachem said tapping his temple, "but we must be smart. Best time to arrive is early morning, maybe four o'clock. Best chance for surprise."

Twenty minutes later, Menachem stopped at a nondescript concrete and cinder block building on a quiet street in the northern outskirts of Jerusalem. While the engine was running, he hurried to unlock the wrought iron gate, and drove inside, locking the gate behind them. Menachem grabbed a remote from the console and opened a garage door at the back of the building. They exited the

Volvo and Menachem turned on the lights. Liam looked around. He was astounded. Hanging from the walls was an incredible array of military gear and equipment. Liam folded his arms across his chest.

"All right, Menachem," Liam said, his arms folded across his chest, "Enough of this 'I am just a lowly driver' bull shit. Who the hell are you? You're no tourist guide. You don't just drive people around to see the sights. Come clean."

Menachem looked puzzled.

"Come clean means tell me everything."

"I am a driver, a special kind of driver. It is true I drive tourists sometimes. At other times I perform other services. Let us make our preparations for the trip to Jericho. On the road I will tell you my story, but it is for your ears only. You must promise not to share the information."

Liam nodded and they got to work. They removed the gas and water containers and the spare tire from the trunk. Menachem unscrewed several wing nuts and bolts and took out its false floor, revealing a hidden compartment.

"Follow me," Menachem said and led Liam inside the cinder block building to what he called his living quarters. He took Liam quickly through a small kitchen and sitting area and into a walk-in gun vault.

"Geez," Liam said. Hundreds of weapons on padded hooks lined the walls of the vault or rested on felt in gun cabinets with glass fronts. "All these in working condition?"

"About half of them are collector's items, different types of guns from all of our wars, going back as far as 1948."

"They ought to be in a museum."

"Maybe so, but I take care of them. Some men collect art or wine. I collect guns that used in the fight to establish my country and to keep it free."

Liam opened a cabinet and removed a high-tech looking black FN Five-seveN with a laser aiming device below the barrel.

"My newest pistol," Menachem said. "Polymer coated. Even the slide. Do you know anything about guns?"

"I trained with weapons in the military. If you have a Baretta or a Colt pistol I'll be right at home. I carry a sidearm in the oil field."

"Why would you do that?"

"Because a lot of times it's just me and my dog Shep in the woods or at a drilling site, and well, you never know. I like to be ready for anything. So far I've only had to shoot rattlesnakes and copperheads."

"America is a violent country."

"Some say it's because we have so many guns."

"And what do you say?"

"That's not it."

"In Israel, it is illegal to own a gun unless you are awarded a special type of permit from the government. The terrorists who bomb our busses and try to kill us with machine guns, they do not obey the gun laws."

"Imagine that," Liam said, "terrorists violating the gun laws."

Liam placed the high-tech FN pistol back into the cabinet. He scanned the walls and cabinets for something more familiar and user-friendly. Liam had been a decent shot in the Army, especially with the M-16, but he was least twenty years behind the times in his knowledge of weaponry. In the service he had trained with the M-16, the Galil and Soviet variants of the AK assault rifle. The only pistols he had fired were Army issued Colt 1911s and M9 Berettas. Liam kept three guns at Grand Oaks: a Remington twelve gauge automatic shot gun, a six-shot Smith & Wesson .357 revolver, and the 9mm Beretta he carried when checking on oil rigs and wells with Shep.

He picked up a nickel-plated 1911. It felt comfortable in his hand, bringing back memories. He slid the external safety off and aimed the pistol, squeezing the familiar beaver tail grip. Menachem reached into a cabinet and pulled out a black matte finish semi-automatic pistol.

"Here, this is a Glock 21, chambered in forty-five. The most simple pistol for you. Rounds go in the magazine, mag goes in gun, pull slide and release to put bullet in chamber. Pull the trigger until you run out of bullets. No external safety, no de-cocker or hammer, just *bang*."

Liam put down the 1911 and held the Glock.

"And here," Menachem said. "This is a Smith & Wesson Airweight snub for backup. A .38 caliber revolver without external hammer, so as not to snag on something. Carry in this ankle holster."

Liam gauged the heft of the S&W. He stuck it in the holster.

"For your rifle, you are familiar with the M-16?"

"Yes."

Menachem took a rifle from the wall and gave it to Liam. "M4A1 carbine," Menachem said. "It's an M-16 short and can be shot in semi, burst, and full auto. I recommend for you controlled bursts. Come with me into the garage."

Menachem led Liam through a small door on the side of the garage. Liam thought it might lead outside, but was surprised when

Menachem flipped the light switch. He found himself at one end of a narrow shooting lane. Padding and baffles lined the cinder block walls and the ceiling. At the other end an outline of a man was silhouetted against a porous fiberboard wall.

"Behind the target and wall is four feet of sand."

"Your own personal indoor shooting range."

"Yes. Load the M4 just like the M-16."

Liam checked the safety and firing selection switch, the bolt and magazine releases. He pushed in a magazine. He pulled the charging handle back and let go. The bolt slammed forward. He raised the M4 to his shoulder, eyeing the target.

"Here. Attach this before you fire the rifle," Menachem said, giving him a black tube-like suppressor. "Screw it in the barrel. It will not eliminate all noise, but it is better. I have one for your Glock as well. None for your backup revolver. In this room and in Jericho use these. We want quiet here to not upset neighbors. In Jericho we do not want noise to bring down P.A. militia on us."

Liam put in ear plugs, screwed in the silencers on the M4 and Glock, and practiced in Menachem's shooting range. He alternated shooting the rifle and the pistol until he was comfortable with his accuracy and his ability to replace the magazines in both guns rapidly and efficiently. With the practice, Liam was satisfied he had the technical ability to hit a live target with either the M4 or the Glock. But he wasn't sure he had the spine to shoot at a living, breathing person, unless that person was firing at him.

Liam visualized the man hitting Mimi. It made his blood boil. Liam visualized plugging the son-of-a-bitch in the chest with a half-dozen M4 rounds, knocking him back ten feet. Then he imagined shooting the prick with the Glock. A double tap right in the upper torso. Liam was no assassin, but he would do whatever it took to get Mimi back, including shooting the bastards. No problem. Save her. Kill them all.

After some time, Menachem tapped on the door to the shooting tunnel. Liam had finished cleaning the M4 and was starting to break down the Glock.

"No need to spend much time cleaning the Glock. It is one of the beautiful things about it. You can abuse it and it will still do the job, dirt and grease and all. Are you comfortable with your firearms?"

"It came back to me," Liam said. "You don't think we should call Peres to get his help?"

"For sure we can do that if you wish. It is up to you. Again I explain. By treaty Jericho is governed by the Palestinian Authority.

Peres is Jerusalem Police. An agency of Israeli law enforcement has no jurisdiction in P.A. territories to make arrests or rescue a hostage unless the victim is an Israeli citizen. If we bring in Investigator Peres, he will have to work through the P.A. and that would be no good for Mimi Stanton. No good for Investigator Peres. He would feel he must go through P.A. because he is already under investigation for taking down the terrorists in Nazareth without permission from his superiors and the P.A. If we go through political channels, the kidnapping might become an international incident. Miss Stanton's captivity could be drawn out for weeks, maybe months. In my experience, it is better to strike immediately than to enter negotiations with these people. It is what landed Peres trouble. We go in, hit fast, grab her and leave. Most effective. We get in trouble with P.A., big deal."

"Forget the protocol. My father was right. He used to tell me it's easier to get forgiveness than permission."

"Do not worry," Menachem said. "I will be with you. We do this together. These Sunni civilians playing soldier will not be so tough."

Menachem and Liam placed their guns and extra magazines in protective cases and put them in the hidden compartment of the trunk. Menachem tied down the gun cases with the bungee cords built into the compartment. He packed plenty of ammunition, night vision equipment, Kevlar vests, and screwed down the false trunk bottom. On top of it they placed the spare tire, gas and water containers, a case of bottled water and a box of MREs. Menachem walked over to the wall next to the garage door and retrieved a laminated checklist, making an imaginary okay in the air with his index finger as he went over each item.

"What else?" Liam asked. "How about flashlights?"

"They are in car already. Small Fenix e01 LED lights no bigger than your finger. We put on our tactical pants and boots, but not tops until we get inside Jericho. We load a few more items, we make sandwiches inside and some coffee, and we..., how you say in America, 'hit the road'?"

It was after two a.m. when they drove away from Menachem's house. Liam had pulled many all-nighters logging wells in Louisiana after reaching total depth, but not recently. No matter. He was not sleepy in the least, still riding the adrenaline that began to flow when they learned from Mahmoud that Mimi was being held in Jericho. As Liam looked down at his black boots and his black tactical pants, his heart started racing at the prospect of invading the Jericho house, his weapon drawn.

"I've never shot a man," Liam said.

"I haven't shot a man...," Menachem said, smoothing the skin on his bald head and looking Liam in the eyes, "recently."

Liam took comfort.

"Do not worry. To live this long in Israel I must be a good judge of character. I judge you to be a man of courage."

"I don't feel courageous at this moment."

"You will, my friend, to save your fiancé."

"Fiance," Liam said, smiling in the dark. "Sounds good."

"And remember. These men who have taken Mimi, who hold her against her will, they will not hesitate to shoot and kill you. They will gladly give up their own miserable lives to keep you from setting her free. If they are martyred in what they believe is the cause of Islam, they are told they will be richly rewarded in heaven, so they are fearless."

Liam was silent a moment. He spoke quietly.

"If that's what it takes to get Mimi, I'll kill them. I'll kill every single one of them."

"Save some for me, my friend."

Liam looked out at the black sky above as they drove out of the neighborhood. No moon or stars. He studied Menachem's face illuminated in the green glow of the dashboard instruments.

"I'm ready for the Book of Menachem."

Menachem laughed. "Where to begin?" he said and thought a moment. "Have you ever heard of 'Operation Wrath of God'?"

Chapter Twenty-Three

"My father, a young engineer in Poland, had the wisdom to leave the country with my mother in the nineteen-thirties. He immigrated to Jerusalem when anti-Semitism in Eastern Europe was being stoked by the Nazis. Of course, Jews had always been hated in Poland. To the east. The *pogroms* in Russia were wiping out hundreds of thousands, perhaps millions of Jews.

"It was not easy for my parents. The British were being pressured by the Arab *Moos-lims* to restrict Jewish immigration. The irony is rich. Jews—they have lived in what is now Israel, the kingdoms of Judah and Israel in the land of Canaan, for more than a thousand years before Muhammad was born."

Menachem jabbed his index finger into his chest. "Yet *we* are the interlopers."

"Back to the story. My father was fortunate. His skills were needed in this country and he had saved the money required to enter. Today, you would call him an electrical engineer."

"So you were born here?"

"In 1949. A year after the State of Israel was born. I am what is known here as a *sabra,* born in the Jewish state."

"You ever marry?"

"Yes, and have a son and daughter. Both have families of their own and live in Israel, one in Tiberius, the other in Haifa."

"From the looks of your place you live alone."

"Yes. My wife and I are not divorced, but we have lived separately for many years. My fault. I was gone much of the time during the marriage. I neglected our children. My wife also."

Liam felt a twinge of guilt. Building Clare Petroleum was an intense, time-consuming undertaking. Ninety per cent of child rearing duties fell on Annette's shoulders. He was at the office or out of town much of the time. When Liam was home—especially when the girls were small—he was often preoccupied with exploration issues. Drill site maps spread on the kitchen table. Annette never complained.

Menachem swerved to miss a pack of dogs on the highway, the headlights reflecting their hungry, primitive eyes.

"Wild dogs?" Liam asked.

"A big problem in these desert hills. Feral dogs are killing many of our native animals. The ibex goat, these dogs, and leopards, too, hunt and kill them for food. Not many left."

With every kilometer they drove east through the darkness, the elevation dropped. Jericho was eight hundred feet below sea level in the Jordan Valley floor, over three thousand feet lower than Jerusalem. Liam looked out at the dark sky above the Judean desert. Two shooting stars flashed, racing toward the Sinai.

"Why were you gone from home so much?" he asked.

Menachem took a deep breath and pointed out Liam's window.

"In the mountains to the south of us is Herodium, the city Herod the Great built to hold his body after death. Just now they dig out two thousand years of sand and dirt covering the magnificent structures he built. His sarcophagus can be seen at the Museum of Israel, pieced together over many years by the archaeologists."

Liam sat in silence in the darkness, waiting for Menachem to reveal his life history at his own pace.

"My wife and I were married in the Spring of 1972. Near the completion of my military service. The Summer Olympics were being held in Munich that year."

"The Olympic Massacre," Liam said. "I remember watching the whole thing on television."

"I did as well," Menachem said. "I felt helpless feeling seeing the Black September cowards in their tracksuits murder my eleven countrymen. Innocent amateur athletes, there to compete for their country. Defenseless. Killed with no mercy.

"I had developed a reputation in my military outfit as a gifted driver. The reputation, it was true. I had raced cars in my youth. Worked with Israeli teams driving the European Grand Prix circuit. I was at home with my wife when the call from the Prime Minister's office came. Mrs. Meir had commissioned Operation Wrath of God.They needed a skillful driver to go on the mission."

"I saw the movie about it," Liam said, "with Eric Bana."

The Volvo's headlights caught a road sign. Highway One. Liam had studied the route on the map. At some point they would turn north on one of the minor roads into Jericho. Liam was torn. He was in a hurry to get to the house in Jericho to free Mimi, but the thought of shooting it out with the kidnappers made him nervous, even scared when he thought of waiting in the dark and shooting it out. Liam was not ready to die, but he wasn't going to let them kill

Mimi or continue to harm her. His fault she was in this mess. He would to get her out of it or die trying.

"So, off and on for years, well into the eighties, I was dispatched with Mossad agents on missions in Europe. And in the Middle East. We eliminated the men who funded and planned the Black September devils who carried out the murders. That, my friend Liam, is where I really learned to drive. I memorized streets and planned escape routes in every city where Wrath of God operations were undertaken. My head was filled with images of the streets and alleys. During the heat of things I never looked at a map or wondered which way to turn. I knew. And I could drive fast. Believe me, when there is a need to drive fast to save your own life, you focus attention on every detail."

"That took a lot of guts," Liam said.

"I didn't look at it that way. It was a privilege. My wife did not think it such an honor. She felt abandoned. I cannot blame her. Every mission she was prepared to hear of my death in some foreign city. In the end we accomplished what we set out to do—deliver justice for our dead Olympic athletes."

"Do you see your two children?"

"I try. As often as I can. My grandchildren as well. To my son and daughter growing up I was a ghost. I would come home without warning, stay a day or two then leave. I was not part of their lives. They never felt close. My wife told them I was performing noble deeds. She could not tell them more. I have tried to make it up to them but it is hard. They made it this far without me. Self-sufficient."

"Do you see your wife?"

"I talk to her as she will let me. She has never re-married. She is pleasant, but her love for me withered. Love is like a flower. It must be nurtured and cared for or it will die."

Liam noticed Menachem's eyes—they glistened with tears.

"I wouldn't give up on her," Liam said. "You still love her? Get her back."

"Perhaps. When this is over. You make me think. You risk your life to save Mimi Stanton. It is a good thing." He paused. "There is nothing so good as the love of a woman."

"You're not just whistling Dixie," Liam said as Menachem furrowed his brow. "That's a saying in the South. It means I agree with you. My life has been easy compared to yours. And to Akiva Peres's. I spent my military duty analyzing intelligence and briefing officers. I was never in the fighting. I could not have done what you did. We had a great generation in the U.S., the men who fought in

World War II. Today, with what we have become in America, I doubt we could have defeated the Axis powers."

"You could do everything I did," Menachem said, "if you had to."

"I'm not sure. Are you still involved with Mossad or the IDF?"

"Most of the time I drive tourists. Make a decent living. And I have a military pension that my wife will inherit when I die. I spend very little money."

"Except on your guns and the other hardware in your garage. Why do you keep it all?"

"What is it your Boy Scouts say in America? Be prepared? If I were called on today—in Israel, you never know. Especially since your current administration has given the Persians permission to go nuclear."

"Our stupid government. Most people think it's a big mistake. Giving away the farm for no reason."

"What farm?"

"Never mind," Liam said, "I'm glad you were prepared to help me. You don't know how glad."

"I feel fortunate to do so. I regret we are driving to Jericho knowing so little of the situation there. In Wrath of God, the men I drove had detailed information about the targets—where each of them lived, worked, and socialized. The executions were carried out efficiently and quietly, except for the ones we killed with explosives."

"I know we're going in blind, but we don't have time to get more intelligence. We have to get her out of there."

"We do not want to do something that will get her killed. We must use our heads. Mahmoud will tell us what he has seen watching the house all night. He will know if people are coming and going. I am relying on Peres's informant who says these men are not trained."

"We don't know what's been going on in there," Liam said.

"No, but we have the element of surprise. And with some luck, these men will be asleep. Perhaps no one is awake, watching for trouble. We can only pray."

"Why would civilians get involved in something like this?"

"Sunni religious zealots," Menachem said, "trying to destroy Yitzhak's scroll, something they believe is blasphemous."

"I cannot understand their thinking."

"Do not try. We will be turning north soon," Menachem said. "If we continued on this road to the Dead Sea and turned south, we would arrive at Masada. You should see it. It will take your breath.

And on the way south to Masada you pass Qumran. From the highway in the daytime we would see the caves in mountains to the west."

"The caves where the scrolls were found?"

"It is walking distance from the parking areas next to the highway. But those caves are off limits. You can get close on government-built overlooks. But the caves are dark. I tell the tourists this, but they insist on climbing up there anyway. They stare into the darkness of the cave and come away satisfied. It is a mystery to me. Masada will be further south from Qumran and west of the salt ponds."

Menachem paused a moment and cleared his throat.

"Mahmoud told me something more. I didn't want it to interfere with our preparations for this drive to Jericho. If we are successful there, what Mahmoud told me will no longer be relevant."

"Come on, Menachem."

"Mahmoud said he might have come across some information on where Yitzhak Palmer may be hiding."

Chapter Twenty-Four

Menachem turned north off Highway One southwest of Bet Ha'Arava and drove the two lane road toward Jericho. He slowed as they approached the checkpoint near the city.

"Most of the guards know me here," Menachem said. "Security is not so strict, especially entering the town."

"Who are the soldiers?"

"No soldiers. Israel Border Police, a branch of Israel National Police force. I come through here with my tourists on a regular basis. You are my American client in Israel on business."

"At three in the morning?"

"We started early to get to Tiberius for breakfast meeting. You want to drive through famous sites like Jericho along the way. So you can tell your friends in America you have seen the places."

"What business am I on?"

"Oil business. Your true profession. We tell them Jerusalem to Tiberius and back in one day. Have your passport ready, but normally they will not ask my tourists to show identification."

"Pretty lax security."

"This checkpoint is merely a symbol," Menachem said. "No terrorists try to slip into Jericho to blow up things. A population around twenty-thousand, almost all *Moos-lim* Arabs and Palestinians. Only a handful of Jews and Christians."

"Jericho goes back ten thousand years before Christ," Liam said. "That's what my Lonely Planet guide book says."

"Correct. Here we go. Checkpoint ahead one hundred meters."

Menachem braked the Volvo at the checkpoint and rolled down his window. The Border Policeman saluted Menachem and smiled. The two of them spoke Hebrew. Menachem pointed to Liam and said something. The guard laughed and waved the Volvo through.

"Thank God," Liam said. "What did you tell him?"

"I told him you were in Israel looking for oil. Foolish. Oil everywhere under the Middle East sand but none here."

"Not true anymore, Menachem. 'Petroleum Weekly' reports a natural gas find off shore in Israeli waters. Some oil production on shore has gotten underway using the new horizontal drilling technology. Israel might be in the money."

"Why am I the last to know these things? I am happy you tell me this. You want to know why?"

"You own some mineral rights somewhere?"

"No," Menachem laughed. "When you tell me these things you do not worry about shooting the Sunnis in Jericho."

"Right. Where is the house?"

"I texted Mahmoud before we left Jerusalem. He will leave his brother to watch the house and meet us many blocks away at a car park near the central market."

Menachem drove slowly on the dusty, narrow street past stone and plaster buildings that had been standing for many centuries. He parked the Volvo next to a crumbling limestone structure off Jericho's central market. The town looked deserted.

"Please to stay here while I speak to Mahmoud," Menachem said.

"He's here?"

"Somewhere. I am sure he already sees us."

"I should have my Glock just in case."

"Guns must remain hidden in trunk compartment until the very last minute in case we are checked out. I can talk us out of anything but guns."

Liam watched Menachem disappear into an alley. The darkness in the Volvo was palpable. It weighed on Liam. He was seven thousand miles from his wheelhouse, the piney woods of northwest Louisiana, sitting in a pitch black parking lot in a ten thousand-year-old city, eight hundred feet below sea level, waiting for word from his Israeli guide to get a Glock and an M4 from the trunk to shoot it out with some Sunni Muslim religious fanatics. He did not know a single Muslim back in Louisiana. Now he was getting ready to kill some.

Menachem returned to the Volvo walking faster than before.

"What did Mahmoud say?"

"We could not talk, not even a whisper. He will meet us where there are not so many houses."

Menachem closed the door quietly and eased the Volvo away from the market. He drove five blocks and turned off the engine.

"Let us get out and walk," Menachem said.

"Where's the house?"

"One block that way. We put on our gear."

Menachem opened the trunk and unloaded the gas and water containers and the spare. He quickly removed the false floor and gave Liam his guns, a tactical vest, and a helmet. They strapped them on quickly in the darkness. Liam jumped when he sensed something on his flank. It was Mahmoud.

Mahmoud led them through a narrow passageway between two buildings. He whispered something to Menachem who told Liam "thirty meters." The three of them hustled to the wall surrounding the house where Mahmoud's little brother crouched against the stones.

Mahmoud spoke quietly to his brother, who jabbed his finger at the house on the other side of the wall and rattled off, his eyes wide. Mahmoud shushed him.

"What's going on?" Liam asked Menachem.

"The brother says less than an hour ago, while Mahmoud was waiting for us near the central market other people came to the house."

"And did what? There's more people in there?"

Mahmoud scampered over the wall and ran without a sound to the back of the house. He disappeared inside. A minute later, Mahmoud stepped out and waved for them to join him.

"Come on," Menachem said and went over the wall.

Liam checked the backup Smith & Wesson on his ankle, his Glock at his side, and screwed the suppressor into the short barrel of his M4. He tumbled over the wall like a good soldier, scraping his Kevlar vest on the stone. Liam felt his heart pounding in his throat as he neared the back door. Liam readied his M4 and his Glock in the unsnapped black holster at his hip.

At the back door with Menachem and the two boys, Liam was confused about what the hell they were doing. All the excited whispering in Arabic. But as he waited to invade the house, his breathing became steady and his hands stopped trembling. The turmoil in his chest was gone. The weight of the M4 in his hands felt good. Liam had been afraid he might panic when push came to shove. But here he was, steady and committed, ready to kill Mimi's captors. It was time to bring her home.

Menachem cracked the back door. Mahmoud rushed past him, opening it wide.

"What are they doing?" Liam said.

"They say there's no one here alive," Menachem said.

"Shit."

"Only dead bodies."

Liam's stomach flipped. All his fault. He never should have come to Israel or met with Ike. The merchants in the Old City were right.

You careless fool.

Menachem turned on his flashlight. A large central room. A puddle of black liquid near a pole crudely secured to the floor and ceiling with boards and nails.

"That's fresh blood," Menachem said. "I can smell it."

"Smell gunfire, too," Liam said.

Liam shined his own light on smears of blood that lead into another room. Mahmoud stood in the doorway, waving him over.

"Let me go in first," Menachem said.

Liam waited. Forever.

"Two dead men inside," Menachem said, coming toward him. "One his throat cut, the other dead from three gunshot wounds. Mahmoud tells me seven dead men in this house."

"Men," Liam said.

Liam, Menachem, and Mahmoud joined Mahmoud's little brother across the room near the pole. The brother said something in Arabic to Mahmoud and Menachem.

"Brother says five dead men in these other rooms," Menachem said, "plus two in room we entered."

"Any sign of a woman?" Liam asked.

Menachem said something to the boys.

"They say no," Menachem said.

A wave of relief washed over Liam.

"All right," Menachem said to Liam, "we have to move quickly. Gather as much information from this house as we can. Examine each body. Any evidence left behind will help us know what happened."

Menachem spoke in Arabic to the two boys.

"Mahmoud will go with you," he said to Liam.

Liam led Mahmoud into the room closest to them, his small flashlight illuminating the entire room. A small man in Western pants and a white shirt lay face down. Liam turned the man over. Though blood covered most of the man's face, Liam could see a large, jagged scar marking the dead man's left cheek. Liam called out to Menachem to come see.

"Yusef. From the café," Liam said.

"Stabbed to death," Menachem said, shining his light around the room. "Let's look at the others and get out of here."

They split up and checked every room.

"One body in a room over here's different," Liam called out. "Not dressed like the others."

"Show me," Menachem said.

Menachem followed Liam into the room and knelt beside a dead man. He wore black tactical gear with a protective vest and a black balaclava covering everything but his eyes and mouth.

"Looks like a SWAT team member," Liam said.

"Except for this," Menachem said, pointing behind the dead man's head to the knife stuck in the base of his skull.

Menachem pulled the balaclava up to expose the man's face and neck. A tattoo on his neck above his shirt collar. Menachem studied it a moment and whispered to Liam.

"Come look in the bathroom."

Inside the small bathroom Menachem shined his light around.

"This is where they held her."

"How do you know?" Liam asked.

"Look at what she did."

Menachem pulled the thin woolen blanket off the wooden table in the cramped room and tapped a spot on the corner. Freshly scratched into the wood in small letters was "Mimi."

"And look at this," Menachem said.

He held up a woman's fingernail covered with red polish.

"Mahmoud's brother found it here on the floor."

Liam held the nail and walked out of the abattoir, careful not to step in the blood. Outside the back door, he took a deep breath of wet early morning air and made the sign of the cross.

Please let her be alive.

Chapter Twenty-Five

"What is Mahmoud's brother's name?" Liam asked as they approached the checkpoint.

"It is unpronounceable in your Western tongue," Menachem said. "Even for me it is difficult. Call him Brother."

Liam rode shotgun in silence. Mimi was not among the seven dead in the house, but was probably in worse jeopardy now than before. The carnage in the slaughterhouse in central Jericho was grisly proof that her new captors, the men who held her *this* time, were willing to kill and skilled at it. He looked at the artificial nail in the palm of his hand, painted the red color Mimi had worn in Italy. Liam didn't always notice such things, but he had a vivid picture of her red fingernails against an Italian wine glass.

Menachem rolled down his window and said something to the same easy-going guard at the Jericho checkpoint. The guard laughed again and waved the Volvo through.

"I told him we had decided to see Qumran before heading north to Tiberius. I told him you have a difficult time making up your mind for an oil man, but I get paid anyway."

"Where are we picking up Mahmoud and Brother?"

"In a few kilometers a small *wadi* intersects with this road above Mezpe Jericho. We will meet them there. Not long to wait. Maybe not at all. They will make good time running through the *wadi*. It is a much shorter distance than we travel."

"Whoever killed those seven men were professionals," Liam said. "Do you have any idea what is going on?"

"Not sure. Mahmoud will have more information."

Menachem pulled off the highway and drove over parched dirt and small rocks to a cluster of palm trees on a promontory overlooking the *wadi*. Liam leaned against the front fender of the dust-covered Volvo, thinking about the killings in Jericho, Mimi in that tiny holding cell. Liam heard shuffling in the *wadi*. Mahmoud and his brother appeared out of the darkness, breathing heavily from their run in the dry stream bed.

"Should we put more distance between us and Jericho before we stop?" Liam asked Menachem.

"It will be days, maybe weeks before those bodies are discovered by the Palestinian police. There's little crime in that city. P.A. officers are lazy and inept. I want to talk to Mahmoud."

Mahmoud and his brother were both slender and looked almost identical. Menachem greeted each of them with busses on each cheek. He clapped their backs. Standing next to the Volvo, Menachem debriefed them in Arabic. Mahmoud always answered first. Brother added details.

"They say," Menachem said, "five men came at three o'clock this morning. Only Brother saw them. Mahmoud was waiting for us near the central market. It was hard to see. Brother stayed well-hidden outside the wall, watching the house through a big crack. Brother says they did not have rifles, just pistols. He says there was no gunfire, just strange sounds and moaning."

"Silencers," Liam said. "Makes sense. How long were they inside?"

"Brother says no more than ten minutes. Only four of them left, one carrying something over his shoulder wrapped in a rug. He thinks it was a rug."

"Mimi," Liam said. "Their mission was to take her."

"Yes," Menachem said. "Brother says he never heard a vehicle."

"The dead man in a black tactical gear and mask?"

"Brother says the four were dressed like the dead one inside. At first, Brother thought the belong to the inside group. Then came the noises, making him think maybe not. Brother waited maybe thirty minutes before he enters into house and sees all the dead men."

Menachem gestured for Liam to join him at the back of the Volvo.

"I need shekels to pay these boys."

Liam pulled a wad of dollars and shekels from his front pocket.

"Take whatever," Liam said. "Give them a bonus. Did they say anything about Ike Palmer?

"Let me talk to Mahmoud," Menachem said.

When Liam and Menachem joined the brothers, Menachem gave Mahmoud and his little brother each a fold of cash. Mahmoud glanced happily at his pay. The boys answered Menachem's questioning at length, both contributing enthusiastically.

"They say their Bedouin cousins tell of a strange man living in the caves between Herodium and Tel Qidron in the mountains of the Judean desert. From the descriptions I think we may have found Yitzhak. The cousins say the man moves from cave to cave."

"They describe him?" Liam asked.

"A small man with much hair and unusual eyes. Walks in a strange way. At times he wears a strange outfit. Some kind of animal fur."

"John the Baptist," Liam said.

Menachem spoke to the boys. After a few minutes, he exchanged light hugs and kisses with Mahmoud and Brother, who came over to share tentative handshakes with Liam. He watched the two boys take off across the road and jog in a southwesterly direction over rocks and boulders.

"Where are they going?" Liam asked.

"They're heading to the mountains to find Yitzak for us. I promised them a substantial reward, more money than they have ever seen. If he can be found they will do it."

"Good going."

Back in the Volvo on the road to Jerusalem, Liam asked Menachem about the tattoo on the dead man's neck.

"The tattoo is a name. Ali ibn Abi Talib. Muhammad's cousin. Muhammad died in the year 632. Some *Moos-lim* scholars claim he was poisoned by a Jewish woman who prepared a goat for him after surviving his conquest of her village of Khaibar. Another reason to hate us. None of Muhammad's sons survived to adulthood, so who would be leader of Islam? Some wanted Muhammad's closest blood relative, his cousin Ali. Others said Muhammad's number one assistant, Abu Bakr, who was appointed successor *caliph* by Muhammad while he was still alive. There was a split in the religion."

"A schism."

"Yes. Abu Bakr and his followers today are Sunni *Moos-lims*. Those who wanted Ali ibn Abi Talib are Shiites. Eighty to eighty-five per cent of the world's *Moos-lims* are Sunni. Shias are the majority sect only in Iran, Iraq, Azerbaijan and Bahrain."

"So this dead guy with the tattoo...."

"Shia, for sure. A Sunni with Ali's name tattooed on his neck would have had his head cut off long ago."

"What does this mean for us?" Liam said. "And for Mimi?"

"I don't know," Menachem said. "Their dress. The icons I saw on prayer beads discarded around the house. The dead men who held Miss Stanton were Sunnis. Yusef, too. The man in the black gear with knife in his kneck was Shia. Shias and Sunnis do not work together. No Sunnis and Shias together on a mission such as this. They hate each other. They would kill each other, rather than the target."

"So the four attackers who carried off Mimi are Shia?" Liam asked.

"My best guess."

"And our next step?"

"Let's go to back to my house. Have some food. Get some rest. I want to think about it."

"Seems to me the men who took Mimi this morning were well-trained and experienced," Liam said.

"Professionals."

"And so Peres's informant was correct. The Sunnis who took Mimi from the Old City were civilians, unprepared for this morning's attack."

"It would seem so. Not prepared in the least. They were asleep," Menachem said. "And from the look of the house the Sunnis did not put up much of a fight except for sticking a knife in the back of the neck of that Shia with the tattoo."

"Maybe Mahmoud and his brother will come through for us again," Liam said. "Those two boys are good."

"If anyone can find Yitzhak, it is Mahmoud and Brother."

Chapter Twenty-Six

Mimi ached all over. The heavy chains hurt her ankles and wrists. At least the smelly rug was gone. With her mouth taped and her sinuses reacting to the dust and grime in the rug, it was a miracle she could breathe in the trunk of the car.

She had to get control of her thinking in the new situation. When the sounds from outside her bathroom cell waked her in Jericho, she had thought she was being rescued. The muffled screams and scuffles outside her door, the strange *pfft* sounds—she just knew she was going home. "Thank You Lord," she whispered, hoping Israeli soldiers and Liam would whisk her away to safety, back to the King David where she could soak in a tub to wash off the dirt and filth. She would drink clean water to rid her digestive system of nasty bugs. She would tell her rescuers everything she knew.

But when the bathroom door burst open, she was grabbed. Duct tape on her mouth and wrists. Out of the bathroom and onto the hard floor. The last thing she saw before the rug enveloped her was a man wearing night vision gear, silhouetted against a dim light. Like she had seen in the Netflix movies she had watched at Grand Oaks with Liam.

Rolled up in the rug, she had realized the men weren't soldiers or policemen. They hoisted her into the air onto someone's shoulders then dumped her onto something hard. She recognized the sound of the car trunk closing and the engine cranking up. As the car began to move, she thought she would die from carbon monoxide poisoning. Wrapped in the rug and imprisoned in the trunk, Mimi could barely breathe. She began to panic.

She said her final prayers, asking God to forgive her sins and let her enter heaven, the same prayers she had repeated in the bathroom cell. In the three days since she was taken from the shop in the Old City, Mimi had thought more about the afterlife than she had in the previous two decades. She hadn't killed anyone. To her knowledge had not slept with a married man. She wasn't very religious, but had never intentionally hurt anyone. She could not believe God would consider divorcing the chronically immature Jimmy Mangum a sin.

Somehow she survived her time in the trunk. The ride was rough and painful. Several times along the way she passed out or slept—she didn't know which. She was relieved to hear the trunk open and felt herself being lifted out and carried, this time by two men, one at her feet and the other at her head. Mimi was elated for a moment. She was alive.

The men unrolled the rug, turning her over and over until she was free. Her head hit the floor, hit it hard. It was already throbbing from the beating she had taken. And her jaw ached. Finally free of the rug, Mimi looked around. Wherever she was, natural light filled the room. She was out of the oppressive darkness of the disgusting bathroom.

Two men stood over her, wearing black balaclavas and all-black clothing. They spoke in a Middle-Eastern language. Another man walked down steps into the room and spoke calmly to the two men. The two lifted her and moved her closer to a wall, where the third man clamped metal bracelets around her ankles and secured her with chains. From somewhere outside she heard a bus motor rev. A sharp blast from a car horn made her wince.

The new man dismissed the other two and squatted next to Mimi. Her lower stomach was churning. She prayed she would not start cramping again. The man wore a black balaclava like the other two. She looked down at her clothing while he studied her. Her linen shirt was filthy and her black pants torn, but at least she was dressed. The man's eyes, different from the dull eyes of the men who had held her at the other house. This man's eyes were intelligent. Mimi fought the urge to thank him for saving her. From the psychology course in nursing school she knew she had to guard against the Stockholm syndrome. She forced herself to repeat silently, over and over, that he was not her friend. He was her enemy, holding her against her will, chaining her to the floor. She resolved to avoid antagonizing the man, but she would do nothing to ingratiate herself with her new captor.

"This may hurt, so I need to do it quickly," the man said in a business-like voice, speaking English with a Middle-Eastern accent.

Before she could react he deftly pulled the duct tape from her mouth. The man was right. It hurt like the dickens.

"I am sorry," he said as he cut away the duct tape on her wrists.

"Who are you? Where am I?"

"Out of that terrible place they were holding you. I cannot tell you where you are. I am sorry that you have to be chained like this, but I have no choice. My men will bring you food and bottled water, a bucket and paper for your bodily needs. They will remove and clean the bucket every four hours. I will have them bring you blankets and towels. I regret we cannot make you more comfortable. This ancient stone floor is cold but I have provided enough chain so that you may stand or sit on the floor. This is the best I can do."

"Who were those men who took me from the Old City? Kept me locked up in...?"

"Ignorant fools. Do not give them another thought. They are no longer a problem."

The way he said it sent a shiver through Mimi. His English was good, but no emotion tempered his voice. She realized he could be a more serious threat to her existence than her previous captors.

"Why are you keeping me prisoner? Is it for money?"

"Your friend Palmer found an ancient scroll in the desert. If your American companion values your life, he will obtain it for me, and I will release you. That is my sole purpose. Nothing personal."

"I know nothing about any scroll. And Ike Palmer's no friend of mine."

"Your friend's friend."

"I wouldn't believe Ike Palmer. He's insane."

"No matter. I must have the scroll. If your friend does not give it up to me, it is unfortunate but I will end your life."

His words took her breath away. No doubt he meant it. His icy nonchalance was frightening. Mimi knew he would have no problem killing her and disposing of her body. All in a day's work.

"As you see steel bars protect the four small windows. Very thick and glazed. No one can see inside. There is no way out of here except through that door at the top of the steps. My men will be guarding there at all times. You may have heard street sounds, but no matter how loud you scream, no one can hear you through these thick walls."

After he was gone, Mimi's stomach cramped and she began to cry.

Out of the frying pan....

Chapter Twenty-Seven

Liam woke up at three o'clock Sunday afternoon. The six hours of sleep on the air mattress in Menachem's compact sitting room were more than the total hours he had slept in the three days since Mimi was taken. He was surprised at how comfortable he was. The oscillating electric fan in the hallway moved the air and provided white noise. Careful not to wake Menachem, he tiptoed through the small hallway, noticing Menachem's open door. Peeked inside but the room was empty. He walked into the kitchen. No Menachem.

Liam opened the door to the garage. The Volvo was there, so Menachem could not be far away. He moseyed into the kitchen and filled the Mr. Coffee carafe on the counter with water and began a search for the coffee, trying to think where a single man would keep his coffee. He opened the freezer and there it was—a can of Folger's Colombian. Liam couldn't find a filter so he made a cradle for the coffee out of a paper towel and turned on the Mr. Coffee. When he lifted a mug to take his first sip, Menachem walked in from the garage.

"Good morning," Menachem said.

"It's afternoon. Where've you been?"

"Outside on the phone. I get better service in my little back yard than in the house. I called Akiva Peres."

"You didn't say anything about Jericho, did you?"

"Of course not. Like I said, it will be many days before those bodies are discovered. I wanted to find out if they have come up with anything. He said they have not."

"Did he ask what we've been doing?"

"He did. I told him Mahmoud is looking for Yitzhak in desert caves and we are calling the number they left at the King David. We are waiting for them to call us back and still trying to get the U.S. government interested."

"Anything to eat?"

"Not so much. You found the coffee I see," Liam asked.

Liam poured Menachem a mug. Menachem grimaced. "Strong."

"What do we do now?"

"Mahmoud will report to me later. I have been thinking about the men who took Mimi from Jericho. They are no doubt Shias and will hold her in a P.A. controlled territory."

"You were right before," Liam said.

"I will make some calls to my people."

"What about the Mossad? Or IDF intelligence?" Liam said. "Since you worked with them in Wrath of God they might be willing to get involved."

"I am afraid even the Mossad is political these days. They err on the side of caution. Besides, all the men I worked with are retired or passed away.Let me go to the market. On the way back I will pick up some pizza at a store run by an Israeli couple I know. The crust is thick, like homemade pita."

"Are they open on Sunday?" Liam asked.

"In Israel, Sunday is our Monday."

"Oh, that's right. Don't get any *falafel*." Liam paused. "I'll go with you just to make sure."

In a few minutes, Menachem cranked the Volvo. They had not been gone ten minutes when Liam's cell phone blared the heavy metal ring tone he had vowed to change. The screen read "Unknown Caller."

"Yes."

"Is this Mr. Palmer's friend?"

"Who is this?"

"I am the person calling you."

"How did you get this number?"

"I came into possession of a telephone."

"Did you find the phone in a house in Jericho?"

"Perhaps. I have your woman. She is safe and living better than before."

"You better not harm her."

"Her well-being is entirely up to you."

"I don't have the scroll."

"That is unfortunate."

"I am trying to find Ike Palmer."

"I wish you luck. All I want is what Palmer possesses. Get it for me; then I will release the woman."

"How do I know you won't kill her anyway?"

"I have no reason to. You may dictate the terms of the exchange to be assured she is safe before you hand over what Yitzhak Palmer has found. Of course I will need to examine the scroll before I release her to you. Those are mere details."

"You could have taken her without spilling all that blood."

"The fools in Jericho? Their deaths are meaningless. I do not want your woman. I want the scroll. Get it for me and I will release her." He paused. "She is very beautiful."

Liam felt his face get hot but controlled himself.

"Do not touch her."

"As long as you act quickly."

"How do I contact you?"

"I will call this number."

"I will double what you are being paid," Liam said. "Let her go."

"Get me what Palmer found."

"I will do my best," Liam said.

"For your woman's sake I hope that will be good enough."

The telephone went dead.

Chapter Twenty-Eight

Liam held the two pizza boxes on his lap. Groceries were in plastic bags across the back seat. Liam was surprised that "the market" in Jerusalem was a modern grocery store, not much different from a Ralph's or Trader Joe's, except he was unable to read the labels on most of the products. The pizzeria was in an ancient limestone building, the proprietors a diminutive husband and wife in their seventies who teased Menachem in Hebrew. Liam couldn't understand a word, but the body language and the rhythms of the good-natured insults and laughter made it clear they were ribbing Menachem.

Liam and Menachem talked only about possible nuances of the phone call, speculating on each detail. The call changed nothing as far as Liam was concerned. Mimi was still being held by thugs promising to kill her if Liam did not deliver the scroll. He didn't know where she was or who had her. The only thing to do was to continue to search for Ike Palmer and hope Akive Peres would come up with something. Liam insisted on talking about something else, even though Mimi's rescue was foremost on his mind.

"What were the old couple on you about?" Liam asked when they left the pizza place to drive home.

"Nothing. They see me shopping by myself and I tell them I am single, so they have lots of women they want to introduce to me."

"You're not interested?"

"No. Only in my wife. A beautiful woman for me these days is like a piece of lovely art work. A pleasure to look at." Menachem glanced at Liam. "You did well in Jericho."

"I didn't do anything."

"You were there. You entered the house with me. Your nerves were steady. You did not seem afraid. Trust me, my friend, most men would not have done what you did in Jericho."

"I was plenty scared."

"As was I. But you did not show it. It did not affect you. Only a fool does not fear to enter a strange house, gun drawn, knowing there are men with guns on the other side of the door. I say to you you did well because it is true."

Liam rode in silence for several blocks. They passed modest, low-rise single family houses on small lots. The pizza warmed Liam's legs.

"Why do Muslims hate Jews so much?" he asked Menachem.

Menachem shrugged. "A small question with a big answer."

Liam summarized what he had had read online before Mimi and he left for Italy. Muhammad announced to the world early in the Seventh Century that he was a prophet. The major religions in Judea and Israel were Christianity and Judaism. Judaism had been around for centuries, going back to Abraham. Christianity had been growing throughout the region for six hundred years. According to the online sources, Muhammad offered first to be accepted by the two religions as a prophet. It would have been the easiest path for his ambitions. But the Jewish and Christian leaders said "no thank you" and turned him away. Muhammad decided he would go it alone, writing down the sacred words he said Allah revealed to him and start his own religion. The sacred words Muhammad wrote contained many disparaging words against Jews, Christians, and other "infidels." Muhammad preached that the followers of Islam must kill Jews and Christians and all other infidels "wherever they hide."

"What you say is correct," Menachem said, "but I think it is most simple to say that Muhammad spread his religion by the sword. He was a great general and ruthless warrior. The people he conquered were given the choice of conversion to Islam or death, so those that wanted to continue living began to worship Allah through Muhammad and Islam. There was no conversion through faith or the doctrines of Islam. By contrast Christianity spread through the preaching of the word of Jesus Christ by his followers. Today *Moos-lims* want to expel Jews from the Middle East by force. Nothing has changed."

"Roman Catholics did the same to the Jews in the Iberian Peninsula," Liam said. "They had to convert to Catholicism or leave Spain and Portugal."

"Yes. The Sepphardic diaspora in the late fifteenth century. Hundreds of years before, Catholic Crusaders killed many of the followers of Islam in the eleventh and twelfth centuries. The Crusaders were unnecessarily cruel in their murders of *Moos-lims*. I must admit much of the anger of *Moos-lims* at Christians and Jews is justified. In the 1930s, the Irgun and other Israeli radicals killed many Arabs, driving them from their villages. And there are many Israelis who believe our treatment of the refugee populations fleeing the 1967 war brought about the terrorist reprisals against our people to this day."

"There's been a lot of misery dealt in the name of religion," Liam said. "And something else. In the short time I've been here in Israel I've seen quite a few Evangelical Christian missions. We've passed their buildings."

"It has to do with eschatology, the part of Christianity dealing with the end times."

"The end of the world?"

"Yes. The fundamentalist Christians believe that when all Jews are converted to Christianity, there will then be the second coming of the Messiah, and after much tribulation, the end of the world."

"Seems like those fundamentalists would want to keep Jews around, keep the world from blowing up."

"Many Christians here in Jerusalem are devoted to reconstruction of the Third Temple on the Temple Mount. They pray for the destruction of Al Aqsa Mosque and the Dome of the Rock and raise money for the building of the Third Temple in their place. It is in their literature. They do not care that *Moos-lims* would take offense at people blowing up their holy sites."

"I was raised Roman Catholic, Menachem. I believe in God, but I have no faith any more in the belief system of any religion. Religions are based on words written on paper that have been translated from one language to another many times. How can anyone rely on something created by humans. I mean, have you ever read about Joseph Smith and the tablets of gold left by the Angel Moroni? No one but Joseph Smith ever saw them. He says he found them under a tree and transcribed the words."

"Yes," Menachem said, "we have Mormon missionaries in Jerusalem and other cities in our country. The Mormons are very good people, very righteous. Who knows what is true about the founding of any religion? As humans we all search for meaning."

"You believe everything in the Torah, Talmud, and Midrash?"

"Valuable lessons are present in all the sacred writings," Menachem said. "I believe in *Eretz Israel,* the Jewish State of Israel. I will fight for this land until my last breath. This small piece of soil, this country of Israel, it is my religion."

"It's as good as any," Liam said.

Liam and Menachem sat around the small dinette table in Menachem's kitchen eating all the pizza they could hold.

"How did the voice on the phone sound? Tell me again," Menachem said.

"Very calm, very business-like. His English was excellent. I can't tell one accent from another, but he's from some country in the Middle East. All he wants is the scroll."

Liam rinsed out the Mr. Coffee carafe and made some more. "When is Mahmoud supposed to check in?"

"Sunset. Unless of course he finds something earlier."

"A lot of mountains and caves lie between Jerusalem and the Dead Sea," Liam said. "I don't think we can count on finding Ike in time to do us any good."

"What are you suggesting? Menachem asked Liam.

"I've been thinking. We need to give them the scroll."

"First we must find Mr. Ike," Menachem said.

"Not necessarily. I remember a scam this oil field promoter ran in South Louisiana. He raised money from investors who lived so far away from the well location they would never appear at the drilling site. He would dummy up a Schlumberger report, send fake logs to the investors, and tell them it was a dry hole. Not enough show to justify setting pipe. Nine of ten wildcats end up dry, so that is not unusual. He got caught when one of the investors called the State Mineral Board about the well location and the Board administrator told him they had never issued a permit for such a well."

"So you are saying give him a scroll that is not real?"

"That's right. Ike says no one's seen the Ishmael scroll except himself and the two *kibbutzniks* from Tel Qidron, the archaeologist and the linguist. And there's a chance he made it all up."

"Yitzhak's scroll is supposed to be two thousand years old and written on parchment in ancient Aramaic."

Liam snapped his fingers.

"The professor who works at the Israel Museum, the one you know, she authenticates artifacts people claim to have found. You mentioned her name and said they uncover phony ones all the time."

"Dr. Sarah Mendheim. She works in the Shrine of the Book."

"And this is probably not the first time someone has claimed to discover a scroll the same vintage as the Dead Sea Scrolls. The Museum examines them."

"Yes," Menachem said. "Some excellent forgeries have taken them months to prove they were fakes. Dr. Mendheim says there are so many crooks doing this she has good job security."

"Well, let's buy or borrow one of the fake scrolls, one that took Dr. Mendheim and her staff a long time to refute. We would also need an ancient jar, like the ones in which the Dead Sea Scrolls were found."

"It might work," Menachem said, "if they are serious about trading Mimi for the scroll. But we must control the terms of the exchange."

"I'll pay whatever the Museum wants," Liam said.

"The Museum might not be willing or able to provide these things," Menachem said. "Regulations may prevent it."

"It's a museum," Liam said. "They're always needing money. They'll sell at some price."

"Well, they are Jews," Menachem said, after thinking a moment. "Pay them enough...."

"How about a million," Liam said.

"Dollars or shekels?"

"Which is the most?"

"That would be U.S. dollars by far."

"Opening bid—one million U.S. dollars," Liam said.

Chapter Twenty-Nine

Menachem turned west off Harav Herzog Street, then drove north into the parking area adjacent to the Israel Museum.

"Just north of here is the center of government," Menachem told Liam as they walked toward the sprawling white stone buildings that housed the Museum. "The Knesset, the Supreme Court, and the Bank of Israel are just beyond."

"Lots of people," Liam said weaving around large groups of students and tourists.

A dozen young soldiers carrying automatic weapons were stationed throughout the grounds.

"This is the number one soft target in Israel," Menachem said. "Many, many people. Very symbolic as well."

The security guard next to the admission counter smiled at Menachem. He shook hands with the guard and spoke to the ticket clerk. She nodded and waved them through. Passing the exhibit areas, they reached the administrative wing of the Museum. Menachem spoke briefly to the receptionist.

"She is expecting you," the woman said. "Office suite 220."

Dr. Sarah Mendheim was waiting outside her office door.

"Hello, Sarah Mendheim," Menachem said, embracing the woman. "This is Liam Connors, the gentleman I mentioned on the phone."

"Dr. Mendheim," Liam said shaking her hand. "It's a pleasure. Thank you for seeing us."

"Menachem tells me you are from Louisiana."

"Yes. The northwestern part of the state."

"I did a year of post-graduate work at Tulane," she said. "I shall never forget New Orleans food."

Dr. Mendheim led them into her office, motioning them to sit in front of her desk. Liam estimated Dr. Mendheim to be in her early sixties, about the same age as Menachem. She was thin, with short salt and pepper hair and a nose that hooked slightly. She wore no makeup to cover the wrinkles and liver spots on her weathered skin. The wide black frames around the thick lenses of her glasses gave her the look of a serious academic.

"My old friend Menachem Wladyslaw warned me you have an unusual request, Mr. Connors," she said, winking at Menachem. "But before we get to business, I want to tell you I am inclined to do whatever you ask if it is within my power. My late husband was named Liam. His father was Irish."

"No kidding," Liam said.

"Yes," she said, "and the name means 'strong-willed,' 'wise,' and 'dog lover'. I assume you have a dog?"

"I do. An Australian Shephard. He works with me every day in the oil business. Shep. He's eight."

"I have a pug," she said. "Mickey snores like my Liam did. It is music to my ears late at night. We had a wonderful marriage. Now, what can I do for you?"

"I would like to make a donation of one million U.S. Dollars to the Museum," Liam said.

"How wonderful! How generous of you, Mr. Connors. Let me call my associate down the hall who works with individual donors and foundations. He will help us...,"

"Not yet. Hear us out," Menachem said, leaning forward in his chair and launching into a fifteen minute explanation of what they needed.

"But you haven't told me *why* you need this pot and scroll, Menachem Wladyslaw. And by the way, some of the Dead Sea Scrolls were written on papyrus, bronze, or copper as well as parchment. You might have many fake documents from which to choose."

Liam felt a surge of excitement. Dr. Mendheim sounded like she was interested in helping them.

"It needs to be written in Aramaic," Menachem said.

"I do not need to hear any more of your specifications until you tell my why Mr. Connors is willing to pay..., or rather donate such a large sum for a counterfeit artifact."

Menachem looked at Liam, who pulled his chair closer to Dr. Mendheim and rested his elbow on her desk.

"The woman I love has been kidnapped and is being held for ransom, Dr. Mendheim."

"Go on," she said and leaned back in her chair.

"I would like what I tell you to stay in this room," Liam said.

"Tell me the rest before I agree to keep your confidence. If I conclude I have to consult with my superiors to do what you ask, it will be up to you to decide to allow me to convey this information or not. If you say no, this conversation never took place."

"Okay," Liam said, looking at Menachem for approval. "A few months ago I received a Fed Ex package from an old friend of mine, Ike Palmer...."

Liam told her about his two meetings with Ike and his claim about Hagar and Abraham. He described where Ike said he found it, Mimi's disappearance from the Old City, and Ike's going into hiding. Liam went into details of the kidnappers' deman to trade Mimi for the scroll. Liam did not mention the seven dead men they found in the abandoned house in the center of Jericho.

"You know," she said, "if such a scroll does exist, it would be a very significant discovery. As your friend Ike said, it would have tremendous geopolitical repercussions."

"If it were authentic," Liam said. "But my old friend Ike may not be dependable. I don't know if he found something authentic or not."

"Is he mentally ill?" she asked.

"Probably," Liam said.

"The men who have Ms Stanton obviously think the scroll is important," Menachem said. "They are willing to kidnap an innocent American to trade for it."

"You know," Dr. Menheim said, "the authorities should be brought into this."

"Investigator Akiva Peres is working with us," Menachem said, "but I am of the opinion his superiors in the Jerusalem Police would not sanction what we are proposing to do with a fake scroll."

"You may be correct," Dr. Mendheim said. "The official policy is to pay no ransom, but what you are asking me to provide, an ersatz pot and scroll, has no actual value, so the authorities may go along."

"Once we involve anyone above Akiva Peres," Menachem said, "I am afraid there would be more interest in obtaining the actual scroll Yitzhak Palmer claims to have found. The authorities may wish to control, perhaps suppress, the contents to appease our enemies."

She took a deep breath and strummed her fingers.

"All I want is Mimi Stanton returned safely," Liam said, "and the substitute pot and scroll might be the only chance we have. We may never find Ike."

"Follow me," she said.

Dr. Mendheim led them down the hall to a reinforced door with an electronic entry system. She slid the card she wore around her neck through the device and pulled the door open. She flipped on a light and the three of them entered a room the size of a large, walk-in closet, much cooler than the hallway. Steel cabinets lined the wall opposite the door and steel shelves ran from floor to ceiling on the side walls. She pulled out a pair of latex gloves from her pocket.

"Let's take a look at this one," she said, opening the door of a small metal safe.

Dr. Mendheim removed an ancient-looking terra cotta jar from the safe and placed it on the adjacent steel shelf. She cradled the pot in her arms and opened it carefully. She pulled out a plastic bag, inside which was a document coiled around two primitive-looking wooden handles.

"This document is parchment, very old parchment. The writing is Aramaic. Our experts took more than four months to conclude it was not authentic. They carbon dated the parchment, which was indeed ancient, but not as old as the proponents claimed. From the time of Christ. Scientific tests showed it to be only a thousand years old. The jar is actually older than the parchment, but not as special. Archaeologists in this country and Jordan have found many hundreds of similar jars, older than this one."

"Where would they get parchment that old?" Liam asked.

"Criminals are very resourceful, Mr. Connors. They apparently bought or found a cache of ancient parchment and hired experts to painstakingly forge Aramaic symbols. They presented it to us along with the jar as relics from the Herodian dynasty."

"How much would it have been worth if it were real?" Liam asked.

"More than priceless," she said. "As it is, its only value is as a teaching tool."

Dr. Mendheim looked around the small room.

"Probably forty, maybe fifty more samples of forgeries and fakes in this room alone. We also have the file on the Ossuary of James that we helped disprove. Several fabricated artifacts here contain writing referring to Solomon's Temple, the Holy Grail for Jewish antiquarians. There is no physical proof the First Temple existed. Only what is set forth in the Torah. Years ago a claim that writing on an ivory pomegranate referred to King Solomon's Temple, but it was proven to be false." Dr. Mendheim caught herself. "I am sorry to bore you with my stories. "Finding your friend must be all you can think about."

"This is all fascinating, Dr. Mendheim. The jar on the shelf, the thousand-year-old parchment with the fake Aramaic writing—how long would it take an expert to invalidate them?"

"We have the best antiquarians in this country working or consulting with us. It took them four months, as I said."

Liam wanted to ask the critical question. Menachem beat him to it.

"Can we use these items to trade for Miss Stanton?"

"I don't see why not," she said.

"I'll call my bank in Louisiana and wire the money," Liam said.

"That's not necessary," Dr. Mendheim said. "At our last meeting, the board asked me to come up with a plan to dispose of these fake artifacts to make room for others. A never-ending process for us here."

"I'm going to do it anyway," Liam said.

"Wait until you have your young lady," she said. "Then if you still want to give the Israel Museum a large sum of money, we will be glad to receive it."

"Count on it," Liam said.

"Can we take it with us now?" Menachem said.

"Yes, but let me put it in a container that will protect it. You don't want to give your criminals a broken jar."

"Thank you, Dr. Mendheim," Liam said.

"I hope this works for you," she said. "It didn't work for the criminals who tried to sell it to us."

Minutes later, Liam and Menachem walked out of the Israel Museum with the thousand-year-old parchment and the terra cotta jar older than the parchment.

"You know why there are no artifacts from Solomon's Temple?" Menachem asked Liam, anger in his voice. "I will tell you. There can be no excavation at Temple Mount, though everyone agrees it is where the Holy of Holies was located. *Moos-lim* authorities say digging would desecrate their holy buildings, the Dome of the Rock and Al Aqsa Mosque. So Israel is prevented from acquiring the proof that the Temple Mount should house a Jewish temple, not Islamic buildings."

Menachem pulled his vibrating phone from his pocket. He listened for a moment and turned to Liam.

"It's Mahmoud."

Chapter Thirty

The back end of the Volvo slid around the curve on the rock strewn dirt road in mountains ten kilometers northeast of Herodium. Liam stared into the dark, rugged mountain landscape searching for the landmark. The two men were to meet Mahmoud and Brother, but it was slow going in the mountains, the roads much worse than they appeared on the map. The Volvo engine groaned and its suspension creaked on the steep, rocky grades.

"What year is this car?" Liam asked.

"Only as old as it feels, and she feels good. Take my word."

"No mountains like this in Louisiana."

"Do not worry. I am a professional."

Menachem chuckled and the Volvo strained to reach another summit. Liam searched for the obelisk.

"It is a rock formation in the shape of an obelisk," Menachem had said after Mahmoud called as they left the Israel Museum, "at the crest of a hill. Mahmoud will hang a white cloth from the remains of a scenic overlook sign. He and Brother will be waiting there."

"We're coming to another hilltop, but it's getting too dark to see anything."

"There," Menachem said, pointing to a flashing light.

"That's got to be Mahmoud," Liam said.

Menachem pulled off the road. They walked to the light.

"Mahmoud?" Menachem whispered in the darkness.

Mahmoud answered. He and Brother followed Liam and Menachem back to the Volvo. Liam strapped on the tactical equipment they had picked up from Menachem's garage, including night vision goggles, six water bottles velcroed to a black belt around their waists, their pistols and Fenix E01 flashlights.

"Ready," Liam said, as he adjusted the Glock in the holster on his hip and adjusted his goggles.

The four of them walked single file from the overlook, Mahmoud in the lead. Down a steep incline, through a *wadi* and up a rocky hill, Liam and Menachem managed to keep up with the boys at first, but gradually lagged behind.

"These guys can cover some ground," Liam said.

"Goats," Menachem grunted.

Liam watched Mahmoud bounce without hesitation up the mountain from one rocky crag to another. Liam's night vision goggles were cumbersome and disorienting. He took his time climbing, and eventually caught up with Mahmoud and his brother, sitting casually on a boulder near the top of the small mountain.

"You guys are fast," Liam said, removing his goggles.

Mahmoud pointed into the darkness and spoke Arabic.

"A cave," Menachem said as he joined them.

"I see it," Liam said, putting his goggles back on. "Let's go."

The cave didn't seem far away until Liam realized they were going to have to descend the back side of the very mountain they just climbed up, then cross a rocky structure to another hill and climb another two hundred feet to the cave.

Mahmoud and his brother beat Liam and Menachem to the cave by fifteen minutes and waited at the entrance. Liam removed his goggles and turned on his flashlight. Menachem followed him slowly into the cave. It was more than ten feet deep inside the mountain and tall enough for them to stand.

"Look at this," Liam said, shining his light on the remnants of a fire near the mouth of the cave.

"Get's cold in here at night," Menachem said, "especially when you're not wearing these."

Liam shined his light a pair of black slacks and a man's white shirt. He examined the clothes.

"This is Ike's waiter's outfit," Liam said.

Chapter Thirty-One

Forty miles east of the cave, Anton Brodie looked out over the lights of Amman from the balcony of his suite in the Four Seasons Hotel on a hill in the center of the city. It had been a smooth flight from Geneva in his Gulfstream 550. The drive from the airport to the Four Seasons in the steel-reinforced Mercedes limousine had also been uneventful. Amman was now his preferred venue for meetings in the Middle East. The Hashemite Kingdom of Jordan was relatively stable, though impoverished in comparison with its neighbors. It was much easier for Brodie to maintain a low profile in Amman than in the glitzy venues of Dubai in the Emirates or the Kingdom of Bahrain. Moving below radar was important to Brodie, whose whereabouts were often tracked by copycat currency traders in London who tried to guess Brodie's monetary strategies by following his travels around the globe.

Amman was becoming a financial center because of its relative stability and receptiveness to Western businesses. Brodie hoped King Abdullah II would be able to hang on to power. The many construction cranes Brodie could see from his balcony were a direct result of forward-thinking economic policies introduced by the youthful-looking, English educated King, a direct descendant of the great grandfather of the Prophet Muhammad. Foreign investment was pouring into the capital city. In spite of Jordan's hosting almost a million Palestinian refugees and more recently Iraqis and Syrians fleeing their war-torn countries, the Arab Spring had not blossomed in Jordan as it had in other Muslim countries in the Middle East. Brodie hoped King Abdullah II enjoyed a long reign. A prosperous Jordan with a healthy financial climate was good for Brodie's business.

Anton Brodie was eighty, but he felt so good he did not think about his age. His hair was white and unruly, his face wrinkled and worn, but his eyes burned bright, reflecting a cunning intelligence that seemed enhanced, not diminished by his years. He had come a long way. His Jewish parents had smuggled him out of the Ukraine into Switzerland in 1935. He was two. The family immigrated to the United States in 1961 and westernized their family name from

Brutkaniuk to Brodie. By the time Anton Brodie was sworn in as an American citizen, he was already on his way to building his currency trading empire.

For twenty-five years, from the mid-sixties to the late eighties, Brodie made incredible profits from global conflicts. He was a genius at predicting outcomes, and would go long or short in currencies, stocks, and commodities, depending on whatever political struggle he was gaming. He placed most of his trades in London, the world's largest foreign-exchange hub. But the remarkable wealth he had accumulated by 1990 was not enough. He had to have more—more than anyone else. When he turned sixty, Brodie decided he would no longer wait patiently for geopolitical disputes and wars to occur organically. He became proactive, inciting conflicts by funding one insurgency or another. On occasion he gave money to *both* sides in an armed struggle for control of a region. Brodie was unencumbered by religious or political beliefs. He was born to Jewish parents, but never religious. At an early age he concluded there was no God. And he had zero allegiance to the State of Israel. He could not have cared less about *Eretz Israel* or Zionism. Nor did he feel any loyalty to the United States or Western Europe, even though free market capitalism had enabled him to amass his wealth.

Anton Brodie's only allegiance was to money.

Brodie glanced at his watch. Al Dub and Hazara were scheduled to knock on his door in fifteen minutes. Brodie had worked with the Syrian Akmal Kassab since meeting with him in the United States in 1992. Looking back, the decision to team up with Al Dub, "the Bear," had been a stroke of brilliance. The Syrian *émigré* to the Boston area burned with religious hatred toward the United States. Al Dub had impressed Brodie with his fervor and the contacts he had made with *jihadists* living on the East Coast from Maine to D.C. The hierarchy of Al Qaeda followers in the U.S. knew him well, as did members of the international organizations that would later become known in the West as Al Qaeda in the Arabian Peninsula (AQAP) and Al Qaeda in the Islamic Maghreb (AQIM). All organizations needed money to fund terror. With Brodie's fortune at his disposal, his emissary Al Dub was welcome in all the *jihadist* circles in the United States, Europe, Africa, and the Middle East.

Brodie had earned huge profits from currency and stock market moves following the WTC bombing in 1993, the U.S. Embassy bombings in Kenya and Tanzania in 1998, and the USS Cole bombing in 2000. But it was the avalanche of money he made in the wake of the financial and currency market crashes after 9/11 that vaulted Brodie near the top of every financial magazine's list of wealthiest people on the planet. Hailed as a market genius in the few interviews he granted, Brodie was suitably humble, the beneficiary of "lucky, educated guesses." In truth, with his singular advance knowledge of terrorist attacks, it was child's play to make tidal waves of money in their wake. And Anton Brodie was the only financier in the world with the information.

Anton Brodie could predict future events because he was instrumental in creating them. Through Al Dub, Brodie had invested in many terrorist incidents that roiled the civilized world, including the event with the greatest financial impact early in the 21st Century: the destruction of the twin towers of the World Trade Center and the attack on the Pentagon on September 11, 2001.

Brodie heard a knock on his door. Peering through the security hole he saw a shiny bald head. Brodie opened the door and welcomed Al Dub, "the Bear," with kisses on each cheek. Putting his arm around Al Dub's shoulders, Brodie ushered him to the sitting area near the balcony. Though he had worked with Al Dub for twenty years, he was always impressed by the Syrian's thick shoulders, barrel chest and his strong arms blanketed with a thick mat of dark hair, the inspiration for his nickname.

"Welcome, my partner," Brodie laughed. "You appear to be in good health for a man of your advanced age."

"Not as spry as I used to be."

"But you have your health. We are both blessed. Tell me how you have faired."

Before Al Dub could answer, they heard a soft knock. Al Dub rose from his seat and hustled to the door. He glanced through the security hole, then opened the door for Hazara, who walked inside, taking long easy strides. Hazara was slender, darker than Al Dub, and at least nine inches taller. He shook hands with Brodie and sat down.

"So, you have the American woman," Brodie said.

"Since this morning at three o'clock. She is now in Bethlehem, well-secured and guarded by The Black and two others."

"Any unexpected difficulty?"

"No. The Sunni zealots were incompetent, sleeping soundly as we moved through the house. I lost one man. He was careless. Not important."

Brodie glanced quickly at Al Dub, expecting him to bristle at the mention of his Sunni faith, but the Syrian remained calm. "The Bear" was becoming more devout as he aged. It had begun to wear on Brodie. Al Dub's simmering rage against Israel and the United

States was based on his belief that the two countries were bent on destroying Islam. Al Dub's religious zeal had been useful to Brodie in the past; it fueled Al Dub's desire to make the acts of terror on which they collaborated as deadly as possible. His devotion to *jihad* also made him willing to work for very little money. In their unusual partnership, Brodie made billions in profits. For the most part, Al Dub drew his satisfaction from the death of infidels.

Brodie was more accustomed to dealing with men like Hazara, who was in it solely for the money. The Afghani was a professional, a mercenary paid to do a job. He was born Shia, a circumstance of no importance to Hazara. He killed Shias, Sunnis, Jews, Christians, even atheists with equal efficiency and lack of remorse. Anton Brodie's identity had remained hidden from Hazara until this mission to obtain the scroll. For the first time, Brodie insisted that Al Dub give Hazara his name and contact information. Brodie told Al Dub it was precautionary, insurance against something happening to Al Dub. Brodie's real purpose was to develop a relationship. He had already spoken to Hazara on three occasions. The Afghan's direct manner and clarity of purpose was refreshing to Brodie, who had grown tired of the religious commentary Al Dub inserted in every conversation with Brodie.

"Is the woman comfortable?" Brodie asked Hazara.

"More than she was in Jericho. She is confined and shackled, but she will be given clean water, better food."

"Keep her unharmed in case we must show her to the American to facilitate the exchange."

"You plan on letting her live?" Al Dub asked.

"It doesn't matter if she lives or dies as long as we get the scroll," Brodie said. "That is an operational matter that doesn't concern me. I leave it in your capable hands. But remember, Akmal Kassab, the scroll is to be preserved at all cost."

"I am out of the money you gave me on Mount Nebo," Hazara said to Al Dub. "I need it tonight."

"What on earth for?" Al Dub demanded.

"Be calm, Akmal," Brodie said laughing. "You act as if it is your money." Brodie turned to Hazara. "Whatever you need."

"Too much money interferes with...."

"Not everyone is motivated by spiritual beliefs, Akmal. People like Hazara and I understand that money is power."

"The lust for money is a sin," Al Dub said.

"Some might say the murder of millions in the name of religion is unholy. Personally, I don't care. How about you Hazara?"

"I do what I am hired to do, Mr. Brodie," Hazara said. "Nothing else is relevant to me."

"There," Brodie said with a smile to Al Dub, "a like-minded soul."

"We should go over some details," Al Dub said.

"I agree. What am I to do when I obtain the scroll?" Hazara asked.

"The girl will have to be held until the experts I've hired verify the authenticity of the document," Al Dub said. "When I'm satisfied it's real, I will call you to release her."

"That will be difficult to arrange," Hazara said. "They will not release the scroll until they have the girl."

"Think of something," Brodie said.

"The American claims he does not possess the scroll and does not know where it is," Hazara said.

"What'd you expect him to say?" Al Dub said. "Tell him you'll kill the girl unless he delivers the scroll."

"She's not to be eliminated," Brodie said, "until we have the scroll in our control."

"We can work this out with the American," Hazara said to Al Dub. "Right now I need money."

Al Dub stood up. Irritated.

"You should have told me before I got here."

"I am telling you now," Hazara said.

Al Dub wanted to slap Hazara down, but decided to save it for another time. No need to argue in front of Mr. Brodie.

"Stay here. I will be back in twenty minutes. You will have your precious money."

"I am good to wait," Hazara said.

Al Dub nodded to Brodie and walked quickly to the door. After he was gone, Brodie looked at Hazara and smiled.

"Now that our devout Muslim is no longer here to be offended by my use of alcohol, how about a drink?"

"American bourbon if you have it."

"Most certainly."

Brodie poured two drinks and sat down.

"Now, Hazara," Brodie said, "tell me about yourself. Is it true that your people, the Hazarajat, are direct descendants of Genghis Khan?"

Chapter Thirty-Two

Isaac Benjamin Palmer woke up with the rising sun. Only an hour's sleep on the hard floor of the cave. Looking east, Ike absorbed the sun's rays, which warmed him and eased his soreness. He stretched and massaged his aging muscles and joints.

"No Spring chicken anymore," he said and chuckled.

Ike slipped out of the rough goat skin tunic he bought from the old Bedouin woman three days before and faced the sun naked. He extended his arms and spread his feet wide like da Vinci's five hundred-year-old drawing, the radiation penetrating him, making him one with Yahweh and his universe. He closed his eyes and spoke in a loud voice.

I am the man I have become. I am Your instrument. You have chosen me though I am not worthy to speak Your Name. You are in me and I am in You. Do with me as You will.

Ike's penis stirred and began to swell.

The time is now. You have led me to Your truth hidden in these holy mountains. I am Your messenger. I will shout Your Truth from on high. It will echo through this land. The land You promised Your people. Those begat of Abraham.

Ike was fully erect and throbbing. His shout became louder, echoing down the mountain and into the *wadi* below.

Hark unto me you descendants of Ishmael. I shall visit upon you the Truth and you shall be ashamed. His Truth shall drive you from this sacred land. I will lead His chosen people in the Truth. They will heed His Truth and follow me.

Ike spasmed and released, his seed spilling onto the rocks below.

Ike woke up grinning after thirty minutes. He had dreamed about ninety-year-old Sarah laughing when the angel Michael told her she would bear a child. *Yitzhak* would be the child's name, as was his own—Hebrew for Isaac, meaning laughter.

He began to laugh and could not stop. He imagined the shocked looks on the faces of the *imams* and *ayatollahs* when he told the world the truth about Ishmael's lineage. It was written in the sacred scroll, there in black and white—the Truth, plainly written. Islam had no right to this land. Its followers were trespassers. Ike laughed louder as he imagined Muhammadans retreating from Israel in shame, settling east of the Euphrates to lay claim to other lands.

He always knew the pills inhibited his path to complete union with The Almighty. He had stopped taking them two weeks earlier and felt his neural pathways opening. A trickle at first, now full bore. Ike was receiving The Spirit and it was good. Twenty-four years of chemical muting gone in two weeks. Like Hercules rerouting the Rivers Alpheus and Peneus to clean the Augean stables. He felt better than he had ever felt in his fifty-three years. No time for sleep. The night before was typical of the last four. Wide awake after the sun dipped behind the mountains, praying, singing, and rejoicing in the Spirit until an hour before daybreak. Resting and rising with the sun. Yahweh was in him. Time for the Awakening of the Chosen People; time to reclaim all of *Eretz Israel*.

But first, he had to tear down and reassemble the rock altar he built the day before on the ledge outside the cave. Looking at it this morning, he knew it was not quite right. He would remove each stone carefully, placing them inside the cave, stone by stone. A backbreaking job, but it was something he was led by The Almighty to do.

He lifted the first stone and laughed with delight. Naked in the morning sun, Ike moved the stones and sang to Yahweh in his mind. At times the interior colloquy erupted in actual shouts and songs of praise, but he was unaware of the difference.

Two hours later he moved the last stone into the cave. He admired his work, twirling his sore naked body on the ledge, a Judaic whirling dervish alone in the mountains. Then he lay on the ledge a moment and closed his eyes. He nodded off, but only for a second. The Spirit of Yahweh infused his brain and Ike was again on his feet spinning. After a few minutes, he stopped to study the stones piled in the cave. Now. Time to begin the holy task of rebuilding the altar on the ledge.

Ike searched the cave for the largest, flattest stone. He laid it carefully on the ledge. Hands on hips, Ike admired his work and began to laugh uncontrollably, doubled over, slapping his naked thighs, roaring out to the mountains. After a while he stopped to give thanks to Yahweh for His guidance in selecting the first stone, the most important one he would choose.

Cornerstone of the Holy of Holies.

He imagined himself standing alone on the dais at a convocation of world leaders, reading from the scroll. Each leader understood Ike in the leader's own language, without the use of electronics or interpreters. Yet another miracle buttressing the legitimacy of the scroll as a message from Yahweh. One by one, the leaders rose to applaud, to shout allegiance to this Yitzhak Palmer and his scroll.

Several hours later, the altar again complete, Ike thought about making a pilgrimage to the other cave—*the* cave where he kept the actual scroll. He squinted into the sun and decided he would begin his ministry, the Awakening of the Israelites, the very next day. He lay down naked to rest his eyes, there on top of the hairy goatskin, and fell asleep.

Chapter Thirty-Three

Liam woke up from a deep sleep. He had no idea where he was. After they found Ike's clothes the night before, they had searched another half-dozen caves in the mountains. No other signs of Ike. At five a.m., Mahmoud's younger brother began to cry. Mahmoud said something to Menachem in Arabic.

"They need rest," Menachem told Liam. "So do I."

Liam and Menachem left the boys in the mountains and returned to Jerusalem. They pulled the Volvo into Menachem's garage at six a.m. Liam handed his night vision goggles to Menachem, vowing he would never wear them again. In the mountains, Menachem had told him he would get used to them, but Liam never did. Seeing everything in an eerie green glow was disorienting. His depth perception was not reliable and he lost his balance several times, catching himself before falling. Menachem hung the goggles from a hook on the garage wall and suggested Liam get some rest.

Liam heard the oscillating fan and propped himself up on the air mattress and looked around. In the kitchen he saw Menachem, dressed and making coffee. Now he remembered. Liam slid on his pants, rolled over on his stomach and pushed himself up. He found it the easiest way from the air mattress to the floor.

"What time is it?" Liam asked Menachem.

"Noon."

Liam picked up the black pants and white long-sleeved shirt from the kitchen floor and held them out to Menachem.

"These are definitely Ike's."

"Yes," Menachem said and poured Liam a cup of coffee. "The clothes have not been in that cave very long."

"It was cold in those mountains last night."

"The fire was not old. Two days maybe. The Bedouins told Mahmoud the man they saw was wearing animal skins. You can buy them in these mountains from goatherds."

"Mahmoud and his brother seemed right at home in those rocks. You and I slowed them down. You think they understood about the bonus for finding him?"

"I made that very clear yesterday," Menachem said. "Believe me, Mahmoud and Brother don't have to be reminded about money."

Liam sipped his coffee and placed his mug on the dinette table. He picked up Dr. Mendheim's box from the counter and placed it on the table. He removed the Styrofoam packing and carefully placed the pot on the table. He took off the top and pointed to the aged parchment inside.

"The Ishmael Scroll. In Aramaic."

"Better to possess the real thing," Menachem said. "Assuming Yitzhak has actually found the real thing."

"A layman wouldn't know just by looking. You heard Dr. Mendheim. It takes months of testing."

"We should offer Dr. Mendheim's jar and scroll only if our search for Ike fails. I am not giving up on Mahmoud and Brother. They are resourceful. Never can they earn such an amount of money."

"We cannot agree to an exchange unless we get Mimi immediately. They won't have time to authenticate it."

"I do not know what to say. Anyone who resides in Israel lives here will be aware. It is in the newspapers. Several times a year a government announcement reveals that an artifact they have examined, a sarcophagus or gold scarab amulet or whatever—is a fake."

"I've been giving the exchange some thought," Liam said.

Menachem's phone rang. He answered and walked through the garage to his back yard to talk. In ten minutes he returned.

"That was Brother," he said. "They've located Yitzhak. Mahmoud is watching his cave now."

"How much further?"

"Not far."

"You can do better than that."

"Maybe twenty minutes," Menachem said.

Liam's Glock was pinching his side. He moved it to his stomach and checked his watch. One-thirty. Four full days since Mimi had been taken. Every hour increased the likelihood she would be harmed. Liam's neck was uncomfortably tight. He fidgeted in his seat and hit his thigh with the bottom of his closed fist. He should have stayed away from Ike Palmer. If Mahmoud actually had him cornered, Liam wasn't giving Ike a choice. Liam was taking the scroll. If Ike didn't have it with him, Liam was going to wring his scrawny neck until he led them to it.

"Dammit," Liam muttered.

He stared out his window at the vivid blue sky and the stark landscape on either side of the dirt road. There was little foliage, just rocks and sand. Moonscape. Jerusalem was arid, but lush compared to these mountains east of the city. Liam rubbed his hands together, squeezing his fingers. Deep in recrimination.

"You promised to tell me what your government did to you," Menachem said, looking over at Liam.

"Huh?"

"On your sale."

"Oh," Liam said, clearing his throat. "As soon as news of my pending sale to Delaware Energy became public the EPA and Louisiana's DEQ began doing one thing after another to shut my fields down."

"Like what?"

"First, the state DEQ sued me. Pollution. They claimed it resulted from my salt water disposal wells. Then EPA decided I had to start measuring the CO_2 off my compressors operating on wells all over northwest Louisiana, something that had never been required before. Finally, for the first time in U.S. drilling history they made a big deal out of naturally occurring radioactive material that had collected in the steel pipes over decades. The industry has known about it for years. There's no way to prevent it. They wanted drillers to collect it, which is the worst thing you could do. Widely disseminated radioactive particles do no harm. I mean, they occur naturally in the soil. If you collect them and get a big pile of radioactive stuff, then you have a problem. They wanted me to create a problem where none existed."

"Sounds like something the Israeli government would do."

"So I filed suit against the EPA and the state DEQ in Shreveport. Then the crap really hit the fan. They tried to shut down my operations, nullify the deal with Delaware. All of a sudden I had audits from the IRS and Department of Energy. OSHA began conducting disruptive inspections of my rigs. Luckily, the Shreveport District Judge ruled in my favor in successive injunction hearings. Delaware wanted the 15,000 acres so badly they agreed to pay the government $5 million to settle all claims. So that's what we did. We closed and Delaware is drilling the deep shale wells as we speak."

"And you made how much?"

"It was a very nice sum."

There was no need to tell Menachem he walked away from the closing with $150 million gross before taxes. Capital gains tax was still 15%, so after all federal and state taxes Liam netted $120 million. The deal he negotiated allowed him to retain his shallow production and keep a small override on Delaware's wells. Liam netted many millions every year from the existing shallow wells. When Delaware's shale production came online, Liam's override would dwarf his current income.

"What did your investigators find out?" Menachem asked. "You said there was one bureaucrat."

"In one of my first deals—leasing up old fields in the mid-nineties—I dealt with a nice lady, Mrs. Lillian Bodenheimer, of Zwolle, Louisiana. She owned a lot of land with wells that had been shut-in, abandoned. I made her a fair deal to lease her properties. She was getting no revenue from the shut-in wells. I agreed to pay her the same bonus and royalty payments I paid everyone. When I began producing the wells, she started getting substantial royalty checks every month. The revenue has continued, even after her death a couple of years ago.

"Mrs. Bodenheimer had one son, David, who has been a federal government employee his entire working career. He's now in the Department of Energy. He looked at the deal his late mother made with me and concluded I had swindled her. Simply not true. It was my standard deal. Fair for the landowner, fair for me. His mother made a ton of money off the royalties, and her estate continues to be paid right now. David Bodenheimer started a one-man campaign against me inside the government, persuading friends and former co-workers in different agencies I was a scam artist, stealing from little old ladies. He used the EPA, Energy, OSHA, and the IRS to try to ruin me. My friend Willie Mitchell Banks, the Mississippi lawyer helped me fight them. He's been in it from the beginning, and still helps me."

"Your own Louisiana Senators refused to help you with the Embassy here?"

"Right. Those two nitwit Senators are scared of the bureaucrats and sided with them in the fight. They called me after it was over. I wouldn't take their calls. They'll hear from me when they have to run for re-election. When Mimi and I return to the U.S., I'm going to sue Bodenheimer and the government and I'm going to find out who's running against each senators and raise money for them from my oil and gas buddies all over America."

"All that trouble from one disgruntled government employee?"

"Scary, isn't it? The Founding Fathers are spinning in their graves. Government controls everything but can't do shit right. You ought to see what they've done with our health care system."

"Look," Menachem said pointing to Mahmoud's brother on the side of the dirt road, jumping up and down and waving at the Volvo.

Menachem pulled off the road and questioned Brother.

"Mahmoud is watching the cave where Yitzhak is hiding," Menachem said to Liam. "We have to go on foot from here."

"I'm taking my Glock."

"Yes, and much water. Let us go have a talk with Yitzhak Palmer."

Chapter Thirty-Four

Mimi sat up when she heard the door open. She had been half-asleep. Her circadian rhythms were getting back to normal, thanks to the light coming through the small, barred windows high on the basement wall. She was pretty sure it was afternoon. Her stomach was feeling better, too, no doubt due to the bottled water her new captors provided. Compared to the pitch black bathroom where she had been kept before, the basement accommodations rated four-stars.

When the light and muffled city sounds had waked her, she began thinking of Liam. How much she missed him and their life together. Before being taken from the Old City, Mimi had been living a fairy tale. Her childhood years and her married life had both been dysfunctional, through no fault of her own. She had resigned herself to a future consisting of her nursing career and many lonely nights. Then she met Liam Connors. What a man. Even if she did not survive this ordeal, she was grateful for her year with Liam, the happiest year of her life.

No one had ever treated her as well as Liam. She knew he had adored his first wife, Annette. He was still grieving when they met in Dr. Vercher's office. Liam referred to Annette's fatal accident early on in their relationship, and Mimi made a point to learn the details from Dr. Vercher. Annette was almost finished with the renovation of Grand Oaks down the river from Natchitoches, when a drunk crossed fifty yards of I-49 median and hit her car head on as she was driving back to Shreveport. It was almost a year-and-a-half after the tragedy when Mimi walked into the examination room and introduced herself to the tall, handsome stranger. Over a year of "dating," Mimi had come to know Liam's daughters: Christine, twenty-five, an up-and-coming fashion designer in Dallas, beginning to get noticed in the Texas fashion world; Rebecca, twenty-three, with a degree from SMU in petroleum engineering and a minor in finance. She had returned to Shreveport after graduation to learn the ropes at Clare Petroleum. Liam began training her to eventually take over the supervision of the shallow production he had retained in the sale to Delaware Energy. He would concentrate on finding and developing new prospects. Protective of their father, Christine and Rebecca accepted Mimi as his "girl friend." The time Mimi spent with Liam's girls had been pleasant, and Mimi liked them both. Their maturity and independence Mimi attributed to learning to live with the loss of their mother. Mimi told them she could not have children. Knowing their father would not be having a second family probably made it easier for them to accommodate Mimi.

After hearing the door Mimi sat with her back against the wall and watched a man she had not seen before walk slowly down the steps, holding several bottles of water. He was dressed in a full length black *thawb*. The black turban draped around the lower half of his face covered all but his eyes.

As he walked closer to Mimi, she noticed his eyes—as black as his clothing and ferocious. The man did not blink. He gave her the bottles of water, then stood over her with his arms crossed and stared at her for several minutes. His eyes were unlike those of the man from the previous day, the man with the cultured voice. Mimi studied the man, shuddered and turned away.

What is he going to do to me?

Mimi kept her head down. She could see his sandals and his long, dirty toenails. Finally, he walked away. She glanced up in time to see him stop on the steps and glare back at her before taking the remaining steps and closing the door.

She heard the bolt slide into place.

Chapter Thirty-Five

Mahmoud's brother stopped at the top of the hill. He sat on a rock waiting for Liam and Menachem. They had been climbing an hour. When they caught up Menachem spoke to Brother in Arabic.

"He says the cave is just over the next hill," Menachem said.

"Let's go," Liam said. "We can rest later."

Menachem said a few words to Brother. He nodded and took off, Liam close behind. Twenty minutes later at the crest of the next rise, Brother stopped and pointed to a cave two hundred yards away, a dark opening on the side of a steep incline. He said something to Menachem.

The white underbelly of a magnificent Nubian ibex goat on a ridge above them caught Liam's eye. He admired the goat's horns, extending back from its forehead and curving down and in like a question mark. The goat studied the awkward two-legged creatures invading his territory, and disappeared over the ridge.

"That cave is where Yitzhak is hiding," Menachem said to Liam. "See Mahmoud? Way up there?"

Brother pointed to an outcropping well above the cave. Liam looked through his binoculars.

"There. Mahmoud," Liam said and gave the binoculars to Menachem.

"That's him," Menachem said and listened to Brother.

"He says we have to approach the cave from above. It is dangerous. We must be very quiet. Our voices carry on the winds. Yitzhak would be able to hear us as though we were standing next to him in the cave."

Liam and Menachem followed Brother along the ridge running south of the cave. Fifteen minutes later, they were a hundred feet above the outcropping where Mahmoud was hiding. Brother asked them to wait while he climbed down slowly. They watched the boy descend, being careful not to dislodge any rocks.

"I didn't realize this incline was so steep," Liam said. "It's almost straight down."

"If we fall we are dead for sure," Menachem said. "My fault we did not bring climbing rope."

Liam watched Brother reach Mahmoud's hiding place and disappear under the outcropping. In a few moments both boys climbed up from the outcropping to join Menachem and Liam. Menachem patted both boys on the shoulders. Liam gave each of them a bottle of water. Menachem whispered to Mahmoud, who responded quickly in animated Arabic, pointing to the cave below.

"Yitzhak is in the cave," Menachem whispered, "but Mahmoud says it is very dangerous to reach from here. Not so dangerous climbing up but going down is difficult. If we slip it is a long way to the bottom."

"What does he think we should do?" Liam asked.

"He says to wait Yitzhak out. He may not have carried much water or supplies. Mahmoud believes Yitzhak cannot stay in the cave much longer."

"Is he sure Ike's still in there?" Liam said.

"Remember the ridge where we first saw the cave? Mahmoud was there. He saw Yitzhak climb down and enter. He has not left."

"He's sure it was him?" Liam asked.

"He says the man was wearing an animal skin," Menachem said.

"John the Baptist," Liam said.

Mahmoud whispered. Menachem looked puzzled. He spoke to the boy again. Mahmoud nodded and grinned.

"What?" Liam asked.

"Mahmoud says Ike has been dancing naked on that ledge in front of the cave. Spinning around with his arms outstretched, shouting to the clouds. He says he has been stacking rocks on the ledge many hours. Naked."

"Naked. He's nutty as a fruitcake," Liam said. "Well, I'm not just going to sit here like a bump on a log. Who knows how much time Mimi has before the men holding her decide they've waited long enough. Let's do this. I'm going down there."

"I will come with you."

"No," Liam said to Menachem. "You and Brother stay here. If Mahmoud and I fall off this mountain go to Akiva Peres. Tell him everything and you two find Mimi. Promise me."

"You have my word."

Menachem spoke to the two boys. He grabbed Liam by the shoulders. "Be careful, my friend."

Mahmoud led the way down. Liam stepped carefully from rock to rock, always leaning against the mountain, testing his footing carefully before putting his full weight on the next step. Fifteen feet above the outcropping where Mahmoud had hidden, Liam dislodged a rock. It tumbled down the incline toward the cave, gathering rocks and debris as it went. They stopped their descent, waiting and watching. After five minutes Mahmoud resumed the climb. Liam followed, checking each step. Within moments they reached the outcropping and waved to Menachem and Brother before the disappeared under the rocks.

The clatter of rocks around the cave startled Ike. He sat up. He had been dreaming about leading a phalanx of Israelites into Nazareth, expelling the trespassing Islamists, using nothing more than the scroll. The Force of His Truth.

He crept out on the ledge and looked around, careful to keep himself well-concealed. Startled, Ike recognized Liam with an Arab boy under the outcropping. His thoughts raced. He knew what had happened. His old friend had sold him out to the Muslims despite his promise of strictest confidence. Liam must have informed the Islamists about the scroll. Son of a bitch. What to do?

It came to him. So obvious. Take the empty jar and run. They would be unable to keep up with him. Find a more remote cave. He put on his goatskin, picked up the terra cotta jar and walked out onto the ledge. He chanted to Yahweh's altar a moment, stood well within the traitor's view and shouted.

"Ammonites. Moabites. Edomites. Babylonians. Get thee behind me. I must be about my Father's business. I am chosen to proclaim His Truth, led to the scroll by Yahweh Himself, commissioned to reveal to the world that Ishmael was not the blood of Abraham."

Ike tucked the jar under his arm. Time to move. Accustomed to moving swiftly among the rocks, he was certain they could not follow. Yahweh would guide his feet.

Lying on the outcropping, eyes glued to the cave entrance, Liam tried to convince himself Ike might have slept through the mini-avalanche. Ike stepped into view wearing his goat hair tunic, shaking his fist toward Liam yelling something.

"Crap," Liam muttered. "So much for surprise."

Liam had never seen Ike like this. Barefoot, his hair wild, his face dark and dirty. Liam could tell he was in some kind of frenzy. Ike shook his fist and screamed. Liam couldn't understand the words, so he edged himself into view, hoping to calm his old friend.

"Hey, Ike. It's Liam. Let's talk. They still have Mimi. Come on, man. I need your help."

Ike shouted. Liam had no clue what he was saying. It was a foreign language. Or maybe insane gibberish.

"What did he say?" Liam asked Mahmoud.

Mahmoud shook his head. Ike screamed louder and disappeared into the cave. A moment later he emerged, clutching something under his arm. A terra cotta jar. Whatever his plan, Ike was taking the scroll with him.

Ike left the ledge, his bare feet stepping from rock to rock in his herky-jerky manner. He squeezed the jar under his arm, using one hand to negotiate his way down the treacherous slope.

A gust of wind blew sand in Liam's face. When he opened his eyes, he saw the Nubian ibex in the rocks below, calmly watching Ike trying to negotiate the steep incline.

"Stay where you are, Ike," Liam said. "No one's going to hurt you."

Ike shook his fist violently at Liam. His foot slipped. He tried to regain his balance with his free hand but the rocks gave way. Ike's feet went out from under him and he fell hard, tumbling headlong down the mountain like a rag doll, hitting one crag then another. Sliding the final hundred feet, his body came to rest in the deep white sand on the floor of the bone dry *wadi*.

Mahmoud and Liam climbed down the slope as fast as they could manage. After seeing Ike fall, caroming from rock to rock, they moved deliberately down the deadly incline, making sure of each step. Above them, Brother led Menachem further along on the ridge before taking a route with less incline to enter the *wadi* from the north. They walked the meandering stream bed to where Ike lay on his back. Liam knelt beside him, trying to make him comfortable. Liam had taken off his own shirt to wad it into a makeshift pillow. Mahmoud stood to the side, watching the crazy American die.

Ike's glacier blue eyes were wide open. His breathing was shallow, his lips dry and cracked.

"Damn, Ike," Liam said. "Why didn't you stay in the cave?"

"You told," Ike rasped. "The scroll. Secret."

"No, I did not. You hang on. We're going for help."

Ike managed a smile, then a quiet laugh that grew into a cough that spewed blood onto Ike's chest. The goat skin tunic had been torn off in the fall. Brother retrieved it a short distance up the incline and handed it to Liam, who draped it over Ike's mid-section.

Liam looked at what was left of his friend. He had open fractures. Bones protruded from bleeding gashes on his arms and legs. His right foot was turned inward at an impossible angle. His face was distorted; his left orbital bones crushed flat causing his eye to bulge. Liam listened to his chest. An ominous rattle. It was all bad, but the worst visible injury was to Ike's head. His skull was fractured. Blood oozed from his temple and the back of his head onto the white sand. Serum and plasma seeped out, leaving small fragments of brain tissue collecting on the surface.

"The jar...?" Ike said. "Ishmael?"

Menachem motioned to Mahmoud to bring over the shards of terra cotta he had collected from the *wadi* and up the rocky incline. Menachem spoke to Mahmoud. Mahmoud shook his head. Menachem held the shards for Ike to see.

"No. Nothing," Ike said, his voice hoarse and wet. "Real one in another cave, not far up...."

Ike squeezed Liam's forearm. He could only whisper now. Liam bent down to listen.

"Get scroll..., tell them I found it. True. I was..., not crazy."

Ike took his last breath. Liam closed his old Louisiana friend's eyes and made the sign of the cross.

"What do you want to...?" Menachem said.

Liam pulled a large wad of U.S. paper money out of his pocket and gave it to Menachem.

"Give this to Mahmoud and his brother. Tell them to get some water and supplies. Check every cave within a five kilometer radius of this spot. I'll pay them the same amount when they finish, triple the amount if they find the other jar with parchment or copper in it."

"Very well. But, I do not think you should expect them to find anything. Yitzhak has caused much trouble with his stories."

"Ike Palmer—a good heart. He may have lived in a fantasy world, but he knew he was dying. Maybe he told the truth this time. I mean, what do we have to lose?"

The boys' eyes widened when Menachem gave them the money. He talked to them. They nodded enthusiastically and took off running through the *wadi*. After they were out of sight, Liam took out his phone and snapped several pictures of Ike lying dead on the bloody white sand.

"Let's rig up something to carry Ike's body back to the car," Liam said. "We'll wrap him best we can. Put him in the trunk of the Volvo. When we get to your place I'm going to call the bastard and send him these pictures. I'll tell him Ike is dead and I now have the scroll. I'm ready to arrange that swap for Mimi."

Three grueling hours later they were on the dirt road to Jerusalem. Menachem was behind the wheel, noticeably silent.

"Ike's death was an accident," Liam said. "We can tell the authorities we couldn't leave him in the mountains for the raptors to devour. With his history, we won't have a problem."

"Will you call Akiva Peres and let him know?"

"After we get Mimi. I don't want the Israeli Police to interfere."

"What about Yitzhak's body?"

Liam paused a moment.

"You got a freezer?"

Chapter Thirty-Six

Al Dub walked up the hill on the crowded sidewalk below the Church of the Nativity. As usual the street was clogged with tourist busses and taxis. Not as bad as in December, when Christians come to Bethlehem to relive the birth of their prophet Jesus.

What ignorant sheep!

The stocky Syrian had no patience with the boarish sybarites from the West, especially the women who showed their naked legs and exposed their breasts corrupting the Muslim men and boys who sold them tourist trinkets and waited on them hand and foot. The open display of flesh at restaurants and decadent hotels where liquor was served was an affront to Allah. The Bear had lived among American Christians in Brookline, Massachusetts for years after his first benefactor, the Turkish financier who taught him about currencies, was murdered. Jews blew up his car on the streets of Istanbul. While in the United States he accomplished many things for his new employer, Anton Brodie. His finest hour was funneling Brodie's money to five of the fifteen Saudis who helped destroy the twin towers and burn the Pentagon on September 11, 2001. Because of the West's ridiculous obsession with privacy and so-called rights, operating in the U.S. was easier in some ways than in Europe and the Middle East. Al Dub would have remained in America if not for the efforts of the secret Special Forces unit that almost killed him in Rock Creek Park, D.C., three years earlier. After Al Dub's brush with death, Brodie insisted he leave the U.S. and pursue opportunities around the Mediterranean.

Al Dub watched a group of white-haired Christians step out of their bus and begin the trek up the hill to the Church of the Nativity. No doubt Jesus Christ of Nazareth was a prophet, although most certainly a lesser prophet. Any fool could see that by comparing the words of the Christian New Testament Bible with the sacred words of the Holy Quran. In some cases the words of Jesus revealed his distorted view of the will of God. Not until The Holy Prophet appeared on earth six hundred years later was the truth of the ages revealed to the world. Allah had spoken through the Angel Jibril to the Prophet Muhammad, who took twenty-three years to transcribe Allah's words for mankind's benefit.

Al Dub gazed up the hill beyond the procession and admired his favorite sign in all of Israel—a banner hanging from the side of the building where the Israelis and Christians had prevented the construction of a massive mosque adjacent to the Church of the Nativity, which infidels claim it was built originally in the Fourth Century by Constantine the Great, after the first Roman Emperor converted to Christianity. The banner proclaimed the truth—those who work to suppress the spread of the words of the prophet Muhammad are losers, and history will judge them accordingly. Al Dub believed the mosque would eventually be built. Over the last year he had invested a substantial sum of Brodie's money in the cause.

Al Dub scratched his hairy forearm and turned onto a side street below the Church of the Nativity. Al Dub scoffed at the Christians' claim that it was the oldest church in continual existence in the world. His fondest memories of the Church were during the siege in 2002, when marauding Jews in the IDF surrounded the church after a dozen Palestinian patriots sought refuge. Israeli forces were trying to kill them. Anton Brodie had sent Al Dub to Bethlehem during the thirty-nine day standoff to see what currency bets Brodie might make based on the outcome of the siege. Al Dub was fresh from the U.S. and hoped the confrontation might set off a widespread revolt by the Palestinians in all of the P.A. controlled areas—Gaza, Bethlethem, Nazareth, Jericho, and Hebron. Anton Brodie felt the situation presented opportunities for a substantial currency play, and was disappointed at the effect on his bottom line when the siege ended in a brokered agreement instead of open warfare between Palestinians and Jews.

Further away from the famous Church, Al Dub made better time. Pedestrian traffic was light on the side streets. He walked as quickly as his short, thick legs would allow. He was anxious to meet with Hazara to discuss the new developments posed by the call Hazara had received from the American oil man. Al Dub turned into an alley and stopped at an old stone structure he thought perfect for holding the woman. The alley was not wide enough for automobile traffic and the pedestrians who walked by were all locals. The entrance to the building was not on the alley, but around to the side, almost invisible. He knocked on the wooden door. Within thirty seconds the door opened.

"Quickly," Hazara said and closed the door.

Al Dub climbed the narrow wooden stairs behind Hazara. At the top of the steps Hazara opened a battered wooden door, paint peeling from it in large strips. Al Dub followed Hazara inside. The main floor was one large room with square brick support columns throughout. Bare mattresses were scattered around. A small refrigerator with rusted hinges sat next to a pedestal sink and lonely toilet. An old wooden table centered the room surrounded by three metal chairs and a red plastic milk case. Very rudimentary, but adequate.

"Excellent choice of property," Al Dub told Hazara.

"Sufficient for this job."

Al Dub knew The Black, but not the other two men in the room.

"Occupy these other men with something. We need to talk," Al Dub said to Hazara.

"The Black stays."

"Of course."

Hazara spoke quietly to the other two men. They looked at Al Dub with dead eyes, opened the door to the basement and walked down the steps carrying their short assault rifles to join Mimi downstairs. Hazara walked to the table and sat down. The Black stood behind him, his back against a column, the end of his turban covering all of his face except for his eyes. Hazara gestured for Al Dub to sit.

"Tell me again what the American said."

"Just as I stated on the phone. He called me. He said he has scroll. Would you like to see the photograph of the dead Jew?"

"Yes."

Hazara pulled out his phone and placed it on the table in front of Al Dub. He tapped an icon to bring up the photograph of Ike Palmer.

"Good," Al Dub said after studying the picture. "It appears real."

"I examined it. The Jew is dead." Hazara paused. "How do you wish to proceed? The American says he will not give us the scroll unless he gets the woman first."

"I have decided to examine the scroll in the American's presence in a public place. If it is authentic, he will leave with the girl and we will leave with the scroll."

"What about scientific tests by an expert?"

"I have an eye for these things," Al Dub said. "An expert, some say. My abilities are well-known."

"And this is acceptable to Mr. Brodie?"

"You work for me," Al Dub said sharply. "I have worked with Mr. Brodie for many years, starting when you were a boy. We have accomplished great things together. Let's keep this straight, Hazara. You are a hired hand. It's up to me to decide these details."

"Very well," Hazara said.

"I brought you something," Al Dub said, regaining his charm.

He reached into the pocket inside his jacket and pulled out a small, thin book. He placed it on the table in front of Hazara, who studied the cover, and opened the book.

"As you can see it is written in Arabic," Al Dub said, "the language of the Holy Quran. The title is <u>The Protocols of the Elders of Zion</u>. Though you follow the Holy Prophet's cousin Ali ibn Abi Talib, I think all Muslims should be made aware of this plan the Jews put into motion centuries ago."

"I follow no one, Akmal Kassab. Why give me this?"

"I want you to know what we are up against. You will see. The original of this document was discovered in Russia over a hundred years ago. The Jews have long planned to dominate the world. Manipulate world economies, control the media, and corrupt the morals of Muslims. The Christians in the West are unwitting allies; the Jews run their banks and media. See the vile movies, the television shows made in Hollywood. You will know what I say is true. I have lived in America. You cannot believe the filth shown or discussed over public airways. And who controls Hollywood? The Jews. This is well-documented. Mayer, Thalberg, Zanuck, Goldwyn—greedy Jews who founded an industry to make money and manipulate world opinion. The Nazis in Germany knew. Adolf Hitler attempted to eradicate the Zionist poison from the world. It was a good start. You and I must continue the fight."

Hazara thumbed through the book, closed it, and slid it back across the table to Al Dub.

"I have no need of this book. None of these things matters to me. Obtaining the scroll—that is my job. Concentrate on the task at hand."

"Yes, well, let me show you something else," Al Dub said, "something that is our future. Not many years from now. This may awaken the word of Allah in you, Hazara."

Al Dub pulled from his inside pocket a folded document the size of a road map, and carefully spread it on the table. Hazara looked it over for a moment.

"A map of Jerusalem?"

"No. It is a map based on a model of Al Quds, one built in the United States when I lived there. I left in such a hurry I couldn't disassemble it, bring it with me. Al Quds is what true followers of Islam call Jerusalem. When the Jews are pushed into the sea, we will re-name the city Al Quds on all world maps. Look closely. See the new mosque on the site of what the Jews call the Temple Mount. They will no longer defile our holy ground in the Old City. All holy sites and properties surrounding them will be placed in a *waqf,* a trust administered by the Grand Mufti and his Holy Council."

"The Church of the Holy Sepulcher," Hazara said, placing his fingertip on the map, "there is no structure there."

"No need in Al Quds for Greek and Russian Orthodox churches or other Christian structures, not even the YMCA tower. Every building that is not Muslim we will raze. I have begun re-building Al Quds in my flat in Amman. I will show you one day."

Al Dub folded the map and returned it to his pocket. Hazara glanced back at The Black.

"You would be wasting your time," Hazara said.

"In time you will see the beauty of Al Quds. We will work together on many more operations in this region. You will come to believe in it."

Hazara shrugged. Al Dub pointed to The Black.

"Does he talk? Can he understand what I'm saying."

"He speaks English, Arabic and a little Farsi. He merely chooses silence."

"Where is he from?"

"He has never told me. I saw no need to ask. You are sure we need no scientists to examine the scroll? It would be unwise to deliver a fake to Mr. Brodie."

"Do not concern yourself," Al Dub said. "Where will we make the exchange? Have you selected a place?"

"I have one in mind."

"Show me," Al Dub said.

Chapter Thirty-Seven

After placing Ike Palmer's broken remains in the chest freezer in the garage, Liam and Menachem sat at the dinette table in the cramped kitchen. Liam had called Mimi's captor on the drive back from the mountains. It was now his turn to call Liam with instructions for the exchange. Liam rubbed and stretched his neck.

"Try to relax," Menachem said.

"Hard to do."

"We have almost ended of Mimi Stanton's ordeal."

"Our scroll's a fake, remember?"

"Maybe their expert is not so smart."

"That's a pretty slim reed to hang Mimi's life on," Liam said. "But we have no other card to play."

Menachem picked up his buzzing phone, looked at the number and answered, "Yes, Mr. Investigator. We will be there right away."

"Who was that?" Liam asked.

"Akiva Peres. He said we must come to the station. Right now. Something important."

"Kind of late for that, isn't it?"

"Six o'clock Monday evening? I suspect it is not unusual for Akiva Peres to work late."

"You go."

"He wants us both. He was very insistent. We need to do as he says. We will need his help later with things."

"You mean like Ike's body in the freezer?"

"Who knows? This is Israel, remember? Peres gave no hint of what he wants. We may be all right. Perhaps he merely wants to bring us up to date on his investigation."

"He could have done that on the phone. Does he know you were in Wrath of God? That you were the driver?"

"I am sure he has no idea. Why would you ask this?"

"Just curious," Liam said. "You just said 'This is Israel, remember?' The government is supposed to know everyone's business."

"Maybe not everything."

Twenty minutes later Menachem parked the Volvo outside the Jerusalem Police Station near the Jaffa Gate. Liam stepped out of the car and stretched, his back and shoulders still stiff from helping Menachem carry Ike's corpse from the *wadi* up the steep, rocky slopes back to the Volvo. Rubbed his neck as he stopped to watch tourists stream out of the Old City toward their busses, then ambled into the station, trying to count the number of times he had been here to see Peres in the 102 hours since Mimi was taken.

The receptionist desk was unoccupied. Menachem pointed to surly Sergeant Leeba's empty chair.

"See? It is another sign our luck is changing."

Akiva Peres appeared at the door to the investigator's office and waved them in. Liam hung back and watched Menachem walk right behind Peres. The two veteran Israeli warriors looked like brothers, the the same age and height, and generally the same build. The only significant difference was Menachem's slick head.

Liam followed them and took the chair next to Menachem across the desk from Peres. Liam glanced at Peres's bad eye. The Investigator's hair was a mess. The mangled stub of a thick cigar balanced on the rim of a glass ash tray on the desk.

"They let you smoke in here?" Liam asked.

"Are you kidding? I take a puff or two outside. I chew on it in here."

"It's a shame how they treat a war hero," Menachem said. "These bureaucrats have no sense of history."

"I don't want to give the *challah* at the reception desk another reason to *kvetch* about me to the Police Board," Peres said to Menachem and Liam. "I do not want to extend my exile to this Jerusalem Police station. They tell me it is against the rules to smoke in here so I comply. You should see how she turns up her big *schnoz* at my little stump of a cigar when she passes my desk."

"You fought to preserve her right to be rude to you," Liam said. "Do you have any idea when you will return to Shin Bet?"

Peres shrugged and spread his arms, palms up.

Lieutenant Colombo!

Finally! It had nagged at Liam from their first meeting. Peres had reminded him of someone. The bad eye, the wavy dark hair, the disheveled look, and the way he gestured when he spoke—Peter Falk. Colombo. Mystery solved. Liam smiled slightly, then realized Peres was talking to him.

"I'm sorry, Investigator Peres," Liam said, "my mind was a million miles away. What is it you were asking?"

"That's all right, Mr. Connors. I understand how upsetting all this has been for you. I wanted to know what you and Menachem Wladyslaw have been doing these past two days. I last saw you here after we found Yitzhak Palmer's apartment turned upside down. From that chair you made the call to the kidnapper. Yesterday and today I hear nothing."

"I remind you that I spoke briefly with you yesterday afternoon," Menachem said. "You said no new developments."

"Yes, but you neglected to tell me what you two were planning," Peres said.

"Looking for Mimi," Liam said. "We knew you were doing everything you could. We were trying to help."

"I see," Peres said, staring at the two men across the desk. "So you've had no further contact with the person we called from this office, the person demanding the scroll."

"You heard them," Menachem said. "They want to trade the scroll for Ms Stanton. We don't have Yitzhak's scroll."

"You have just been sitting around your hotel, Mr. Connors?"

"No, indeed," Menachem said quickly. "We have walked many miles through the Old City showing the picture."

"And we attempted to contact Ike Palmer," Liam said. "Have you a clue to where he has been hiding?"

"No, Mr. Connors." Peres paused, tapping his nose. "This is telling me I am not receiving the whole story. Let me say how important it is that all leads in the investigation be reported to this office. I must be made aware of whatever you are doing. And let me make this clear. Do not try to deal with these people yourselves. A big mistake for you. A very big mistake. It could doom your fiancé. And you."

"Absolutely," Liam said. "You have the experience. We appreciate your help."

"In my earlier response to one of your questions I may not have been clear," Menachem said. "Earlier this afternoon Mr. Connors called and spoke to the people holding her. He told them we continue to search for the scroll. They will not release her until the scroll is in their hands. So, nothing has changed."

"And there is nothing else you would like to tell me?" Peres asked.

Chapter Thirty-Eight

On their way back from the outdoor restaurant Hazara had chosen for the exchange, he and "the Bear" walked up the hill toward the Church of the Nativity. Al Dub had a difficult time keeping up with the long, easy strides of the much-younger and taller Hazara. They turned onto the side street leading to the building where Mimi was being held.

"There is no need for such haste," Al Dub said.

"I'm just walking," Hazara said, slowing his steps. "If the restaurant I selected is not to your liking, where do you wish to meet with the American to make the trade?"

"Not 'we.' I will meet with the American to examine the scroll. The girl will be with me. You and The Black will be close enough to act if something goes wrong."

"And this will take place where?"

"The Buraq Wall."

Hazara stopped and looked down at Al Dub as if the stocky Syrian had lost his mind. "Too many people, too much security. In order to get into the main area we must pass through metal detectors and X-rays."

"Exactly. It is perfect. No weapons. At least not the conventional sort. I have worked it out. You will see. I want you to call the American. Tell him to meet us at noon tomorrow. Use the term the People of the Book use—the Western Wall."

"It is a big place, crowded with people. You must be more specific."

"Facing the Wall I will be with the woman in the far left corner. Tell him to walk down the hill to the plaza."

"What if ceremonies are underway...?"

"Enough," Al Dub barked. "You work for me. I pay you. You will do as I say. Tell him the woman will be in a wheelchair. Unharmed. The chair is only to secure her, to prevent her from running."

Hazara nodded. He wanted to wring the Syrian's neck.

"The American is to deliver the scroll and walk away. Ten meters. He is not to talk to me or the woman. He is to wait. I will examine it."

"How much time will you need to verify?"

"Not long. Shortly after I see it I will know if it is authentic. I will examine certain parts closely and perform a brief chemical test."

"Mr. Brodie wants it undamaged."

"The test will not destroy any part of the document," Al Dub said, irritated at the insolence. "You forget your place, Hazara."

"Perhaps, but I know Mr. Brodie will be very displeased if the exchange does not go smoothly or if the document is defaced. In our previous collaborations, you have never concerned yourself. Such details you have always left to me. What is different?"

"Do as I say, Hazara. Make the call."

Hazara and Al Dub walked up to the main floor. Hazara's two hired guns sat at the dinette table smoking cigarettes and drinking dense coffee from tiny ceramic cups. Hazara spoke in Arabic. They pointed to the basement door. Hazara gestured for Al Dub to wait. He opened the basement door and disappeared down the steps. The Black was standing against the wall opposite Mimi, his back straight and his eyes locked on the American woman. Hazara spoke quietly to him, then to Mimi.

"I am about to call your friend to set up our meeting for tomorrow at noon. If all goes well, you will be reunited with him then."

Mimi sat up. "Oh, thank you," she said, smiling through trembling lips. "Thank you very much."

"Do you need anything?"

Mimi glanced at The Black and whispered.

"Does he have to stay down here?" she asked.

"Why do you ask?"

"He just stares at me. He scares me."

"There is nothing to fear. He will not touch you unless I authorize him to do so—unless something goes wrong tomorrow."

Mimi's fragile stomach did a flip. Back to reality. Her jaw ached and head pounded. Elation dissipated into fear. Tears filled her eyes.

Mimi shivered. "What if it does?"

Hazara smiled and nodded toward The Black. "He will be the one to cut your lovely throat."

Hazara motioned to The Black to return to the main floor. Hazara followed him up the basement steps. Al Dub waited at the small table. The two hired men sat on mattresses on the other side of the room, watching Al Dub, who ended his phone conversation as Hazara joined him. The Black stood by, his back against the brick column, his raptor eyes on Al Dub.

"I have confirmed my arrangements. When I return in the morning I will have clothing for her, a wheelchair, the pharmaceuticals, and other items I need. Now, call the American."

Hazara sat at the dinette, punched re-dial and waited. Liam answered.

"I have instructions," Hazara said. "Do you know the Western Wall in the Old City? She will be there with one man who will be unarmed. The expert. You give him the scroll and walk away ten meters while he examines it. If he is satisfied, he will leave with the scroll and the girl will be yours. Understand?"

Hazara listened a moment and ended the call.

"The American will be there at noon," Hazara said to Al Dub. "For your sake, Akmal Kassab, I hope you know what you are doing."

Chapter Thirty-Nine

As usual, controlled bedlam ruled the Western Wall. Eleven-thirty in the morning. Worshippers and curious tourists filled the plaza, walking with purpose or wandering, praying or gaping. The tourist busses began disgorging their pilgrims at the Jaffa Gate at nine a.m., an hour after local foot traffic through Herod's Gate, New Gate, and Damascus Gate had begun. Every day it was the same.

Waves of devout Jews and tourists crowded the Western Wall. Liam walked the stone pavement of the plaza alone. He carried the terra cotta pot in a white cotton tote strapped on his shoulder. He studied the plaza layout for thirty minutes—the Wall, the points of entrance and egress. The exotic people mesmerized Liam: men with beards, curling side locks, black suits, white shirts buttoned to the neck, heavy wide-brimmed woolen hats in all shapes and sizes; Jewish men without hats wore patterned *yarmulkes;* Western non-believers covering their crowns with delicate, white *yarmulkes* given them in the security line.

The crowd was vibrant, the air electric. Women segregated, set apart at their end of the Wall. Believers and tourists alike stuffed prayer notes in the cracks between the giant stones. Though Thursday was the major *Bar Mitzvah* day, Menachem had warned Liam that several were scheduled for today. They would add a significant number of worshippers in the small plaza.

Liam spied Menachem across the plaza and walked toward him. Menachem was dressed as an *Hasid*—black suit, white shirt buttoned to the neck, and a furry black hat shaped like a small automobile tire. Menachem had sewn fake side locks into the hat. Liam, dressed like the secular American visitor he was, wore a thin white *yarmulke*. Few people noticed it because he was at least a head taller than most visitors to the Western Wall.

By the time Liam caught up with him, Menachem was at the Wall, his eyes closed, hands in prayer, head nodding, over and over again. His fake curlicue sideburns bounced and swayed. Liam stood next to Menachem and aped him, mumbling and nodding. Menachem's prayers grew louder and louder, until the only other worshipper near him grumbled and moved away.

"Still no sign," Liam whispered, his eyes closed.

"When I finish praying I will walk away from the Wall. Wait for a moment. Then do the same."

"I'll keep my distance."

"A man pushing a woman in a wheelchair will stand out in this crowd. Remember what I say. The man will have a weapon of some kind on him, possibly in the chair. He will appear to have no defense, but I tell you he has a deadly weapon somewhere. Do not take a chance. Do as he says or he will harm Mimi Stanton."

"At the Wall at noon."

"I would not miss it," Menachem said, studying prayer book as he walked away.

Al Dub waited in the security line on the limestone walkway watching the excavation crews at work. The Jews were constantly digging around the wall of the Old City, claiming to discover this and that, all in an effort to justify their illegal occupation of the holy site. Al Dub recalled rumors the Zionists had spread three years earlier of the discovery of columns from Solomon's Temple, fifty feet below the Western Wall plaza. Muslim archeologists exposed this lie. To this day, there is no archeological evidence that the First Temple existed. Al Dub believed Solomon's Temple a fiction—concocted by Jews to justify their trespass. Had it been real, some physical proof of it would have been found.

Al Dub rested Mimi's head against the frame of the chair. Perhaps he had given her too much of the drug. He adjusted the black *burqa* which covered her from head to toe.

When he finally arrived at the special security checkpoint for the disabled, going through was a breeze. Pushing a woman who appeared to be suffering from ALS through the checkpoint elicited only pity for the woman and her elderly father, not suspicion. The women guards could see through the *burqa's* mesh eye slit, but Al Dub knew from his own observation that the guards could not tell through the mesh that her eyes were glazed and unfocused. When her head lolled against her chest from time to time, at times striking the frame of the chair, he moved her gently to make her more comfortable. Al Dub explained to the guards in decent Hebrew his daughter's lungs were weak and warned the security X-rays might show three small inhalers in her *burqa*. Al Dub did not share with the guards that the inhalers were filled with a cyanide aerosol that would kill in seconds, nor did he let them know about the same deadly spray in a flat container attached to the wheelchair's seat belt. If the buckle were not loosened exactly right, it would envelope Mimi Stanton and anyone around her in a brown cloud of death. The *jihadist* pharmacist had charged too much for the aerosol weapons and the wheelchair, but Al Dub would have paid a hundred times more in the pursuit of the heretical scroll.

He pushed the wheelchair along the ramp watching the Zionist puppets nod and mumble their gibberish at Al Buraq. He made steady progress and exited the walkway onto the uneven stones of the plaza. Al Dub set a course for the Wall, down the gradual slope toward the left corner. On the ramparts above he saw Hazara eyeing the plaza. Further along the sides of the Wall he saw The Black begin his descent to plaza level, his signature black turban blending nicely with the myriad black hats bobbing and nodding toward the Wall.

A hundred feet from the corner, Al Dub saw the tall American carrying a bag on his shoulder. He nodded slightly at the man and continued down the slope until he was five feet from the huge stones of the Wall. The American walked to the wheelchair, gave Al Dub the cotton bag, and knelt beside Mimi. When Al Dub looked into the bag to feel the jar, Liam lifted Mimi's veil.

"You drugged her, you bastard," Liam said through gritted teeth.

"Keep your voice down. She is only sedated. It is for her safety. You see she is alive. When the drug wears off she will be fine."

"She better be."

"Walk away while I examine this scroll. Ten minutes."

It took all the will power Liam could summon. He wanted to knock the man flat on his back and push Mimi up the incline. He did consider lifting her out of the chair and carrying her away. But he knew Menachem was right: the sly son-of-a-bitch had something up his sleeve, some weapon, some means of harming Mimi. Nor would he show up alone. Liam had not seen them, but knew there were others with the old man to help him make good on his threat to hurt her. Liam shook his head and as he walked away from the old man and the wheelchair, he spotted Menachem moving toward him.

Hazara and The Black also drew closer to Liam. They appeared deep in prayer, like hundreds of men around them. Liam focused on Al Dub and Mimi. The old man opened the jar and carefully removed the parchment. He concentrated on the parchment, at times holding it inches from his eyes. Al Dub rubbed the parchment between his thumb and fingers, checking the texture.

"Hurry up, you son-of-a-bitch," Liam muttered under his breath.

Chapter Forty

Liam's eyes locked onto Mimi. The space around him had become thick with men. But nothing interfered with his concentration on her. Strangers shuffled past him to the Wall, praying, nodding, mumbling—gathering between him and the wheelchair. Liam moved slightly so as to keep Al Dub in view. More men were amassing, moving and murmuring, jostling one another. By the time Liam recognized what was happening, it was too late.

Al Dub stuck his arm through the straps and hoisted the cotton bag on his shoulder. He pushed Mimi to Liam's left, toward the stone wall perpendicular and connecting to the Western Wall. Liam eyed a passage through the adjoining wall beneath a Corbel arch. Al Dub pushed Mimi straight for it. Liam moved to intercept them. A wave of three dozen men jammed together like a rugby scrum. Stopped Liam in his tracks. He tried to force his way through. The men absorbed and folded in on him until Liam realized he was blocked.

Liam saw Menachem, also trying to shove his way through the mass of men. Under the arch and in the passageway beyond, more men, perhaps fifty, intentionally choked the corridor. They closed in behind Al Dub and Mimi like quicksand. Liam grabbed one of the men and shook him, asking him where Al Dub was taking Mimi. From his blank stare, Liam realized the man could not understand him, knew nothing of the old man's escape plan. Liam pushed him into the others and hustled up the slope with Menachem.

"Where does that corridor lead?" Liam demanded.

"I have been through that archway many times. It leads under the wall into the tunnels. It is a maze under there. If he has an accomplice who knows the underground, we will never find him."

"We can't just stand here."

"Hundreds of places he can surface in the Old City from the tunnels below."

Liam slammed his fist into his palm. "Where did all the men come from? Who were they?"

"I am guessing. Probably among the many unemployed Palestinians who enter the city every day hoping for a day's work.

They want cash and will do anything for it. The old man created that human shield. Most likely paid a labor broker twenty U.S. dollars for each man. Perhaps the old man told them it was a domestic dispute."

"What now?"

"We will have to think of another plan."

Liam was sick. He rubbed his neck. Mimi was in more danger than before. They had both her *and* the scroll. A *fake* scroll. If they found that out they would kill her.

Liam removed the *yarmulke* from the crown of his head and studied the walls and ramparts around the plaza.

"Security cameras everywhere," Liam said to Menachem. "How can we get a look at what they recorded?"

"Akiva Peres," Menachem said.

"Let's go," Liam said. "We have no other choice."

Hazara and The Black arrived at the house in Bethlehem an hour later. Hazara spoke briefly to his two hired guns, sat down at the small table and made a phone call. The Black stood by.

"Al Dub has disappeared with the scroll and the girl," Hazara told Anton Brodie. He gave him details of what happened at the Western Wall. "Once the crowd of men gathered between us, we could not follow him into the corridor leading down into the tunnels. At least a hundred men blocked our way."

Hazara listened a moment.

"No. I have no idea how he arranged it. It is obvious he wanted to evade us as well as the American."

Hazara listened for several minutes more then hung up.

"He says we must find the old man and get the scroll," Hazara told The Black. "Mr. Brodie wants the traitor Al Dub dead. He does not care what we do with the woman."

The Black barely nodded, unperturbed. Hazara thought a moment.

"I am tired of this cat and mouse game. We will kill her, too."

Chapter Forty-One

Menachem's phone buzzed. He pulled the Volvo into the parking area adjacent to the police station and glanced at the number.

"I must take this call. Go on in."

Liam entered the station and stood before Sergeant Leeba.

"I have to see Investigator Peres. Right now, please."

She continued to study her computer screen, ignoring Liam.

"Listen to me. This is very important."

Sergeant Leeba looked up at him and shook her head, as if Liam were causing her a huge inconvenience.

"Yes, it's me again. Why do I seem such a bother to you? My fiancé is in a lot of danger. I'm going to come across this counter if you don't get out of that chair and get Akiva Peres for me."

Startled, Sergeant Leeba moved quickly into the investigators' office. Getting reinforcements, perhaps. Liam knew intimidating the woman cop might get him arrested. But she returned and seemed to have a helpful attitude for the first time.

"He is out, Mr. Connors. Where he is or when he will return nobody knows."

Liam was surprised. He had finally discovered how to get her attention.

"Thank you, Sergeant Leeba," he said politely and walked out of the station.

"We need to call Peres on his cell," Liam said to Menachem in the Volvo. "He's not here and no one knows when he's coming back."

"I just tried that. No answer. But I have another resource. Let us return to the Wall."

Twenty minutes later, Liam and Menachem stood in the center of the stone plaza two hundred feet from the Western Wall.

"I have a friend who works in the *Kotel* security office...," Menachem said. "I believe he will let us see what the cameras captured."

"*Kotel*?" Liam said.

"The Western Wall."

"His office is right over there."

Menachem pointed to a small building near the primary security checkpoint for the plaza. They walked up the slight incline. Menachem looked into the camera over the door and pushed an intercom button. A voice speaking Hebrew answered. After Menachem responded to several questions, the thick, reinforced steel door opened. They stepped into a small foyer and waited inside a steel holding cage. No one else in the foyer.

Minutes passed. The cage door popped open and Menachem pushed through. They waited another five minutes. A steel door on the foyer wall opposite the cage opened. An Israeli policeman gestured for Menachem and Liam to follow him.

Up well-worn stone steps, they climbed to the upper level. They entered a room with two dozen black and white monitors on the walls. Four Israeli policemen sat at keyboards watching images of different parts of the plaza, the Wall, the ramparts, and the security checkpoints. Another door opened and the police officer gestured for them to follow.

They climbed another flight of stone steps to a smaller room with an additional bank of computers. The officer said something to a technician who tapped into his keyboard. A large screen on the wall in front of them came alive. Liam watched himself walking toward the man pushing Mimi in the wheelchair, give the tote to the man, and kneel by the chair. Liam and the old man spoke a moment before Liam backed away to watch the old man examine the pot and the scroll.

"There. Look at that," Liam said, and they watched as the men began to swarm the area between Liam and the wheel chair.

Liam's stomach felt hollow as he watched the old man strap the bag on his shoulder and push Mimi into the archway. He saw himself sink into the wall of men running interference, then watched Menachem do the same thing.

"Freeze it. There," Liam said, pointing to two other men trying to get through the mass of men shielding Al Dub. "Those two, the one in the black turban and robe and the taller one who looks like Usama bin Laden. They're trying to follow the old man, too. Run it back. Now forward in slow motion."

They watched Hazara and The Black trying to push through the human blockade and finally give up. When they turned to walk up the slope, the camera had a better angle on their faces.

"Can you make us a copy of that shot?" Liam said.

The technician nodded and said something in Hebrew to Menachem. The image on the screen changed. A camera inside the corridor captured the image of the old man scampering by pushing Mimi. For a moment, Mimi seemed to look into the camera. The system switched again and showed the back of the man heading down the ramp and disappearing into the darkness of a tunnel.

"Are there any cameras in the tunnels?" Liam said.

Menachem spoke to the policeman, who shook his head no.

"Go back to the previous screen," Liam said, "where we get a better shot of the old man's face.

Menachem spoke to the technician. The screen filled with the old man's face.

"There," Liam said. "Can he freeze that and clean it up?"

Menachem asked the technician. Liam watched him tap into his keyboard. The computer segregated the old man's face, enlarged and enhanced it, creating a vivid black and white close up. The technician tapped his keyboard again and three copies of the photograph of Al Dub slid into the print tray.

"We can take these?" Menachem asked the officer.

The officer nodded and spoke in Hebrew.

"What did he say?" Liam asked.

"He said they will run the man's image through their face recognition software. It is the best in the world."

Chapter Forty-Two

Anton Brodie stood on the balcony outside his suite in the Four Seasons Hotel sipping a light red wine and enjoying the evening, now quiet except for the muted sounds of traffic hundreds of feet below. Watching the city lights emerge after sunset from his private balcony was a simple pleasure he relished. Earlier he had retreated from the balcony and shut the glass door to escape the calls to prayer emanating from mosques all over downtown Amman. He missed the time not so long ago when it was pleasant to listen to the calls, even haunting. In those days, devout *muezzins* sang in person from the tops of minarets. A personal call to prayer without artificial amplification. Now the songs blared from loudspeakers, sounding tinny and overdone, electronic recordings rather than human voices in real time.

He wanted several hours to pass before he called Al Dub. Let the emotions of the moment cool down. Hazara's report of the action at the Western Wall was not surprising, but disturbing nonetheless. Brodie had known this day was coming. Al Dub had worked for him the past twenty years. They had done amazing things together, but Al Dub's zealotry in the name of Allah had become a real problem now. With today's events at the Wall, Al Dub's religious devotion seemed to have reached the tipping point. Brodie had already put into place some of the currency positions and stock options that would make him many billions when the content of the scroll became public.

Timing was everything in currency and option trades, and Anton Brodie had lost control of the big reveal. He had to convince Al Dub their individual goals were not mutually exclusive: Brodie could reap his profits and Al Dub could refute the blasphemy without a conflict. It was a blatant lie, but Brodie could pull it off. He had convinced Al Dub of some equally ridiculous postulates in the past, but none involved the core of Al Dub's religious beliefs like this one.

He moved inside the suite and stood in front of the large, gilded mirror in the living area to smooth his rambunctious white hair. He studied the deep wrinkles that made him appear so old. Looks were deceiving, as the half-dozen young women he had entertained in the last two days would attest. All black-haired Arabian beauties with soft, golden skin, dark eyes, and luscious brown nipples. He satisfied each of them, one after another, in this very suite, all without pharmaceutical help. His remarkable sexual prowess arose from the prospect of making billions from the Ishmael scroll trades—all the aphrodisiac he needed. Brodie raised his wine glass to his image in the mirror and took a final sip. Time to call Akmal Kassab.

"Yes," Al Dub answered.

"My old friend," Brodie said, "how did it go today?"

"I duped the American. I have the scroll."

"And you still have his woman."

"Yes."

"It makes no difference to me, but why was it necessary to keep the woman?"

"I need time to prove it a fabrication. This was the only way I could do it. Had I released the woman I would lose my leverage."

"You are not able to examine it yourself?"

"Of course not. The pot and the parchment are very old. They appear authentic, but they must be tested using scientific means."

"If the scroll is as old as the ones found at Qumran and the Aramaic says what the crazy American claimed, what will you do?"

There was silence on the other end.

"Do you plan on destroying it?" Brodie asked.

"It is a vile thing, an abomination."

"So you say, but preserving it might help your cause more than its destruction."

"How could that be?"

"Jewish Aramaic was the language of Jesus and the vernacular of first century Jews, was it not?"

"Yes."

"And many, many documents from the early centuries after Jesus's death support the fact that Ishmael was of the blood of Abraham, that Ishmael was the product of Abraham's intercourse with the slave girl Hagar, are there not?"

"Well, yes, many," Al Dub said.

"And many Christian scholars are convinced the original text of Genesis proves that Ishmael *is* the biological son of Abraham."

"Correct."

"So, here you have a wild instrument from ancient times. No doubt written by Jews in their Hebrew dialect of the time. Discovered in a cave by a Jew. All further proof of their perfidy and hatred of Islam. The scroll in your possession proves the Jews have been spreading falsehoods going back two centuries. Even before the Holy Prophet Muhammad appeared on earth to spread the word of Allah. Believe me, Akmal Kassab, I know these people. How they think. They make me ashamed of my heritage. You have read the Protocols of the Elders of Zion. My conniving Israelite forebears spread lies throughout history. And here is another one."

"It is true," Al Dub said as he sat down, beginning to second-guess himself. "I understand what you are saying. You make a valid point, but in my opinion it's better to destroy the scroll and eliminate its falsehood from the world."

Brodie knew he had additional convincing to do, but at least he had the Syrian thinking.

"What if it is not the original? What if the American gave you a fraudulent scroll and has hidden the original somewhere, ready to reveal it to the world?"

"That is why I will have the scroll tested."

"Let me help you with this," Brodie said. "Use my resources. We will hire the world's finest scientists from the most reliable laboratories on the planet to carefully examine this document. We must control the information."

"I have my own resources…, and friends."

"Not equal to mine." Brodie paused. "We have been through much together, my friend. You know I am loyal to you and your cause, but we must plan carefully. If I make the profits I anticipate, there will be more money for you to begin the final push of Zionists into the sea."

"Let me think," Al Dub said. "I must think. I will call you later."

"Very well. It is my hope you will agree with me, remain my friend," Brodie said, ice forming on each word. "You have seen what happens to my enemies."

"How well I know. I have carried out your instructions many times. Tell me. What about the woman?"

"After we have the scroll tested, we will have no further need of her. If it is determined to be a forgery, we will use the woman to force the American to give us the real scroll that his friend Palmer found."

"I should keep her alive for now?"

"That is correct. Later you may dispose of her. Where are you? Still in Jerusalem?"

"I am safe."

"Call me soon," Brodie said.

Anton Brodie ended the call, poured himself another glass of red wine, and returned to his balcony. He looked down on Amman. Three million people in its metropolitan area, and almost all of them still as ignorant as the Bedouins and other nomadic tribes from whom they descended centuries before. But that was the way of the world, six billion souls and only a handful with enough sense to come in out of the rain. Even in the West, ignorance was thriving. In the United States, Brodie had influenced many elections, sponsoring ad campaigns through one of his many NGOs or non-profit organizations, or paying canvassers to get out the "low information voters." Idiots whose vote counted just as much as the businessmen and women who read newspapers and follow the issues of the day. Brodie chuckled. What an easy system for rigging an outcome. He always laughed at the ludicrous principle of one-man-one-vote. The underclass in America had finally learned that with their votes they can take more and more money from the rich and successful. Forty-nine per cent of the American population now received government benefits. And the racial animus growing worse every day in the U.S. was an added bonus. Hatred for the white people and Jews who controlled the money was an easy sell. Democracies were easy to manipulate. All it took was money.

Riots, civil unrest, and violence on the streets—all good for Brodie's currency portfolios. Turmoil produced opportunities to make money. Quiet, uneventful times were anathema to Brodie. Like all traders, he needed movement, one way or the other. It didn't matter which. It had taken Brodie years of planning and distributing seed money, helping fund groups like ACORN and Occupy Wall Street in the U.S.; various anarchist groups in Europe including the Free Workers' Union in Germany and National-Anarchism in England; and the Al Qaeda spinoffs in the Middle East and Africa, AQIM, AQAP, and al-Shabab. Now he was reaping his rewards. He had his hand in so many seething situations—Pakistan, Indonesia, Somalia, Mali, Bangladesh, some of the former SSRs in eastern Europe, the Kurds in Turkey and Iraq, and many, many others—he was well on his way to becoming the richest man in the world.

This thing with Al Dub was a minor irritant. Brodie could achieve his goal without the scroll. He had people in Reuters, the Associated Press, and free-lance stringers throughout the Middle East. It was time to give them a call. Time to contact a few of his non-profits operating in the occupied territories on the West Bank, too.

"Now to awaken the great unwashed," he said as he swirled his remaining red wine.

Al Dub shifted in the ragged easy chair in the small cinder block house. It sat on a dirt street on the outskirts of Hebron in the Palestinian controlled H1 sector of the ancient town. His distant cousin, the rug merchant, who had fled Syria two decades ago to settle in Hebron, was glad to rent the house to him, especially when Al Dub offered to pay two month's rent in advance.

Al Dub had selected Hebron over the other Palestinian Authority cities in Israel because of his cousin's house. He knew his kin to be trustworthy, capable of keeping his mouth closed. Al Dub needed his privacy. He didn't share with his cousin why he rented the house. Given the paucity of tenants in Hebron capable of paying cash, the cousin was happy to accommodate Al Dub and promised to leave him alone, especially after Al Dub hinted his need of the house had to do with a young woman.

He considered it ironic that the so-called Ishmael scroll he took from the American at Al-Buraq was now located in Hebron, the West Bank city most closely associated with Abraham, who acquired the Cave of the Patriarchs from the Hittites and was later entombed in the city himself. Al Dub had traveled the twenty-six miles early Saturday morning south from Jerusalem to Hebron to rent his cousin's house. He considered it a secure place to hide. Al Dub stocked it with food and supplies, and briefly visited the Cave of the Patriarchs and Abraham's sepulcher. He had read the history of the Muslim conquest of Hebron, the village of the prophet Abraham al Khalil, "the friend of God," as the followers of Muhammad referred to the founding father of the Israelites.

His conversation with Anton Brodie had filled Al Dub with foreboding. He knew Brodie was much smarter and craftier than he. Brodie was always many moves ahead of Al Dub, just as with his counterparties in the currency trades. Al Dub knew Brodie would say and do anything to get what he wanted, including lie. The threat from Brodie was real. Al Dub wondered if his plan to destroy the scroll was worth his life. He would earn a higher place in Allah's heaven. But he wasn't certain he was ready to accept such a prize just yet. True, he was growing older and felt tired much of the time. Spreading *jihad* for Anton Brodie was lonely work. Heaven might be more pleasant. Allah knew how he had fought the Jews and Christians. He had already secured an exalted place in heaven. He would think about what Anton Brodie said.

Al Dub walked through the small house to check on the American woman. He looked through the door into the room where he had tied her securely to the bed. She was still out from the additional injection. He had followed the dosage the *jihadist* pharmacist recommended for deep sedation. He walked into the room and looked down on the woman. She was drooling. The American would not think his short-haired woman so attractive now, saliva oozing down her cheek.

Al Dub left the woman and sat in the overstuffed chair again. He removed the thick map of Al Quds from his pocket, took his time unfolding it and studying the city. In his mind's eye he pictured how Al Quds would look when all the Christian churches and Jewish holy sites and synagogues were destroyed. His plans called for covering the sloping stone plaza in front of Al-Buraq with another great mosque, removing forever the Western Wall the Jews considered so sacred. He folded the map, rolled out his prayer rug, knelt, and placed his forehead on the floor. He closed his eyes and pictured the new mosque obscuring Al-Buraq.

Praise be to Allah. What a glorious day that will be.

Chapter Forty-Three

Liam said little on the drive home with Menachem. Of every misstep he had made in his five day search for Mimi, today was the worst. He had been right there, kneeling beside her. How easy to cold-cock the old man and take Mimi in his arms.

"Stop blaming yourself," Menachem said.

"I could have pushed the chair away from him," Liam said, pounding his knee. "I blew it."

"Believe me. That old man had the capability of killing you and Mimi had you tried something like that. He may not have had a gun, but he did not come to the Western Wall without a weapon of some kind. You did the right thing. At least, we now know who has her."

"I'm an idiot," Liam muttered as they turned the corner onto Menachem's street.

Night had fallen by the time Menachem opened the gate to his house and drove in. They entered through the garage into the kitchen. Liam's heart leapt into his throat, pushing out a laugh that sounded more like a bark.

Jerusalem Police Department Investigator Akiva Peres sat at the dinette table in the dim light above the stove, a mug of coffee in his hand. His black stump of a cigar butt rested in a metal ash tray. Liam felt adrenaline pumping as he stared at Akiva Peres. Peres raised the cup.

"Excellent coffee, Mr. Wladyslaw. Why don't you and Mr. Connors join me for a cup? You must be tired."

"Too late for coffee," Menachem said.

"We were just about to call you," Liam said, holding out his phone and clearing his throat.

Heavy metal music blared from the phone and it flew out of Liam's hands. Peres caught it in mid-air.

"Dammit," Liam said. "I hate that music."

Answering the phone, Peres said a few words and hung up.

"Wrong number," Peres said. "Let me select for you a decent ring tone. So you will not go to a Jerusalem hospital from a heart attack."

Peres tapped the settings icon. In a matter of seconds he had executed several deft maneuvers and returned the phone to Liam.

"I understand you have a photo of the man who now holds Miss Stanton."

"I do," Liam said, puzzled. "Here. Take a look."

With his good eye Peres squinted at the photo. After a moment he tossed it onto the table. "Akmal Kassab. Also known as Al Dub, meaning 'the Bear'."

His brain in a fog, Liam sat down at the small table with Peres. Menachem leaned against the kitchen cabinet, his arms crossed. Peres rubbed his knuckle into his bad eye.

"His bad eye," Menachem said. "Always it bothers him. Akiva Peres and Moshe Dayan, they saw eye to eye before the General passed away."

"Funny," Peres said and turned to Liam. "Sometimes he compares me to Sammy Davis, Jr."

Peres looked the same as always, his dark, wavy hair messy and his clothes rumpled. *Lieutenant Colombo.*

"I am sure you know," Peres said, "our country is under constant threat of destruction. From both inside and out. So, we have eyes everywhere. Small drones, smaller than you have developed in the United States, constantly patrol our borders, our cities, our deserts, our shores. We have CCTV cameras everywhere, more per square mile than in London. Human eyes keep watch in every city and village. Whether controlled by the Israeli government or the PLO."

"Palestinian Authority," Menachem said.

"Same thing. The point is...."

"You've been watching us the whole time," Liam said.

"Most, not all. We have limited visuals in the Old City and of course, nothing in the tunnels. A vulnerability imposed by our leaders for political and religious reasons to appease our enemies. A mistake, for sure, but nonetheless the way it is. Our surveillance is not perfect. You saw everything we had on the abduction of Miss Stanton. We have images of her entering into the Old City last Thursday. We could not see how she was abducted in the Armenian Quarter and we do not know how she was smuggled out of the Old City."

"You knew she was being held in Jericho?" Liam asked.

"From a human source. We knew men had been gathering in that house for several days, men who should not have been there. Unfortunately, there was insufficient information to link those suspicious characters to Miss Stanton's disappearance. We did not know they were holding her inside."

"Do you know those men were murdered?" Liam said.

"Yes. We cleared the house of the bodies and any evidence of their deaths. The men who killed them were highly skilled professionals. All well-planned, unnoticed by anyone in the neighborhood. I want you to continue your search and rescue operation. Now with my assistance and resources."

"Your agents and policemen?" Liam said.

"No. I believe you are fully capable of retrieving Miss Stanton without our bureaucracy getting in the way. The dissension I anticipate within our government on how to handle this scroll must be avoided. From today forward we will share our information on the whereabouts of Al Dub and whoever else is working with him."

"You saw more than the old man at the Wall?"

"Two others. One wore a black turban concealing his face and a full-length black *thawb*. The other is slender, almost as tall as you, Mr. Connors. With a beard going gray. These two men are unknown to us."

"These two guys?" Liam said, tossing onto the table the black and white photograph the technician had printed, showing Hazara and The Black trying to push through the wall of men to follow Al Dub.

"Yes," Peres said focusing his good eye on the photograph. "Those are the two men."

"Do you know where this Al Dub took Mimi?" Liam asked.

"Not yet. He is very good. He knows our cameras and surveillance systems. He moves accordingly. Tracking Al Dub is not as simple a task as following you. We do know he disappeared into the tunnels with Miss Stanton in the wheel chair. The other two men did not. We were unable to follow those two. They are also apparently well-trained and avoided cameras after they left the Wall."

"Does that mean anything?" Liam asked.

"We don't know. Perhaps that was planned."

"Al Dub has the Ishmael scroll," Liam said.

"You mean, he has the scroll you gave him."

Liam glanced up at Menachem, waiting for the other shoe to drop.

"The scroll you obtained from Dr. Sarah Mendheim at the Museum of Israel," Peres said. "It is not very old. She will be happy to receive the gift you discussed after we rescue Miss Stanton."

"You had cameras in the museum as well," Liam said.

There was silence in the small kitchen. Liam looked at Menachem leaning against the cabinet then across the table at Peres.

"I see. I knew Menachem was more than a driver. You two have been working together on this from day one."

Investigator Akiva Peres stood up and shambled over to Menachem Wladyslaw, placing his hand on Menachem's shoulder.

"Mr. Connors, this man Menachem Wladyslaw is the finest driver in all of Israel, even to this day."

Peres embraced Menachem, kissing each cheek.

"The hero of Wrath of God if you ask me," Peres said. "Had he not driven like a Formula One racer through the congested streets of Rome after the first assassination, there may have been no others. We would have been discovered and the remaining plans to render justice thwarted."

"Did you say we?" Liam asked.

"Akiva Peres was one of the men I drove," Menachem said.

"I'll be damned," Liam said. "You guys have been working together for thirty years."

"Soon to be forty," Peres said.

"All the calls you've excused yourself to make," Liam said. "You've been reporting to Investigator Peres, keeping him informed."

"Not all the time," Menachem said. "Sometimes he called me."

"This old bald eagle is still associated with Mossad and works with them on occasions like this. They arranged for Menachem to answer Yitzhak Palmer's call for a driver many months ago. The agency had heard rumblings about what Palmer was proclaiming to have found. The man could not keep his mouth shut. When you came into the picture last week and Palmer disappeared, they asked Menachem to stay involved and help you.

"And I authorized the security station supervisor at the Wall to show you the recordings of what happened," Peres said, "and to give you copies of the photographs of Akmal Kassab and the other two men."

Liam turned to Menachem. "Maybe you should tell him about Ike."

"I have already moved Mr. Palmer's body from Menachem's freezer to the morgue," Peres said. "His death was an unfortunate accident. Perhaps Yitzhak Palmer will at last have peace. He was a tortured soul."

"The pot that shattered into the *wadi* was empty," Liam said to Peres. "Before he died he said he hid the real scroll in another cave. Do you have any idea...?"

"Only God knows," Peres said. "We have no cameras in the desert. Our drone coverage over the rocks and sand is intermittent. What do you think, Menachem?"

"It is possible," Menachem said with a shrug. "Who knows? Maybe he did."

"All this trouble. A two thousand year old document," Liam said. "I don't understand how it could arouse the hatred...."

"It is difficult for outsiders to understand," Akiva Peres said. "This country is the birthplace of Judaism and Christianity. Islam, too, arose in this immediate region. Muhammad rode with his armies over these very hills and deserts. His followers believe he ascended to heaven from the limestone mound preserved under the Dome of the Rock. His followers who want *jihad* against the West live by the ancient words of the Quran. These words are holy and anything that challenges their beliefs is evil. From the Devil himself. Their religion justifies violence, murder, and genocide are justified by their religion. A Seventh Century mentality. They want the world to be as it is described in their Holy Quran."

"If Ike Palmer's scroll really exists and proves that Ishmael was not the blood of Abraham," Liam said, "what will happen?"

"Nothing. Jerusalem is controlled by Israel, not because the Torah is correct and the Quran is wrong. It is because the Israeli army and air force are stronger now than our enemies' forces. Only by the sword do we hold on to this little sliver of earth. If our resolve grows weaker, if Iran continues to strengthen Hamas and Hezbollah and the criminal regime in Syria, if Iran gets a nuclear bomb, it is over for Israel. It does not matter if Hagar was already pregnant when she slept with Abraham. It does not matter if the scroll proves the Israelis hold a historic claim to the Promised Land and the Muslims have none. True-believers do not care. *Jihadists* will kill all Jews and Christians or banish them from here.

"In America, you wrested the land from the Native Americans by force, killing all but a few. You took the Southwest and California from Mexico by force. The American Indians and Mexicans have historical claims to the land superior to those of white Americans. Do you think it makes any difference? No. The U.S. will never give back the land to the Native Americans or to Mexico. They took it by force and will keep it by force. It is the same in this country. Whoever wins the war writes the history."

"Akiva Peres is right," Menachem said.

"I don't give a damn what the scroll says," Liam said. "I want Mimi back. How do we manage that?"

"We must find Al Dub," Peres said. "Let me tell you about the Bear."

Chapter Forty-Four

Mimi smelled something. She opened her eyes. Light leeched through the blinds covering the windows. She tried to get up but the effort made her dizzy. Her hands and feet were tied. She waited a moment for the fuzz in her brain to settle down. Carefully this time, she moved her head. Her right wrist was bound to the bedpost with rope and duct tape. So was her left wrist. She checked her feet. Each one was tied to a corner of the footboard. She laid back and closed her eyes, spread-eagled and helpless. Thankful someone had the decency to cover her.

Coffee!

That's what she smelled. At least she was being held by someone civilized enough to brew coffee. How many days had it been? How had she come to be here, wherever this was? The bed was more comfortable than the dark, filthy bathroom and the cold stone of the basement floor. She suppressed a sudden wave of encouragement. She was still a prisoner.

"Hello," she croaked.

Not much sound came out. She swallowed, trying to moisten her parched throat.

"Hello? Anyone?"

The door creaked open. A stocky, bald man stood in the door holding a steaming mug. He wore slacks and a short-sleeved shirt revealing the blanket of hair covering his forearms. He walked over to stand next to the bed and looked down at Mimi. He took a sip of his coffee and checked her bindings.

"Who are you?"

"No one."

"Will you let me go?"

The man pulled the sheet and blanket off Mimi.

"No," she cried. "Please."

He stood over her, studying her naked body as if she were a lab specimen. She closed her eyes tightly. Tears ran down her cheeks. She had never felt so vulnerable.

"Please," she whispered and began to sob.

She felt the sheet and blanket being pulled back over her body and tucked around her neck.

"Thank you," she said, trying to stop crying.

She heard the man walk away from the bed, and close a door. Mimi opened her eyes and looked around, grateful to be alone again. Her fingers felt numb. She wiggled them, trying to keep her blood moving. She clinched her toes, then released them and clinched them again. She tugged on the rope and tape, trying to rip them from the bed posts.

Mimi stopped struggling against her bindings, fatigued from the slightest effort. How many days had it had been since she had walked? She could feel weakness in her leg and arm muscles. After resting a moment, she began a systematic check of her muscles, flexing and releasing, exercising her body isometrically. The effort caused her joints and muscles to ache. She felt as if she had been hit by a truck and dragged many blocks.

Mimi thought back to Deborah Fowler in Natchitoches. Surviving a bad car wreck, the fifteen-year-old was in a coma for several days. When she came out of it, she was determined to exercise her muscles in the hospital bed. Mimi helped her develop a regimen, flexing and stretching muscles to regain strength. Arms and ankles bound, Mimi began the routine she helped the young girl develop. First, tighten the abdominals and count to ten. Release. Tighten again. Release.

After thirty minutes she was exhausted, but the exercise seemed to help her mind work better. She began mental exercises, too, quietly singing the ABCs and mumbling her multiplication tables. She named the muscles of the body, recalling the mnemonic devices she used in nursing school. She tried to relive each day of her trip to Tuscany and Umbria with Liam, beginning with the flight out of Atlanta and their arrival in Rome. She retraced her steps in the Old City the morning she was taken at the *mezuzah* shop. Her time in the inky darkness of the small bathroom. The events in the basement, the needle stick in her upper arm. She wondered what happened to the tall, thin man with the salt-and-pepper beard, nice smile, and soft voice saying he might have to slit her throat if they didn't recover the scroll. And his sidekick who wore the black turban, whose eyes seemed to bore a hole right through her as she shivered on the stone floor.

Minutes later, she began her exercise routine again. She knew it was important to keep her muscles active, build her strength. She would need them when she made her escape.

Chapter Forty-Five

The next morning Liam sat on a stack of cinder blocks behind Menachem's house doing an internet search on Akmal Kassab. He had borrowed Menachem's laptop. He found nothing. None of what Peres had told them about Al Dub was online.

It seemed hopeless. Unless Al Dub contacted them or surfaced, unless he was spotted by a drone or camera pushing a woman in a wheelchair, Liam didn't think there was any way they could find him. In Israel, thousands of stocky, bald men in their sixties looked like Al Dub. The wheelchair set him apart, but it wasn't likely he would be seen with it again, especially if he was as crafty as Peres described. Peres had detailed Al Dub's history of supporting terrorists of all stripes, going back to his involvement with the Saudi hijackers who flew into the World Trade Center and hit the Pentagon on 9-11.

Liam waded through breaking news items on a British newspaper site. The stories were brief, a mix of international politics, news, sports, and entertainment items. An item entitled "Ancient Scroll Disputes Quran" caught his eye. He read it quickly and hurried through the garage into the kitchen where Menachem sat at the table sipping coffee.

"You need to read this," Liam said.

Liam placed the laptop on the table.Menachem studied the news item. He pushed the computer back to Liam.

"What do you think?" Liam asked.

"I am wondering how this newspaper obtained this information."

"Notice how the article details the contents of the scroll. It says Hagar was already pregnant with Ishmael, says the scroll was found and authenticated by Israelis. But doesn't give basic information like Ike's name, where it was found, who authenticated it, or where the scroll is being stored and protected."

"Yes," Menachem said. "Only the most incendiary details are emphasized in the story. The scroll you gave Al Dub at the Wall says nothing about Ishmael. And only one thousand years old. No expert antiquarian would authenticate it."

"Someone planted this story," Liam said.

Menachem turned on the small television on the kitchen counter. One station he checked had live footage of young men throwing rocks at a border wall manned by Israeli soldiers. The words across the screen under the images said *Protests in Gaza over New Dead Sea Scroll.*"

"Why do they call it a Dead Sea scroll?" Liam asked.

"Those are highly charged words. Full of meaning for *Mooslims* who live in the territories. The original Dead Sea scrolls were controlled by Israel for so many years after their discovery. Many *Mooslim* holy men claim they were fabricated by Jews to undermine Islam."

"But the Dead Sea scrolls don't say anything about Islam or the Quran," Liam said. "They were written at least five centuries before Muhammad came on the scene."

Menachem took a sip of coffee and leaned back in his chair.

"Why would you think logic and reason would make any difference to these fanatics?" Menachem said. "Even the facts cannot diminish their hatred for Israel."

"The article in the British newspaper claims the unnamed Israeli expert says the document proves entire Muslim religion is based on a false premise," Liam said. "Someone fed the writer this story."

"You see this rock-throwing on the television?" Menachem said, pointing to the small screen. "This is nothing. The crowds and the violence will grow. In Gaza it takes very little to cause young men to take to the streets. They have no jobs. Nothing else to do. Their leaders encourage violence and hatred rather than grow their economy to provide work for their people. The louder they scream, the more money the brain-dead United Nations will send them. The world blames us for the poverty of the Palestinians. Yet Yasir Arafat diverted nine hundred million dollars of aid money to his own personal bank accounts in Europe, money he stole from his own people. The IMF discovered this, not Israel. An audit after Arafat's death. But no one discusses this." He paused. "It is too easy to blame the Jews, so they do. This violence in the streets will get much worse—there will be deaths. Mark my words."

"This is being orchestrated," Liam said. "But why?"

"If we find the answer to that," Menachem said, "maybe we will find Miss Stanton."

Menachem's cell phone vibrated on the counter next to the television. Liam handed it to him. Menachem listened.

"Yes. We have seen the report on the television."

Menachem listened and nodded.

"We will be here waiting." He ended the call. "That was Akiva Peres. One of his stringers in Bethlehem saw an older man pushing a woman in a wheelchair yesterday. He can identify the building they left."

"Let's go," Liam said, jumping up from his chair.

"Not yet. Peres said to wait here for him. He is on his way."

Chapter Forty-Six

Al Dub opened the door for the dour-looking cleric in the ankle-length white *thawb* and black turban. He welcomed the *imam*, bowing slightly with his palms out, making way for the *imam* to enter. The guest was a holy man, a scholar of the Quran and ancient languages. He looked the part—a long, white beard; dark, intimidating eyes; a stern visage. Raising his right hand to the level of his shoulder, palm inward, the *imam* walked inside.

Al Dub hustled ahead of him and gestured for the holy man to be seated at a table. Al Dub went into the kitchen of his modest rental and returned with a small cup of thick, black coffee. The cleric tasted the coffee and nodded his approval. Al Dub bowed and backed out of the room. Within thirty seconds, he returned with the terra cotta jar in Liam's cotton tote. Al Dub placed the bag on the table and carefully removed the jar. The *imam* studied the pot for several minutes without touching it. He finished his coffee and removed from a pocket a pair of latex gloves.

He placed the jar on the table in front of him, gently removing the lid. He tilted the jar toward him, looked at the document inside, then removed it, placing it flat on the table. The cleric pored over the first page then carefully turned to the following pages of the parchment. After fifteen minutes he closed the scroll, put it back into the pot, and replaced the lid.

"Do you have what we discussed?" the *imam* said in Arabic.

"Yes. Yes."

Al Dub scurried into the kitchen and returned with a white business envelope stuffed with U.S. currency. The cleric flipped through the money and put it in his pocket. Al Dub sat down across the table.

"What can you tell me?" Al Dub asked in Arabic.

"The pot is old, but it is not significant. The document inside is old parchment, less than one thousand years. The writing is not what you were told it was. Not even one part of it."

"How can you tell without testing the paper or the writing?"

"I read the first three pages. The writer describes a battle in great detail. From the First Crusade. I know from my own studies this battle occurred in 1098 in the Common Era. There is no need for a laboratory test. The writing on the document is less than 915 years old. The battle had to have occurred before it could be written about."

Al Dub leaned back in his chair.

The American thought he was dealing with a fool.

"The writing is in Aramaic. Unusual. By the time this document was written, the late Eleventh Century, Aramaic was used primarily for documents in religious worship."

"There is no mention of Ishmael?"

"Not in the first three pages. If you wish I can read the entire document, but there would be additional cost to you. I have fulfilled my contract. I will read more if you wish to waste your money."

"No, *imam,* I will accept your word."

The old cleric stood up and walked to the door. Al Dub hustled quickly to open it. The *imam* raised his right hand to his shoulder and walked slowly outside. Al Dub closed the door behind him. He placed the parchment inside the jar, the jar inside the cotton bag, and returned it to the kitchen. With a sigh he seated himself in front of the small television. It was time for the ten a.m. news.

"...riots in Gaza and Jericho this morning over a controversial discovery in Israel," the newsman said. "So far this morning, at least twenty young Palestinian men are dead at the hands of the IDF. A spokesman for the Israeli government has issued a statement denying knowledge of any so-called 'ancient scroll,' allegedly discovered only recently in Israel. Israeli officials regret the deaths in Gaza. The spokesman claimed the IDF soldiers were not the aggressors, and were only defending themselves against the waves of Palestinians storming the security gate at the Erez Border Crossing checkpoint. Further reports indicate the unrest has become widespread. We have reports of violence in all occupied territories administered by the Palestinian Authority. Scores of students were also injured by IDF troops this morning in Nazareth and in Bethlehem. At least two are dead and many others wounded. We go now to our reporter at the scene of the rioting in Bethlehem."

Al Dub watched the videotape. Pandemonium in the center of Bethlehem near the Church of the Nativity. Mere blocks from where they had kept the American woman in the basement. He had known when he saw television coverage of the rock-throwing in Gaza at daybreak that trouble would spread. The rioting was not spontaneous. True believers had been driven into a religious frenzy overnight when their leaders revealed the contents of the blasphemous scroll. He watched as a sixteen-year-old Palestinian boy screamed into the reporter's microphone, livid about the scroll. Al Dub knew the youngster was parroting his religious leaders. The young man did not know the clerics were functionaries, lackeys on the payroll of Hamas and Hezbollah, operating on orders that emanated from Tehran. Al Dub hated Israel more than Hezbollah or the clerics and rioters in Gaza and Bethlehem, but it made him angry that these Muslim youths were dying for nothing. There was no ancient scroll. Had there been, the American would have turned it over to Al Dub. Not this fabricated document. The American was not a Jew. He would not have sacrificed his woman's life for a scroll from Biblical times that had no meaning for him.

Al Dub turned off the television and thought about the events of yesterday and this morning. He knew of only one man who had the network of contacts in the Middle East and the money to stir up such outrage and rioting overnight: Anton Brodie. Al Dub had seen the man roil the local hotheads many times before—in Kashmir, Belfast, Tunis, Kabul. Many other times, many other places. Al Dub knew the script. He himself had helped Brodie instigate civil unrest by spreading misinformation resulting in thousands of deaths all over the world. Al Dub had personally tended to the details—planting lies, delivering money, sometimes weapons. Creating havoc and roiling the markets. Al Dub was as guilty as the cold-blooded Hebrew he worked for, and just as responsible for the deaths.

Everything Anton Brodie did was for money. Brodie cared nothing about any cause or any life. He manipulated entire populations to line his pockets. Al Dub was proud to go along with Brodie's plans in order to advance his faith and diminish the influence of the Zionists and Christian infidels in the Middle East. But this time, Brodie's lies were resulting in the senseless deaths of devout young Muslim men. Al Dub buried his face in his hands. For over two decades he had helped Brodie amass his obscene wealth and power. No more.

Time to put a stop to these killings. Time to tell the world the truth about Anton Brodie.

He would travel to Bethlehem. Announce to the world the scroll was a fake and reveal Brodie's role in the deadly riots. Only thirty-three kilometers from Hebron. Television reporters in Bethlehem were already covering the demonstrations and fighting. He would show them the scroll, speak directly into the camera, tell the world the scroll was trickery and reveal the truth about Anton Brodie. The rioting and mayhem would cease. Al Dub would be saving lives for a change.

He walked into his room and strapped on his pistol. Al Dub put on a light jacket to hide the gun, and retrieved the bag holding the jar and parchment from the kitchen. He was ready for the drive to Bethlehem.

He paused before leaving the rental house, debating what he should do with the woman. Al Dub put down the scroll and removed the last vial of the sedative from the refrigerator. He would inject her with another dose. Make sure she would remain unconscious until he returned. He looked at the last vial, not sure how much of it to administer. Too much might prove fatal.

After a moment, he decided it did not matter. He would give her all that remained of the drug. He stuck the needle through the rubber top and drained the vial into the syringe.

This would be her last injection. One way or the other.

Chapter Forty-Seven

Menachem drove the Volvo south toward Bethlehem. Liam rode shotgun, Akiva Peres in the back seat. It was only eight kilometers from the Old City to Bethlehem's center, but Menachem's house being on the outskirts of Jerusalem added an additional four or five klicks. Menachem suggested they enter Bethlehem from the south. Althought it would add a few more kilometers, it would save time. Less traffic flowed into the city center from the south and the checkpoint guards were more efficient.

Liam was uncomfortable. The Kevlar vest under his shirt kept riding up on him, leaving everything below his rib cage exposed. He struggled to pull the vest down to cover his navel.

"You need to stock some bigger vests," Liam said, tugging at it.

"Very inconsiderate of you, Menachem," Peres said.

"The vest is fine. Liam should not be so tall."

Liam carried his Glock in the holster at his waist and his backup, the .38 S & W revolver, holstered at his ankle. He had watched Menachem double check his own two pistols before they left. Liam had extra magazines and plenty of loose ammo in his pockets. They couldn't carry semi-automatic rifles on the streets of Bethlehem without being accosted so they had left them in Menachem's garage. Menachem brought additional equipment they might need in a black backpack.

"You are too tall for this kind of work," Peres said to Liam in the front seat. You will stick out in Bethlehem like a white thumb."

"Sore thumb," Menachem said.

Menachem stopped the Volvo at the security checkpoint on the edge of Bethlehem. Peres opened the back window and gestured for the Israeli Border Policeman to come close. He spoke quietly to the guard, who motioned for Peres to follow him into a administrative building no larger than a tool shed. Menachem pulled the Volvo out of the travel lane. After a few minutes Peres returned to the back seat. The Border Policeman spoke briefly to the other guards and waved the Volvo through.

"What was that all about?" Liam asked.

"There is much unrest in the city, very dangerous," Peres said. "He told me to be cautious. Two Palestinians have been killed, a dozen or more wounded. The protestors gathered at Nativity Square very early this morning. Speeches inflamed the crowd. They began to destroy barricades and throw rocks at our forces. They rushed a security fence. Israeli soldiers fired rubber bullets at first, but real ammunition after one of our soldiers was shot. Our soldiers had to defend themselves. The checkpoint guard tells me the situation is very tense in the city center."

"The birthplace of Jesus," Liam said. "Where is Nativity Square in relation to the house we're checking out?"

"Two blocks away."

Menachem maneuvered the Volvo through the narrow, winding streets, passing small groups of young Arabs who shook their fists and shouted at the Volvo as it passed.

"What's the makeup of the population here?" Liam asked.

"Seventy per cent Arab *Mooslims,*" Menachem said. "We are not welcome. Especially on a day like today."

Menachem turned into a narrow alley, driving in the shadows of three and four story buildings. Liam felt relatively safe in the confines of the alley until the Volvo's rear window exploded. Liam turned to see Peres with his head between his knees and a cantaloupe-sized stone cradled in the center of the Volvo's shattered rear window. Menachem stopped in the alley. The three of them jumped out of the car with their pistols drawn. They surveyed the buildings and rooftops. After a few minutes, Menachem removed the stone from its crater in the safety glass.

"Everyone all right?" Menachem asked.

"Your window, not so much," Peres said.

Menachem opened his trunk and pulled out a tire tool. He smashed, then gouged the Volvo rear window until it pulled away from the frame. Liam helped him lift out the glass and toss it to the side of the alley.

"The glass was dirty, Wladyslaw," Peres said. "You can see behind you much better now. It's not much farther to the building. We leave the car here and walk the rest of the way."

"Might not be much left of the Volvo when we return," Liam said.

"Time for a new one anyway," Peres said.

Chapter Forty-Eight

Hazara drove the stolen vehicle, a 2005 Peugeot Partner two-door white van with dark-tinted side windows, slowly down the dusty streets of Hebron, trying to find the house Al Dub had rented from his cousin. Hazara and The Black had stolen the van from a delivery service in Jerusalem. Hazara told The Black it would be less conspicuous in Hebron than his plaster-spattered Toyota truck. He hoped Anton Brodie would pay him well enough on this current assignment to enable him to abandon his Toyota and the tools of the plaster trade forever.

Al Dub was apparently unaware of Anton Brodie's practice of keeping an up-to-date computer file on the extended family of each of his employees and associates. Had Al Dub known, he surely would not have rented a safe house from his cousin. Especially a cousin so cowardly that mere proximity to The Black had caused him to blurt out that Al Dub had paid him two months in advance. The cousin gave Hazara exact directions to his Hebron rental house. Hazara did not have to threaten him. Politely asking questions with The Black glaring at the cousin seemed to work well enough.

"Please do not damage my rental house," the cousin whimpered. He neglected to request the same treatment for his cousin Al Dub.

Hazara glanced over at The Black sitting very still in the Peugeot's passenger seat. Never before had he encountered a man who could sit silently for so many hours in one position. Without moving. He and The Black had worked together in the two years since their release from the United Nations encampment on the Mediterranean shore west of Tripoli near Libya's border with Tunisia. The U.N. claimed to be holding them in connection with the death of Muammar Gaddafi. Hazara knew they had no proof, at least not the kind of proof they needed to satisfy the U.N.'s ridiculous legal standards. Playing by their rules of engagement and their standards of evidence and criminal procedure guaranteed the U.N. could never prove that anyone did anything, especially during the riots and civil unrest endemic in the "Arab Spring" uprisings.

Hazara and The Black did not appear on the gruesome videotape of the beating and eventual shooting death of the Libyan dictator, nor in the video of his naked body being desecrated by the Misrata fighters on the dirty streets outside Sirte. Hazara chuckled thinking of the image of the "rebels" dragging the simpering Gaddafi from the concrete culvert where he made his last stand. It reminded him of the footage of Saddam Hussein surrendering meekly as the hatch of his spider hole was opened by U.S. forces, then being shown later to the world in his filthy underwear with an American doctor checking his head for lice like an impoverished Baghdad schoolboy.

Hazara and The Black weren't seen on the digital video. They had fought side-by-side in Libya, however, and were heavily involved in Gaddafi's capture and death on behalf of Al Qaeda in the Islamic Maghreb. In retrospect, the thirty days they were held in the U.N. encampment had been an important time in Hazara's life. It was there he decided to jettison what little remaining allegiance he had to the principles of Islam or *jihad*. He had no objection to violence and war, but Hazara had fought and killed all his life, and had nothing to show for it. He decided in the encampment that he would find someone who would pay him handsomely for his ability to kill, instead of making him absurd promises of virgins in heaven. Hazara had seen too much killing and destruction in the name of religion. He no longer had faith in Allah, or God, or Jesus, or Yahweh, or the Prophet. The distinctions between his Shia upbringing and the Sunni beliefs meant nothing. Nor did distinctions between Muslims, Jews, and Christians. The so-called holy wars were really about power and hegemony. If the Jews did not have such a powerful military force and strong allies, only Arabic would now be spoken in Jerusalem.

Someone told him at an AQIM planning meeting that The Black was Lebanese. Hazara did not think so. His features indicated his forebears came from farther east. In the encampment, he watched The Black beat to death a Chadian U.N. peacekeeper, who made the mistake of striking him with the butt of his rifle. Hazara was the sole witness to the murder. He watched The Black walk away from the Chadian's corpse, not even breathing hard. It was at that moment Hazara decided to ask The Black to join him—for money, not religious or political reasons. Dark, threatening, The Black eyed Hazara. After a moment, he nodded an almost imperceptible yes.

After the U.N. released them, Hazara and The Black were in a Cairo hookah bar when a stocky Syrian with hairy forearms struck up a conversation. Hazara was the kind of man Al Dub had been looking to hire, but Hazara's sinister companion puzzled him. Hazara assured Al Dub The Black was an accomplished killer. Since that day, the two had worked many missions for Al Dub. Hazara had saved all the money Al Dub paid them. As far as he could tell, The Black placed no value on the money they were paid. Hazara deposited The Black's pay into a Jordanian bank account with his own, planning to divide it when they had saved enough to quit or decided to part ways. It was a strange feeling. For the first time in his life Hazara had a nice sum of money in the bank in Amman. Anton Brodie's promise of a big payday for dispatching Al Dub to his eternal reward was all the motivation Hazara needed.

Hazara drove the Peugeot van from street to street in Hebron, looking for Al Dub's rental house. He had orders from Brodie to find the scroll and kill Al Dub. But even if they could not get the scroll, Brodie told Hazara to make sure Al Dub was dead.

Hazara slowed when he saw Al Dub walking quickly from the house toward the white Fiat sedan he drove the week before to Mount Nebo. The Black had spied Al Dub, too. His black eyes locked on the stocky Syrian with the white cotton bag slung over his shoulder.

Al Dub sped off towards Bethlehem. They followed. To Hazara, the Syrian appeared to be a man on a mission. His last.

Chapter Forty-Nine

Not far from Nativity Square, Liam and Menachem caught the signal. Peres walked a half-block ahead. Moments later the two of them slipped into the small opening between the target house and the old building next to it. The street was deserted. With demonstrations in Bethelem, Liam had expected more pedestrian traffic. The two men screwed suppressors onto their pistols.

Menachem and Liam had convinced Peres to let the two of them handle the incursion into the building.

"Someone should be left to continue the mission of freeing Mimi, someone with some credibility," Menachem said, "in case things do not go so well in there for Liam and his famous driver."

"He's right, Investigator Peres," Liam said.

Peres squeezed Liam's arm.

"You call me Akiva, please. You are about to risk your life. It is time to dispense with formalities."

"Thank you again for all you've done," Liam said.

"Anyway, old man," Menachem added, "you are already in such trouble with your bosses. If they learn of your role in this adventure, you will never make it back to Shin Bet. And that, my friend, would be very bad news for the security of our country."

Peres bristled at being sidelined, but he knew Menachem was right. It was too risky for all three to go in.

"Go rest your old bones at that café we passed," Menachem said, elbowing Peres lightly. "It is important you keep an eye on things."

Peres squinted and wagged his finger at his old friend.

"Remember we are the same age, Mr. Wladyslaw. And I have hair."

Peres grew serious. He reminded them that his informant had noticed no activity at the house this morning, no one coming in or going out. It was very likely the house was empty. Mimi Stanton had probably been moved again after the incident at the Wall. Peres walked away to take a seat in the empty sidewalk café.

Menachem easily picked the old lock on the outside door and opened it. He reached inside his backpack, removed a flexible camera snake, and activated it. He eased the snake past the door jamb to have a look inside.

"A narrow, wooden staircase. A single long flight up to another door made of wood."

Liam nodded.

"Let us go," Menachem said, replacing the camera in the backpack on his shoulder.

"Me first," Liam said.

"No. You follow me."

"My fight," Liam said with force. "I'm grateful for your help but I'm going first. Back me up."

Menachem read Liam's eyes. No reason to argue.

"I will be with you," Menachem said and backed out to let Liam take the first step inside.

Liam had never felt such resolve. No jitters, no case of nerves like Jericho. His hands were calm, his breathing even. He had been waiting for this moment for six days. He would rescue Mimi or die trying.

Both hands on his Glock, pointed toward the ceiling. His back against the wall to help balance his move up the steps. Softly on the first step, then the next. Menachem waited a moment, then followed, pistol in hand, ready to fire. Halfway up, the steps creaked. Liam turned to Menachem. If a gunman appeared at the door above them they were toast, trapped in the narrow stairway with nowhere to take cover.

After a few moments, Menachem tapped Liam, who gingerly moved to the next step. Liam held his breath and proceeded carefully. In a minute he faced the wooden door at the top of the stairs. No landing. It was awkward, no platform to give them leverage to smash open the door.

Liam pointed to the half-inch crack under the door and signaled Menachem to remove the camera from his backpack. Liam slid the snake under the door to check out the other side. It was one huge room. Brick columns were spread throughout. Sitting at a small table in the corner of the room across from the door were two Arabs slouching in their chairs

Liam quietly tested the door. Locked. Liam gestured for Menachem to try the pick again. Menachem shook his head and aimed his pistol at the lock. Liam turned his back to the door and gripped his Glock. Menachem unleashed a torrent of bullets at the door lock. Liam burst through the door into the room.

The two men jumped from the table. Liam screamed.

"Stop where you are!"

One man grabbed an assault rifle from the table but Liam shot him twice in the chest before he could raise his weapon. Liam spun toward the other man running for the basement door and sprayed him with gunfire. The man tumbled head first into the stone wall. Menachem walked quickly to kick away the first man's SAR and check him. Dead. Glock pointed at his torso, Liam walked to the second man, splayed against the stone wall. Liam turned the man over. Blood gushed from a shot through his neck. Liam checked him for a gun.

"Where's the woman?" Liam asked.

The man's eyes were wide. He stared at Liam, opened his mouth and died.

Liam slammed in a new magazine and chambered a round. They spread out, checking everywhere. Menachem opened the basement door. Liam pulled out the camera snake from Menachem's backpack and extended it as far into the basement as he could.

"Can't see from here," Liam whispered to Menachem.

Liam took the first step and listened. Silence. He walked slowly, step by step, both hands on the Glock, ready to fire. On the basement floor, Liam spun in each direction, his weapon ready. Nothing.

"No one here," Liam called up to Menachem.

Liam saw a heavy chain and clothing on the floor. He kicked the chain away and picked up the clothes—a woman's filthy linen blouse and black slacks. Mimi's.

"Dammit to hell," he said and climbed the stairs.

He held out the pants and blouse to Menachem. "These are Mimi's." Liam stuffed them inside his shirt. "Let's go."

They descended the stairs and hurried toward the sidewalk café. Peres saw them on the street and walked toward them. The three men turned to head back to the Volvo.

"Only two men inside," Menachem said as they walked. "Mr. Liam Connors of Louisiana, U.S.A., killed them both."

"Who were they?" Peres asked.

"No time for introductions," Menachem said.

Liam showed Peres the blouse and slacks.

"They're Mimi's," he said. "From the basement."

"My information was good," Peres said, "just a little late."

"What now?" Liam asked.

"We have to get out of here," Peres said. "Back to Jerusalem."

In minutes they were in the Volvo. Menachem looked through the empty rear window frame and backed out of the alley. After maneuvering expertly through the winding streets, Menachem had the Volvo at the checkpoint heading south out of Bethlehem. Peres spoke briefly to the same Border Policeman. He said something to the guards and waved the Volvo through.

As they pulled off, Liam noticed a white, two-door Peugot Partner commercial van in the checkpoint line heading north into Bethlehem. The windows were tinted, but the windshield was almost clear, enabling Liam to study the two men in the van. Liam turned in his seat to watch the oddly-shaped van go through the checkpoint into Bethlehem.

"Hey," he said to Peres in the back seat. "Those two guys in that little white van. They were the ones at the Western Wall. Trying to get to Akmal Kassab. The driver looks like Bin Laden and the other wears the black turban and long tunic."

"You sure?" Peres asked.

"Positive."

Menachem did a u-turn just as the Volvo cleared the concrete barricades outside the checkpoint. Peres signaled the Border Policeman. He smiled and waved them back through.

"Buckle your seat belts," Menachem said.

Chapter Fifty

Mahmoud and his younger brother were tired and hungry. They rested on boulders below the next cave to be explored. For two days they had worked the rugged mountains and foothills southeast of Jerusalem. Beginning at the incline where Yitzhak Palmer had hidden before falling to his death, they searched in concentric circles, moving farther and farther away from his cave. They were surrounded by the rugged mountain desert northeast of Herodium, southwest of Mar Saba. The middle of nowhere.

"Let's go," Mahmoud said in Arabic to his brother.

"No," Brother muttered. "I quit."

"We are not quitting. We will search every cave. We will find it."

"It does not exist. A crazy man wearing no clothes."

Mahmoud reached into his loose fitting pants and pulled out a wad of U.S. currency.

"You see this? Three times this much when we locate it. We will be rich. More rich than any Bedouins our age in all of Israel."

"Give me my share of what he already paid."

"You leave now, I keep it all."

"You are a cheater."

"I am the oldest. I make the rules."

"I am hungry."

"Check this cave and we go find something to eat."

"And you should pay the goat herders we have been mooching off."

"You fool. No one must know we have this money. They are required to feed us and give us water. It is our custom. They see how pitiful you look, little brother. The nomads will give us our next meal."

Mahmoud began to climbing toward the next cave. Brother dragged himself up the rocks behind him.

"There will be nothing here but dried up shit like the others," Brother said. "You are dreaming."

Mahmoud continued to climb until he reached the mouth of the cave. Waiting for his brother to join him, he pulled a small flashlight from his pocket and clicked it. Nothing. He hit the bottom of the light against his palm. It flickered. He unscrewed the bottom and reversed the order of the batteries and tried again. Light!

He walked inside. Brother waited at the mouth. It was small, no more than three meters deep into the mountain. Mahmoud crouched down and shined his light into the corners. It flickered and went out.

"*Khabeez*," Mahmoud cursed.

"No matter. There is nothing here," Brother said.

Mahmoud again struck the metal bottom of the flashlight against his open palm. "*Aywa!*" The light shone long enough for Mahmoud to see something tucked against the back wall. He jammed the flashlight in his pocket, dropped to his hands and knees and crawled in darkness to the back wall. He reached out put his hand on something, something smooth, round, and cool to the touch.

"I have found something here," Mahmoud yelled to his brother.

"A large goat bone," Brother laughed. "Fool."

Mahmoud picked up the object carefully. He moved toward the mouth of the cave. When he could stand up, he cradling the object in his arms. Coming into the light, he shouted with joy.

"Here it is," Mahmoud said, holding out the terra cotta jar for his brother to see. "I told you."

"What is this?" Brother said as he touched a small piece of paper held against the neck of the pot with a well-worn leather string.

"Let us see," Mahmoud said when his eyes adjusted to the light.

"Can you read it?" the brother asked.

"No. The note is in the English."

"Untie the string and take the paper," Mahmoud said.

He moved out of the direct sunlight and opened the top of the jar long enough to see an old document inside. He quickly replaced the top.

"What is it?" the brother asked.

"An old book or something. We must keep the top on the container. Away from air."

"Why?"

"So it won't be damaged. Give me the note."

Mahmoud glanced at the note and stuck it and the leather string in his pocket.

"Let's go," Mahmoud said. "We must find Menachem."

Chapter Fifty-One

Al Dub abandoned his Fiat sedan and walked up the hill. A crowd was spilling onto the Bethlehem street from the small, rectangular plaza outside the limestone walls of the Church of the Nativity. Someone was speaking to the crowd but Al Dub could not see him. He began pushing his way through the people, the cotton bag holding the scroll still hanging from its straps on his shoulder.

The square was packed, the demonstrators almost all young men. At the edge of the square closest to the church a small, flat bed truck was serving as a platform. A speaker addressed the crowd through a bullhorn. Above the crowd on the walls and parapets, heavily armed Israeli soldiers looked down on the angry Palestinians. Al Dub caught glimpses of the speaker, whose rhetoric was getting more intense as Al Dub neared the platform. The crowd roared rhythmic responses to the speaker's questions. Al Dub sensed that the seething mass was on the verge of erupting. He pressed through the crowd. He would reach the platform and show them the fake scroll. Defuse their anger. If he failed, many more young Muslim men would die senselessly.

Finally, the flatbed. He made a push to climb onto the truck but an angry young man in front of him shoved him back. Al Dub reached into his pocket for a small roll of currency and grabbed the young man closest to him. He yelled into the young man's ear and gave him the money. The young man took the roll of dollars and summoned his friends to help. Together, they pushed Al Dub up onto the platform where he sprawled on his face.

Al Dub picked himself up, removed the jar from its cotton bag, and walked toward the startled speaker. The Bear held out the jar and shouted. The speaker listened to Al Dub for a moment as the crowd grew quiet. Al Dub removed the top of the jar and pulled out the parchment. He crumpled it and shook the parchment at the speaker.

The speaker grabbed the bullhorn and yelled to the crowd. Al Dub listened a moment and began shaking his head.

"No. No." Al Dub said, grabbing the bullhorn. "It is a fake. You must tell them. This is all a mistake."

Jerking the bullhorn from Al Dub, the speaker screamed at the crowd. The young men nearest the truck swarmed onto the platform, engulfing Al Dub in a sea of bodies. One man grabbed the jar and threw it into the crowd where it broke into pieces. The angry young demonstrators on the plaza stomped the jar into dust.

The speaker wrested the parchment from Al Dub, held it high above his head and screamed into the bullhorn. The crowd surged forward, shouting, chanting. The speaker barked at the men holding Al Dub on the platform to clear a small area. The speaker pulled a lighter from his pocket and lit the parchment. He tossed it onto the flatbed. It burned quickly and the young men surrounding it stomped the ashes and pumped their fists at the Israeli soldiers on the battlements.

"There it is," Liam yelled, pointing to the small Peugeot Partner van parked awkwardly, half on the sidewalk behind a white Fiat sedan.

Menachem slammed on the Volvo's brakes. Peres, Liam, and Menachem hit the pavement running toward Nativity Square. A block from the demonstration, Peres veered off the street toward a group of five reinforced Israeli Humvees barricaded behind sandbags. He held up his badge calling out in Hebrew. The officer in charge waved Peres inside the barricades. Peres spoke quickly. The officer ordered one of his men to lead Peres and the others into the Church of the Nativity. The soldier made double-time racing through the church, leading the three of them up the stairs to a loft where a door opened onto a narrow parapet overlooking the plaza filled with angry Palestinians. A dozen Israeli soldiers aimed their rifles at the demonstrators below.

"There's Al Dub," Liam said pointing to the flatbed where Al Dub was being restrained as the parchment burned at the feet of the speaker. "What are they doing?"

All eyes were glued on Al Dub in the grasp of a half-dozen aggravated young Palestinians on the flatbed. They heaved Al Dub off the platform onto the concrete plaza amid the screaming, apoplectic demonstrators.

"Damn," Liam said.

"He is up," Menachem said when Al Dub staggered to his feet and began slogging through the screaming mass.

"Look," Liam said. "There they are."

Hazara and The Black moved through the crowd toward Al Dub like sharks slicing through churning water. The stocky Syrian confronted the violently inflamed young men immediately in front of him and pushed them aside. He could not have known the two killers he himself had hired for Anton Brodie were headed straight for him.

Al Dub had lost patience. He had tried to show the young Palestinian men the truth, but he was unable to overcome the ignorant hot blood of the crowd. He pushed his way through them, intent on getting back to Hebron.

When he shoved a screaming protestor out of his way he looked up to face The Black only inches away. Al Dub cried out but The Black shoved a curved, razor sharp blade under Al Dub's sternum, driving the tip of the knife into the old Syrian's heart. Al Dub grunted and grabbed The Black's arms and squeezed. Al Dub felt his life ebbing away.

The Black twisted the knife and pulled Al Dub closer. Al Dub's eyes locked onto the savage eyes below the black turban. They were the last thing he saw.

The Black released him. Al Dub's body slid to the stones. The Black followed Hazara closely. They pushed their way through the crowd, out of the plaza, and into the Peugeot van.

"We kill the woman and return to Jordan," Hazara said.

The Black cleaned his knife, wiping off the remainder of Al Dub's blood on the bottom of his *thawb*. He stared blankly into the Bethlehem street, squeezing the knife handle under his black tunic. He pictured this very blade slicing through the American woman's pale, white neck.

Chapter Fifty-Two

Mimi fought the drug, slipping in and out of consciousness. The man had given her another dose. She had watched him inject her, the pistol on his hip persuading her that resistance was futile. Mimi didn't know what sedative he was using but it was powerful. But so was Mimi's will to live. She knew she must concentrate, generate enough adrenaline to fight off the drug. Down deep, she realized if she didn't escape now, she was dead.

Mimi became feral, stretching her neck to reach her left wrist, gnawing at the duct tape and rope like a wolf with its leg in a trap. Her exercise regimen had loosened her bindings somewhat, but they still held her fast. And she could contort her upper body only a few minutes at a time, stretching her neck so that her teeth could reach her wrist. When she tired and fell back onto the mattress, she had to fight off the drug to remain awake. It would have been so easy to give in to unconsciousness. All she had to do was stop resisting. She imagined she was floating near the ceiling, looking down on herself strapped to the bedposts, the stocky man injecting her. It made her angry. She was not helpless—she could do this.

She thought of Liam. He made her so happy. Her life had become meaningful for the first time. She didn't want it to end. She wanted to be with him again. She wanted to go home.

Got to stay awake.

She took a deep breath and stretched toward her wrist, spitting out the small pieces of tape and rope she managed to rip away with her teeth. Mimi locked her incisors on the frayed edge of the gray tape and pulled with all her might. The tape tore in half, leaving only the slender rope holding her left wrist to the bed post. She rested a moment, thinking of Liam, then lunged at the rope, grabbing and tearing at it, biting a few strands at a time until there was little left of it.

Mimi rested to gather her strength. She jerked her upper body and ripped apart the remaining strings with a ferocious bite, freeing her left hand.

She fell back onto the bed. She twisted her body and with her free hand grabbed her right wrist, pulling at the tape. No good.

With all the strength she could muster, she grabbed the tape in her teeth and tugged, making a tear half way through its width. She felt like screaming for joy but settled for a whispered *"yes."* Then she went to work with her teeth again. In moments it was done.

Mimi sat up and rubbed her wrists. Now to work on her ankles. Both hands tore the tape. That was the easy part. She could not reach her ankles with her teeth. She was forced to picking at it with her fingernails. It took a long time. Her back ached from sitting up with her legs splayed. Finally she broke through the rope on her left ankle. She scooted to the foot of the bed, bent her knees, and tore through the rope on her left ankle in short order.

"Oh, God, please, no," Mimi said when she began to feel the sedative engulfing her, making a final run at her consciousness. In her state of fatigue, she would be an easy mark. She tried to concentrate through it, but the room grew dark and she collapsed back on the mattress.

Her heart pounding, Mimi's eyes popped open. She leapt from the bed. She had lost consciousness again, but had no idea how long she was out. Time to move or die.

Standing up caused her brain to float. Light-headed, she almost fainted. She grabbed the bed post and hugged it until her brain stopped spinning.

She looked down at her black undergarment and shuddered. She thought about being nude, her body handled, turned this way and that, by that strange old man—God knows how many strangers—dark memories of the black hole of a bathroom and the heavy chains in the basement overwhelmed her for a moment. Willing those thoughts away, she looked around the room to find some clothing.

She let go of the bed post and lurched across the room to a chair against the wall. Draped over the chair was a *burqa*. She looked around the room. No shoes. She threw on the *burqa*, covering herself from head to toe, a mesh rectangle over her eyes. Mimi opened the door to her room and staggered out. She prayed the man was not there. Moving toward the front door, she looked around. Moving her head made her dizzy. She leaned against the wall to steady herself. No sign there was anyone in the house with her.

Mimi opened the front door. The glare hurt her eyes. She shuffled outside in her bare feet. When she made it to the street she started walking. The rocks and crumbling asphalt hurt her feet. But the pain felt good. She was free. She could move on her own, go where she wanted. But where was she? Mimi had no idea.

Keep walking. Move. Keep walking. Move.

She passed houses and side streets. The locals paid her no attention. Thank God for that. She came to a dusty intersection. An old Arab couple in a ramshackle truck stopped on the intersecting street. They watched Mimi for a moment. The man waved her over. She stumbled on her way. Mimi stood outside the driver's door. He had a white beard and wisps of white hair sticking out from under his brown *kufi*. He said something to Mimi. She shrugged.

"I can't understand. But I need help," she slurred as she put her hands together as if she were praying. "Can you take me somewhere?"

"Telephone," she said, pretending to talk on a phone. "Telephone."

The old man smiled. Crooked, brown teeth. His wife said something to him. Mimi watched the old woman talk. Her face was brown as a pecan and wrinkled; toothless. Finally, she smiled and nodded at Mimi. The old man gestured for her to get in the back of the truck. Mimi managed to climb into the bed of the pick up and crawl toward the front, resting her back against the cab. The old man said something out his window. Mimi didn't know what he said, but she gave him a thumbs-up. The truck pulled slowly away from the intersection.

Mimi took a deep breath and passed out.

Chapter Fifty-Three

Menachem raced south toward Hebron. The Border Policeman at the checkpoint did remember the white Peugeot Partner van and told Peres the two men headed south. Peres called a friend at Shin Bet who connected him with drone surveillance.

The technicians picked up the Peugeot van driving south at forty-five miles an hour. Six miles north of Hebron. More than halfway there.

"What's in Hebron?" Liam asked.

Peres ordered the technician to review the surveillance footage.

"I want to know where the Peugeot has been this day," Peres barked into his cell phone. "And I need this information now."

"We will not catch them unless you drive like the old days," Peres said to Menachem.

Menachem accelerated the Volvo from eighty to over a hundred miles an hour. He passed other cars like they were parked.

"Yes," Peres said, listening to the technician's report. "Good work. Now stay on them."

Peres tapped an icon on his phone and entered a Hebron address.

"They are traveling to a house in Hebron," Peres shouted. "My tech said they parked outside that house in Hebron this morning and then followed another vehicle to Bethlehem."

"Al Dub," Liam said. "They followed him to get the scroll."

"And to kill him," Menachem said. "Now they are returning to the house in Hebron to finish their business."

"Eliminate all witnesses," Peres said.

"Go. Go," Liam said, slapping his hand on the dash.

Liam pulled his Glock from its holster. The magazine was full. He made sure a bullet was chambered. He was ready.

He had always wondered how he would perform under fire. Kill or be killed. He felt strangely indifferent about killing the two men in Bethlehem. Not how he thought he would feel. But they were bad guys, going for their guns.

They would have killed me.

Killed Menachem, too. Liam would kill again to save Mimi, to save Menachem—Liam was okay with that. No remorse. The time to think was before the shooting. He thought of the double tap on the first man's chest in Bethlehem. No thought process involved. It was all instinctual. His military weapons training from decades earlier had kicked in when he went through that door. Like riding a bike.

"Where are they?" Liam asked Peres.

Peres barked at the technician on the phone.

"Two miles ahead of us," Peres said. "Maintaining speed."

Menachem floored the accelerator. Liam glanced at the speedometer needle hard against the right edge of the dial—the Volvo had maxed out. Menachem gripped the wheel, totally immersed in the road and his machine.

Liam tapped the Glock against his leg as he spoke to God. No recitation of words learned in catechism or church. Just plain talk.

Help me get to her. Help me save her.

Seconds later, Menachem slowed behind a semi. No way to pass. He beat the steering wheel, saw an opening and stomped it. He whipped the Volvo around the truck in no time. Back at full speed in seconds.

"Hebron ahead," Menachem said.

Peres barked into the phone at the technician and looked up.

"We should see them," Peres said.

Liam strained to spot the van in the distance. They were in Hebron now, passing small stone houses at warp speed. No Peugeot van.

"They turned off," Peres said, looking at the map on his phone. "Turn around. Turn around."

Menachem skidded into a u-turn and raced back to the side street they had passed.

"Right. Turn right," Peres said.

"There," Liam said. "The black turban."

Menachem raced toward the small house where the white Peugeot Partner van had stopped. The Black walked from the van toward the house. Menachem skidded to a halt and Liam jumped out pointing the Glock at The Black, running straight toward him.

"Stop," Liam roared. "Take one more step and I'll kill you."

The Black half turned toward Hazara. Liam watched the slender driver with the brown and white beard signal The Black to return to the Peugeot.

Liam hustled to the driver's side, the Glock aimed directly at Hazara. The Black stared at Liam over the hood of the van, puzzled.

Menachem and Peres caught up with Liam. Standing beside him, Menachem aimed his pistol at The Black. Peres stared at the two men in the Peugeot.

"What now?" Liam said to Peres.

Peres put his hand on Liam's Glock, guiding it down, and Menachem lowered his. Peres locked eyes with Hazara. Peres said something to him. Hazara nodded and drove slowly away.

"You're letting them go," Liam said.

"Go get the girl," Peres said.

Liam raced inside the small house. Menachem stayed with Peres to watch the Peugeot van turn the corner and drive away.

Moments later, Liam walked out the front door.

"Dammit," he shouted. "There's no one inside."

Chapter Fifty-Four

"She was here," Liam said standing over the bed in the house, "tied to these bedposts."

Peres studied what was left of the rope and the tape.

"She must have chewed through these," Peres said.

"A very determined young woman," Menachem said.

"Why'd you let them go?" Liam asked Peres.

"They thought she was here," Peres said with a shrug. "They were here to kill her I am sure."

"Akiva Peres was never in Bethlehem or here in Hebron," Menachem said. "He is banned from all Palestinian Territories until they finish his investigation."

"We watched the guy in the black turban murder Al Dub."

"I did not," Menachem said. "And the elderly investigator Akiva Peres did not because, I repeat, the old gentleman was never in Bethlehem or here in Hebron."

Liam was beginning to understand.

"This man Al Dub," Menachem said, "was a kidnapper. He was killed in a riot in Nativity Square. Unless, Mr. Liam Connors, you want to spend many months, maybe years in Israel being detained by the Palestinian Authorities as a witness in connection with the death of Al Dub and as a suspect in the murder of two Arab men who died suddenly from being shot with your Glock pistol in Bethlehem."

"And," Peres added, "if I file a report you would have to remain in Israel to attend the coroner's inquest. Answer questions about the death of Israeli citizen John the Baptist, also known as Yitzhak Palmer from Louisiana, U.S.A."

Peres answered his phone. He listened for several moments.

"Start the Volvo," Peres said to Menachem. "We have to take another short ride."

Liam jumped from the Volvo and raced inside the security checkpoint station on the southeast edge of Hebron. A woman in a *burqa* sitting in a metal chair caught his eye. Liam stared at her bare white feet.

Thank you, God.

With a muted sob, Mimi stood from the chair and tried to move toward Liam. She stumbled and he rushed to catch her. He lifted her in his arms, tenderly removing the black veil from the *burqa* and looking into her eyes. He kissed her, tears running down his cheeks.

Menachem and Peres watched for a moment, then had to look away. They considered what Mimi Stanton had been through, the long journey they had all shared since the American couple first arrived in Israel.

Menachem wiped his eyes. He would go see his own good wife, get on his knees and beg her to let him come home to spend what remained of their lives together. Perhaps she would take him back. It would be a miracle. But, it was also a miracle seeing Mimi and Liam in each other's arms in the middle of the Hebron security station.

Peres elbowed his old friend and wrapped him in a hug.

"We have become sentimental in our old age," Peres said. "But it is a fact you are still the greatest driver in all of Israel."

Menachem looked around the room. With open mouths the Israeli soldiers and policemen watched the tall American spin around the short-haired woman in the *burqa*.

"What's the matter with you guys?" Menachem chided them in Hebrew. "Haven't you ever seen a man and woman kiss? It's in all the Hollywood movies."

Chapter Fifty-Five

Menachem drove from the Hebron checkpoint directly to the Hadassah University Medical Center on Mount Scopus. Akiva Peres rode in front, Liam in back, holding Mimi close. He checked her into the hospital where physicians examined her immediately. They started her on a regimen of broad spectrum antibiotics and treated the burns and lesions on her wrists and ankles. X-rays revealed a broken rib from being a punching bag in Jericho, but no fractures to her skull or jaw.

Liam stayed with her until the doctors forced him to leave. He walked out to join Menachem and Peres in the hallway outside the examining room.

"How is she?" Menachem asked.

"So far, they think okay. They used the "date rape" drug, Rohypnol."

"Salzman from the King David called," Peres said. "He was concerned about Miss Stanton's welfare."

"I need to shake that man's hand," Liam said. "The only place Mimi knew to call was the King David Hotel. Salzman took it from there."

"There is news for you," Menachem said.

"What?"

"Come. It is better to show you."

Menachem led Liam down the hallway with Peres following closely behind. They went through a swinging door into a family waiting room where Mahmoud and Brother sat in orange plastic and aluminum chairs.

"Mahmoud," Liam said. "What are you doing here?"

"Payday," Mahmoud said with a big grin.

"I thought he didn't speak English," Liam said.

"He doesn't," Peres said. "Menachem taught him the word just now to surprise you."

Brother pulled out a wrinkled brown paper bag from under his orange chair. He held it out for Liam, his grin as expansive as his big brother's. Liam opened the bag and removed an ancient terra cotta jar. Mahmoud reached in his pocket and gave Liam the note and leather string he had removed from the jar's neck. Liam read the note.

For Liam Connors. Tell everyone back home Ike Palmer found this.

Chapter Fifty-Six

Anton Brodie buckled his seat belt as his Gulfstream 550 taxied the runway to take its place in the queue for takeoff. His pilots had filed the flight plan for Kabul. Brodie's meeting with the *de facto* treasurer of the Taliban was scheduled for the next day. Brodie chuckled. He no longer had to listen to Karzai's paranoid ramblings. Soon out of office, Hamid Karzai would have plenty to be paranoid about.

Brodie swirled the red wine in his crystal goblet and held it to his nose, inhaling deeply. His Ishmael gambit had ended with a whimper. It was time to move on.

When Brodie's stringers spread the news of the Ishmael scroll throughout the Middle East, currencies in the region immediately lost value, as he had known they would. Flare ups of hostilities between Israel and the Arab nations surrounding it always moved the currencies. He had closed out all of his positions an hour before arriving at the airport, netting a profit of one-and-a-half billion U.S. dollars. Financial pundits would say it was significant coup for Brodie, but he was disappointed. Had it not been for the irrational behavior of Al Dub, he would have made twice the amount. Had he gained control of the actual scroll instead of having to leak information about its contents to the media through his sources, the firestorm would have been more widespread and deadlier. Much more international attention. Brodie's currency moves would have been protracted and involved more markets. As it was, governments were beginning to issue statements denying such a scroll's existence, and values were beginning to stabilize. Brodie had timed his own trades perfectly. The currencies ticked up minutes after Brodie had sold every position.

Al Dub disappointed Brodie, but it was no surprise. The religious fervor that made the Syrian such a valuable advance man finally had reached the tipping point. His beliefs proved to be the Bear's undoing. Brodie would miss Al Dub's connections in the worldwide *jihadist* network. The currency movements he had helped manipulate had been highly profitable for Brodie. He sipped his wine and recalled the dramatic devaluations of the U.S. dollar after terrorist attacks in the previous twenty years. Brodie traded each crisis, making billions. But the pinnacle of his symbiosis with Al Dub came in the weeks after 9-11. The Saudi hijackers needed a small amount of money. Brodie supplied it. Al Dub delivered it. Brodie made tens of billions in profits during the worldwide financial turmoil afterwards.

Brodie raised his goblet in a silent toast to his late associate. Besides the modest financial reward, some additional good had come of the scroll venture. Brodie had added Hazara and The Black to his stable of assassins and operatives. Since their meeting at the Four Seasons in Amman, Brodie had communicated directly with Hazara, who kept him aware of Al Dub's treachery. Brodie was impressed with Hazara's focus on the mission and lack of interest in its religious, political, or legal implications. Brodie had not met The Black. He did not intend to.

The Gulfstream 550 shot skyward into the clear blue sky like a bullet. Brodie sipped his wine and gazed southward out his window as the jet banked hard toward its flight path to Afghanistan. As the horizon slipped away, Brodie thought he saw smoke rising into the atmosphere from the area where Bethlehem would be, but he could not be sure.

Chapter Fifty-Seven

The following Monday, eleven days after Mimi's disappearance from the Armenian Quarter in the Old City, she sat with Liam, Menachem, and Akiva Peres in the office of Dr. Sarah Mendheim at the Museum of Israel. She was feeling human again.

After her release from the hospital, Jerusalem Police escorted Mimi and Liam to the King David Hotel, where she spent the weekend recovering. Salzman provided ample security, even stationing two burly men in blue blazers on the sixth floor. Liam and Mimi ventured out of the room only once, to enjoy a quiet dinner Sunday evening in in a secluded corner of the hotel restaurant under the watchful eye of Salzman himself.

Mimi wore long sleeves in the meeting at the Israel Museum Monday morning to cover the burns and scabs on her wrists. She listened as Dr. Mendheim read from the written report detailing the intense examination of the jar and scroll by experts at the Museum.

"Our preliminary conclusion is subject to further scientific testing," Dr. Mendheim said, "but all of us believe this scroll appears to be authentic. We think it was produced during the same period as the Dead Sea Scrolls, in the same vernacular, and within fifty years of the death of Jesus Christ of Nazareth. The jar is identical to those containing the Dead Sea Scrolls. Initial carbon testing shows both the jar and the parchment to be approximatly two thousand years old. Of course, we will conduct more thorough carbon testing over the next several months.

"As for the portion of the writing concerning the relationship of Ishmael, son of Hagar, to Abraham, our linguistic experts verified the claim of this man Yitzhak Palmer. The scroll says explicitly that Hagar, Abraham's servant girl, was already with child when she lay with Abraham the first time."

"What will come of all of this?" Liam asked.

Dr. Mendheim put down the report. She removed her black-rimmed glasses and patted her salt and pepper hair.

"This document," she said solemnly, "this scroll, is very problematic for all of us here at the Museum."

"I am certain of that," Liam said.

"A problem for our country," Akiva Peres said.

"Everyone here knows the destructive forces it would unleash," Dr. Mendheim said. "The countless deaths and injuries occurring this past week, riots over all the Palestinian Territories. On mere rumors of the discovery of such a document. Some peace has been restored as news has spread that the scroll burned at Nativity Square in Bethlehem last Thursday was a fake. Imagine what would happen now if the Israel Museum confirmed the existence of an authentic Ishmael scroll and published its contents."

"But other ancient documents affirm that Ishmael *was* the blood of Abraham," Menachem said.

"Yes," Dr. Mendheim said, "but none of the ancient scribes writing on Hagar and Ishmael provide as much evidence as the writer of this scroll. The author of the document we studied over the last three days writes with great authority. The facts he sets forth make it difficult for our experts to doubt what he says."

The room was silent for a moment.

"It is my understanding," Dr. Mendheim said, "that the only people who know of the existence of this scroll are in this room."

"That's right," Liam said.

"The two Bedouin boys who found it for us," Menachem said, "do not know what it is or what it says."

"Do you not think the Prime Minister and a select committee of the Knesset should be consulted?" Akiva Peres said.

"Those in the government who need to know of this have been briefed. They agree that this scroll and this jar should be protected from deterioration. Kept in a vault here in the museum. Tomorrow they will issue a strong statement renouncing the rumors of the Ishmael Scroll's existence."

"To be clear," Menachem said. "You said only the four of us seated before you know of the authentic scroll. But your scientists and government officials—what of them?"

"Yes. I worked only with staff I trust. And with government officials I know to be trustworthy."

"So, if there is a leak...," Menachem said.

"Your point is taken, Menachem Wladyslaw," Dr. Mendheim said.

"I will send you the money we discussed last week," Liam said. "Use it to build a special vault for the scroll."

"No," Dr. Mendheim said. "We need no link between you and the Israel Museum, Mr. Connors. Your offer is most generous, but such a grand donation would have to be disclosed. Someone might decide to investigate why a Christian from Louisiana is suddenly taking such an interest in Jewish heritage. We would have no good answer."

Dr. Mendheim walked around her desk.

"May we here at the Museum depend upon your silence in this matter?" she asked, shaking Liam's hand.

"Absolutely," Liam said, his arm around Mimi.

"And you two?" Dr. Mendheim asked Menachem and Peres.

"What do we know?" Menachem said.

"We know nothing," Akiva Peres said.

They held their palms open and shrugged as if rehearsed.

The four of them left Dr. Mendheim's office and walked to the huge public room just inside the entrance to the Museum. Droves of tourists and students from all over the world walked past them.

"We owe you an apology," Menachem told Liam and Mimi.

"For what?" Liam asked.

"Akiva and I were to drive you to Tel Aviv to catch your flight. But we must attend a meeting instead."

"Do not listen to this old bald-headed joker," Peres said. "It is not a meeting."

"It is a celebration," Menachem said, clapping Peres on the shoulder. "This dinosaur of a warrior is back at Shin Bet. They need him to keep an eye on things."

"A very tired joke, Wladyslaw. You must get new material."

"Congratulations," Liam said to Peres, "great timing."

"It is not a coincidence, my friend Liam," Menachem said. "Those trustworthy souls in government who were told of the scroll were also told of the brilliant investigator who masterminded its recovery."

"Menachem told them," Peres said. "He knows everybody."

"Me? I am just a driver."

Peres laughed and rubbed Menachem's bald head.

"We cannot thank you enough," Mimi said as she hugged both men.

"How do do you say in your country? Peres said. "It is not such a big deal. We handle this sort of thing all the time."

Liam's smile grew serious. He began to say something to the two old Israeli warriors, but choked up. Menachem wrapped him in his arms.

"You have much to be proud of, my friend."

He turned to Mimi. "This is a very brave man."

"I know," Mimi said.

◆ ❖ ◆

Liam concentrated on the bulkhead between first class and the captain's cabin. The tiny white plane on the monitor was approaching the east coast of the United States.

Mimi had slept most of the way, but Liam had spent the flight planning. He had received a call in the Tel Aviv airport from his friend Willie Mitchell Banks. David Bodenheimer had been suspended for thirty days with pay from the Department of Energy. No additional punishment. Energy Department bigwigs were treating him as a whistleblower. Bodenheimer had violated conflict of interest rules, that was all. They said his claims must have been justified: the investigations into Liam Connors and Clare Petroleum resulted in Delaware Energy paying $5 million to settle.

What Liam did in Israel he had never done before. He killed two men and would have killed another. He dispensed justice, enabling Mimi to survive her close call with death. He did what he had to do. He could do it again.

When the captain announced their final descent into Newark, Liam raised his seat back and nudged Mimi awake.

He closed his eyes. He had decided on the path he was about to take.

Acknowledgements:

Much thanks to Tim Lockwood for lending me his expertise on Middle East security; Woods Eastland for his biblical insights; Chuck Thomas and Rudy Atallah for comments early in the process; and Curtis Wilkie for sharing his knowledge of the region. Thanks for the constancy and support of indefatigable readers Francine Luckett and Mike Hourin; to insights and comments from David Fite, Martha V. Whitwell, Christine Maynard, Kaye Bryant, Eddie Ahrens, Julie Sample, and Pat Austin. Thanks to friend and neighbor Dickie Scruggs for his help; to the lovely, elegant Gayle Gresham Henry for her support; and to the creative mind of William Henry. Special thanks to editor Mary Ann Bowen for her sharp insights and bright red pen.

Author Biography

Michael Henry graduated from Tulane University and University of Virginia Law School. FINDING ISHMAEL is his seventh novel. He currently resides and writes in Oxford, Mississippi.